Robert Ludlum's

THE
ALTMAN
CODE

Also by Robert Ludlum and Gayle Lynds in Large Print:

Robert Ludlum's The Hades Factor

Also by Robert Ludlum in Large Print:

Bourne Supremacy
Gemini Contenders
Holcroft Covenant
Parsifal Mosaic
Aquitaine Progression
Icarus Agenda
The Matarese Countdown
The Prometheus Deception
The Sigma Protocol

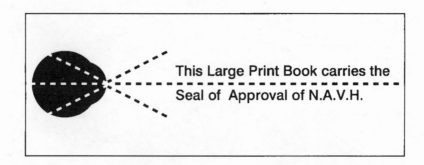

This Large Print Book carries the Seal of Approval of N.A.V.H.

Robert Ludlum's

THE
ALTMAN
CODE

A COVERT-ONE NOVEL

Series Created by
ROBERT LUDLUM

Written by
GAYLE LYNDS

WHEELER PUBLISHING

Published in 2003 by arrangement with St. Martin's Press, LLC.

Wheeler Large Print Hardcover.

The text of this Large Print edition is unabridged.
Other aspects of the book may vary from the original edition.

Set in 16 pt. Plantin by Christina S. Huff.

Printed in the United States on permanent paper.

Library of Congress Cataloging-in-Publication Data

Ludlum, Robert, 1927–
  [Altman code]
  Robert Ludlum's The Altman Code / Robert Ludlum and Gayle
Lynds.
    p. cm.
  ISBN 1-58724-532-9 (lg. print : hc : alk. paper)
    1. Smith, Jon (Fictitious character) — Fiction.
2. International relations — Fiction.   3. Intelligence officers —
Fiction.   4. Americans — China — Fiction.   5. Conspiracies —
Fiction.   6. Large type books.   I. Lynds, Gayle.   II. Title.
PS3562.U26A7 2003b
                                                    2003057584

Robert Ludlum's

THE
ALTMAN
CODE

As the Founder/CEO of NAVH, the only national health agency solely devoted to those who, although not totally blind, have an eye disease which could lead to serious visual impairment, I am pleased to recognize Thorndike Press* as one of the leading publishers in the large print field.

Founded in 1954 in San Francisco to prepare large print textbooks for partially seeing children, NAVH became the pioneer and standard setting agency in the preparation of large type.

Today, those publishers who meet our standards carry the prestigious "Seal of Approval" indicating high quality large print. We are delighted that Thorndike Press is one of the publishers whose titles meet these standards. We are also pleased to recognize the significant contribution Thorndike Press is making in this important and growing field.

Lorraine H. Marchi, L.H.D.
Founder/CEO
NAVH

* Thorndike Press encompasses the following imprints: Thorndike, Wheeler, Walker and Large Print Press.

Prologue

On the north bank of the Huangpu River, giant floodlights glared down on the docks, turning night into day. Swarms of stevedores unloaded trucks and positioned long steel containers for the cranes. Amid the squeals and rasps of metal rubbing metal, the towering cranes lifted the containers high against the starry sky and lowered them into the holds of freighters from across the world. Hundreds streamed in daily to this vital port on China's eastern coast, almost midway between the capital, Beijing, and its latest acquisition, Hong Kong.

To the south of the docks, the lights of the city and the towering Pudong New District glowed, while out on the swirling brown water of the river itself, freighters, junks, tiny sampans, and long trains of unpainted wood barges jostled for position from shore to shore, like traffic on a busy Paris boulevard.

At a wharf near the eastern end of the docks, not far from where the Huangpu curved sharply north, the light was less bright. Here a single freighter was

7

being loaded by one crane and no more than twenty stevedores. The name lettered on the freighter's transom was *The Dowager Empress*; her home port was Hong Kong. There was no sign of the ubiquitous uniformed dock guards.

Two large trucks had been backed up to her. Sweating stevedores unloaded steel barrels, rolled them across the planks, and set them upright on a cargo net. When the net was full, the crane arm swung over it, and the cable descended. On its end was a steel hook that caught the light and glinted. The stevedores latched the big net to the hook, and the crane swiftly lifted the barrels, wheeled them around, and lowered them to the freighter, where deckhands guided the cargo down into the open hold.

The truck drivers, stevedores, crane operator, and deckhands worked steadily on this distant dock, fast and silent, but not fast enough for the large man who stood to the right of the trucks. His sweeping gaze kept watch from land to river. Unusually pale-skinned for a Han Chinese, his hair was even more unusual — light red, shot with white.

He looked at his watch. His whispery voice was barely audible as he spoke to the foreman of the stevedores: "You will finish in thirty-six minutes."

It was no question. The foreman's head jerked around as if he had been attacked. He stared only a moment, dropped his gaze, and rushed away, bellowing at his men. The pace of work increased. As the foreman continued to drive them to greater speed, the man he feared remained a looming presence.

At the same time, a slender Chinese, wearing Reeboks and a black Mao jacket over a pair of Western jeans, slid behind the heavy coils of a hawser in a murky recess of the loading area.

Motionless, almost invisible in the gloom, he studied the barrels as they rolled to the cargo net and were hoisted aboard *The Dowager Empress*. He removed a small, highly sophisticated camera from inside his Mao jacket and photographed everything and everyone until the final barrel had been lowered into the hold and the only remaining truck was about to be driven away.

Turning silently, he hid the camera inside his jacket and crab-walked away from the brilliant lights until he was wrapped again in darkness. He arose and padded across the wood planks from storage box to shed, seeking whatever protection he could find as he headed back toward the road that would return him to the city. A warm night wind whistled above his head, carrying the heavy scent of the muddy river. He did not notice. He was exultant because he would be returning with important information. He was also nervous. These people were not to be taken lightly.

By the time he heard footsteps, he was nearing the end of the wharf, where it met the land. Almost safe.

The large man with the unusual red-and-white hair had been quietly closing in, taking a parallel path among the various supply and work sheds. Calm and deliberate, he saw his target tense, pause, and suddenly hurry.

The man glanced quickly around. To his left was the lost part of the dock, where storage and seagulls found their haven, while on the right was a pathway kept open for trucks and other vehicles to go back and forth to the loading areas. The last truck was behind him, heading this way, toward land. Its headlights were funnels in the night. It would pass soon. As his prey darted behind a tall pile of ropes on the far left, the man pulled out his garotte and sprinted. Before the fellow could turn, the man dropped the thin cord around his neck, yanked, and tightened.

For a long minute, the victim's hands clawed at the cord as it tightened. His shoulders twisted in agony. His body thrashed. At last, his arms fell limp and his head lolled forward.

As the truck passed on the right, the wood dock shuddered. Hidden behind the mountain of ropes, the killer lowered the corpse to the planks. He released the garotte and searched the dead man's clothes until he found the camera. Without hurrying, he walked back and retrieved two of the enormous cargo hooks. He knelt by the corpse, used the knife from the holster on his calf to slash open the belly, buried the points of the iron hooks inside, and sealed them there by winding rope around the man's middle. With alternating feet, he rolled him off into the dark water. The body made a quiet splash and sank. Now it would not float up.

He walked toward the last truck, which had paused as ordered, waiting, and climbed aboard. As the truck sped away toward the city, *The Dowager Empress* hauled up her gangway and let go her lines. A tug towed her out into the Huangpu, where she turned downriver for the short journey to the Yangtze and, finally, the open sea.

PART ONE

Chapter One

There was a saying in Washington that lawyers ran the government, but spies ran the lawyers. The city was cobwebbed with intelligence agencies, everything from the legendary CIA and FBI and the little-known NRO to alphabet groups in all branches of the military and government, even in the illustrious Departments of State and Justice. Too many, in the opinion of President Samuel Adams Castilla. And too public. Rivalries were notoriously a problem. Sharing information that inadvertently included misinformation was a bigger problem. Then there was the dangerous sluggishness of so many bureaucracies.

The president was worrying about this and a brewing international crisis as his black Lincoln Town Car cruised along a narrow back road on the northern bank of the Anacostia River. Its motor was a quiet hum, and its tinted windows opaque. The car rolled past tangled woods and the usual lighted marinas until it finally rattled over the

13

rusted tracks of a rail spur, where it turned right into a busy marina that was completely fenced. The sign read:

ANACOSTIA SEAGOING YACHT CLUB
PRIVATE. MEMBERS ONLY.

The yacht club appeared identical to all the others that lined the river east of the Washington Navy Yard. It was an hour before midnight.

Only a few miles above the Anacostia's confluence with the broad Potomac, the marina moored big, open-water power cruisers and long-distance sailing boats, as well as the usual weekend pleasure craft. President Castilla gazed out his window at the piers, which jutted out into the dusky water. At several, a number of salt-encrusted oceangoing yachts were just docking. Their crews still wore foul-weather gear. He saw that there were also five frame buildings of varying sizes on the grounds. The layout was exactly what had been described to him.

The Lincoln glided to a halt behind the largest of the lighted buildings, out of sight of the piers and hidden from the road by the thick woods. Four of the men riding in the Lincoln with him, all wearing business suits and carrying minisubmachine guns, swiftly stepped out and formed a perimeter around the car. They adjusted their night-vision goggles as they scanned the darkness. Finally, one of the four turned back toward the Lincoln and gave a sharp nod.

The fifth man, who had been sitting beside the president, also wore a dark business suit, but he

14

carried a 9mm Sig Sauer. In response to the signal, the president handed him a key, and he hurried from the car to a barely visible side door in the building. He inserted the key into a hidden lock and swung open the door. He turned and spread his feet, weapon poised.

At that point, the car door that was closest to the building opened. The night air was cool and crisp, tainted with the stench of diesel. The president emerged into it — a tall, heavyset man wearing chino slacks and a casual sport jacket. For such a big man, he moved swiftly as he entered the building.

The fifth guard gave a final glance around and followed with two of the four others. The remaining pair took stations, protecting the Lincoln and the side door.

Nathaniel Frederick ("Fred") Klein, the rumpled chief of Covert-One, sat behind a cluttered metal desk in his compact office inside the marina building. This was the new Covert-One nerve center. In the beginning, just a few years ago, Covert-One had no formal organization or bureaucracy, no real headquarters, and no official operatives. It had been loosely composed of professional experts in many fields, all with clandestine experience, most with military backgrounds, and all essentially unencumbered — without family, home ties, or obligations, either temporary or permanent.

But now that three major international crises had stretched the resources of the elite cadre to the limits, the president had decided his ultrasecret

15

agency needed more personnel and a permanent base far from the radar screens of Pennsylvania Avenue, the Hill, or the Pentagon. The result was this "private yacht club."

It had the right elements for clandestine work: It was open and active twenty-four hours a day, seven days a week, with intermittent but steady traffic from both land and water that followed no pattern. Near the road and the rail spur but still on the grounds was a helipad that looked more like a weed-infested field. The latest electronic communications had been installed throughout the base, and the security was nearly invisible but of cutting-edge quality. Not even a dragonfly could cross the periphery without one of the sensors picking it up.

Alone in his office, the sounds of his small nighttime staff muted beyond his door, Klein closed his eyes and rubbed the bridge of his longish nose. His wire-rimmed glasses rested on the desk. Tonight he looked every one of his sixty years. Since he had accepted the job of heading Covert-One, he had aged. His enigmatic face was riven with new creases, and his hairline had receded an inch. Another problem was on the verge of erupting.

As his headache lessened, he sat back, opened his eyes, put his glasses back on, and resumed puffing on his ever-present pipe. The room filled with billows of smoke that disappeared almost as soon as he produced them, sucked out by a powerful ventilating system installed specifically for the purpose.

A file folder lay open on his desk, but he did not look at it. Instead, he smoked, tapped his foot, and

16

glanced at the ship's clock on his wall every few seconds. At last, a door to his left, beneath the clock, opened, and a man with a Sig Sauer strode across the office to the outer door, locked it, and turned to stand with his back against it.

Seconds later, the president entered. He sat in a high-backed leather chair across the desk from Klein.

"Thanks, Barney," he told the guard. "I'll let you know if I need you."

"But Mr. President —"

"You can go," he ordered firmly. "Wait outside. This is a private conversation between two old friends." That was partly true. He and Fred Klein had known each other since college.

The guard slowly recrossed the office and left, each step radiating reluctance.

As the door closed, Klein blew a stream of smoke. "I would've come to you as usual, Mr. President."

"No." Sam Castilla shook his head. His titanium glasses reflected the overhead light with a sharp flash. "Until you tell me exactly what we're facing with this Chinese freighter — *The Dowager Empress*, right? — this one stays between us and those of your agents you need to work on it."

"The leaks are that bad?"

"Worse," the president said. "The White House has turned into a sieve. I've never seen anything like it. Until my people can find the source, I'll meet you here." His rangy face was deeply worried. "You think we have another *Yinhe*?"

Klein's mind was instantly transported back: It was 1993, and a nasty international incident was

17

about to erupt, with America the big loser. A Chinese cargo ship, the *Yinhe*, had sailed from China for Iran. U.S. intelligence received reports the ship was carrying chemicals that could be used to make weapons. After trying the usual diplomatic channels and failing, President Bill Clinton ordered the U.S. Navy to chase the ship, refusing to let it land anywhere, until some sort of resolution could be found.

An outraged China denied the accusations. Prominent world leaders jawboned. Allies made charges and countercharges. And media around the globe covered the standoff with banner headlines. The stalemate went on for an interminable twenty days. Finally, when China began to noisily rattle its sabers, the U.S. Navy forced the ship to stop on the high seas, and inspectors boarded the *Yinhe*. To America's great embarrassment, they uncovered only agricultural equipment — plows, shovels, and small tractors. The intelligence had been faulty.

With a grimace, Klein recalled it all too well. The episode made America look like a thug. Its relations with China, and even its allies, were strained for years.

He puffed gloomily, fanning the smoke away from the president. "Do we have another *Yinhe*?" he repeated. "Maybe."

"There's 'maybe' remotely, and 'maybe' probably. You better tell me all of it. Chapter and verse."

Klein tamped down the ash in his pipe. "One of our operatives is a professional Sinologist who's been working in Shanghai the past ten years for a

18

consortium of American firms that are trying to get a foothold there. His name's Avery Mondragon. He's alerted us to information he's uncovered that *The Dowager Empress* is carrying tens of tons of thiodiglycol, used in blister weapons, and thionyl chloride, used in both blister and nerve weapons. The freighter was loaded in Shanghai, is already at sea, and is destined for Iraq. Both chemicals have legitimate agricultural uses, of course, but not in such large quantities for a nation the size of Iraq."

"How good is the information this time, Fred? One hundred percent? Ninety?"

"I haven't seen it," Klein said evenly, puffing a cloud of smoke and forgetting to wave it away this time. "But Mondragon says it's documentary. He has the ship's true invoice manifest."

"Great God." Castilla's thick shoulders and heavy torso seemed to go rigid against his chair. "I don't know whether you realize it, but China is one of the signatories of the international agreement that prohibits development, production, stockpiling, or use of chemical weapons. They won't let themselves be revealed as breaking that treaty, because it could slow their march to acquiring a bigger and bigger slice of the global economy."

"It's a damned delicate situation."

"The price of another mistake on our part could be particularly high for us, too, now that they're close to signing our human-rights treaty."

In exchange for financial and trade concessions from the U.S., for which the president had cajoled and arm-twisted a reluctant Congress, China had all but committed to signing a bilateral human-

19

rights agreement that would open its prisons and criminal courts to U.N. and U.S. inspectors, bring its criminal and civil courts closer to Western and international principles, and release longtime political prisoners. Such a treaty had been a high-priority goal for American presidents since Dick Nixon.

Sam Castilla wanted nothing to stop it. In fact, it was a long-standing dream of his, too, for personal as well as human-rights reasons. "It's also a damned dangerous situation. We can't allow this ship . . . what was it, *The Dowager Empress?*"

Klein nodded.

"We can't allow *The Dowager Empress* to sail into Basra with weapons-making chemicals. That's the bottom line. Period." Castilla stood and paced. "If your intelligence turns out to be good, and we go after this *Dowager Empress,* how are the Chinese going to react?" He shook his head and waved away his own words. "No, that's not the question, is it? We know how they'll react. They'll shake their swords, denounce, and posture. The question is what will they actually *do?*" He looked at Klein. "Especially if we're wrong again?"

"No one can know or predict that, Mr. President. On the other hand, no nation can maintain massive armies and nuclear weapons without using them somewhere, sometime, if for no other reason than to justify the costs."

"I disagree. If a country's economy is good, and its people are happy, a leader can maintain an army without using it."

"Of course, if China wants to use the incident as an excuse that they're being threatened, they might invade Taiwan," Fred Klein continued. "They've wanted to do that for decades."

"If they feel we won't retaliate, yes. There's Central Asia, too, now that Russia is less of a regional threat."

The Covert-One chief said the words neither wanted to think: "With their long-range nuclear weapons, we're as much a target as any country."

Castilla shook off a shudder. Klein removed his glasses and massaged his temples. They were silent.

At last, the president sighed. He had made a decision. "All right, I'll have Admiral Brose order the navy to follow and monitor *The Dowager Empress.* We'll label it routine at-sea surveillance with no revelation of the actual situation to anyone but Brose."

"The Chinese will find out we're shadowing their ship."

"We'll stall. The problem is, I don't know how long we'll be able to get away with it." The president went to the door and stopped. When he turned, his face was long and somber, his jowls pronounced. "I need proof, Fred. I need it *now.* Get me that manifest."

"You'll have it, Sam."

His big shoulders hunched with worry, President Castilla nodded, opened the door, and walked away. One of the secret service agents closed it.

Alone again, Klein frowned, contemplating his next step. As he heard the engine of the president's car hum to life, he made a decision. He swiveled to the small table behind his chair, on which two phones sat. One was red — a single, direct, scrambled line to the president. The other was blue. It was also scrambled. He picked up the blue phone and dialed.

Wednesday, September 13
Kaohsiung, Taiwan

After a medium-rare hamburger and a bottle of Taiwanese lager at Smokey Joe's on Chunghsiao-1 Road, Jon Smith decided to take a taxi to Kaohsiung Harbor. He still had an hour before his afternoon meetings resumed at the Grand Hi-Lai Hotel, when his old friend, Mike Kerns from the Pasteur Institute in Paris, would meet him there.

Smith had been in Kaohsiung — Taiwan's second-largest city — nearly a week, but today was the first chance he'd had to explore. That kind of intensity was what usually happened at scientific conferences, at least in his experience. Assigned to the U.S. Army Medical Research Institute for Infectious Diseases — USAMRIID — he was a medical doctor and biomolecular scientist as well as an army lieutenant colonel. He had left his work on defenses against anthrax to attend this one — the Pacific Rim International Assembly on Developments in Molecular and Cell Biology.

But scientific conferences, like fish and guests, got stale after three or four days. Hatless, in civilian clothes, he strode along the waterfront, marveling at the magnificent harbor, the third-largest container port in the world, after Hong Kong and Singapore. He had visited here years ago, before a tunnel was built to the mainland and the paradisaical island became just another congested part of the container port. The day was postcard clear, so he was able to easily spot Hsiao Liuchiu Island, low on the southern horizon.

He walked another fifteen minutes through the sun-hazed day as seagulls circled overhead and the clatter of a harbor at work filled his ears. There was no sign here of the strife over Taiwan's future, whether it would remain independent or be conquered or somehow traded off to mainland China, which still claimed it as its own.

At last, he hailed a cab to take him back to the hotel. He had hardly settled into the backseat when his cell phone vibrated inside his sport jacket. It was not his regular phone, but the special one in the hidden pocket. The phone that was scrambled.

He answered quietly, "Smith."

Fred Klein asked, "How's the conference, Colonel?"

"Getting dull," he admitted.

"Then a small diversion won't be too amiss."

Smith smiled inwardly. He was not only a scientist, but an undercover agent. Balancing the two parts of his life was seldom easy. He was ready for a "small diversion," but nothing too big or too engrossing. He really did want to get back to the conference. "What do we have this time, Fred?"

From his distant office on the bank of the Anacostia River, Klein described the situation.

Smith felt a chill that was both apprehension and anticipation. "What do I do?"

"Go to Liuchiu Island tonight. You should have plenty of time. Rent or bribe a boat out of Linyuan, and be on the island by nine. At precisely ten, you'll be at a small cove on the western shore. The exact location, landmarks, and local designation have been faxed to a Covert-One asset at the American Institute in Taiwan. They'll be hand-delivered to you."

"What happens at the cove?"

"You meet another Covert-One, Avery Mondragon. The recognition word is 'orchid.' He'll deliver an envelope with *The Dowager Empress*'s actual manifest, the one that's the basis for the bill to Iraq. After that, go directly to the airport in Kaohsiung. You'll meet a chopper there from one of our cruisers lying offshore. Give the pilot the invoice manifest. Its final destination is the Oval Office. Understood?"

"Same recognition word?"

"Right."

"Then what?"

Smith could hear the chief of Covert-One puffing on his pipe. "Then you can go back to your conference."

The phone went dead. Smith grinned to himself. A straightforward, uncomplicated assignment.

Moments later, the taxi pulled up in front of the Hi-Lai Hotel. He paid the driver and walked into the lobby, heading for the car rental desk. Once the courier had arrived from Taipei, he would drive down the coast to Linyuan and find a fishing boat to take him quietly to Liuchiu. If he could not find one, he would rent one and pilot it himself.

As he crossed the lobby, a short, brisk Chinese man jumped up from an armchair to block his way. "Ah, Dr. Smith, I have been waiting for you. I am honored to meet you personally. Your paper on the late Dr. Chambord's theoretical work with the molecular computer was excellent. Much food for thought."

Smith smiled in acknowledgment of both greeting and compliment. "You flatter me, Dr. Liang."

"Not at all. I wonder whether you could possibly join me and some of my colleagues from the Shanghai Biomedical Institute for dinner tonight. We are keenly interested in the work of both USAMRIID and the CDC on emerging viral agents that threaten all of us."

"I'd very much like that," Smith said smoothly, giving his voice a tinge of regret, "but tonight I have another engagement. Perhaps you are free some other time?"

"With your permission, I will contact you."

"Of course, Dr. Liang." Jon Smith continued on to the desk, his mind already on Liuchiu Island and tonight.

Chapter
Two

Washington, D.C.
Wide and physically impressive, Admiral Stevens Brose filled his chair at the foot of the long conference table in the White House underground situation room. He took off his cap and ran his hand over his gray military buzz cut, amazed — and worried — by what he saw. President Castilla, as always, occupied the chair at the head. But they were the only two in the large room, drinking their morning cups of coffee. The rows of seats at the long table around them were ominous in their emptiness.

"What chemicals, Mr. President?" Admiral Brose asked. He was also the chairman of the joint chiefs.

"Thiodiglycol —"

"Blister weapons."

"— and thionyl chloride."

"Blister and nerve gases. Damn painful and lethal, all of them. A wretched way to die." The admiral's thin mouth and big chin tightened. "How much is there?"

"Tens of tons." President Castilla's grim gaze was fixed on the admiral.

"Unacceptable. When —" Brose stopped abruptly, and his pale eyes narrowed. He took in all the empty chairs at the long table. "I see. We're not going to stop *The Dowager Empress* en route and search her. You want to keep our intelligence about the situation secret."

"For now, yes. We don't have concrete proof, any more than we did with the *Yinhe*. We can't afford another international incident like that, especially with our allies less ready to back us in military actions, and the Chinese close to signing our human-rights accord."

Brose nodded. "Then what do you want me to do, sir? Besides keeping a lid on it?"

"Send one ship to keep tabs on the *Empress*. Close enough to move in, but out of sight."

"Out of sight maybe, but they'll know she's there. Their radar will pick her up. If they're carrying contraband, their captain at least should know. He'll be keeping his crew hyperalert."

"Can't be helped. That's the situation until I have absolute proof. If things turn rocky, I expect you and your people to not let them escalate into a confrontation."

"We have someone getting confirmation?"

"I hope so."

Brose pondered. "She loaded up the night of the first, late?"

"That's my information."

Brose was calculating in his mind. "If I know the Chinese and Shanghai, she didn't sail until early on the second." He reached for the phone at his elbow, glanced at the president. "May I, sir?"

Samuel Castilla nodded.

Brose dialed and spoke into the phone. "I don't care how early it is, Captain. Get me what I need." He waited, hand again running back over his short hair. "Right, Hong Kong registry. A bulk carrier. Fifteen knots. You're certain? Very well." He hung up. "At fifteen knots, that's eighteen days, give or take, to Basra with a stop in Singapore, which is the usual course. If she left around midnight on the first, she should arrive early in the morning on the nineteenth, Chinese time, at the Strait of Hormuz. Three hours earlier Persian Gulf time, and evening of the eighteenth our time. It's the thirteenth now, so in five-plus days she should reach the Hormuz Strait, which is the last place we can legally board her." His voice rose with concern. "Just five days, sir. That's our time frame to figure out this mess."

"Thanks, Stevens. I'll pass it on."

The admiral stood. "One of our frigates would be best for what you want. Enough muscle, but not overkill. Small enough that there's a chance she'll be overlooked for a time, if the radar man's asleep or lazy."

"How soon can you get one there?"

Brose picked up the phone once more. This time, his conversation was even briefer. He hung up. "Ten hours, sir."

"Do it."

Liuchiu Island, Taiwan

By the green glow of his combat watch, agent Jon Smith read the dial once more — 2203 — and silently swore. Mondragon was late.

Crouched low in front of the razor-sharp coral

formation that edged the secluded cove, he listened, but the only sound was the soft surge of the South China Sea as it washed up onto the dark sand and slid back with an audible hiss. The wind was a bare whisper. The air smelled of salt water and fish. Down the coast, boats were harbored, motionless, glowing in the moonlight. The day tourists had left on the last ferry from Penfu.

In other small coves up and down the western coast of the tiny island, a few people camped, but in this cove there was only the wash of the sea and the distant glow of Kaohsiung's lights, some twenty kilometers to the northeast.

Smith checked his watch again — 2206. *Where was Mondragon?*

The fishing boat from Linyuan had landed him in Penfu harbor two hours ago. There he had hired a motorcycle and driven off on the road that encircled the island. When he found the landmark described in his directions, he hid the cycle in bushes and made his way here on foot.

Now it was already 2210, and he waited restlessly, uneasily. *Something had gone wrong.*

He was about to leave his cover to make a cautious search when he felt the coarse sand move. He heard nothing, but the skin on his neck crawled. He gripped his 9mm Beretta, tensed to turn and dive sideways to the sand and rocks, when a sharp, urgent whisper of hot breath seared his ear:

"Don't move!"

Smith froze.

"Not a finger." The low voice was inches from his ear. "Orchid."

"Mondragon?"

29

"It's not the ghost of Chairman Mao," the voice responded wryly. "Although he may be lurking here somewhere."

"You were followed?"

"Think so. Not sure. If I was, I shook them."

The sand moved again, and Avery Mondragon materialized, crouching beside Smith. He was short, dark-haired, and lean, like an oversized jockey. Hard-faced and hungry looking, too, with a predator's eyes. His gaze flitted everywhere — around the shadows of the cove, at the phosphorescent surge of the sea on the beach, and out toward the grotesque shapes of coral jutting like statues from the dusky sea beyond the surf.

Mondragon said, "Let's get this over. If I'm not in Penfu by 2330, I don't make it back to the mainland by morning. If I don't make it back, my cover's blown." He turned his gaze onto Smith. "So you're Lieutenant Colonel Smith, are you? I've heard rumors. You're supposed to be good. I hope half the rumors are true. What I've got for you is damn near radioactive."

He produced a plain, business-size envelope and held it up.

"That's the goods?" Smith asked.

Mondragon nodded and tucked it back inside his jacket. "There's some background you need to tell Klein."

"Let's get on with it then."

"Inside the envelope's what *The Dowager Empress* is really carrying. On the other hand, the so-called official manifest — the one filed with the export board — is smoke and mirrors."

"How do you know?"

"Because this one's got an invoice stamped with the 'chop' — the personal Chinese character seal — of the CEO, as well as the official company seal, and it's addressed to a company in Baghdad for payment. This manifest also indicates three copies were made. The second copy is certainly in Baghdad or Basra since it's an invoice for the goods to be paid for. I don't know where the third copy is."

"How can you be sure you don't have the copy filed with the export board?"

"Because I've seen it, as I said. The contraband isn't listed on it. The CEO's seal is missing."

Smith frowned. "Still, that doesn't sound as if what you've got there is guaranteed."

"Nothing's guaranteed. Anything can be faked — character seals can be counterfeited, and companies in Baghdad can be dummies. But this is an *invoice* manifest and has all the correct signs of an interoffice and intercompany document sent to the receiving company for payment. It's enough to justify President Castilla's ordering the *Empress* stopped on the high seas and our boys taking an intimate look, if we have to. Besides, it's a lot more 'probable cause' than the rumors we had with the *Yinhe*, and if it *is* fake, it proves there's a conspiracy inside China to stir up trouble. No one can blame us, not even Beijing, for taking precautions."

Smith nodded. "I'm convinced. Give it to —"

"There's something else." Mondragon glanced around at the shadows of the tiny cove. "One of my assets in Shanghai told me a story you'd better pass on to Klein. It's not in the paperwork, for obvious reasons. He says there's an old man being held in a low-security prison farm near Chongqing — that's

31

Chiang Kaishek's old World War Two capital, 'Chungking' to Americans. He claims he's been jailed in one place or another in China since 1949, when the Communists beat Chiang and took over the country. My asset says the guy speaks Mandarin and other dialects, but he sure as hell doesn't look Chinese. The old man insists he's an American named David Thayer." He paused and stared, his expression unreadable. "And, hold on to your hat . . . he claims he's President Castilla's real father."

Smith stared. "You can't be serious. Everyone knows the president's father was Serge Castilla, and he's dead. The press covers that family like a blanket."

"Exactly. That's what caught my interest." Mondragon related more details. "My asset says he used the exact phrase, 'President Castilla's *real* father.' If the guy's a fraud, why make up a yarn so easily disproved?"

It was a good question. "How reliable is your asset?"

"He's never steered me wrong or fed me disinformation that I've caught."

"Could it be one of Beijing's tricks? Maybe a way to make the president back off about the human-rights accord?"

"The old prisoner insists Beijing doesn't even know he's got a son, much less that the son's now the U.S. president."

Smith's mind raced as he calculated ages and years. It was numerically possible. "Exactly where is this old man being —"

"Down!" Mondragon dropped flat to the sand.

Heart racing, Smith dove behind a coral outcrop as shouts in angry Chinese and a fusillade of automatic fire hammered from their right, close to the sea. Mondragon rolled behind the outcropping and came up in a crouch beside Smith, his 9mm Glock joining Smith's Beretta, aiming into the dark of the cove, searching for the enemy.

"Well," Mondragon said gloomily, "I guess I didn't shake them."

Smith wasted no time on recriminations. "Where are they? You see anything?"

"Not a damn thing."

Smith pulled night-vision goggles from inside his windbreaker. Through them, the night turned pale green, and the murky coral formations out in the sea grew clear. So did a short, skinny man naked to the waist, hovering near one of the statuelike pillars. He was knee-deep in water, holding an old AK-74 and staring toward where Smith and Mondragon hunched.

"I've got one," he said softly to Mondragon. "Move. Show a shoulder. Look like you're coming out."

Mondragon rose, bent. He thrust his left shoulder out as if about to make a run for it. The skinny man behind the pillar opened fire.

Smith squeezed off two careful rounds. In the green light, the man jerked upright and pitched onto his face. A dark stain spread around him as he floated facedown in the sea.

Mondragon was already back down. He fired. Someone, somewhere in the night, screamed.

"Over there!" Mondragon barked. "To the right! There's more!"

Smith swung the Beretta right. Four green men had broken cover and dashed away from the sea toward the inland road. A fifth lay sprawled on the beach behind them. Smith fired at the lead man of this outflanking group. He saw him clutch his leg and go down, but the two behind him grabbed him by each arm and dragged him onward into cover.

"They're flanking us!" Sweat broke on Smith's forehead. "Move back!"

He and Mondragon leaped up and pounded across the coral sand toward the ridge that sealed the cove in the south. Another fusillade behind them said a lot more than three of their attackers were still standing. With a jolt of adrenaline, Smith felt a bullet sear through his windbreaker. He scrambled up the ridge into thick bushes and fell behind a tree.

Mondragon followed, but he was dragging his right leg. He flopped behind another tree.

A fresh fusillade ripped through leaves and small branches, spraying the air and making Smith and Mondragon choke with the dust. They kept their heads down. Mondragon pulled a knife from a holster on his back, slit his trousers, and examined his leg wound.

"How bad is it?" Smith whispered.

"Don't think the bullet hit anything serious, but it's going to be hard to explain back on the mainland. I'll have to hide out 'on vacation,' or fake an accident." His smile was pained. "Right now, we've got more to worry about. That small group's on our flank by now, probably up on the road, and the gang in the cove is going to drive us to them. We've got to keep moving south."

Agreeing, Smith crawled ahead through the brush, forged hard and tough under the sea-bent trees by the constant wind and spray of the South China Sea. They made slow progress, Smith clearing a path for Mondragon. They used only their feet, knees, and elbows, as they cradled their pistols. The bushes gave reluctantly, the branches tearing at their clothes and hair. Smaller twigs broke and scratched their faces, drawing blood from forearms and ears.

At last they reached the high bank above another less-sheltered angle in the island's coastline. It was far too open to the sea to be called a cove. As they crawled eagerly on toward the road, voices carried in the windless night from there. Behind them, four silent shadows materialized ashore, while two remained ankle deep in the sea. One of the shadows, larger than the rest, motioned the others to spread out. Bathed in gentle moonlight, they broke apart and emerged as four men dressed completely in black, their heads covered by hoods.

The man who had ordered them to fan out bent over. Smith heard a whispery version of a deep, harsh voice give instructions over what was probably a handheld radio.

"Chinese," Mondragon analyzed quietly, listening. His tones were tight. He was in pain. "Can't make out all of the words, but it sounds like the Shanghai dialect of Mandarin. Which means they probably did follow me from Shanghai. He's their leader."

"You think someone tipped them?"

"Possibly. Or I could've made a mistake. Or I

could've been under surveillance for days. Weeks. No way to know. Whatever, they're here, and they're closing in."

Smith studied Mondragon, who seemed to be as tough as the ocean-forged brush. He was in pain, but he would not let it stop him.

"We could play the odds," Smith told him. "Head on for the road. Are you up for that? Otherwise, we'll make a stand here."

"Are you crazy? They'll massacre us here."

They crawled deeper into the brush and trees, away from the sea. They had gone a slow twenty more feet, when footsteps approached from the rear, grinding through the undergrowth. Simultaneously, they saw the shadows of the inland group pushing toward them and the sea. Their pursuers had guessed what they would do and were closing in from front and back.

Smith swore. "They've heard us, or found our trail. Keep moving. When the ones from the road get close, I'll rush them."

"Maybe not," Mondragon whispered back, hope in his voice. "There's a rock formation over there to the left that looks like good cover. We can hide in there until they pass. If not, we might be able to hold out until someone hears the shooting and shows up."

"It's worth a try," Smith agreed.

The rock formation rose out of the brush in the moonlight like an ancient ruin in the jungles of Cambodia or the Yucatan. Composed of odd-shaped coral groupings, it made a crude kind of fort, with cover on all sides and openings to fire through, if that was what they had to do in the end.

It also contained a depression in the center, where they could sink low, nearly out of sight.

With relief, they hunkered in the basin, their weapons ready, as they listened to the sounds of the island in the silvery moonlight. Smith's scratches and small puncture wounds stung with sweat. Mondragon eased his leg around, trying to find a position that was less painful. Their tension was electric as they waited, watching, listening . . . Kaohsiung's lights glowed against the sky. Somewhere a dog barked, and another took it up. A car passed on the distant road. Out on the sea, the noise of the motor of a late-returning boat growled.

Then they heard voices, again murmuring in the Shanghai dialect. The voices came closer. Closer. Feet crackled against the tough brush. Shadows passed, broken up by the brush. Someone stopped.

Mondragon raised his Glock.

Smith grabbed his wrist to stop him. He shook his head — *don't.*

The shadow was a large man. He had removed his hood, and his face was colorless, almost bleached looking, under a shock of oddly pale red hair. His eyes reflected like mirrors as they searched the coral formation for any shape or movement. Smith and Mondragon held their breaths in the depression inside the rocks.

For a long moment, the man continued his slow surveillance.

Smith felt the sweat trickling down his back and chest.

The man turned and moved away toward the road.

"Whewwww." Mondragon let out a soft breath. "That was —"

The night exploded around them. Bullets slammed into coral and whined away into the trees. Rock chips showered down in a violent hail. The entire dark seemed to be firing at them, muzzle flashes coming from all sides. The large, redheaded man had seen them but had made no move until he had alerted the others.

Smith and Mondragon returned fire, searching frantically among the moonlit shadows of the brush and trees for a visible enemy. Their cover had now become a disadvantage. There were only two of them. Not enough in the darkness to beat off at least seven, possibly more. Their ammunition would soon run low.

Smith leaned close to Mondragon's ear. "We'll have to make a break for it. Head for the road. My motorcycle's not far away. It can carry both of us."

"There's less fire coming from the front. Let's pin them down and break that way. Don't worry about me. I can do it!"

Smith nodded. He would have said the same thing. Right now, with adrenaline pumping through them like lava, either of them could run from here to the moon, if they had to.

On a count of three, they opened fire and rushed out of the rocks toward the road, running low while still moving fast, dodging brush and trees. Moments later, they were through the circle of attackers. At last the gunfire was from behind, and the road was close ahead.

Mondragon gave a grunt, stumbled, and went

down, ripping through the tangled vegetation as he fell. Smith instantly grabbed his arm to help him up, but the agent did not respond. The arm was without energy, lifeless.

"Avery?"

There was no answer.

Smith fell to his haunches beside the downed agent and found hot blood on the back of his head. Instantly, he felt for a pulse in his neck. None. He inhaled, swore, and searched Mondragon's pockets for the envelope. At the same time, he heard the killers approach, trying to be quiet in the heavy undergrowth.

The envelope was missing. Frantically he checked every pocket again, taking whatever he found. He felt around Mondragon's body, but the envelope was gone. Definitely gone. And there was no more time.

Cursing inwardly, he sprinted away.

Clouds had built over the South China Sea and drifted across the moon, turning the night pitch-black as he reached the road. The deep cover of darkness was a rare stroke of good luck. Relieved, but furious about Mondragon's death, he ran across and dropped into the cover of the low ditch that bordered the two-lane road.

Panting, he aimed both Mondragon's Glock and his Beretta back at the trees. And waited, thinking . . . The envelope had been in an inside pocket. Mondragon had gone down at least twice that Smith had seen. The envelope could have fallen out then, or perhaps when they were crawling through the brush, or even when they were running, their jackets flapping.

Frustrated and deeply worried, his grip tightened on the two weapons.

After a few minutes, a single figure emerged warily at the road's edge, looked right and left, and started across, his old AK-74 ready. Smith raised the Beretta. The motion attracted the killer's attention. He opened fire blindly. Smith dropped the Glock, aimed the Beretta, and shot twice in rapid succession.

The man slammed forward onto his face and lay still. Smith grabbed the Glock again and opened a withering, sweeping fire with both weapons. Shouts and screams sounded from the far side of the road.

As they echoed in his mind, he leaped out of the ditch and tore away through the trees toward the center of the island. His feet pounded and his lungs ached. Sweat poured off him. He did not know how far he ran, or for how long, but he became aware that there were no sounds of pursuit. No trampling of brush. No running feet. No gunshots.

He crouched in the cover of a tree for a full five minutes. It seemed like five hours. His pulse pounded in his ears. Had they given up? He and poor Mondragon had killed at least three, wounded two more, and perhaps had shot others.

But little of that was important right now. If the killers had quit their pursuit, it meant only one thing — they had what they had come for. They had found the secret invoice manifest of *The Dowager Empress*.

Chapter
Three

Washington, D.C.
Golden sunlight drenched the Rose Garden and made warm rectangles on the floor of the Oval Office, but somehow it seemed menacing this morning, President Castilla thought as Charles Ouray, White House chief of staff, stepped inside the door.

Ouray looked as unhappy as he felt, the president decided. "Sit down, Charlie. What's up?"

"I'm not so sure you want to hear, Mr. President." He sat on the sofa.

"No luck with the leaks?"

"Zero," Ouray said, shaking his head. "Leaks of such extent and accuracy over an entire year should be traceable, but the secret service, FBI, CIA, and NSA can't find a thing. They've investigated everyone in the West Wing from the mail room to the whole senior staff, including me. The good news is they guarantee the leaks aren't coming from any of us. In fact, the entire White House roster down to cleaning crews and gardeners is clear."

The president tented his hands and scowled at his fingers. "Very well, what does that leave?"

Ouray looked wary. "Leave, sir?"

"Who's left, Charlie? Who haven't they investigated who could've had access to the information that's been leaked? The plans . . . the policy decisions. They were high-level."

"Yes, sir. But I'm not sure what you mean by who's left? No one, I can —"

"Have they investigated me, Charlie?"

Ouray laughed uneasily. "Of course not, Mr. President."

"Why not? I certainly had entree, unless there were leaks I didn't hear about."

"There weren't, sir. But suspecting you is ridiculous on the face of it."

"That's what they said about Nixon before they found the tapes."

"Sir —"

"I know, you think I'm the one harmed most. That's not true. It's the American people, but I think you get my point now."

Ouray said nothing.

"Look higher, Charlie, and look around. The cabinet. The vice president, who doesn't always agree with me. The joint chiefs, the Pentagon, influential lobbyists we sometimes talk to. *No one* is above suspicion."

Ouray leaned forward. "You really think it could be someone that high, Sam?"

"Absolutely. Whoever it is, he — or she — is killing us. Not so much the information . . . the press, and even our enemies, knowing our plans before we revealed them . . . that's been simply embarrassing so far. No, the worst damage is to our confidence in each other and to the potential

42

threat to national security. Right now, I can't rely on any of our people with something really sensitive, not even you."

Ouray nodded. "I know, Sam. But you can trust me now." He smiled, but it was not a humorous smile. "I've been cleared. Unless you can't trust the FBI, CIA, NSA, or secret service."

"See? In the back of our minds we're beginning to doubt even them."

"I guess we are. What about the Pentagon? A lot of the leaks involve military decisions."

"Policy decisions, not military. Long-range strategy."

Ouray shook his head. "I don't know. Maybe we've got a foreign mole somewhere, so deep the security people can't find him. Maybe we tell them to dig deeper? Look for a professional spy hidden behind one of us?"

"All right, tell them to pursue that angle. But I don't think it's a spy, foreign or domestic. This deep throat isn't interested in stealing secrets — he's interested in changing the public debate. Influencing our decisions. Someone who secures an advantage, if our policy changes."

"Yeah," Ouray agreed uneasily.

The president returned to the papers on his desk. "Find the leaker, Charlie. I need answers before this situation paralyzes me."

Thursday, September 14
Kaohsiung, Taiwan

The windows of Jon Smith's room on the twentieth floor of the Grand Hi-Lai Hotel displayed a breathtaking panorama of Kaohsiung's sparkling night, from the horizon-to-horizon lights up to the black, star-studded sky. Tonight, Smith had no interest in it.

Safely back in his room, for the third time he read through everything in Mondragon's wallet and notebook. He had hoped there would be some clue to how the murdered Covert-One agent had secured the manifest. The only unexplained item was a crumpled cocktail-sized napkin from a Starbucks coffee shop with a name scrawled on it in ink — Zhao Yanji.

His cell phone buzzed. It was Fred Klein returning his call.

Klein's greeting was a question: "You delivered the article to the airport?"

"No," Smith told him. "I have bad news. Mondragon was killed." The silence at the other end was like a sigh.

"I'm sorry. I worked with him a long time. He was a fine agent, and I'll miss him. I'll contact his parents. They'll be shocked. Distraught."

Smith breathed deeply. Once. Twice. "Sorry, Fred. This must be hard on you."

"Tell me what happened, Jon."

Smith told him about the envelope, the attack, and Mondragon's death. "The killers were Chinese, from Shanghai. The invoice manifest must've been the real thing. I have a lead, but it's remote." He told Klein about the Starbucks napkin.

"You're sure the napkin's from Shanghai?"

"Was Mondragon anywhere *but* Shanghai in the last few months?"

"Not that I'm aware of."

"Then it's a possibility, and it's all I have anyway."

"Can you get to Shanghai?"

"I think so. There's a scientist at the conference here, Dr. Liang, whom I think I can convince to take me to his facility there for a tour." He explained about the Chinese microbiologist buttonholing him. "There are three problems. I don't know a damn word of Chinese, and I don't have a clue where the Starbucks coffee shops are there. Then there's my Beretta. I have no way to slip it into China."

"I'll have the Starbucks information faxed to Taipei. I'll have an interpreter waiting for you in Shanghai, and he'll bring you a weapon. Recognition words: 'double latte.' "

"One more thing." Smith told him about the old man in the Chinese prison farm who claimed his name was David Thayer. He repeated the details Mondragon had passed on.

"Thayer? I've never heard of a connection by someone named Thayer to the president. Sounds like a dodge of some kind."

"Mondragon's asset said the old man is definitely American."

"Is the asset reliable?"

"As much as any," Smith said. "At least, according to Mondragon."

"I'll tell the president. If the man's an American, no matter who he really is, Castilla will want to know."

"Then I'll start working on finding the invoice manifest in Shanghai. What about the other copies?"

"I'll take care of the one that should be in Baghdad. With luck, we won't care where the third is." He paused. "You should know, Colonel, that the time frame's tight. According to the navy, we've got only five days, maybe less, until the *Empress* reaches the Persian Gulf."

Wednesday, September 13
Washington, D.C.

In the Oval Office, President Castilla ate lunch at the heavy pine table he had brought with him from the governor's residence in Santa Fe. It had served as his desk there as it did here. With a sense of nostalgia, he put down his chile-and-cheese sandwich and swiveled in his new chair to stare out his window at the lush green grounds and distant monuments he had grown to love. Still, another view blotted it from his mind — the wide red sunsets and vast, empty, yet perpetually alive desert of his ranch far down on the borderlands of his native New Mexico, where even a wild jaguar might still be found roaming. He was feeling suddenly old and tired. He wanted to go home.

His reverie was interrupted by the entry of his personal assistant, Jeremy. "Mr. Klein is here. He'd like to speak with you, sir."

The president glanced at his desk clock. What time would it be in China? "No calls or visitors until I tell you otherwise."

"Yes, sir." The assistant held open the door.

Fred Klein hurried in, his pipe stem sticking up from the handkerchief pocket of his Harris tweed jacket.

46

As Jeremy closed the door, Castilla waved Klein to the London club chair that had been a gift from the queen. "I'd have come to the yacht club tonight."

"This can't wait. With the leaks, I didn't want to trust even the red phone."

The president nodded. "Do we have the manifest?"

Klein heaved a sigh. "No, sir, we do not." He repeated Smith's report.

The president grimaced and shook his head. "Terrible. Has your agent's family been notified?"

"Of course, sir."

"They'll be taken care of?"

"They will."

The president glanced out his high window again. "Do you think they'd like to visit the Oval Office, Fred?"

"You can't do that, Mr. President. Covert-One doesn't exist. Mondragon was in private business, nothing more."

"Sometimes this job is particularly hard." He paused. "All right, we don't have what I have to have. When will we have it?"

"Smith has a lead in Shanghai. He's working on a way there now, as a guest of the Chinese government. He'll be talking to microbiologists from China's research establishments. Meanwhile, I have people in Beijing, Hong Kong, Guangzhou, and some of the new manufacturing cities that have sprung up there over the last few years. They're looking for any sign Beijing orchestrated this, as well as information about *The Dowager Empress*, even rumors. And there's a possibility we can find a second copy in Baghdad. I'm assigning an agent to it."

"Good. I have the navy sending a frigate. Brose says at the most we'll have ten hours before the *Empress* tumbles to what we're doing. After that, China knows, and probably the world."

"If the Chinese want them to." Klein hesitated. Klein was not a man who hesitated.

"What is it, Fred? If it involves those chemicals, I'd better know it."

"It doesn't, Mr. President." Klein paused again, choosing his words.

This time the president didn't prompt him, but he frowned, puzzled by what could be unsettling the iron chief of Covert-One.

At last Klein continued: "There's an old man being held in a prison farm in China who claims to be an American. He says he's been a prisoner since Chiang's defeat in 1949."

President Castilla nodded, his face sober. "Things like that did happen to our people after World War Two. Probably to many more than we actually knew about or suspected. Nevertheless, it's outrageous and totally unacceptable, as well as unconscionable, that he's still being held today. It's one of the reasons I insisted the human-rights treaty include outside inspectors to investigate foreign prisoners of war. In any case, if it's true and we have firm intel, we'll have to do something about him immediately. Does this American have a name?"

Klein watched the president's face. "David Thayer."

The president showed no reaction. No reaction

at all. As if he had not heard. As if he still waited for Klein to say a name. Then he blinked. He swiveled in his chair. Abruptly he stood up, strode to the window behind his desk, and stared out, hands clasped in a white knot behind his back.

"Sir?"

Samuel Castilla's back was rigid, as if he had just received a beating. "After all these years? How is it possible? There was no way he was still alive —"

"What happened — ?" Klein began but did not finish. With a sinking stomach, he knew the answer to the question.

The president turned, sat down again, leaned back, his eyes seeing somewhere faraway in both space and time. "He disappeared in China when I was in diapers. The State Department, the military, and Truman's own staff people tried to find him, but we were heavily opposed to Mao's Communists, as you know, and they had no love for us. But we did manage to get some clandestine information from the Soviets and some American and British sources in China, and all of it indicated Thayer was dead. Either he'd died fighting, had been captured and executed by the Communists, or killed by Chiang's own people for trying to talk to the Reds. He'd told my mother he was going to try to do that before he left."

He inhaled deeply and gave Klein a small smile. "Serge Castilla was another State Department man, a close friend of Thayer's. He led State's efforts to locate him, which threw him into almost weekly contact with my mother. Because I was so small, there was no way she could explain what was happening. By the time I was four, everyone finally

49

accepted Thayer was dead. With Serge and my mother, one thing led to another, and they married that year, and he adopted me. By then, as far as I was concerned, Serge was my father, and David Thayer was just a name. When I was in my late teens, she filled me in on everything they'd learned about his time in China, which was damn little. I didn't see any purpose in telling the world, because Serge was my dad. He'd raised me, had been there for me through chicken pox and spelling tests, and I loved him. Since we had the same last name, people never bothered to ask whether he was my biological father."

The president shook his head, bringing himself back to the present. He met Klein's worried gaze steadily. "David Thayer is part of my history, but at the same time, I have no memory of him."

"It's a thousand to one this man is simply an opportunist, possibly a common criminal, probably not even American. He could've met Thayer back before he vanished. So now he's on a low-security farm, has heard about you and your efforts to make China give more respect to human rights, and he sees an opportunity to get out of there."

"If that were true, how could he have guessed Thayer had a son who'd grow up to be an American president, especially one with the last name of Castilla?"

Klein frowned. "For that matter, sir, how would the real David Thayer know about you? He knew he had a son, but he couldn't know his widow would marry Serge Castilla."

"That's simple enough. If this man really is David Thayer, he could've simply put two and two

50

together. He knew he had a son named Samuel Adams, and a close friend named Castilla. Spelled the way our family does, Castilla is hardly common. My age would fit exactly."

"Of course, you're right," Klein admitted. "But what about the leaks? Maybe we have a spy in the White House who told Beijing and this is one of their convoluted setups."

The president shook his head. "I never tried to hide that Serge adopted me, but it wasn't something that tended to come up in conversation. No one beyond my immediate family, not even Charlie Ouray, knows exactly who and what my birth father was and what happened to him. Not even you knew that. I didn't want to trade on sympathy or embarrass my mother."

"Someone always knows, and remembers, and has a price."

"And you're always the cynic."

"It's part of the territory." Klein smiled thinly.

"I suppose it is."

Klein hesitated again. "All right. Say we can't be sure he's not real. He *could* be your father. If he is, what do you want to do?"

The president leaned back in his chair again, took off his glasses, and ran his big hands over his face. He sighed heavily. "I want to meet him, of course. I can't think of anything right now that would make my jaded old heart sing the way that would. Imagine, my real father is alive. Imagine that. Incredible. When I was a little boy, despite all my love for Serge, I used to dream about David Thayer." He paused, his face filled with melancholy and long-ago loss.

He shrugged and waved a hand in dismissal. "All right. So that's the dream. Realistically, what does the president of the United States want? I want him out of China, of course. He's an American. Therefore, he deserves the complete support of his country. As I would with any American who has been through the ordeal that he has, I want to meet him, thank him for his courage, and shake his hand. But that said, there are international consequences to consider. There's *The Dowager Empress*, and there's the potential of deadly cargo that it's ferrying to a country that would like to destroy us."

"Yessir, there is."

"If we find the ship *is* carrying the chemicals and we have to board it, I can't imagine the treaty will be signed. Certainly not this year, probably not until a new administration takes over. There'll be more delays as the Chinese feel out the new Oval Office China policy. Thayer, given his age, will probably never get out."

"Probably not, Sam."

The president grimaced, but his voice was hard, unyielding as he continued, "And that can't matter. Not for a second. If she's carrying chemicals for weapons, the *Empress* must be stopped, or sunk if necessary. For the moment, we do nothing about this old man in China. Is that clear?"

"Absolutely, Mr. President."

Chapter Four

Thursday, September 14
Shanghai, China

The Air China jet from Tokyo flew in over the East China Sea and arced across the vast delta of the Yangtze River. Through his window, Jon Smith studied the green land, the dense buildings, and the haze that had settled like wisps of cotton in the low areas of what was one of Asia's most powerful cities.

His gaze swept from the congested Yangtze River north to Chongming Island, as he silently grappled with the problem of the missing manifest and the alarming cost of its loss. When the jet landed at Pudong International Airport at exactly 1322 hours, he had come to no conclusion except that if the human-rights treaty were imperative, keeping more chemical weapons out of Saddam Hussein's hands was probably even more so.

With their colleagues smiling around them, Dr. Liang Tianning escorted Dr. Jon Smith from the jet. Not large by Western standards, the terminal was ultramodern, with potted plants and a high blue ceiling. The ticket counters were packed with

53

men in business suits, both European and Chinese, a symptom of Shanghai's drive to become the New York City of Asia. A few glanced at Smith and his companions, but the looks showed idle curiosity, nothing more.

Outdoors, a black limousine was waiting among the eager taxis. The instant they were seated in the rear, the driver pulled into traffic. He managed to dodge three taxis and two pedestrians, who leaped for their lives. Smith turned to see whether they were safe, while no one else paid the slightest attention, which said a lot about local driving customs. Also it gave him a clear view of a small, dark-blue car that appeared to be a Volkswagen Jetta. It had been parked among the taxis but was now directly behind the limo.

Was someone else expecting him — someone who had nothing to do with biomolecular science and was unsure whether he was who and what Dr. Liang said? The Jetta driver might simply be an ordinary Shanghainese, who had mistakenly parked among the taxis instead of inside the garage while waiting to pick up a returning friend or relative. Still, it was remarkable that the driver had chosen the identical moment to leave the terminal.

Smith said nothing about it to Dr. Liang. As the men discussed viral agents, the limo glided onto an express highway, heading west through the soggy delta, which was barely above sea level for the entire nineteen miles. Shanghai's toothy skyline came into view — a new city, almost entirely the work of the last decade. First came the sprawling Pudong New District, with the needle-sharp point of the Oriental Pearl Tower and the squarer but also

54

soaring eighty-eight-story Jin Mao Building. Expensive architecture with all the accouterments of luxury and high technology. Only a dozen years ago, this land had been a flat marsh that supplied the city with vegetables.

The conversation turned to plans for Smith's visit as the limo continued through Pudong, under the Huangpu River, and into Puxi and the Bund, which until 1990 had been the heart of old Shanghai. Now a phalanx of glistening skyscrapers towered above the neoclassical business offices of the city's colonial period.

At People's Park, Smith had a close view of the cars, bicycles, and individuals who mobbed the streets, a sea of life on the move. For a few seconds, he paused to contemplate it all: The massive new construction. The evidence of outrageous wealth. The tooth-to-jowl humanity. Shanghai was China's most populous city, larger even than Hong Kong or Beijing. But Shanghai wanted more. It wanted a prominent place on the world's economic stage. It gave nodding obeisance to the past, but its interest was focused on the future.

As the limo made a right turn toward the river, Dr. Liang came close to wringing his hands. "You are sure, Dr. Smith, that you do not wish a room at the Grand Hyatt in Jin Mao Tower? It is a modern hotel, magnificent. The restaurants and amenities are beyond compare. You would be most comfortable there, I assure you. In addition, it is far more convenient to our Biomedical Research Institute in Zhangjiang, where we will go when you are settled. The Peace Hotel is historic, yes — but it is scarcely four star."

Covert-One's research people had informed him that there were only three Starbucks coffee shops in Shanghai at the moment, and all were on the Puxi side of the river, two not far from the Bund.

He smiled and said, "I've always wanted to stay at the old Peace Hotel, Dr. Liang. Call it the whim of a history buff."

The scientist sighed. "Then of course. Naturally."

The limousine turned south onto the scenic street that skirted the river, with the Bund's colonial buildings on one side and the Huangpu broad and flowing on the other. Smith gazed out at the row of stately businesses and houses that overlooked the river. Here was the heart of the old British Concession, which had established itself in 1842 and held convulsively to power for nearly a century, until the Japanese finally captured the city during World War II.

Dr. Liang leaned forward and pointed. "There is your Peace Hotel."

"I see it. Thanks."

Crowned by a green pyramid, it was twelve stories of Gothic architecture by way of the Chicago School. A notorious Shanghai millionaire, Victor Sassoon, had built it in 1929, after making a fortune trading in opium and weapons.

As the limousine pulled to a stop before the arched entrance, Dr. Liang informed Smith, "I will register you in the name of the Biomedical Institute." He climbed out.

Smith followed, casually making a 360-degree survey. He saw no sign of the dark-blue car that had left Pudong International with them. But as he stepped into the revolving doors, he noted their driver had also left the limo, raised the hood, and seemed to be examining the engine, which had been operating with the perfection of a Swiss timepiece, at least to Smith's ear.

The lobby was Art Deco, little changed since the Roaring Twenties, which had roared especially loudly in Shanghai. Dr. Liang steered Smith left, across the white Italian-marble floor, to the registration desk. The haughty desk clerk looked down his nose at Dr. Liang as he registered and then over at Smith. He made little effort to conceal his arrogance.

Dr. Liang spoke to him in low, harsh Chinese, and Smith heard what sounded like the name of the research institute. Fear flashed in the clerk's eyes. Instantly he became almost obsequious toward the Western guest. Despite the aura of freewheeling capitalism that had enlarged the city, Shanghai was in China, China was still a Communist country, and Dr. Liang appeared to be a great deal more influential than he had let anyone at the Taiwan conference see.

As the clerk summoned a bellman, Dr. Liang presented Smith with his room key. "I regret a suite could not be authorized, but your room will be most spacious and comfortable. Do you wish to freshen up before we continue to the institute?"

"Today?" Smith acted surprised. "I'm afraid I wouldn't be at my best, Dr. Liang. I was in meetings and consultations until the small hours last night. A day of rest, and I'll be able to do justice to our colleagues in the morning."

Dr. Liang was startled. "Well, of course, that will be fine. I will alert my staff to rearrange our schedule. But surely you will join us for dinner. It would give all of us a great pleasure to reveal to you the beauty of Shanghai after dark."

Smith resisted an urge to bow; it was not a Chinese custom. "I'd be delighted, thank you. But perhaps we can have a late start? Would nine o'clock do?"

"That is agreeable. We will be here." Liang smiled and nodded understandingly. But there was an edge to his voice as he added, "We will not keep you up too late, Dr. Smith. That is a promise."

Was there suspicion behind the words and the smile? Or was Dr. Liang simply losing patience? For a simple scientist, he seemed to inspire a little too much fear in the desk clerk. Smith was acutely aware he might have raised his colleague's doubts by putting him off in Taiwan, then seeking him out a few hours later, and, finally — no matter how subtly he had tried to make the invitation seem to come from Liang — hinting he would not turn down an immediate invitation. But with the time pressure, he'd had to take the risk.

Suspicious or not, the scientist was at least smiling when he left. Smith watched through the glass doors as he stopped at the limo. The driver appeared from somewhere and spoke swiftly and urgently. Both got in, and the limo sped away.

The bellman had taken his suitcase. Smith rode the elevator up to his floor and found his room, still contemplating Dr. Liang, the limousine driver who had inspected an engine that had given no indication it needed inspecting, and the dark-blue Jetta. His bag was waiting, and the bellman was gone — tipping was frowned upon in the People's Republic, although, as Shakespeare wrote in *Hamlet*, it was a custom more honored in the breach than in the observance.

The room was everything Dr. Liang had promised. As large as a small suite in most modern American or European luxury hotels, it was atmospheric, with a king-sized bed and side tables recessed in a wood-paneled alcove lighted softly by antique table lamps. There was also a cozy sitting area with armchairs and coffee table, a leather-inlaid desk, green ivy plants, and a full bathroom behind a paneled wood door. With the chintz prints and piecrust tables, it looked very British. The windows were expansive, but the view was far from spectacular — neither the river, Pudong, the two suspension bridges, nor the Bund. Instead, Smith looked out on the older, lower office buildings and residences of the millions who staffed, fed, and operated the great city.

Smith checked inside his suitcase. The all-but-invisible filament he'd had installed in the interior was unbroken, which meant no one had searched it. He decided he must be too jumpy, probably overreacting. . . . Still, somewhere out there was the true manifest of the *Empress* as well as the people who had created it and the people who had stolen it from Mondragon. They might or might not be the same group. In any case, he was reasonably certain some had seen him close enough that they would recognize him again. By now, they might already know his name.

At the same time, all he had was a short glimpse of the big, tall leader of the attackers — a Han Chinese with unusual red hair — and a meaningless name scribbled on a coffeehouse napkin.

He was just starting to unpack when he heard footsteps in the corridor. He slowed, listening. The sounds stopped outside his door. His pulse accelerating, he padded across the room and flattened against the wall, waiting.

As Dr. Liang Tianning entered the biomedical center, the staff secretary nodded toward his private office. "There's a man waiting, Dr. Liang. He said he came to talk to you about your phone call. I . . . I couldn't keep him out." She looked down at her hands in her lap and shivered. She was young and shy, the way he preferred his secretaries. "I don't like him."

Dr. Liang admonished her. "He is an important man. Certainly not one you should dislike so openly. No phone calls, please, while he is here. You understand?"

She nodded, still looking down.

When Dr. Liang entered his office, the man was leaning against his filing cabinet, across from the desk. He was smiling and idly whistling, like a mischievous little boy.

Dr. Liang's voice was uneasy. "I don't know what I can add to what I reported over the telephone, Major Pan."

"Possibly nothing. But let's find out."

Major Pan Aitu was small and pudgy, with soft hands, a gentle voice, and a benign smile. He wore a conservative gray European suit, clip-on floral bow tie, and horn-rimmed glasses. There was nothing about him to frighten anyone, until you looked behind the glasses. The eyes were completely unresponsive. When he smiled, the eyes did not. When he conversed in his quiet voice, the eyes did not animate or listen. They watched. They looked at you, but they did not see you. It was impossible to say at any given moment what they did see.

"Explain what has alarmed you about this Dr. Jon Smith," Major Pan said. "Has he been asking questions?"

"No, no. Nothing like that." Liang fell into his desk chair. "It is only that in Taiwan he was so eager, and then when we have arranged an immediate visit to the research center here, he is quite suddenly too tired. He says that tomorrow would be better."

"You don't think he's tired?"

"In Taiwan, at the conference, he did not seem tired. At the airport in Taipei, he was quite eager."

"Explain to me exactly what happened in Taiwan."

Liang described his approach to Smith, his invitation to dinner with himself and his colleagues from the institute, and Smith's excuse and suggestion another time would be good.

"You thought he had no other engagement that night?"

Dr. Liang clicked his teeth, considering. "He was . . . well . . . evasive. You know how you can sense when someone has been taken by surprise and is quickly thinking of a polite way to refuse?"

Major Pan nodded, as much to himself as to

61

Liang. "That's when you left it that you'd contact him for a more convenient occasion to confer about your biomedical matters?"

"Yes." There was something about Major Pan — perhaps the way he always seemed to be waiting — that compelled people to say more. "It seemed the right thing to do. His work at USAMRIID is important. We are anxious to understand what they are doing. Perhaps there is something there to aid our own research."

"He is, then, a legitimate scientist?"

"A fine one."

"But also an officer in the U.S. Army?"

"I suppose so. A colonel, I believe."

"A lieutenant colonel," Major Pan corrected absently, his expressionless eyes turned inward, as he thought. "I have studied his record since your call. There are, shall we say, odd occurrences in his past."

"Odd? How?"

"Gaps. They are usually explained in his record as 'leave time,' which is military vocabulary for a holiday. A vacation. One occurred after the death of his fiancée from a virus she was working with."

"Yes, I know that virus. Frightening. Surely an absence is understandable after such a cruel misfortune?"

"Possibly." Major Pan nodded as if he had really heard, but his eyes said his mind was somewhere else. "You did not see Smith again last night?"

"No."

"But you attended various talks and meetings?"

"Of course. It was why we were there."

"Would you have expected that he'd be around, too?"

"Yes." Liang frowned. "There were two in particular. One by an American colleague, and another by a personal friend of his from the Pasteur. But remember, he did tell me he was in meetings late into the night. There were many to choose from."

Major Pan considered. "It was the next morning that he suddenly approached you to come to Shanghai to visit your institute?"

"Well, not in so many words. But I would say . . . he made it quite clear he would be interested in an immediate invitation."

"How so? How did he happen to be with you this morning?"

Dr. Liang thought. "He joined us for breakfast. Usually he ate with his friend from the Pasteur. During the meal, he casually mentioned he would like to see our facility and speak to us about USAMRIID's work. When I said I could certainly arrange it in the near future, he became regretful, suggesting it was difficult for him to travel so far, which meant he was rarely in Asia. At that point I, of course, suggested that since he was so close, why not now?"

"And he liked the idea?"

"He hemmed and hawed, but I could see it appealed to him."

The major nodded to himself again. He abruptly slid off the filing cabinet and was gone.

Dr. Liang stared at the closed door of his office, wondering what had happened. He was certain he had reported everything by phone to the Security

Bureau, as he was required to do after every trip outside China. Why had Major Pan come here, and what could he have learned just now that made him leave so suddenly? The major had a reputation as a man who succeeded in his work where everyone else failed. Liang shook his head, feeling a disorienting chill of fear.

Beijing, China

The highly secure conclave of Zhongnanhai stood in the shadow of the legendary Forbidden City in central Beijing, where China's emperors and empresses once played and governed. For centuries, Zhongnanhai was the imperial court's pleasure garden, where horse races, hunts, and festivals were held for nobility and their retainers on the green banks of two lakes. In fact, Zhongnanhai meant "Central and Southern Lake."

After the Communists captured the country in 1949, they moved into the vast complex and refurbished and remodeled the pagoda-roofed buildings. Today, Zhongnanhai was alternately revered and reviled as the all-powerful national seat of Chinese government — the new Forbidden City. Here the Politburo, which numbered twenty-five, held forth in regal splendor. Although ultimate authority rested with them, the truth was that it was the Politburo's Standing Committee that really ruled. They were the elite of the elite. Recently, the Standing Committee had been increased from seven members to nine. Their decisions were rubber-stamped by the Politburo and implemented by ministries and lower-level departments.

Many lived on the highly secure grounds with their families, in traditional courtyard-style estates of several buildings, surrounded by walls. Top staff members did, too, in apartments far more comfortable than most of those available outside, in the metropolis.

Still, this was not the White House or 10 Downing Street or even the Kremlin. Secretive, media-averse, Zhongnanhai showed on few tourist maps, even though its general office address at 2 Fuyoujie was printed clearly on Communist Party stationery. Surrounded by a vermillion-colored wall like the one that had once shut the old Forbidden City off from the world, the compound was so well designed that seeing in or over the high walls from anywhere in Beijing was impossible. Ordinary Chinese were not welcome. Foreigners even less so, unless they were ruling heads of state.

Some of this pleased Niu Jianxing, but not all. Although he was one of the elite Standing Committee and worked in Zhongnanhai, he chose to live outside it, in the city itself. Instead of being decorated with ornamental scrolls, dragons, and photographs, his office was spartan. He believed in the basic socialist principle of from each according to his abilities, to each according to his needs. His physical needs were simple and unpretentious. His intellectual needs were something else again.

Niu Jianxing leaned back behind his cluttered desk, entwined his fingers, and closed his eyes. He was still within the circular pool of light cast by his old desk lamp. It glared on his sunken cheeks and delicate features, which were partially hidden behind tortoiseshell glasses. The harsh light did not appear to bother him, as if he were so deep in concentration he did not know there was any light at all, as if nothing disturbing could exist in the tranquil world inside his mind.

Niu Jianxing had become a very important man by acquiring power step by clandestine step. Ever since entering the party and the government, he had found repose to be a great aid to concentration and correct decisions. He would often sit silently like this at Politburo and Standing Committee meetings. At first, the others had thought he was asleep and had dismissed him as a lightweight from the countryside of Tianjin. They talked as if he were not there — in fact, as if he did not exist at all — until it became clear, to the permanent regret of a few who had spoken too freely, that he heard every word and usually had their problems solved or dismissed before they could even articulate them.

After that, his admirers nicknamed him the Owl, a catchy name that spread through the ranks and made him someone to be remembered. A savvy politician as well as tactician, he had made it his personal chop.

At the moment, the Owl was pondering the disquieting rumor that some of his colleagues on the Standing Committee had second thoughts about signing the human-rights agreement with the United States he had worked so hard to negotiate. He had spent the morning putting out feelers to identify who those backsliders might be.

Strange that he'd had no warning of such serious dissension. This concerned him, too, hinting as it did of an organized opposition waiting for the right moment to reveal themselves and kill the treaty. Now that China was entering the capitalist world, it was inevitable that some in government would be determined to destroy it to preserve their own dominance.

A light knock yanked him from his reverie. His eyes snapped open. His windows were shuttered against the bright Beijing day and the magnificent gardens of Zhongnanhai. The years had taught him the importance of his secluded office. The single knock came again — one he recognized only too well. It always signaled trouble.

"Come in, General."

General Chu Kuairong, PLA (Ret.), marched into the cloistered room, took off his hat, and sat. Hunched forward in the hard wood chair that faced the desk, he had a scarred face, thick shoulders, and barrel chest. His tiny eyes were sunk in deep, wind-and-sun creases. They squinted at Niu as if looking through the raw desert sunlight. His shaved head reflected like polished steel in the circle of light from the desk lamp. In his medal-bedecked uniform, he resembled some old Soviet marshal, contemplating the destruction of Berlin in World War II.

Only the thin cigar clamped between his teeth spoiled the image. "It's the spycatcher."

"Major Pan?" The Owl hid his impatience.

"Yes. Major Pan thinks Dr. Liang could be jumping at shadows, but he's not sure." General Chu was the chief of the Public Security Bureau, one of the organs under the Owl's control. Major Pan was one of the general's top counterintelligence operatives. "It's possible Colonel

Smith is a spy who's maneuvered an invitation for a specific purpose. Perhaps scientific espionage."

"Why does Major Pan think that?"

"Two things. First, there are some oddities in Smith's paper record. Brief, more-or-less unexplained periods away from his lab at USAMRIID. It turns out that Smith is more than a medical doctor or scientist. He has far more combat and command training than most pure scientists even in their military."

"What's the second thing?"

"Major Pan has a 'feeling' about him."

"A *feeling?*"

General Chu blew a neat circle of rich cigar smoke. "Over the years that I've been running the security forces, I've found Pan's 'feelings' are based on his experience and are therefore often accurate."

Of the many agencies under his charge, Niu liked the Public Security Bureau least. It was an octopus with fangs and claws — an enormous, covert bureau with far-ranging police and intelligence power. The Owl was a builder, not a destroyer. In his position as bureau minister, the decisions he sometimes had to approve, or even make, were distasteful.

"What does Major Pan propose?" he asked.

"He wants to keep a close eye on this Colonel Smith. He wants authorization to surveil him and to hold him for interrogation if he does anything remotely suspicious."

The Owl closed his eyes again, mulling. "Surveillance is probably wise, but I want concrete evidence before authorizing interrogation. These are sensitive times, and at the moment we're fortunate to have an American government peculiarly disposed toward peace and cooperation. We'd be fools not to take advantage of this rare occasion."

General Chu blew another cloud of smoke. "Pan suggests there may be a connection between Smith's sudden interest in visiting Shanghai and the disappearance of our agent in the same city."

"You still have no knowledge of exactly what your man was working on?"

"He was on vacation. We think he must have stumbled onto something that made him suspicious and was checking it out before reporting in."

The last situation the Owl wanted was a confrontation with the United States. It would cause a public furor in both countries, posturing by both governments, tie the U.S. president's hands when it came to the human-rights agreement, and cause the Standing Committee to listen to the hardliners on the Politburo and Central Committee.

But the prestige and security of China were more important than any treaty, and a possible spy in Shanghai and a missing internal security agent were matters of sober concern. "When you know the answer, come to me," Niu ordered. "Until then, Major Pan has the authorization to watch Smith closely. Should he feel it is time to detain him, he will need to convince me."

The general's small eyes gleamed. He blew another perfect smoke circle and smiled. "I'll tell him."

Niu did not care for the look in the old soldier's

eyes. "Make sure that you do. I'll report Pan's suspicions and actions to the Standing Committee. Pan and you, General, will answer not only to me, but to them."

Chapter
Five

Shanghai

Smith's spacious room in the Peace Hotel was suddenly claustrophobic. Pressed flat against the wall next to the door, he listened for the footsteps to move. Instead, there was a knock. It was as faint as the footsteps had been. Smith did not move. There it was again — a light tapping, now insistent, nervous. Not a bellman or a maid.

Then he knew. "Damn." It had to be the interpreter Fred Klein had arranged. He opened the door, grabbed a tall, thin, Chinese man by the front of his oversized leather jacket, and jerked him into the room.

The fellow's blue Mao cap flew off. "Hey!"

Smith seized the cap in midair, heeled the door closed, and glared at the skinny man who struggled while at the same time looking aggrieved.

"What's the word?"

"Double latte."

"You're undercover, for God's sake," Smith told him. "Undercover agents don't skulk!"

"Okay, Colonel. Okay!" he protested in a completely American accent. "Get your paws off me."

71

"You're lucky I don't strangle you. Are you *trying* to draw attention to me?" He let go, still scowling.

"You don't need me for that, Colonel. You've done a hot job all by your lonesome." Indignant, the interpreter straightened the collar of his voluminous jacket, brushed his unpressed blue work shirt, and snatched his peaked Mao cap from Smith.

Smith swore, at last understanding. "I'll bet your car's a dark-blue Volkswagen Jetta."

"Yeah, okay, you spotted me at the airport. And damn lucky I was back there, or I'd never have caught on to the surveillance."

Smith's shoulders tightened. "What surveillance?"

"I don't know who it is. You never do in Shanghai these days. Cops? Secret police? Military? Some tycoon's goons? Gangsters? Could be anyone. We've got capitalism now, and more-or-less free enterprise. It's a lot harder to tell who's out to get anyone."

"Swell." Smith sighed. He had been concerned, and now he knew he had been right. Small compensation. "What's your cover?"

"Interpreter and chauffeur. What else? Definitely not gunrunner, so here, take it quick." As if it were scorching his fingers, he handed Smith a canvas holster encasing a duplicate of his 9mm Beretta.

"You have a name?" Smith stuck the semiautomatic into his belt at the small of his back and tossed the shoulder harness into his suitcase.

"An Jingshe, but you can call me Andy. That's

what I was at NYU. The Village, not uptown. I liked it down there. Plenty of chicks and good space you could share sometimes." Adding proudly, if a little wistfully, "I'm a painter."

"Congratulations," Smith said drily. "It's an even more unstable living than a spy's. Okay, Andy, let's go get coffee at a Starbucks and see whether we can figure out who's on my tail."

He restored the invisible filaments inside all his suitcases, shut them, and walked to the door, where he smoothed a thin sheet of see-through plastic on the carpet so that anyone entering would step on it before they saw it. He hung the DO NOT DISTURB sign on the doorknob.

They took the elevator down. On the lobby floor, Smith asked An Jingshe, "Is there a way out through the kitchens?"

"There's gotta be."

The uniformed maintenance man polished the brass fittings and shined the marble walls in the corridor from the lobby to the bank of elevators. A wiry man, his long face, sharp black eyes, pale brown skin, and drooping mustache were unlike any other Chinese or Westerner in the lobby. He worked in silence, head down, apparently concentrating on what he was doing, but his gaze missed nothing.

When the tall, skinny Chinese and the tall, muscular Westerner left the elevator, they stopped for a moment to converse. Too far away to hear the low conversation, the maintenance worker polished another brass sconce and assessed the big man with practiced eyes. No more than an inch over six

73

feet, he was broad through the chest and shoulders, trim and athletic. His hair was smoothed back from a high-planed face, and his blue eyes were clear and intelligent. All in all, the maintenance man saw nothing unusual about him in his dark-gray, American-cut business suit. Still, there was an unmistakable military bearing about him, and he had arrived at Pudong International from Taiwan with Dr. Liang Tianning and his biomolecular team.

The maintenance man was still studying him when the pair turned and headed toward the doors into the kitchen. As they pushed through, he packed his cleaning materials and hurried across the lobby and out to busy Nanjing Dong Lu, one of the world's greatest shopping streets. He ran west through the throngs and honking vehicles toward the pedestrian mall. But before he reached the first cross street, he stopped at the alley that edged the hotel.

He waited where he could watch the employees' entrance as well as the lobby entrance through which he had just left. It was always possible he had been seen, and the men's entry into the kitchen a calculated ruse.

Neither the tall American nor the Chinese exited, but the maintenance man saw something else: He was not the only one observing the hotel. Two cigarettes glowed and faded inside a black car, parked so it blocked the narrow sidewalk across from the hotel's revolving doors. The Public Security Bureau — China's dreaded police and intelligence agency. No one else would be that arrogant.

He studied the vehicle longer. By the time he

74

looked back into the alley, the American and the Chinese were running toward a Volkswagen Jetta parked so that it faced the street. The maintenance man shrank back into the crowd that surged along the sidewalk.

The Jetta's right wheels were flat against a wall. The Chinese unlocked the car door, while the American surveyed all around as if expecting an attack. They jumped inside, the Jetta pulled into the traffic, and it turned west toward the pedestrian mall, which reached all the way to the French Concession. No vehicles were allowed there.

The maintenance man wasted no time. He gave a piercing whistle. Seconds later, a battered Land Rover pulled up. He dropped his toolbox in back and vaulted into the front beside the driver, who wore a round white cap and had leathery brown skin and round eyes like his.

When the driver spoke in a language that was neither Chinese nor European, the maintenance man responded in the same language and jabbed a thumb at the Jetta, less than a half block ahead in the jammed traffic.

The driver nodded and forced the Land Rover through the congestion. Abruptly, the Jetta turned left.

Bellowing curses, the driver snaked, bumped, and banged the Land Rover to the left and followed the Jetta, which turned west again on Jiujiang Lu. And quickly north once more, back toward Nanjing Dong Lu.

Swearing again, the Land Rover driver tried to follow but was momentarily blocked. He burst his vehicle out to turn into the same street. The maintenance man caught another glimpse of their quarry far ahead — and then the car vanished.

The driver pushed the Land Rover on, stopping just before Nanjing Dong Lu, where an all-but-hidden alley ran off to the south. The maintenance man cursed. The Chinese driver and the American with the military posture must have spotted him. The Jetta had pulled into this alley and by now could be anywhere in the teeming area.

Two hours later, Andy dropped Smith at the second Starbucks and drove off to park. This one was on Fixing Dong Lu, another bustling street, not far from the river in the Nanshi district — Shanghai's Old Town.

The first Starbucks had been in Lippo Plaza on Huaihai Zhong Lu. That coffee shop had been filled with locals and Westerners alike, and Smith and Andy had seen no connection to the *Empress* there or when they had walked the streets, reading nameplates on doors and studying the low buildings filled with shops and small stores.

This second Starbucks was less crowded. Only Chinese sat at the tables and ordered coffees to go. Most were well dressed in suits, both Western and Chinese, and appeared to be rushing back to desk jobs.

Smith carried his second double latte of the day to a table at the front window. This was a business district, which accounted for the lack of Westerners. The buildings were a mixture of four-, five-, and six-story structures dating back to the late colonial era as well as taller modern buildings and a few shiny glass-and-steel high-rises. One of the newest was directly across the street. Smith focused on a vertical row of brass plaques beside the entrance doors.

Andy joined him. "I'll get me a mocha, and we can start walking. Are you buying?"

Smith handed him money. When the interpreter-chauffeur returned, Smith stood up. "We'll try that new building across the street first."

Carrying their Styrofoam cups, they dodged among the bicycles, cars, and buses to cross with the skill that came from maneuvering through Manhattan's traffic. Smith headed to the brass nameplates at the entry. Most were in Chinese characters, some transliterated into Pinyin.

Andy translated for Smith.

"Hold it!" Smith said at the tenth plaque. "Read that again."

"Flying Dragon Enterprises, International Trade and Shipping." Andy pontificated: "A dragon's the symbol of heaven in China."

"Okay."

"And, therefore, of the emperor."

"The emperor's been dead a long time, but thanks. Finish the list."

As it turned out, Flying Dragon was the only shipping company. As they drank their coffee, they hurried through the directories of the other office buildings on the block. They found four more companies that could have ties to global transportation. Then they found a street vendor who sold *jianbing,* an egg and green-onion omelette folded over chili sauce. This time, Andy bought.

As soon as they had finished their omelettes,

Smith was on the move again. "Time to check the last Starbucks."

It proved to be in a shopping center in the new business development zone around Hongqiao Airport on Hongqiao Lu. There were no companies connected to shipping nearby, and Smith told Andy to drive back to the hotel.

"Okay, we've got five possibilities," Smith said, "all close enough to the second Starbucks for an informant to use it as a place to pass his information on to Mondragon. How good are you on a computer?"

"How good was Grant at winning battles?"

"Access the five companies on the Internet, and look for the name Zhao Yanji among their staff."

"Consider it done."

They drove on. As they neared the Bund, Jon said, "Is there another way into the Peace Hotel besides the front and employees' entrances?"

"Yeah. Around the corner on an intersecting street."

"Good. Take me there."

As Andy drove through a dizzying tangle of thoroughfares and alleys, Smith looked him up and down. "You're almost my height. Your pants should be long enough, and that leather jacket of yours is big enough for a buffalo. With your Mao cap, I'll pass for Shanghainese, unless someone gets too close to my face. You'll be a scarecrow in my suit, but you don't have to wear the jacket."

"Thanks. I think."

As they approached the hotel, Smith told Andy where to park. He struggled out of his clothes in the small car. Andy turned off the motor and did

78

the same. The leather jacket was fine on Smith. The trousers were an inch short, but they would do. He pulled the Mao cap down almost to his eyes and stepped out of the Jetta.

He leaned down to the open window. "Do that research, have an early dinner, and pick me up here in two hours."

Andy brightened. "That's too soon for shows or club hopping. What's our gig?"

"You don't have a gig. You're waiting in the car. I'm going to do a bit of breaking and entering. How much'll depend on what you find out."

"I can help on the b and e, too. I'm a cat."

"Next time."

Andy frowned, disappointed. "I'm not the patient sort."

"Work on it." Smith liked the interpreter. He grinned and walked off.

The noise was clamorous, the streets as always mobbed. He saw no one tailing, but he took no chances. Blending into the surge of Shanghainese, he let the throngs carry him toward the Bund. Only when he reached the doors to the hotel did he push his way free and stride inside.

At dusk two hours later, purple light enveloped Shanghai, and a sense of Asia's lush beauty softened the hard-edged skyline. Andy An paused his car to let Smith off a block from the building that housed Flying Dragon Enterprises, International Trade & Shipping. Since most of the night's action had already headed off to Old Town, the French Concession, and Huangpu, the street was very different now, half deserted.

Andy's research had made the target definite: Zhao Yanji was the treasurer of Flying Dragon, which was housed in the high-rise directly across the street from the second Starbucks they had visited that day. It made sense to Smith. A clandestine seller of highly sensitive material who conducted sales during working hours would want to be away from his or her job as short a time as possible and on a believable errand, such as getting coffee at a nearby Starbucks. If Zhao Yanji was that person, he had a perfect outlet at the obviously popular Starbucks.

If all went well, Smith would be back in plenty of time for dinner at nine o'clock with Dr. Liang and his fellow scientists. If events went against him . . . well, he would deal with that, too.

As the Jetta plowed off into the twilight, Smith walked toward the high-rise office building, covertly watching everyone and everything. He was dressed in a black sweater, black jeans, and soft-soled, flexible shoes. On his back was a light pack, also black. He looked up. The building that housed Flying Dragon blazed with light, a contributor to the city's dazzling night skyline. Across the street, the Starbucks was still open, a scattering of coffee drinkers sitting at the small round tables in a hyperrealistic display reminiscent of an Edward Hopper painting. The air had that faint diesel odor of all cities, with touches of Asian spices and garlic.

Through the high-rise's plate-glass windows, Smith saw a single uniformed guard, dozing behind a security desk in the lobby. Smith might be able to slip past, but the risk was unnecessary.

The modern building should have all the customary features.

He continued past to the driveway that led down into a lighted, but closed garage. About ten feet beyond the ramp was an exit door to the fire stairs. Just what he needed. He tried it. It was locked from inside. He used the picklocks disguised as surgical instruments he carried in his medical kit. The door opened on the fourth try.

He slid inside, closed it quietly behind, returned the picklocks to his backpack, and listened in the empty stairwell. It stretched upward out of sight. He waited two minutes and began climbing. His soft-soled shoes made little sound. Flying Dragon Enterprises was on the eighth story. Twice he froze, remaining motionless as a door opened somewhere above and footsteps reverberated.

At the eighth floor, he took a stethoscope from his backpack and used it to listen through the door. Satisfied there was neither sound nor movement on the other side, he pulled open the door and stepped into a green-carpeted, white-walled waiting area decorated in ultramodern chrome, glass, and suede.

A wide corridor, with the same white walls and emerald carpet, led to a cross corridor of double doors — some of glass and others of polished wood. The corridor stretched in both directions. Flying Dragon Enterprises turned out to be the third set of double-glass doors. Smith glanced in casually as he passed. There was a lightless reception area. Behind it was a large, lighted office of long rows of empty desks, with a wall of windows behind the desks. Solid doors lined the inner walls right and left.

On his third pass, he tried the entrance doors. They were unlocked. Eager but wary, he slipped inside and wove soundlessly among the furniture to the solid door in the far corner. The door was marked in both Chinese and English gold lettering: YU YONGFU, PRESIDENT AND CHAIRMAN. No light showed beneath the door.

He slid inside and, using the illumination from the open doorway, crossed to a large desk. He switched the lamp there onto low beam. The small column of yellow light gave the office a dim, ghostly effect that would not be evident down on the street.

He closed the outer door and surveyed the room, impressed. It was not a prized corner office, but it was so mammoth that its size more than compensated. The view was pure prestige, too — sweeping from the river and the towers of Pudong to the historic Bund, northeast Shanghai across Suzhou Creek, and finally back to the river as it curved east and headed downstream to the Yangtze.

The most important piece of furniture to Smith was a three-drawer filing cabinet, which stood against the left wall. There was also a white suede sofa with matching armchairs, a glass Noguchi coffee table, a wall of leather-bound books to the right, original Jasper Johns and Andy Warhol paintings here and there, and a panoramic photo of turn-of-the-nineteenth-century British Shanghai. The desk itself was mahogany, and enormous, but in this office seemed small. The office told a story:

82

Yu Yongfu, president and chairman, had made it big and gaudy in New China, and he wanted everyone to know it.

Smith hurried to the cabinet. It was locked, but his picks made short work of it. He pulled out the top drawer. The folders were filed alphabetically — in English, with the words duplicated in Chinese. Another of Yu Yongfu's grandiose affectations. When he located the file for *The Dowager Empress*, he exhaled. He had been holding his breath without realizing it.

He opened the file right there, on top of the cabinet, but all he could find were useless internal memos and the manifests of old voyages. His worry growing, he kept at it. Finally, with the last document, there it was — the manifest. His excitement dimmed as he studied it. The dates were right, as were the ports on both ends of the journey, Shanghai and Basra. But the cargo was wrong. It was a list of what the freighter allegedly carried — radios, CD players, black tea, raw silk, and other innocent freight. It was a copy of the official manifest, filed with the export board. A smoke screen.

Angrily he returned to the cabinet, searching through the other file drawers, but found nothing more that related to the *Empress*. As he closed and relocked the cabinet, he grimaced. He would not give up. There must be a safe somewhere. He scanned the huge office and considered what sort of person would create it — vain, self-congratulatory, and obvious.

Of course. *Obvious*. He turned back to the filing cabinet. Above it hung the panoramic picture of old British Shanghai. He lifted the framed photo from the wall, and there it was — the safe. A simple wall safe, with no time lock or any other advanced electronics he could see. His picklocks would . . .

"Who are you?" demanded a voice in heavily accented English.

He turned slowly, quietly, making no provocative move.

Standing in the gray light of the doorway was a short, heavy Chinese man who wore rimless glasses. He was aiming a Sig Sauer at Smith's belly.

Beijing

Night was one of Beijing's best times, when the slow transformation from terrible pollution and gray socialist lifestyles to unleaded fuels and cutting-edge fun was apparent in pockets of vibrant nightlife under a starry sky that was once impenetrable through city smog. Karaoke and solemn band music were out. Discos, pubs, clubs, and restaurants with live music and fine food were in. Beijing was still firmly Communist, but seductive capitalism was having its way. The city was shrugging off its dreariness and growing affluent.

Still, Beijing was not yet the economic paradise the Politburo advertised. In fact, ordinary citizens were losing their fight against gentrification and being forced out of the city, because they could no longer afford the cost of living. It was the dark side of the new day. This mattered to the Owl, if not to some of the others on the Standing Committee. He had studied Yeltsin's failure to stop Russia's greedy oligarchs and the near-destruction of the Russian economy that resulted. China needed a more measured approach to its restructuring.

But first, the Owl had the human-rights treaty with the United States to protect. It was critical to his plans for a democratic, socially conscious China.

Tonight was a special meeting of the nine-member Standing Committee. From under his half-closed eyes, he studied the faces of his eight colleagues at the ancient imperial table in the Zhongnanhai meeting room. Which man should concern him? In the party and, therefore, in the government, a rumor was not merely a rumor — it was a call for support. Which meant one of the solemn older men or the smiling younger ones was reassessing his position on the human-rights agreement, even as Niu waited to make his report.

Half blind behind his thick glasses, their leader — the august general secretary — was unlikely to resort to spreading a rumor, Niu decided. No one would oppose him openly. Not this year. And where he went, his acolyte from their days in Shanghai would always follow. That one had the face of an executioner and was too old and too committed to his boss to ever be secretary himself. He had no reason to bother with fighting the treaty.

The four beaming younger men were possibilities. Each was assembling backers to strengthen his power base, but at the same time all were modern men and, as such, strong proponents of good relations with the West. Since the treaty was important to the current U.S. president, persuading them to reverse their support would be difficult.

That left two potentials, one of which was Shi Jingnu, with the fat, grinning face of the silk merchant's clerk he once was. To paraphrase Shakespeare, he smiled and smiled but was a villain. The second possibility was bald, narrow-eyed, never-smiling Wei Gaofan, who as a young soldier had once met the incomparable Chu The and never moved beyond that moment.

The Owl nodded to himself inside his own sleepy smile. One of those two. They were old guard, fighting to maintain power as the specter of irrelevance breathed chills down the backs of their ancient, wrinkled necks.

"Jianxing, you have not commented on Shi Jingnu's report?" The general secretary smiled to show he knew the Owl was not sleeping.

"I have no comment," the Owl — Niu Jianxing — said.

"Then do you have a security report to make?"

"One matter came up today, Chairman," Niu said. "Dr. Liang Tianning, the director of the Shanghai Biomedical Research Institute, invited an eminent American microbiologist, Lieutenant Colonel Jon Smith, M.D., to visit his institute and speak to his researchers. He —"

Wei Gaofan interrupted, "When did the Americans begin to give military rank to scientists? Is this another example of the warmongering of —"

"The Colonel," Niu snapped back, "is a medical doctor and works at the United States Army Medical Research Institute of Infectious Diseases, a world-renowned Level Four installation similar to our biomedical establishments in Beijing and Shanghai."

The general secretary supported the Owl: "I know Dr. Liang well from my time in Shanghai. We can trust his judgment concerning whom his researchers need to hear."

"Actually," Niu continued, "Dr. Liang has some doubts about the American." He went on to repeat what General Chu Kuairong had told him. "I tend to agree with Major Pan's first assessment of the matter. Dr. Liang is something of an old rag man, always jumping at shadows."

"You take a possible American spy very lightly, Niu," Shi Jingnu criticized, his gaze flicking from one colleague to the other to gauge their reactions.

"The key word here is 'possible,'" Niu answered, ignoring Shi and addressing the room in general. "We shouldn't have quite as much faith in Major Pan's 'feeling' as our Public Security Bureau chief does. It's his — and Pan's — job to jump at shadows. It's not our job."

"So what did you decide?" the secretary's disciple wanted to know.

"I have instructed General Chu to have Major Pan keep a close eye on Colonel Smith. I've not authorized them to arrest and interrogate him. First they must present me with concrete evidence of sufficient gravity. These are sensitive times, and at the moment we have an American government disposed toward peace and cooperation."

He did not mention the Public Security agent who had gone missing in Shanghai. So far, there was nothing to tell, and he wanted to add no support to whoever was vacillating over the human-rights accord.

There were nods of general agreement, even

from Shi Jingnu and Wei Gaofan, which told him whoever was considering opposing the treaty at this late date was not yet ready to commit himself openly.

Wei, however, could not resist a final word of caution. His narrow eyes were slits as he said, "We must not appear too eager to cooperate with the Americans. Remember, shadows can be dangerous."

Chapter Six

Shanghai

Twilight had deepened into night. In an expensive Shanghai suburb, Yu Yongfu paced across his study, gazing out through his French doors at the garden. The scent of freshly cut grass floated in. Floodlights illuminated the specimen plants and trees, sometimes from above, sometimes from beneath, seeking perfect harmony. This English garden was a replica of one created for a British tea tycoon in the early twentieth century, whose mansion was demolished long ago. Yu had bought the plans and enjoyed showing the renowned landscape to his Western guests.

But tonight, it gave him little solace. He checked his Rolex every few minutes.

A tycoon at just thirty-four years, Yu looked even younger. Trim and athletic, he worked out daily in an exclusive health club near his trade and shipping company — Flying Dragon Enterprises. He watched his weight as closely as he watched the international stock, currency, and commodity markets, and he dressed in slim Italian suits custom-made in Rome. His regimental ties and ankle-high dress boots were handmade in England, his shirts in Paris, and his underwear and pajamas in Dublin. He had risen to this rarified affluence in the last seven years. But then, this was a new China . . . a brash, self-indulgent China . . . a very American-century China . . . and Yu considered his attitudes, business methods, and ambitions all American.

This had given him little comfort when his man, Feng Dun, called yesterday to tell him about agent Mondragon and the missing invoice manifest. *The Dowager Empress* venture had been risky, he had known that, but the profit involved was stratospheric, plus there would be enormous *guanxi*, because the cargo was connected to the illustrious Wei Gaofan himself, a longtime powerful member of the Standing Committee.

But now, something was very wrong. Where was that blasted Feng? Where was the manifest? The death of ten thousand cuts to the one who had given it to the American!

"Are you all right, husband?"

Yu whirled to snap at his interfering wife and stopped. That was not the kind of wife Kuonyi was or ever would be. Theirs was a modern marriage, a Western marriage.

He managed to control his voice. "It's that damnable Feng. He should've been back from Taiwan by now."

"The invoice manifest?"

Yu nodded.

"He'll get it, Yongfu."

Yu resumed pacing, shaking his head. "How can you be so sure?"

"That one could bring the devil back from hell. He's invaluable, but he's also dangerous. You must never trust him."

"I can handle Feng."

His wife stopped her response, and Yu froze in his pacing. A large vehicle had driven into their walled courtyard.

"It's him," he told her.

"I'll wait upstairs."

"Yes."

In China, despite the law of the Party that proclaimed women fully equal to men, to treat one's wife like a partner was considered weak. Yu forced himself to sit behind his desk. He assumed a composed mask as he heard the maid open the front door.

Measured steps crossed the hardwood floor, coming toward his study, and a large man appeared in the open doorway as suddenly as if he had materialized there. Unusually light skinned, he had close-cropped hair that was ashy red mixed with stark white. He was tall — perhaps three inches over six feet — and powerfully built, but he was hardly heavy — a muscled two hundred pounds or so. He dwarfed Yu Yongfu, who scowled up at him.

Yu made his voice harsh, as befitted an important employer. "You have it?"

Feng Dun smiled. A small smile, nothing more, as if pasted on the face of a wood marionette. He padded across the study to a leather armchair and sat with hardly a sound.

His voice was low and whispery. "I have it . . . boss."

91

Yu could not suppress a sigh of relief. Then he held out his hand and made his voice stern. "Give it to me."

Feng leaned forward and handed him the envelope. Yu ripped it open and scanned the contents.

Feng noted the hands trembled. "It's the real manifest," Feng assured him. His light brown eyes were almost colorless, giving them the appearance of emptiness. They darkened and focused on Yu's face. It was a stare few had been able to meet.

Yu was not among them. He quickly looked away. "I'll lock it in my safe upstairs. Fine work, Feng. There'll be a bonus in it for you." He stood.

Feng stood, too. He was in his late forties, once a soldier and career officer who had started as an "observer" in the American war against North Vietnam and the late Soviet Union. He gave it up when he realized there was far greater profit in the profession of mercenary in the would-be armies of the restless Central Asian republics, particularly as the Soviets collapsed. He considered himself a good judge of men and situations, and he was underwhelmed by what he saw in Yu Yongfu.

As they walked through the study's doorway, Feng said, "I suggest you burn the manifest. That way, no one else can steal it. It's not over, boss."

Yu jerked back as if pulled on a leash. "What do you mean?"

"Perhaps you should hear what happened on Taiwan."

Where he stood, one foot out of the room like a confidence man poised to make a clean getaway, Yu hesitated. "Tell me."

"We killed the American agent, and we retrieved the manifest . . ."

Yu wanted to scream with frustration. Why was this not finished? What the hell did Feng mean? "I know that! If that's all —"

"— but Mondragon wasn't alone. There was another man on the beach. A well-trained man, clever and skilled. Almost certainly another American spy sent to ferry the information to Washington while Mondragon returned to his cover in Shanghai. The beach was merely a transfer point. There is no other logical explanation for the presence of the second man, since he had the training and skill to escape us."

Yu fought panic. What was so bad about that? The Americans had failed; the manifest was now safely in his pocket. "But he failed, we have the manifest. What —"

"The man's in Shanghai now." Feng watched every move the entrepreneur made, every twitch of a muscle. "I doubt he's here for a holiday."

A sour taste rose into Yu's throat. *"Here?* How could such a thing happen? *You let him follow you back?* How could you be so *stupid?"* He heard his voice rise like that of a hysteric. Instantly, he stopped his tirade.

"He couldn't have followed us. Mondragon must have given him some other information, or he found some on Mondragon's corpse. One of those two brought him here."

Yu struggled to regain control. "But how did he get into the country?"

"That's the question, isn't it? It appears he's actually a well-known microbiologist and medical

93

doctor, who also happens to be a soldier. Lieutenant Colonel Jon Smith, M.D., a biomedical researcher. What he does *not* appear to be is an operative with any known U.S. agency. Yet he was the one who met Mondragon on the beach. And then he invited himself into our country."

"Invited himself?"

"On Taiwan, our eminent Dr. Liang Tianning expressed interest in meeting with him. Smith put him off. Then this morning, Smith changed his mind. He hinted strongly to Dr. Liang that he would honor us by addressing our microbiological research institute here in Shanghai immediately. But once here, he pleaded fatigue. He wanted to remain alone in his hotel. Dr. Liang was surprised and a little suspicious. Of course, he informed Zhongnanhai. Zhongnanhai now has him under surveillance."

"How do you know this?"

"Knowing such things is why you pay me so well."

It was true. Feng's *guanxi* sometimes appeared to be greater than Yu's own, and it could make him impudent. He constantly needed to be reminded who was boss. "I pay you to do your job, nothing more. Why is this American still alive?"

"He's not easy to approach, and we must be careful. As I said, Zhongnanhai is watching."

Yu tasted bile in his throat. "Yes, yes, of course. But he must be killed. Killed quickly. Have you discovered who gave Mondragon the invoice manifest?"

"Not yet."

"Find him. And when you do, kill him, too."

Feng smiled. "Of course, boss."

In the dim light of the Flying Dragon office, Smith saw the short, heavy man stare at the file folder still open on the filing cabinet. The man's gun wavered as his gaze swept to the exposed safe on the wall above the cabinet. He had not asked, *What are you doing?* or *What's going on here?* He had demanded only, *Who are you?* He knew why Smith was in the office headquarters of Yu Yongfu, president and chairman.

Smith said, "You must be Zhao Yanji. It was you who gave Avery Mondragon the *Empress*'s real manifest."

The muzzle of the Sig Sauer began to shake. "How — ?"

"Mondragon told me. They killed him before he could pass it to me."

"Who has it now?"

"They do."

Zhao Yanji grabbed the shaking pistol with both fleshy hands to try to steady it. "How . . . how do I know you're telling the truth?"

"Because I know about Mondragon, I know your name, and I'm here looking for the manifest myself."

Zhao blinked, the Sig Sauer dropped to his side, and he sank cross-legged to the floor, head in his hands. "I am a dead man."

Smith picked the Sig Sauer from his fingers. He transferred his Beretta to his jacket pocket, shoved the Sig Sauer into his belt, and looked down at Zhao. Zhao sat with the back of his neck exposed, as if waiting for the slice of an executioner's axe.

Smith asked, "They can trace the manifest back to you?"

The head nodded. "Not today. Perhaps not tomorrow. But eventually. Feng is a sorcerer. He can see behind any screen."

"Who's Feng?"

"Feng Dun. Yu Yongfu's security chief."

Smith frowned, wondering. . . . "What does he look like?"

Zhao described his height and strength, the red-and-white hair, and the viciousness that was hidden behind the calm exterior. "You've seen him?"

"I have." Smith nodded, not surprised. At last, he had a name for him. "Start at the beginning. Why did you do it?"

Zhao looked up, suddenly angry, his terror forgotten. "Yu Yongfu is greedy, a pig! *He* is why I gave the manifest to Mondragon! The honored grandfather of my friend Bei Ruitiao founded Flying Dragon Enterprises while the English and Americans were still among us. We were an honorable company. . . . We . . ."

As Smith listened to the harangue, he pieced together a story that was all too common in the new People's Republic: Flying Dragon had been a relatively small, conservative company, primarily ferrying cargo up and down the Yangtze and along the coast as far as Hainan Island. Bei Ruitiao was president until Yu Yongfu, using muscle, connections in the Party, and Belgian financing, grabbed the company in a Mafia-like takeover. Yu made himself president and chairman and, with the help of the Belgian shipping firm, expanded into international transport. The entire time, he skated on the edge of both Chinese and international law.

Zhao's voice shook with emotion. "My friend Ruitiao is ruined because of Yu. I gave the manifest to Mondragon to expose Yu and ruin him in return!" All his bravado vanished as quickly as it erupted. "But I have failed. I am a dead man."

"How did you manage to steal it?"

He nodded to the exposed safe above the file cabinet. "It was in a secret file in Yu's safe. I am the treasurer of Flying Dragon. I pretended to welcome Yu, and he made the mistake of retaining me. One day he forgot he had taken the file from the safe, and I found it. I returned it to the safe after I took the manifest. At the time, he did not remember he had left it out. But he will remember now. The manifest had to come from somewhere." His body slumped more, beaten.

"Where do you the think the manifest is? In the safe here again?"

Zhao shook his head. "No. Yu would be too afraid to leave it here now. It must be with him at home. He has a safe there, too."

"Where does he live?"

"Far beyond Hongqiao Airport. An obscene mansion that would have shamed an official of the Yuan Dynasty." He related an address that meant nothing to Smith, but Andy would be able to find it.

"Mondragon said there were three copies?"

"Yes," Zhao said dully. "Three."

"Where are the other two?"

"One must be in Basra or Baghdad, with the re-

97

cipient company. That would be normal procedure. I don't know where the other is."

Smith gazed at the woeful Zhao. "I can arrange to get you safely out of China."

The heavy little man sighed. "Where would I go? China is my home." He pulled himself to his feet, walked across the room, and collapsed in one of Yu Yongfu's suede armchairs. "Perhaps they do not find out."

"Maybe not."

"May I have my pistol?"

Smith hesitated. Then he took the Sig Sauer from his belt, checked the chamber, unloaded the clip, and handed him the weapon. "I'll put the clip beside the door."

He left him there, seated in the stately armchair, staring out into the new Shanghai night.

Inside Yu Yongfu's walled compound, Feng Dun sat patiently in his Ford Escort, hidden in the black umbra beneath a branching plane tree. As a breeze carried the sweet scent of blooming jasmine in through his rolled-down window, he studied the shadows that moved behind the curtains of the mansion's windows. They were Western curtains at the windows of Yu's big Western house, which the entrepreneur had built as a modern replica of the baronial manses of the tea and silk taipans of the British and French hongs in the Concession era.

The shadows gestured — the taller one pacing, arms waving, while the smaller one remained still, with sharp gestures. That would be Li Kuonyi, Yu's wife. She was more sure, more emphatic, and

Feng had always treated her with caution. Her husband could not be relied upon to keep his head if the situation deteriorated more. It was unfortunate for all of them that she was not in charge.

Feng had seen enough. As he fingered his old Soviet Tokarev with one hand, he punched numbers into his cell phone with the other. He waited for the series of rings and silences that formed the intricate relays that protected the man he was calling, Wei Gaofan.

"Yes?" a voice answered.

"I must speak with him."

The voice instantly recognized him. "Of course."

From the Ford, Feng saw the silhouette of Yu Yongfu, slumped now, and the slimmer shape of Li Kuonyi standing over him. Her hand was on his shoulder, no doubt comforting him.

"What has happened about the American?" the gruff voice of Wei Gaofan asked from distant Beijing.

Feng reported, "Jon Smith is apparently still in his hotel. The security police are watching it. My people are staked out to intercept him should he try to retrieve the manifest as we suspect he will."

"Which hotel is he in?"

"The old Peace."

"So? A curious choice for a modern American microbiologist whose interest is, presumably, in our research institute in Zhangjiang. I believe it tells us all we need to know, you agree?"

"His interest is in more than microbiology."

"Then continue your efforts."

99

"Of course." Feng paused. "There's another problem. Yu Yongfu will not hold up."

"You're sure?"

"Already he's cracking. Should the slightest detail be uncovered, he'll break. Reveal everything. Perhaps he'll do that even before." With finality, he pronounced, "We can no longer trust him."

"All right. I'll take care of it. You liquidate the American." There was a silence, then, "How did all this happen, Feng? We wanted the information to reach the Americans, nothing more. Never the proof."

"I don't know, master. I made sure word of the cargo leaked to Mondragon, as you instructed, but I don't know who then found and stole the invoice manifest, but I will."

"I am sure you will." The line went dead.

Feng sat for a time in the car. All of the mansion's windows were dark now, except those of the upstairs master bedroom. No shadows moved behind the curtains. Feng smiled his unreadable smile and envisioned Yu's wife, Kuonyi. She had always appealed to him. He gave a short laugh, a shrug, and redialed his cell phone.

Hong Kong

Once the last British-occupied corner of China, Hong Kong had lost some of its brash luster since the mainland resumed ownership in 1997. While Beijing envisioned itself as the future capital of Asia, and Shanghai thought of itself as an eastern version of New York City, Hong Kong only wanted to remain itself — freewheeling, money-making, and joyfully exciting, hardly the reputa-

100

tion of any other modern metropolis in China.

From the penthouse balcony of the Altman Group, Hong Kong's sea of twinkling lights seemed to spread forever, a testament to the vigorous city. In the teak-paneled dining room, a dinner party was winding down. The aromas of expensive meats and French sauces filled the room. The genial host, Ralph McDermid — founder, CEO, and chairman of Altman — held forth for the benefit of his last two guests.

A man of medium height, with a bland face that would never be noticed in a crowd, McDermid was in his mid-sixties, slightly overweight, and jovial. "The future of world commerce lies around the Pacific Rim, with the United States and China its twin financial pillars and major markets. I'm sure China recognizes that as much as the United States. Whether they like your semi-independence or not, they'll have to live with it for a long time to come."

Both Hong Kong natives, the Chinese couple were power players in the financial community. They nodded in sober agreement, but they had little influence, because Beijing's heavy political fist constantly threatened all businesspeople in the Special Administrative Zone.

But being wined, dined, and reassured by a man of Ralph McDermid's importance in such a luxurious Western setting fed their pride and hopes. The penthouse crowned the most expensive high-rise on Repulse Bay Road. While they continued their discussion, the husband and wife paused occasionally to enjoy the multimillion-dollar view.

As a phone rang somewhere, the Chinese businessman told McDermid, "We are pleased to hear your views and hope you'll make them clear to our mayor. America's support is critical to our relations with Beijing."

McDermid smiled graciously. "I think Beijing is well aware —"

Making an almost soundless entry, McDermid's private assistant spoke quietly into his ear. McDermid gave no acknowledgment, but he apologized to his guests. "I regret I must take this call. It's been a grand evening, educational for me as well as particularly enjoyable. Thank you for your company. I hope you'll be available to join me again so we can continue sharing views."

The businesswoman said, "It will be our pleasure. You must visit us next time. I think we can promise you an interesting evening, but not such sumptuous food. The wine was exquisite."

"Simple American fare, nothing more, and a small country vintage hardly worthy of such distinguished guests. Lawrence will give you your coats and show you out. Thank you again for honoring me with your presence."

"Many thanks from two humble shopkeepers."

The compliments properly offered and rejected, McDermid hurried through the penthouse to the master suite.

His jovial smile vanished. He snarled into the phone: "Report."

"All went well," Feng Dun told him. "As you expected, there was another American agent on the island. We killed Mondragon, retrieved the manifest, but let the American escape. They will now be fully alarmed."

"Excellent."

"There's better," Feng continued. "That same American agent, a Lieutenant Colonel Jon Smith, is a microbiologist from USAMRIID."

"Why is that better? Who is he?"

"He isn't with any of the U.S. intelligence organizations."

McDermid nodded, wondering. "Curious."

"Whoever sent him, Smith is in Shanghai now, which will work to our favor. I'll handle him. But that leaves us with another large problem. One we had not expected."

"Who? What?" he demanded.

"Yu Yongfu. He pretends to be a fox, but he's a frightened rabbit. A rabbit will gnaw himself to death when he feels cornered. Yu is terrified. He will destroy himself and us."

There was a thoughtful pause. "You're right. We can't take the risk. Get rid of him."

When McDermid rang off, the information about Smith continued to resound in his mind. A knock at his door roused him from his reverie. "Yes?"

"Ms. Sun is in the living room, sir."

"Thank you, Lawrence. Give her a drink. Tell her I'll be along."

He remained mulling for another few minutes and then roused himself. Sun Liuxia was the daughter of an important official he could not afford to offend. She was also stunning and young.

Smiling, he freshened up, changed his dinner jacket, and left the bedroom. It was still early. Through the penthouse windows, the lights of Hong Kong spread before him as if all the world were his. By the time he entered the living room, his good humor had fully returned.

Shanghai

Still seated in Yu Yongfu's exotic armchair in the Flying Dragon offices, Zhao Yanji sighed. Miserable and discouraged, he stared down at the empty pistol in his lap. Perhaps the American actually could help. Maybe the answer was to leave Shanghai at last. Or he could always retrieve the clip, put the pistol to his head, and pull the trigger.

He studied the weapon thoughtfully, stroking it with a finger. He imagined the bullet shooting from the chamber, exploding like lightning from the barrel, and blasting through his skull and the soft tissue of his brain. He did not shudder as he contemplated this. In fact, he had a moment of peace. At last, his battle would be over, and he would no longer feel the terrible burden of the company's dishonor.

He looked around Yu Yongfu's office, so familiar. As treasurer, he had spent a lifetime here, it seemed, trying to educate the selfish entrepreneur and rescue the company from him. He took a deep breath and found himself shaking his head. A surge of resentment, almost of determination, rushed through him. No, he was not ready to die. He still wanted to fight. The company could still be saved.

He should get out of here before he was discovered. He pushed himself up to his feet, feeling relieved. To make a decision was to reaffirm the future.

There was a small sound. No more than a sharp click.

Puzzled, he turned. The office door was open. A figure stood silhouetted against the outer office's light. Before Zhao could speak, there was a loud *pop*. As his sight went blank, he realized what it was — a silenced gunshot. Abruptly, pain burst from his heart. It was so overwhelming he did not feel himself topple face first to the carpet.

Chapter Seven

In their mansion on the outskirts of Shanghai, Yu Yongfu and his family had an important guest. His arrival had surprised them. He was a fat old man with many chins, who sat behind Yu's massive desk as if he owned it. Yu said nothing, trying to forget the aggravations of having such a meddling father-in-law. At least the *Empress*'s manifest was safely locked away now, and all that remained to be handled was the American spy. He must have faith that Feng would eliminate him.

With pride, he watched the old man beam at the small boy who stood shyly to his side. He turned to study the boy, who wore Western-style pajamas with the face of Batman emblazoned on his thin chest. He was small for his age and smelled of Western peanut butter.

The old man — Li Aorong — patted him indulgently on the head. "You are how old now, Peiheng?"

"Seven, honored Grandfather." With a glance at his mother, he continued, "I will be in a month anyway." He added proudly, "I'm in the American school."

Li laughed. "You like being in school with the children of Westerners?"

"Father says it'll make me important in the world."

Li glanced at his son-in-law, Yu Yongfu, who sat rigid in one of his suede armchairs. Still, despite his obvious tension, Yu was smiling at his son.

Li said, "Your father is an intelligent man, Peiheng."

From where she stood near the door of the study, Li Kuonyi interrupted, "You have a grand-daughter, too, Father."

"So I do, daughter. So I do. And a most beautiful little one." Li smiled again. "Come, child. Stand with your brother. Tell me, are you, too, in American school?"

"Yes, Grandfather. I'm two grades higher than Peiheng."

Li feigned astonishment. "Only one year older, and *two* grades ahead? You take after your mother. She was always smarter than my sons."

Yu Yongfu spoke sharply, "Peiheng learns his numbers quickly."

"Another businessman." Li chuckled with pleasure. He stroked the faces of both children as if touching rare and delicate vases. "They will go far in the new world. But it's past their bedtime, eh?" He nodded gravely to Yu and his daughter. "It was kind of you to allow them to remain awake."

"You don't visit us often enough, Father," Kuonyi told him, an edge to her voice.

"The affairs of Shanghai keep an old man busy."

"But you are here tonight," Kuonyi challenged. "At such a late hour."

107

The father and daughter stared. Kuonyi's gaze was as hard and bold as that of her powerful father, demanding an explanation.

He said, "The children must be in bed, Daughter."

Kuonyi took their hands and turned toward the door. "My husband and I will return."

"Yongfu will stay. He and I will speak together," he said. Now the edge was in his voice. "Alone."

Kuonyi hesitated. She straightened her back and took the children away.

Above the mantle in Yu's Western-style office, the Victorian clock ticked quietly. The two men sat for some minutes in silence. The older man stared at his son-in-law until Yu Yongfu said politely, "It's been too long since your last visit, honored father-in-law. All of us have missed your wise counsel."

Li said, "A man's first responsibility must be to his family. Is that not so, son-in-law?"

"As has long been written."

Li fell silent again.

Yu waited. The old man had something on his mind, perhaps an important position for Yu that might be seen as favoring his own family too much. He needed to be sure Yu was equal to the task. Yu wanted good news tonight. His problems with the *Empress* were draining him.

At last, Yu echoed, "A man must never bring disrepute to his family."

"Disrepute?" The older man lifted his head and repeated the word in a tone almost of wonder. "You have a wife and two children."

"I've been blessed, and they are my soul." Yu smiled.

"I have a daughter and two grandchildren."

Yu blinked. What had happened? What was he supposed to say to that? His mouth turned dry as the deserts of Xinjiang, because something had changed in the room. Fear riveted him. He was no longer looking into the eyes of the indulgent grandfather of his son and daughter. Instead, this was the flinty, unrelenting gaze of an official of the Shanghai Special Administrative Zone, a politician who was owned by the immensely powerful Wei Gaofan.

"You've made an irredeemable mistake," Li told him in an emotionless voice. His large, fat-encrusted face was as still as a waiting snake's. "The theft of the true manifest to *The Dowager Empress* puts us in grave jeopardy. *All* of us."

Yu felt himself dissolve in fear. "A mistake that's been corrected. No harm has resulted. The manifest is locked in my safe upstairs. There is no —"

"The Americans know what the *Empress* carries. An American spy is sniffing around Shanghai because of it. He cannot be disposed of without many questions being asked. You have imperiled me, and — worse — you have imperiled Wei Gaofan. What was secret is no longer secret, and what is no longer secret can come to the ears of Wei Gaofan's enemies on the Central Committee, the Politburo, even on the Standing Committee itself."

"Feng will dispose of this American!"

"What comes to the ears of the Politburo will be investigated. *You'll* be investigated."

Yu Yongfu was desperate. "They'll learn nothing —"

"They'll learn *everything*. It isn't in you to resist, son-in-law." Li's tone softened. "It's sad, but it's true. You'll reveal everything, and if you live, you'll be ruined. Which means the ruin of all of us. *All* of the Yu's. *All* of the Li's."

"No!" Yu Yongfu shuddered. His stomach was a fist. He could hardly breathe. "I'll go away. Yes, I'll leave . . ."

Li dismissed him with a wave. "The matter is decided."

"But —"

"The only question now is how it is to be done. That is your choice. Will it be prison, disgrace, and ruin for our family? Many questions asked and answered, and the loss of the favor of Wei Gaofan for all of us? Without the great Wei, I will go down. Your wife — my daughter — will fall with me, and there will be no future for my other children and their families either. Most crucial to you, there will be no future for *your* children."

Yu trembled. "But —"

"But you are right, none of that need happen. The honorable way will save all of us. The responsibility will end with you. Without you to speak, and no question as to the manner of your death, nothing can lead to Wei Gaofan or myself. My position remains secure, because we will retain Wei's favor. Your wife and children will still have an unlimited future."

Yu Yongfu opened his mouth to answer, but no sound came out. Fear paralyzed him as he saw his suicide.

★ ★ ★

Far to the west of downtown Shanghai, beyond the ring road expressway, Andy cut his engine and allowed his Jetta to glide to a stop on a tree-lined suburban street. There were no streetlights. The houses were mostly dark at this late hour. Nothing moved in the blue-steel moonlight.

In the passenger seat, Smith checked his watch. It was after nine o'clock. Before he had rendez-voused with Andy, he left a message on Dr. Liang's answering machine that he was indisposed and un-able to join him and his colleagues for dinner. He hoped that would cover his activities tonight.

Now he had something far more crucial to worry about. He listened intently. He heard nothing except the faint noise of traffic back on the ring. Something was wrong about this street of af-fluent homes. He gazed around, trying to under-stand . . . then he saw what it was, and inwardly laughed at himself. He had lived in the Eastern Seaboard corridor so long he had become culture bound. The answer was, no cars were parked at the curbs.

"That's the address over there." Andy pointed across the street. "Yu Yongfu's mansion."

Smith saw no numbers. "How the hell do you know?"

Andy grinned. "In Shanghai, you just know."

Smith grunted. There was a high, solid wall right on the edge of the dark street, occupying the entire block. Through the barred metal gate, he could make out an impressive compound in the court-yard style of the long-ago estates of rich land-owners. Deep inside, the mansion was barely

111

visible. Unlike anything he had seen in this Asian metropolis, Yu's estate seemed to come straight from the last imperial dynasty.

Smith grabbed his night-vision binoculars and focused on the distant manse and had a shock. It looked American, as if it had been built around 1900. It was big, rambling, and airy. So far, the perimeter wall was the only trace of old China.

He handed the binoculars to Andy, who was as surprised as Smith. "It's like one of those big houses the opium taipans had back in the eighteen hundreds. You know, in the British, American, and French Concessions? Those were the dudes who ran the trading companies, built the Bund, and made millions swapping Indian opium for Chinese tea and silk."

"That's the impression Yu probably intended," Smith guessed. "Judging from what I saw at his office, and what you've told me, the man thinks of himself as a modern taipan."

Smith continued to study the silent estate. There was no light in the house, no movement, and no sign of security guards on the grounds. That also surprised him. While the Communist government would certainly not permit elaborate private electronic security that could keep their police out, manpower here was both cheap and plentiful.

"Okay, Andy, I'm going in. Give me two hours. If I'm not back, get out of here. Better give me my suit in case we get separated."

Andy handed him the suit in a tightly rolled bundle tied by his belt. "What if someone comes before two hours?"

"Leave fast. Try not to let them see you. Hide the car then slip back on foot and hunker down out of sight. But don't wait longer than the two hours. If I'm not back by then, I'm probably not coming back. Notify your contact and tell him about Flying Dragon and Yu Yongfu."

"Jesus, don't scare me any more than I am. Anyway, my contact's not a him. She's a her."

"Then tell *her*."

Andy An swallowed and nodded. Smith climbed out of the car and pulled on his backpack. Inside were his tools. In his black work clothes, he trotted through the darkness toward the compound as traffic hummed far away, reminding him again how quiet this neighborhood was.

At a corner of the wall far from the Yu mansion, a tree with thick branches hung over the side. The municipal government would not trim or cut down trees for the safety of a private tycoon, anymore than they would permit electronic security. Smith grabbed the branch and pulled himself up the wall. At the top, he paused. Blooming jasmine perfumed the air. He had a sense he was on the edge of a forest, so dense were the trees and underbrush. He dropped over into dry leaves. They crunched under his feet. Crouching, he waited motionless, hoping no one had heard him.

There was still no sign of security. It made him uneasy. A man of the ambition and ostentation of Yu would have some sort of protection. Most likely, a phalanx of personal guards.

He trotted toward the house and soon came out of the trees into a garden that brought him up as short as the house and the forest had. It was an elaborate, nineteenth-century English garden with narrow paths winding among rosebushes and immaculate flower beds, elaborate topiary, quaint benches, a gazebo, and even a lawn for croquet and bowling. There was the scent of freshly cut grass. He could imagine a homesick British tea tycoon finding solace here.

The garden gave less cover in the ghostly moonlight, but the grotesque shadows cast by the topiary would serve well enough. Moving swiftly, he was soon inside a stand of trees near the house. He circled, discovered a six-car garage at the side that contained only two cars — a large, black Mercedes sedan and a silver Jaguar XJR. He could see no light in the house or an open window.

He worked his way around to the front again. The ornately carved entrance door was mostly in shadow. The brass knocker was oversized and silvered by the moonlight. He studied the door. It was not set back inside a recess, so the moonlight shined directly on it. Moonlight distorted perspective, and depth perception became difficult. The door should not be shadowed at all. Where did the shadow that seemed to cover a quarter of the door come from?

The answer was, there was no shadow. The door was a quarter open, and what appeared to be a shadow was the house's dark interior.

A trap? People had been watching and following him, but he had taken a multitude of precautions driving here. To all appearances, the estate was deserted. Still, there was the possibility he had missed something or someone.

He drew his Beretta, circled left, and worked

his way back to the front door. He listened once more.

Everything was still, silent. Beretta in both hands, he inched the door farther open with the toe of his athletic shoe. The door was well oiled and swung soundlessly. Where were the servants who should be tending this post? He let the door open fully. A broad foyer of polished wood, floor to ceiling, came into view, illuminated by a wash of pewter-colored moonlight through the door and windows. An elegant, winding staircase led up at the rear.

He stepped inside, his soft-soled shoes making little sound. He paused to peer into the room to his left. It was a Victorian-style dining room, but everything in it was Chinese, from the carved-wood dinner table to the screens that hid various corners.

He padded to the right. Another open archway showed a living room twice the size of the dining room. It was dark and nearly silent. He listened, frowning. Inside he could hear the soft sound of someone's weeping.

Baghdad, Iraq

The one commodity in Baghdad that was not in short supply or impossible to afford was petrol. As usual, traffic at five P.M. was congested on every major street of the ancient metropolis. Behind the wheel of his shiny Mercedes, Dr. Hussein Kamil was thinking bitterly of the shortages of anything that had to be imported or manufactured as he fought the sluggish river of cars and trucks toward the commercial center of the city. He was on a terrifying errand. His patients depended on the life-saving medicines that came from outside Iraq. So did his wealth, privileges, and the future of his family. His patients were among the country's elite, and if he failed to find the antibiotics, tranquilizers, antidepressants, and all the other sophisticated Western pharmaceuticals they demanded, they would go somewhere else . . . or worse.

He did not know how the elegant Frenchwoman had discovered how he obtained his contraband pharmaceuticals. But she knew every name and place, every contact, every devious arrangement, every secret drop. If a syllable of it were ever to come to the ears of the government or the Republican Guard, they would kill him.

His throat dry with fear, he arrived at a soaring high-rise that had been constructed in happier times. He parked in the garage beneath and rode the elevator up to the headquarters of Tigris Export-Import, Ltd., Agricultural Chemicals. It was rumored to be one of the thousands of companies owned through fronts by the president and his family.

Nadia, the anxious secretary, was waiting to meet him, wringing her hands. "He just collapsed, Dr. Kamil. Without warning. One moment he was —"

"He's still unconscious?"

"Yes. We're so frightened."

She led him at a trot past the cubicles of dozens of employees preparing in grim silence to go home for the day and into the large, quiet office of his patient, Nasser Faidhi, CEO and chairman. The view over the city and far out into the desert beyond the Tigris and Euphrates rivers was imposing. He took it in with a brief glance and rushed to Faidhi, who was lying on a leather couch, unconscious. He checked his vital signs.

Nadia whispered, "Is he going to die?"

Dr. Kamil had no idea how the Frenchwoman had created this medical crisis, but he knew she had, since she had told him he would get the call at precisely 4:45 P.M., and she had been right. He doubted Faidhi's death was in her plan, because it would provoke an official investigation. The good news was that Faidhi's heart beat strongly, his pulse was steady, and his color good. He was simply unconscious. Some kind of quick-acting but essentially harmless drug, Dr. Kamil guessed.

He told the secretary, "Not at all, but I'll need to make some tests." He glanced at her. "I must undress him. You understand?"

Nadia flushed. "Of course, Doctor."

"Thank you. And see that we're not disturbed."

"No one would dare." She left the office. She would guard the door like a fire-eating beast.

The moment he was alone with the unconscious businessman, Dr. Kamil hurried to the wall of filing cabinets where he found the file the Frenchwoman had described: Flying Dragon Enterprises of Shanghai. Inside were four sheets of paper. Two were letters from the company's Basra office, describing negotiations with a Yu Yongfu, president of Flying Dragon, concerning a cargo of agricultural implements, chemicals, electronics, and other goods to be delivered to the company on a ship named *The Dowager Empress*. The other two were Faidhi's responses, containing instructions on the handling of the arrangements by the Basra office. There was nothing else.

Dr. Kamil's heart pounded with joy. The invoice the Frenchwoman wanted either did not exist or was in the Basra office. He jammed the file back inside the drawer, closed it, and strode back to his patient.

Twenty minutes later, there was a low cough followed by a sigh from Faidhi. His eyelids fluttered. Dr. Kamil marched to the office door, opened it, and smiled to the distraught secretary, pacing outside.

"You may come in now, Nadia. He's reviving and should be fine."

"Allah be praised!"

"Of course," Kamil said solemnly, "I'll need to examine him further, a complete checkup. Call my office and make an appointment for him." He smiled again. There would be a fat fee and much gratitude. He would tell the Frenchwoman that if she wanted that invoice, she would have to go to Basra, where, of course, he could not go without arousing suspicion. Everything had turned out well, just as he had expected.

Chapter Eight

Shanghai

A beautiful woman sat alone in the darkened living room, in the midst of heavy, museum-quality antique side pieces. She was curled up on a brown-leather Eames chair. Small and slender, she wore her shiny black hair pulled back in a simple ponytail. In one hand, she held a half-full brandy snifter. An uncorked bottle of Remy Martin cognac stood on the chrome-and-ebony table next to her. A large cat watched from a luxurious couch nearly half as long as the mammoth living room.

The woman gave no sign she saw Smith, the cat, or anything else. She was staring into space, a fragile presence dwarfed by her surroundings.

Smith scanned the room for a sign the woman was not alone. He saw and heard nothing. The house was eerily silent. He stepped carefully into the room, his Beretta still in both hands. The woman raised the snifter and drank it dry in a single gulp. She reached for the open bottle, poured it half full again, set the bottle down, and continued to stare ahead, her movements automatic, like a robot.

Smith walked closer, making no sound, the Beretta still up and ready.

Suddenly she was looking straight at him, and he realized he knew her from somewhere, had seen her before. At least her face, the high-necked Chinese dress she wore, the imperious expression . . . Of course, it was in the movies. Some Chinese movie. She was a film star. Yu Yongfu's trophy wife? Whoever she was, she was staring straight into his face, seemingly oblivious to his pistol.

"You're the American spy." Her English was flawless, and it was a statement, not a question.

"Really?"

"My husband told me."

"Is Yu Yongfu here?"

She looked away, staring again into the distance. "My husband is dead."

"Dead? How did he die? When?"

The woman turned to face him again and then did something odd. She looked at her watch. "Ten or perhaps fifteen minutes ago. How? He didn't tell me. Possibly a pistol like the one you're holding. Do all men love guns?"

Her matter-of-fact, emotionless voice, her morbid calm, chilled Smith. Like a sharp wind blowing across a glacier.

"It was you," she continued. "They feared you. Your presence. It would cause questions they didn't want asked."

"Who are 'they'?"

She drained her cognac again. "Those who required my husband to kill himself. For me and the children, they said. For the *family*." She laughed. It was abrupt, like an explosion. A macabre sound more like a bark than a real laugh. There was no humor in it, only bitterness. "They took his life to save themselves. Not from danger, mind you. From *possible* danger." Her smile at Smith was mocking. "And here you are, aren't you? Looking for my husband, just as they said you would. They always know when there's a threat to their interests."

Smith seized on the acerbic mockery. "If you want to avenge him, help me bring them down. I need a document he had. It'll expose them for the international criminals they are."

She considered. There was speculation in her gaze. She searched his face as if to find some trick. Then she shrugged, picked up the bottle of Remy Martin, poured her snifter almost full, and gazed away.

"Upstairs," she said woodenly. "In the safe in our bedroom."

She did not look at him again. Instead, she sipped the brandy and studied the empty air above her head as if it were full of answers she could not quite read.

Smith stared. Was this an act? Perhaps to lull him into going upstairs where he would be trapped?

In the end, it did not matter. He needed the document in the safe. Too much was at stake. He half backed out of the baronial room, rotating his Beretta to cover both it and the dark entry hall. But the house remained as silent as a tomb.

He slipped upstairs to the second-floor landing, where the shadows were denser, since there were no windows to let in the moonlight. Nothing moved up here either. There was no odor of gun smoke and no corpses. The only sound came from down below — the clink of the bottle of cognac against the snifter in the echoing living room, where the grieving woman poured her next brandy.

The master bedroom was at the far end of the hall. The size of two normal bedrooms, it was completely Chinese. There was a six-post, curtained canopy bed from the late Ming Dynasty, two Ming couch beds, Qing wardrobes and lady's dressing table, and chairs and low tables from various other dynasties. Everything was heavily carved and decorated in the most elaborate Chinese style. Silks and brocades curtained the bed and hung from the walls. Screens decorated every corner.

The wall safe was behind a hanging depicting some ancient battle from what looked like the Yuan Dynasty of Kublai Khan. Smith took out his picklocks, laid them on the cabinet closest to the safe, and inspected the combination lock.

He took hold of the dial knob — and the safe door moved. Full of misgivings, he pulled on the knob. Just as the door swung toward him, a powerful car engine roared to life outside the house.

Smith sprinted to the window, which overlooked the garage and driveway, in time to see the taillights of the Jaguar disappear down the long driveway toward the street. *Damn.*

He tore out of the bedroom and down the stairs two at a time to the living room. The snifter and bottle were on the table beside the Eames chair, and the woman was gone. Had it all been a setup?

A trap? The woman's purpose to distract him with her bitter tale of forced suicide?

He listened, but there were no sounds of any vehicles coming up the driveway.

He rushed back upstairs to a bedroom at the front of the house to get a different view. It was a boy's room. From the window, he looked past the garden and trees toward the distant wall. He heard nothing now out on the street. Saw nothing moving anywhere in the gardens below.

Maybe he was wrong. Maybe she really was distraught and half drunk, running away because of her horror to some private sanctuary. Or to join her husband in death.

He could not take the chance. He raced back upstairs, emptied the safe, and dumped the contents on one of the couch beds. There were jewels, letters, documents. There was no money and no manifest. He shook his head angrily, his disappointment raw. He searched through the letters and documents twice more, swearing to himself. The invoice manifest was definitely missing.

There was one item that was interesting — a typed note on the letterhead of a Belgian company: Donk & LaPierre, S.A., Antwerp and Hong Kong. Written in French, it was addressed to Yu Yongfu at Flying Dragon Enterprises. It assured Yu the shipment would arrive in Shanghai on August 24 in plenty of time for *The Dowager Empress* to sail, and it expressed great optimism for "our joint venture." It was signed by Jan Donk and listed a phone number in Hong Kong under the sender's name.

Relieved he might have found something solid at

123

last, Smith jammed the letter into his backpack and hurried out of the bedroom. He was at the head of the stairs when he saw shadows flit across the moonlit windows on either side of the front door. His pulse accelerated as he forced himself to stay motionless, listening. Out in the night, quick footsteps ran close to the house.

With a jolt of adrenaline, he sprinted back to the master bedroom and peered out the rear windows at the formal English garden. No one was in sight, but there were no trees and no other way down except to jump.

He dashed to the windows on the other side of the room, which faced away from the driveway and garage. The manicured lawn was the color of tarnished copper in the moonlight. There were trees, but none close enough to reach. There was, however, a drainpipe that ran from the gutters at the edge of the roof above him down to the grass.

As he studied the drainpipe, two figures ran around the front corner of the mansion close to the house. They tested each window for entry.

If no trap had been intended when he arrived, it was a trap now. They would soon find the front door unlocked, if they had not already. He had seconds to get out of the house before they were inside, up the stairs, and on him.

He waited until the figures vanished toward the rear. He opened the window, climbed out, sat on the sill with his legs dangling, and leaned to the drainpipe, which was sheet metal and looked well attached to the house. Holding it, he swung himself out. It groaned but held. Using the toes of his shoes, he literally walked down the side of the mansion. As soon as he touched grass, he bolted out across the moonlit lawn toward the stand of trees that had sheltered him when he first arrived.

Angry shouts in Chinese carried across the night from the windows of the master bedroom. They had found the open safe and spotted his escape.

As soon as he reached the trees, he began weaving, dodging the dark vegetation. Shouts followed across the distance, and then it was a single hushed version of a deep, harsh voice giving whispery orders like a drill sergeant instilling steadiness in his men. Smith had heard the voice before — from the leader of the attackers on Liuchiu Island. The big Chinese with the red-and-white hair that the treasurer of Flying Dragon had called Feng Dun.

Suddenly an ominous silence filled the night. Smith guessed they had been ordered to spread out, to methodically force him toward the wall where it bordered the street and the gate. Feng Dun would have more of his people waiting there. It was the same pincer movement he had used in the attack on Liuchiu Island. Military minds tended to favor the same tactics — like Stonewall Jackson's outflanking night marches.

Smith turned and trotted softly toward the back wall. As he slipped through the shadows, he pulled his walkie-talkie from his pocket. "Andy? Come in, Andy."

"Shit, Colonel. Are you okay?"

"You saw them?"

"Sure did. Three cars. I got out of there fastest."

"Where are you now?"

"Out front, like you said. I stashed the car and walked back. The three cars are right here on the street, too close for comfort."

"Did they leave men there, too?"

"You bet."

"How many?"

"Too many, as far as I'm concerned. Three drivers. And another five just came out through the gate to join them."

"Let's skip their greeting party. Go back to the car fast and drive around to meet me at the back corner of the wall on the side street. Got that?"

"Side street, rear corner."

"Get going."

Smith ended the transmission and resumed his race toward the rear. He was just beginning to think he had outwitted his pursuers when he heard a noise that meant danger. He spun and dropped flat, Beretta in hand. There it was again — the hard sound of metal striking wood. There was a low, muttered oath.

From the ground, he strained to see anything that stirred. The little forest had turned quiet, and the only movement seemed to be caused by the wind rustling through branches and leaves.

There was a thicket of bushes to his right, near the wall. He inched toward it, all his senses on high alert. He slid in between two bushes that hid him from above, and he forced his breath to slow, grow shallow. He waited.

The only reason he saw the big shape pass was that the wind blew an opening in the leaf cover high above. Moonlight shone through and illuminated a half-crouched man and his raised AK-74 passing by.

Disgusted with himself, Smith knew he had guessed wrong. Feng Dun had reasoned Smith would expect another pincer movement, so he had sent most of his people to the street, while doubling back the opposite way alone, in hopes of taking Smith by surprise. But he would not be alone ahead; he would have men in position, waiting.

Smith slithered out from under the thicket, the spiny branches scratching his head and hands. He hardly felt the discomfort. As soon as he was out, he trotted left to where the wall bordered the side street. There was no tree close enough to be useful, but fallen branches and other debris had collected in a pile high enough to help. Fortunately, Yu Yongfu preferred appearance over substance — taking care of one's wooded grounds where they were out of sight was not something that interested him. Or if anything his wife had said were true, *had* interested him.

Smith ran, jumped up onto the pile, and leaped. He grabbed the wall, pulled himself to the top, and straddled it as he surveyed the street. On the other side near the far corner, Andy An's Jetta was parked.

He turned on his walkie-talkie. "Andy?" he said in hushed tones. "We've got company all over the compound. I can't get to the corner. Drive away, circle, and come back to the center of the block. Slow down, and I'll meet you. Then we'll burn rubber."

He waited. There was no answer. Was Andy's radio out?

"Andy? Are you there?"

Silence.

"Andy?"

His stomach went loose with fear. A chill swept through him. He dug his night-vision binoculars from his backpack and focused on the Jetta. Andy sat behind the wheel, motionless as he kept watch on the street ahead. There was no one else in the small car.

Smith frowned, studying the car and the green night all around. Andy still did not move. Smith watched him for two more long minutes, an interminable length of time. But nothing changed. Andy moved not an inch. Not a muscle. Not the blink of an eye.

Smith heaved a sad sigh. Andy was dead. They had taken him out.

He put away his binoculars and dropped down to the street, sprinted across into the cluster of smaller neighborhood estates, and tore off through their grounds. He heard no shouts behind him this time. They would be too focused on the Jetta, expecting him to connect with Andy.

Furious and weary, he slowed to a lope. He wove along streets and past gardens, fences, and the walls of gated communities built for the expatriate businessmen who would flock more and more into the People's Republic to live off its billions. Finally he reached a major street. Dripping with sweat, he hailed a taxi.

Beijing

The telephone rang in the family room of the main house of Niu Jianxing's old-fashioned court-

128

yard complex on the outskirts of the Xicheng district, one of the older sections of the city. The Owl liked to think of himself as a man of the people. He had refused to join the many members of the Central Committee who had built expensive mansions far out in the Chaoyang district. Instead, although his complex was large and comfortable, it was far from flashy.

Niu had been watching the tape of an American legal drama with his wife and son and, consequently, was annoyed by the interruption. Partly because it was an intrusion on his family time, something he cherished but could indulge in less and less since his elevation to the Standing Committee. But perhaps even more because it broke into his fascinated study of American concepts of crime, law, society, and the individual.

Still, no one would dare call him at this late hour unless the matter were urgent. He excused himself, went into his private study, and closed the door, drowning out the television and the happy sounds of his wife and son.

Niu picked up the receiver. "Yes?"

General Chu Kuairong's rasping voice wasted no time on preambles. "Our scientist friend, Dr. Liang, reports that Jon Smith failed to keep the dinner engagement he arranged. The doctor found a message on his answering machine from Smith. He went to Smith's hotel room, hoping to change his mind. When there was no response, he had the manager open the door to be sure Smith was well. The room was empty. Smith had not checked out and not taken his belongings, but he was gone."

Niu did not like that. "What does Major Pan say about Smith?"

"His surveillance did not see Colonel Smith leave the hotel. Ever."

Niu knew the chief of state security was enjoying Pan's embarrassing failure. Still, that was hardly the point. "Smith must have suspected Dr. Liang had become suspicious, knew he would be watched, and found a way to slip out."

"Clearly." On the edge of sarcasm.

Niu repressed his irritation. "Has Smith been to Shanghai before?"

"Not that we know."

"Does he speak Chinese? Have friends or associates here?"

"His military and personnel records give no indication of that."

"Then how is he functioning?" Niu wondered and answered his own question: "Someone must be helping him."

The general had had his fun; now he became serious. "Someone Chinese. An insider who speaks English or another language Smith knows. He would have a vehicle and know his way around better than most. We are particularly puzzled because Smith is totally unknown to us, and yet he clearly has help in our midst, perhaps from someone recruited years ago to spy among us."

Niu contemplated his own private spies. Without them, he would be nearly blind and deaf in the byzantine world of Chinese national politics. "Whatever the case, we must now detain this colonel and interrogate him. Tell Major Pan to do so immediately."

"Pan has his people searching Shanghai."

"When they find Smith, notify me. I will speak to him myself." Niu scowled as he hung up. He had lost all pleasure in his family time and the American television program.

Why would the Americans send this sort of agent now, at such a politically sensitive time, and allow him to operate when he surely knew he had been discovered? Why would they risk their own treaty?

He fell into his office chair, leaned back, and closed his eyes, allowing his mind to sink into that quiet place where it seemed as if he were floating. There was no weight on his body, or on his mind. . . . Minutes passed. An hour. Patience was necessary. Finally, with a soaring burst of clarity, he knew the answer: It would happen if a faction in the American government opposed the treaty, too.

Chapter Nine

Washington, D.C.

In the big conference room next door to the Oval Office, the air was heavy with anticipation. The chairs encircling the long table were filled, as were the chairs lining the walls, where assistants, advisers, and researchers sat and stood, waiting to hear what decisions would be made so they were prepared to find answers to their bosses' questions. This packed meeting was just a preliminary discussion, but it was for the all-important, annual multibillion-dollar appropriations package for military weapons. The new secretary of defense, Henry Stanton, who sat to the right of the president, had called it.

Stanton was a man of medium height and hot disposition. From his balding head to his restless hands, he exuded energy and charm. His sharp features had softened with age, making him look almost avuncular. In his midfifties, he used that reassuring affect to great advantage in press conferences. But now, out of sight of the media, he was all business.

He continued in his blunt style, "Mr. President,

gentlemen, and lady." He inclined his head to the only woman at the long table, former Brig. Gen. Emily Powell-Hill, the president's National Security Adviser. "Think of our military as if it were an alcoholic. Like any alcoholic, if it — and our nation — is to survive, it must make a clean break from the past."

The irritation on the other side of the table was visible in the grimly set jaws and audible in the low rumbles of the military commanders. *Alcoholic? Alcoholic! How dare he!* Even President Castilla raised an eyebrow.

Emily Powell-Hill jumped in to soothe the offended egos. "The secretary is, of course, asking for input from all of you, as well as from many experts in the field and our allies."

"The secretary," Secretary Stanton snapped, "is *asking* nothing. He's *telling* you the way it is. It's a brand-new day and a brand-new world. As the man said, we've got to stop preparing for last year's war!"

"The secretary's pronouncements and analogies might make him a great man in the headlines he appears to crave," Admiral Stevens Brose, chairman of the joint chiefs, growled from his seat directly facing the president and Stanton, "but his armchair views won't matter a plugged nickel on a battlefield." His gray buzz cut seemed to bristle with disgust. He sat awkwardly, his ankles crossed, his big chin jutting forward.

Secretary Stanton instantly retorted, "I resent the implication, Admiral, and —"

"That was no implication, Mr. Secretary," Brose said flatly. "That was a fact."

The two matched glares.

Stanton, the new man, gazed down at his notes. Few people had ever out-stared the implacable chairman of the joint chiefs, and Stanton was not going to be one of them today.

Still, Stanton did not give an inch. He looked up. "Very well. If you wish to make this adversarial . . ."

The admiral smiled.

Stanton reddened. As a former empire-building CEO of General Electric, Stanton was a long way from doubting his convictions. "Let's just say I got your attention, Admiral. That's what counts."

"You're too late. The world situation already did that," Brose rumbled. "Like an anchor between the eyeballs."

The president raised a hand. "All right, gentlemen. Let's call a truce. Harry, enlighten us poor laymen. Tell us specifically what you're suggesting."

Stanton, accustomed to cowing corporate boards that rubber-stamped his every whim, paused for effect. His analytical gaze perused the assembled generals and secretaries. "For more than a half century, America's been arming to fight a short, highly intense war in Europe or the old Soviet Union from large, permanent bases that were relatively convenient distances away. Targets were within striking range of carrier-based fighters and bombers, plus there were the giant bombers that could fly out of America. To prevent war, we relied on containment and massive deterrence. All that must change radically. It must change *now*."

Admiral Brose nodded. "I'm in full agreement, if you're suggesting a leaner military. It has to be quick to respond, fast to deploy anywhere at any time, and equipped with lighter, smaller, stealthier, more expendable weapons. The navy's already implemented its 'street fighter' concept of small carriers, missile ships, and submarines to fight in the narrow coastal waters we expect we'll be operating in more and more."

Air Force General Bruce Kelly was next to Brose. He sat erect, his patrician face florid, his uniform immaculate, and his eyes clear and calculating. His enemies complained he was an emotionless machine, while his supporters bragged he had one of the shrewdest intellects the military had ever produced. "I assume the secretary isn't suggesting we abandon our deterrent capability," he said in a mild voice. "Our nuclear weapons — long-range or short-range — are critical."

"True." Stanton offered his charming smile, since he and Kelly were in fundamental agreement. "But we should consider reducing stockpiles and trimming research for bigger and 'better' bombs and the giant missiles capable of carrying them. It's also probably unwise to build more carriers and subs beyond what we need to replace what we have."

Emily Powell-Hill said, "Cut to the bottom line, Henry. This is a meeting about appropriations. Exactly what are you suggesting we build and don't build?"

"As I said, Emily, I'm not suggesting anything. I'm telling you what we must do to keep our military superiority. We must shift funding from giant carriers, huge tanks, and fighter jets with overwhelming power to light, small, almost invisible weapons."

The army chief of staff, Lt. General Tomás Guerrero, was seated to the far right of Admiral Brose. His big, square-fingered hands knotted on the table. "No one's going to tell me we won't need tanks, heavy artillery, and large forces trained to fight big wars. Russia and China are still out there, Secretary Stanton. You're forgetting them. They've got massive armies, enormous territories, and nuclear weapons. Then there's India, Pakistan, and a united Europe, too. Europe's already our economic adversary."

Stanton was not about to back down. "That's exactly what I *am* telling you, General."

NSA Powell-Hill chimed in, "I doubt anyone believes — or wants — our current military power scrapped, Mr. Stanton. As I understand it, your opinion is that we need to intensify our direction in developing smaller weapons and capabilities."

"I — " Stanton began.

Before the defense secretary could continue, Admiral Brose used his commanding presence and voice to bull his way in. "No one in this room disagrees with the concept of a leaner, meaner military. Hell, that's what we've been working on since the Gulf War. We just haven't made the complete commitment you're asking for."

From the far end of the table, Lt. General Oda, the marine commandant, boomed, "I sure don't disagree. Light and fast, that's what the marines want."

Nods of consensus filled the room. Only President Castilla, who was usually a full participant in any serious discussion of the military, remained si-

136

lent. He appeared to be brooding, waiting for something else to be said.

Secretary Stanton glanced at him, sensing uncertainty. He moved ahead boldly. "As far as it goes, I'm glad you agree with my analysis. But I get the impression you're talking about beginning tomorrow. That's not good enough. We have to start today. *Now.* At this moment, we have weapons in various stages of development — the air force's F-22 short-range fighter jet, the navy's next generation DD-21 battleship and aircraft carriers, and the army's Protector long-range armored artillery system. They're too big. Every one of them. They're elephants when we need jaguars. They're going to be completely useless in the kinds of future engagements we're most likely to face."

Before the chorus of outrage could gain steam, Admiral Brose abruptly raised a hand. As the voices subsided to aggrieved rumbling, he said, "All right. Let's deal with them one at a time. Bruce, lay out the case for the F-22."

"That won't take long," General Kelly said. "The F-16 is getting old. The F-22 will establish absolute control of the skies over any battlefield. The new generation provides first-look, first-shot, and first-kill. They're faster, more maneuverable, and more powerful, and their stealth is increased to where the jets are essentially undetectable."

"Succinctly put, General," Stanton said approvingly. "I'll try to match. No country's building air capability equal to our air force. What they *are* building are relatively cheap, powerful, and accurate missile systems. The problem is, many of the missile systems will end up in the hands of terrorists. At the same time, despite its supercruise capability, the F-22 remains a short-range fighter. That means it's got to have bases close to battle. But what happens when the enemy takes out those bases with missiles? *Our new and expensive fighters will be useless.*"

"I'll speak for the navy," Brose said. "We're already rethinking our carriers and other surface vessels. In confined waters or waters close to a coast, they'll be sitting ducks for missiles. If it's a war deep inside a continent, no ships or short-range aircraft will be able to get to the battlefield anyway."

"That leaves the army and the Protector artillery system," secretary of the army, Jasper Kott, announced. He was an elegant man with fastidious manners. Smooth-cheeked, with a quiet face and expressive eyes, he was also unflappable under the most trying circumstances. "I'll anticipate Secretary Stanton by agreeing we need the quickly committed army he envisions. If a ground war had erupted in Kosovo, our tanks would've needed months to arrive, and when they did, the massive weight of the seventy-ton Abrams would've crushed ten of the twelve bridges between the port and the battlefield. That's why we're training 'interim' brigades now. They'll ultimately have a new armored vehicle far smaller than the Abrams, and we can ship it by air."

"Then we don't need the Protector system at all, do we, Secretary Kott?" Stanton challenged.

Kott's voice remained polite, almost neutral. "As a matter of fact, we do need it. We need it very much. As General Guerrero said, we've got serious potential adversaries out there — China, Russia, Serbia, India, Pakistan, India, and — don't forget — Iran and Iraq. Our long-range bombers are powerful but not always accurate. Artillery's still the key to winning a major battle. We like the Protector because it's far superior to our current Paladin system. It gives us the superiority to deter big military adversaries. By the way, the Protector is easily airlifted."

"It's easy to fly into remote areas only if it remains at the forty-two tons you stripped it down to. You discarded a lot of the armor you really want. Everyone knows you'll put it back on as soon as you can. Then the damn thing'll be too heavy to fly anywhere."

"It will remain airlift capable," General Guerrero retorted.

"I doubt that, General. The army loves heavy armor. You'll find a way to regain that weight once you've got the government's commitment to build it. Just remember what the Germans learned in Russia and the Ardennes in World War Two: Poor roads, old bridges, narrow tunnels, and bad terrain can torpedo any advantage heavy tanks and artillery have. Throw in bad weather, and you might as well dig your grave on the spot."

"On the other hand, light forces fail every time against heavy weapons and large manpower," Secretary Kott pointed out. "That's impossible to deny. What you want, Stanton, is a recipe for disaster."

As the men around the table bristled, ready to resume arguing, Admiral Brose raised his voice, "I believe we have defined our positions sufficiently.

Funds for weaponry are not unlimited, right, Emily?"

The National Security Adviser nodded soberly. "Unfortunately."

"So I tend to side with the defense secretary on this," Brose told them. "Our first priority is to develop the fleeter forces our experiences from Somalia to the present tell us we need. We also need to hold the line on what we have and keep a wary eye on the military developments of potential enemies." He gazed across the table to the president. "What do you say, sir?"

Although President Castilla had remained oddly silent through the lengthy discussion, he was known to favor a sparer military. He nodded almost to himself. "Each of you has made cogent arguments that must be considered. The need for a quick-response force large enough and powerful enough to handle any brushfire war or Third World threat, or to protect our citizens and interests in developing nations, is clear. We can't have a repeat of Somalia. At the same time, we can't rely on nations doing nothing while America builds up massive forces on their borders, as Saddam Hussein allowed us during the Gulf War."

The president nodded to Admiral Brose and Secretary Stanton. "On the other hand, the generals and Secretary Kott are reminding us we may face conflicts on a monumental scale as well, against major-league opponents with nuclear weapons. We may have to fight on vast landmasses where light forces are inadequate." He seemed to brood again. Finally he announced, "We may have

140

to consider a larger military allocation than we anticipated."

Puzzled, everyone in the room looked at one another and back at the president. He was vacillating, a rare occurrence for such a firm decision maker. Only Admiral Brose had an inkling of what could be causing the uncharacteristic hesitancy — *The Dowager Empress* and China's strategic interests in her.

The president stood. "We'll meet again soon to discuss this further. Emily, I need to speak with you and Charlie on another matter."

The assorted generals, cabinet members, and assistants filed out, frowning and exchanging cryptic comments about what they obviously considered an unsatisfying meeting. President Castilla watched them go, his expression grave.

Shanghai

In the taxi, Smith changed into the suit and tie he had retrieved from poor Andy earlier. Every few minutes, he looked over his shoulder at the jockeying headlights on the street behind. He could not shake the sense of being followed. At the same time, the faces of Andy An and Avery Mondragon haunted him. Was there something he could have — should have — done that would have saved their lives?

In his mind, he went back over the last two days, searching for what he might have missed. For a decision that would have altered everything. Anger surged through him again. His muscles tensed. His chest ached with rage. Who were these people who killed so easily?

At last, he shook off the worst of it. Too much fury clouded the mind. He needed all of his intelligence, because finding the manifest was critical.

He finished dressing and shoved his black work clothes into his backpack. He had a job to do. A job made more vital by Mondragon's and Andy's deaths.

The taxi dropped him two blocks up the Bund, and he blended into the throngs out for an evening walk by the river. When he reached the corner across from the Peace Hotel, he turned into Nanjing Dong Lu. Here the famed shopping paradise reverted to the narrow, stinking, teeming street it had been before the mall was built. The sidewalks were so constricted that most of the shoulder-to-shoulder crowd walked in the street.

Across from the hotel's revolving door, Smith shrank back into an alley. He focused on the hotel entrance, hoping to spot the red-and-white hair of Feng Dun. One vendor of fake Rolex watches who buttonholed everyone going in or out of the hotel could have been someone he had spotted at Yu Yongfu's mansion. A dumpling seller on the sidewalk beside his steaming pot definitely was — one of the two who had passed under the windows of the master bedroom.

They looked their parts, but they also showed the telltale signs of men on stakeout: They were uninterested in what they were selling, never really looked at anyone who stopped to inspect their wares, and never bothered with the customary loud pitches. Instead, they strained to scrutinize everyone who moved through the hotel's doors. There was no point in checking the other entrances; they would be similarly covered. These people were organized and adept.

He needed to draw them away or somehow remove them. Showing himself as bait was risky. This was their city, not his, and he spoke no Chinese. At last, he joined the crowds walking back to the Bund, located a public telephone, and used the IC card Dr. Liang had given him. He dialed the hotel.

The desk clerk answered in Chinese but switched quickly to English the moment Smith gave his name.

"Yes, sir. How may we help you?"

"It's a bit embarrassing, but I have a small problem. Earlier today, I had an unpleasant altercation with a pair of street vendors. Unfortunately, they're back, watching the hotel entrance. That makes me uneasy about my safety. I mean, why are they out there?"

"I will take care of it. Can you describe them? There are so many on this part of Nanjing Dong Lu."

"One is selling fake Rolexes, and the other Shanghai dumplings."

"That should suffice, Dr. Smith."

"Thank you. I feel safer already." He hung up and wove back through the swarming pedestrians to stand by a planter where he could watch.

Less than two minutes later, a municipal police car honked and bulled its way through to stop in front of the hotel. Two officers in dark-blue pants and light-blue shirts jumped out, and the fake street vendors made a mistake: They showed no interest, which made the police immediately suspicious. Street vendors everywhere started looking over their shoulders when the police appeared. Seconds later, the phony vendors were in a shouting match with the officers.

Smith waited. Soon, the door of a large black sedan that had been parked across the street opened, and two men in street clothes got out. They pushed through the crowds, everyone cringing back, quickly giving them space. Public Security Bureau. They joined the municipal policemen. One spoke sharply. Instantly, the police officers and the vendors turned their shouts onto the Public Security agents, each side screaming its case. The vendors waved permits. The police pointed to the hotel. The Public Security people shouted back.

When a large black Lincoln stopped at the entrance and disgorged three European businessmen and three young Chinese women in slit dresses, Smith attached himself to their happy party, laughing with them as they sauntered into the lobby while a larger and larger crowd encircled the arguing police and vendors.

Pulling out his cell phone as he entered his room, Smith stopped in his tracks. The thin sheet of see-through plastic on the carpet was gone. He returned his cell phone to his pocket, drew his Beretta, and surveyed the floor. He did not have to look far. The plastic sheet was wadded up against the floorboard only feet from the door. Someone had entered, stepped on the plastic, and kicked it away without thinking what it meant.

He returned to the hallway, removed the DO

NOT DISTURB sign, and examined the door lock. It looked untouched. Back in the room, he locked the door again and checked his suitcases. The filaments were intact. Someone with a key had entered, was unconcerned about stepping on an invisible sheet of plastic, and had no interest in his suitcases. That did not sound like Public Security, local cops, or tonight's thugs. It sounded more like hotel personnel.

He frowned. Still, the DO NOT DISTURB sign had clearly been hanging on the knob. Had someone — not necessarily from the hotel — been simply checking to see whether he was there?

Frowning, he could take no chances. He turned on the TV set, raised the volume, went into the bathroom, and turned the faucets in the tub on full. With the jarring noise for background, he sat on the toilet seat, pulled out his cell phone again, and dialed Fred Klein's scrambled Covert-One line.

"Where in hell are you?" Klein demanded. "What's all that noise?"

"Just making sure I'm not overheard. There's a possibility my hotel room's been bugged."

"Swell. You have good news for me, Colonel?"

He angled back his head, stretching his neck. "I wish. My only break was I found who owns the *Empress* — a Chinese company called Flying Dragon Enterprises. A Shanghai businessman, Yu Yongfu, is — or was — president and chairman, but the true manifest wasn't in any of Yu's safes." He filled in the Covert-One chief about the company's treasurer, Zhao Yanji, and the information the distraught fellow had relayed. "Of course, I

145

went to Yu's mansion." He described his conversation with Yu's wife. "She might have been playing me, or she might not. She's an actress, and a damn good one from what I remember. Still, I had the feeling her story and her bitterness were real. Someone forced Yu Yongfu to kill himself, and whoever that was has the manifest."

He could hear Klein puffing hard on his pipe. "They've been one step ahead of us from the start."

"There's worse. Andy — An Jingshe — has been killed, too."

"I assume you're speaking of the interpreter I sent. I didn't know him, but that doesn't make me less sorry. You never get used to the deaths, Colonel."

"No," Smith said.

There was a moment of silence. Then, "Tell me more about the attack on the Yu mansion. What exactly makes you think it wasn't a trap?"

"It didn't have the feel of one. I think they'd been watching me and finally decided to make a move when the wife drove off. From how they acted, they obviously didn't expect to find the front door open."

"Public Security Bureau?"

"They were too open and clumsy. My guess is they were private killers."

"Killers who forced Yu to commit suicide and took the manifest?"

"If so, why did they go back to the mansion? Does the name Feng Dun sound familiar?"

When Klein said no, Smith described his run-ins with him.

146

"I'll have my people identify him."

Klein paused, and in his mind, Smith could see him scowling and pondering in the distant office at the yacht club on the Anacostia River.

At last, Klein rumbled, "So our main lead is dead, and the manifest we need is gone. Where does that leave us, Colonel? I could pull you and regroup for a try from another angle."

"Try any angle you can think of, but I'm not ready to give up yet. Maybe I can pick up the trail of the attackers. There's the man who says he's the president's father, too. I'll look for a lead on him."

"What else have you found?"

"Something very important . . . Flying Dragon isn't alone in the *Empress* venture. A Belgian company named Donk & LaPierre, S.A., supplied some of the cargo, if not all. Donk & LaPierre has an office in Hong Kong. It'd be logical for them to have a copy of the real invoice manifest, too."

"Good idea. Get to Hong Kong fast. I'll send someone to see what they have in Belgium, too. Where's the headquarters again?"

"Antwerp. I take it our people came up empty in Baghdad."

"They did. I'm arranging for a more reliable agent in Basra to investigate further."

"Good. I'll make some excuse to Dr. Liang and fly to Hong Kong on the first China Southwest plane I can get."

"Now . . ."

He barely heard the knock on the room door over the TV and the tub faucets. "Hold on." Smith drew his Beretta and walked out to the door. "Who is it?"

147

"Room service, sir."

"I didn't order room service."

"Dr. Jon Smith? Hairy crab dinner? A Bass ale? From the Dragon-Phoenix restaurant."

Hairy crab was a prized Shanghai dish, and the Dragon-Phoenix restaurant was in the hotel, but that did not change the fact that Smith had ordered no food. He told Fred Klein he would be in touch.

"What's going on there?" Klein demanded. "Is something wrong?"

"Tell Potus what I said. I may need that dental appointment after all." He severed the connection, pocketed the cell phone, and gripped his Beretta. He cracked open the door.

A lone man in a waiter's jacket stood beside a serving cart draped in white linen. The hot smell of seafood drifted from covered dishes. Smith did not recognize him. He was short and very lean, but there were muscles under his uniform, and the sinews of his neck were thick ropes. There was a tension and purpose to him like a coiled spring. Darker than any Han Chinese Smith had ever seen, he could have been carved from sun-browned rawhide. His long, high-boned face was lined and deeply seamed, although he was no more than forty, probably younger. The mustache was an elegant touch. Whatever and whoever he was, Smith decided, he was not the usual Chinese.

Before the door was fully open, the waiter shoved the cart into the room. "Good evening, sir," he said loudly in English thick with a Cantonese accent. A couple was swinging along the hall, holding hands. They passed Smith's room.

"Who are you?" Smith demanded.

The waiter glanced at Smith's Beretta, gave no sign he was perturbed, and used a heel to push the door closed behind him.

"Don't give a fuss, Colonel," the man said, with a flash of his black eyes. Gone was the Cantonese accent, replaced by an upper-class British one. "If you would be so kind." He reached under his serving cart and tossed a bundle of clothes to Smith. "Put these on. Quickly. There are some blokes downstairs looking for you. No time for full disclosure."

Smith caught the bundle with his left hand, while his right continued to point his Beretta at the man. "Who the hell are you, and who are *they?*"

"*They* are the Public Security Bureau, and I'm Asgar Mahmout, alias Xing Bao in the People's Republic." He still did not acknowledge Smith's Beretta. "I'm the 'asset' who got the word to Mondragon about the old man in the Chinese prison."

Chapter
Ten

Washington, D.C.

Near their offices in the Pentagon, Secretary of the Army Jasper Kott parted with General Tomás Guerrero in the corridor. They had been discussing various strategies for gaining more support from both the government and the military, including publicity to educate the general public. Kott continued on toward his office until General Guerrero disappeared.

The secretary changed directions and ducked into the men's restroom. It was deserted, so he went into a stall, locked the door, and sat on the toilet top. He dialed his cell phone and waited while the call was relayed through a maze of electronics.

The robust voice that finally came on asked, "Well?"

"I think it's working. The president's vacillating."

"That doesn't sound like our leader. What exactly is he doing?"

"You know what a bulldog he is. Well, he hardly took any part in the discussion. Stanton rode his horse hard, but he rode alone. Except for Brose and Oda, of course. But we expected that."

150

"Give me the details."

Kott described the high points of the appropriations meeting. "No one knew why the president seemed so moody, preoccupied, and waffling. Only maybe Brose. I caught a look between them."

There was a bitter laugh. "I'll bet you did. We need to talk more about this."

"Anytime. We'll make another phone appointment."

"No. In person. Just the two of us. There's too much to discuss, and it's too important."

Kott considered. "I need to visit our bases in Asia anyway."

"Good. I'll be waiting." The line went dead.

Kott returned the phone to his pocket, flushed the toilet, and left.

President Castilla often had the feeling Fred Klein lived in perpetual midnight. In the Covert-One office hidden in the ANACOSTIA SEAGOING YACHT CLUB, heavy curtains covered the windows against the late-morning sunlight, the noise of the bustling marina, and the sounds of boats and wildlife from the river. The president sat facing Klein, who leaned back behind his desk, his hands in the light of the lamp, and his head in the gloom of the office's shadows.

Klein repeated what Jon Smith had just reported. "And we may have to get him out of China quickly." Klein described the abruptly ended phone call from Shanghai that included the code words "Potus" — president — and "dental appointment" — extraction.

"Let's not lose Smith, too." The president shook

his head worriedly. "We still don't have the manifest, and we don't know who has it or where it is."

"Smith thinks the Belgian company may have a copy."

"*May* have?"

"I have people in China trying to track down who attacked Smith, and in Iraq looking for the second copy of the invoice manifest. I'll get the ball rolling in Antwerp to find out whether the third copy is there. But if we don't find one in Shanghai, Basra, or in Antwerp, then only Hong Kong is left."

The president nodded. "All right. I trust your judgment. We have a few days of grace before the freighter arrives." He hesitated then grimaced. "I have to consider what we do if no copies of the manifest are ever found. I can't let that ship unload its cargo in Iraq. In the final analysis, we'll have no choice but to board it, and that means I have to anticipate the consequences and prepare."

"A military confrontation with China?"

"A confrontation is a very real — and frightening — possibility."

"Would we go it alone, without our allies?"

"If necessary. They'll demand documentation if we ask them to back us. And if we have no documentation —"

"I see your point. We'd better get the manifest."

"I don't like to think about what we'll have to do if China is foolish enough to actually challenge us." Castilla shook his head, his broad face cloudy with unspoken worries. "Imagine, I wanted this job. I worked my ass off to get it." He hunched forward and said softly, "Tell me what's happening about David Thayer?"

"As soon as I can pinpoint the prison farm's exact location, I'm going to send in an agent to make contact and assess the accuracy of his story."

The president nodded again. "I've been thinking about the possibility the human-rights accord may never be signed. I don't like that at all."

"If that's what happens, a rescue mission for Thayer would come on the table."

"What kind of rescue mission?"

"A small unit. Exactly how large, with what personnel and equipment, will depend on the prison farm's security and location."

"You'll have whatever you need."

From the shadows, Klein studied his longtime friend. "Do I understand, sir, that you're ready to give the go-ahead for such a mission?"

"Let's say I'm keeping my options open." The president closed his eyes a moment, and melancholy seemed to fill his face. It was gone quickly. He stood up. "Keep in touch. Day or night."

"As soon as I hear anything."

"Good." He opened the door and walked out, heavy shoulders square and dignified. He was immediately surrounded by three secret service agents, who escorted him toward the outer door.

Fred Klein listened to the Lincoln's engine come to life and the tires crunch gravel as the vehicle rolled off. He stood up and crossed to a large screen on his right wall. His mind tumultuous with ideas and concern, he touched a button. The screen lit up. A detailed map of China came into view. He clasped his hands behind his back, studying it intently.

Shanghai

In his hotel room, Smith continued to point his Beretta at the man disguised as a waiter. "Who's 'Mondragon,' and what does he care about some old man?"

"This is hardly the time to be coy, Colonel." He stripped off his white jacket and loose trousers to reveal the typical young Shanghainese man's ubiquitous white shirt, cheap navy wash-and-wear slacks, and navy coat. "We sent a man to track Mondragon to make certain he gave the information to you Yanks. Remember Liuchiu Island? The ambush? That's where Mondragon took the long trip. Then you returned to Kaohsiung. We've never stopped keeping a bead on you. Satisfied?"

Still, Smith's weapon remained trained on him. "Why would Public Security care about me?"

"Oh, bloody hell! Back off. David Thayer could just be our ticket to worldwide recognition of what's actually going on here in China. Public Security's after you for *their* reasons, not ours."

"You were in the Land Rover?"

Asgar Mahmout gave an exaggerated sigh. "It wasn't Queen Elizabeth. Put on those clothes before they hoist both of us up by our gonads."

Asgar Mahmout was no Chinese name, and with his round eyes and dark complexion, he did not look Chinese. He spoke of "we." *We sent a man to track Mondragon.* And our. *Our ticket.* Some kind of underground dissident group? Exactly who or what would have to wait, because what he said was logical: They could have found him if they had been tracking him since the time he met Avery on

154

Liuchiu. Which meant Public Security was likely downstairs, lying in wait.

Smith laid his Beretta on the coffee table, peeled off his suit, and dressed quickly in the clothes — an old man's deep-blue Mao suit, a People's Liberation Army cap, a pastel-blue shirt with a grimy collar, and Chinese sandals.

"Grab only what you must." Mahmout had wheeled the serving cart around to face the door. He opened it.

Smith snatched up his backpack, shoved the Beretta into his pocket, and sprinted after him into the hotel corridor. It was deserted. Mahmout ran the cart to the right, away from the bank of regular elevators, and around the corner to a service elevator.

It was open. "Bit of luck that," he said approvingly.

He pushed the cart into it, Smith on his heels. As the doors closed, they heard a guest elevator stop on their floor. The doors *whooshed* open, and footsteps rushed down the corridor. Their elevator descended, with the noises of harsh, impatient knocking and sharp orders in Chinese so loud they penetrated the walls.

"Sounds as if they're at your room," Asgar said.

Smith nodded, wondering how long it would be before the security police figured out what had happened and where they had gone.

At the first floor, Mahmout pushed the cart into the lobby.

"There's a way out through the kitchen," Smith said.

"I know. You used it earlier today with that young Han. Who is he? *Where* is he?"

"An interpreter." Smith's voice dropped. "He's dead, too."

Mahmout shook his head, his expression hard. "You're a good-luck charm, Colonel. I'll be sure to watch not only your back, but mine. Who killed him?"

"I suspect a man named Feng Dun and his people."

"Never heard of him." Mahmout hurried off through the aromatic corridors behind the kitchen to the employees' exit, Smith by his side. They abandoned the cart and crept outdoors, where they were instantly assaulted by city noises. The dark alley stretched left to Nanjing Dong Lu and its crowds, and to the right toward the street behind the hotel.

"You have the Land Rover?" Smith asked.

"Are you mad? Not with me."

The shouts came from neither left nor right, but from behind, inside the hotel. The security police had figured out where they had gone sooner than Smith expected.

"Run!" Like a greyhound, Mahmout tore off to the right.

Smith raced along the dim alley beside him, following his lead as the babel of Nanjing Dong Lu faded in the distance. At the corner, more shouts exploded and feet hammered, chasing them. They turned left, away from the Bund and the river, plunged across the narrower side street and into the mouth of another alley, and twisted through into a third alley. Checking over their shoulders, they shot out across another street.

As they entered a new alley, Mahmout settled into a punishing, distance-devouring trot. Sweating, confused, Smith had no idea where they were or where they were going. Mahmout took him through a bewildering maze of back streets and anonymous alleys, where they dodged, eluded, jumped over, and bounced off swearing pedestrians, bicycle parking lots, construction sites, strewn debris, street vendors, cars parked up on the sidewalks, and cars that ran red lights — right and left — without even a token pause.

As they panted on, they were assailed by a hundred raw, stinking odors and earsplitting dins. They ducked under hanging laundry, leaped over cooking fires, skidded around garbage, and dodged both bicycles and motorcycles that made no distinction among streets, alleys, and sidewalks. All this while shouts and the racket of running feet continued to dog them, sometimes closer, sometimes farther back, but always there, like a bad dream.

Twice, Mahmout darted sharply right or left, as new pursuers suddenly appeared ahead, trying to block their path. Once an unmarked car skidded to a screeching stop just meters before them. They swerved into a dwelling and blasted through and out into yet another alley.

Their pursuers were relentless. There was no time for talk or questions. No time for rest. No respite of any kind.

Smith lost his sense of direction, although he was certain he had run miles. His muscles ached, and his lungs felt raw. By now, they must be in old Shanghai or the French Concession. But then they emerged into the packed masses of Nanjing Dong Lu again, where the world swarmed with shoppers, bar hoppers, sightseers, thieves, pickpockets, and men on the prowl for the women who had reappeared in the city as if by magic when the economic "free" market became the new goal of socialism.

"The metro! There, old boy. *Come along!*" Mahmout skidded downstairs, used his Y90 prepaid ticket to enter, and handed it back to Smith.

Smith pounded after, to a well-lighted platform marked HE NAN LU. At this late hour, few people waited for trains. On edge, drenched in sweat, Smith and Mahmout paced the loading area and studied the various entrances. When a train finally came, they leaped aboard.

Smith took a deep breath as the cars rolled from the station, leaving the platform behind. "Nice job," he said in the mostly empty car. "But you'll never make a tourist guide. You don't schedule in enough time to enjoy the sights."

Mahmout's face was shiny with sweat, and his expression as always ranged between grim and neutral. Suddenly he gave a sardonic grin. The skin around his black eyes crinkled with humor. "Obviously, Colonel, you don't understand." Smith was adjusting to the strong Brit accent from the fellow who looked as if he might be Chinese but probably was not. "I require very special tourists, those more interested in endurance than a photo op. In any case, one must have a permit. That simply won't happen here, for me."

"You can't get one?"

"Not if the police are involved. They have a habit of chasing me."

"This sort of thing happens to you often?"

"Why do you think I'm such a fine physical specimen? I may live in China, but I still talk openly about the Party, the government, and the minorities. I'm far from popular with those hired by the crooks at the top."

The subway car was clean, fast, and comfortable. When they reached the next station, Mahmout stepped off and looked up and down the platform. After one survey, he returned to the car, shaking his head.

"Trouble?"

"The city police are watching the exits, which tells me the Public Security people know we took the metro."

"But how would they know which direction?"

"They don't. If they knew, we'd be seeing Public Security agents on the platform, not city police. The security guys are waiting for us to be spotted."

"I don't like that."

"I do," Mahmout said. "It gives us a small advantage. The city cops won't arrest us — they'll wait for Security to arrive."

The train pulled out again. Mahmout let two more stations pass before telling Smith, "The next stop is Jing An Temple. We'll get off there. They never did get a sharp look at me, and in these clothes, I could be anyone. As for you, I doubt they'll stop you in the station, but I can't be certain. I'll tell you which exit to take, and you swarm out with the crowd. I'll be right behind, in case you're spotted. We'll jump them together."

"Then what?"

159

"Then we run again."

"Good. Can't wait."

Mahmout grinned widely, showing white, even teeth beneath his black mustache. As the train burst into the lighted station and rolled to a stop, he looked out the windows. "Go out with everyone else. Turn left toward the far end of the platform. There'll be three exits along the way. Take the next to last."

As they watched, the doors rattled open.

"Got it." Smith stepped off the car with the surge of passengers. He followed those who turned left. Fewer than a quarter chose the next-to-last exit. He stayed among them, not daring to look back to be sure Mahmout was near.

At the exit, two Shanghai policemen were scrutinizing each passenger. The attention of the first officer passed right over Smith, but the second, after an initial cursory inspection, jerked back and fixed on his face.

Smith walked faster, with a glance back. The policeman was bent to his communications unit, talking.

Smith had made it to the stairs, when a shout behind erupted first in Chinese, then English: "Stop! Tall European, you will stop!"

A hand pushed him in the back. "Go, old man. Like the wind!"

Smith leaped up the stairs, raced forward, and burst out into a dark street.

Mahmout passed him. "Follow me!"

More shouts reverberated through the night, above the sounds of traffic. "Halt! You, *Colonel Smith*. Stop, or we shoot!"

Public Security had arrived. Vehicle headlights blazed on, and motors roared.

"Stop them, you idiots!" This was in the best English.

Smith thundered after Mahmout, both trapped in the glare of headlights, like antelope fleeing across the African veldt. There was no shelter to hide behind. The street was open and straight.

"We can't outrun them!" Smith snapped to his side.

"We don't have to." Mahmout turned ninety degrees and darted down an inky side street.

They passed a stately European house from the early 1800s, and Smith realized they must be in the old French Concession at last.

The headlights closed in. Mahmout turned again onto an even narrower and darker side street. They sprinted past rows of what looked like attached terrace villas enclosed by walls that were of an architectural style that did not match the villas. Before the headlights of the security police could round the corner, too, Mahmout flung open a gate in a wall.

He dashed in and darted to the side as Smith bolted through after him. Immediately, Mahmout closed the gate. As headlights illuminated the street, the two men ran past a row of the brick villas. They left a broader alley for what became a labyrinth of passageways, each smaller than the last, with doors opening from all sides. Laundry hung between windows in rising rows, two and three stories up, still out in the warm night. Battered bicycles leaned against brick walls. Rusty air conditioners stuck out of windows like rectangular tumors. Greasy cooking odors permeated every-thing.

"Is that gate we came through the only way out?" Smith asked.

"Usually," Mahmout said. "Come along now. In here."

He ducked into one of the buildings along the most constricted alley Smith had seen so far. Smith followed through small rooms where men with long, dusky faces similar to Mahmout's, all wearing white or mosaic skullcaps, sat in chairs or lounged on rugs and pillows. Most slept, but others studied him curiously, without fear.

Mahmout stepped lightly, making as little noise as possible, as he headed toward an irregular hole in the wall. He crawled through. "Come along, Colonel. Don't dawdle."

"What's this?" Smith asked dubiously, following.

"Safety."

They were in another room, this one furnished with beds, chairs, small tables, and standing lamps. They were alone.

"We're in the French Concession, but where?" Smith wondered. His heart still hammered from their long marathon, and he was drenched in sweat.

Mahmout's face was not only sweaty but deep red from the exertion. "In the *longtangs*." He wiped an arm across his forehead.

"What's that?"

"Attached European-style brick houses built in the late eighteen hundreds. However, the houses are clustered, and the walls around the clusters are in the Chinese style. The *longtangs* were designed on the old Chinese courtyard pattern — many houses inside each set of walls, most connected by walkways."

"You mean alleys."

"You noticed. Yes, in this case. The Europeans realized they were losing money by keeping the Chinese out of the concessions. So they built the *longtangs* to rent mostly to the wealthiest Chinese. All native Shanghainese used to live in them. Maybe forty percent still do. These in the French Concession are the most habitable. Sometimes whole families, groups of friends, or people from a particular village share the same courtyard."

Smith heard a noise. He glanced back in time to see an entire section of brick wall, the exact shape of the hole they had come through, being fitted back into the opening.

"From the other side, the hole's essentially invisible now," Mahmout explained.

Smith was impressed. "What the hell *is* this place?"

"A safe house. Hungry?"

"I could eat the imperial palace."

"For myself, I'm regretting those crabs we left behind." Mahmout opened a door, and they entered another room. This one contained a long table, a stove, and a refrigerator. Mahmout started to open the refrigerator, but his hand stopped in midair.

Smith heard it, too.

On the other side of the far wall, heavy feet walked, and male voices argued and discussed. They sounded like the security police, and only a room away.

Mahmout shrugged. "They won't find our hole in the wall, Colonel. You'll adjust to a feeling of safety. We're not even in the same *longtang* they are. When we came through the wall, we entered the next one, and . . ."

He stopped again, and his head whipped around. Smith was already staring. There were new commanding voices, but they were not on the other side of the bedroom wall. These were outside the building.

"What — !" Smith began.

A heavy knocking hammered a door not twenty feet away from where they stood.

Asgar Mahmout chuckled silently as he reached into the refrigerator. "Take a seat at the table, Colonel. They won't find us."

Smith was doubtful as he listened to the voices and heavy feet walking on a wood floor. They sounded even closer.

But Mahmout showed no more interest. "Our hole is the only way any of them can find us. No one will notice it." He had decided where their pursuers were, and he trusted his security. He pulled out more food, carried everything to two microwave ovens, and turned them on. As their dinner heated, he found two bottles of ale and sat at the table.

He pointed to the second chair. "Trust me, Colonel."

The voices and feet continued to sound, but no one had appeared, and Smith was hungry. He sat, facing Mahmout, who opened bottles of Newcastle Brown Ale and poured them into common English pub imperial pint glasses, etched crowns and all.

"Cheers and safe passage." Mahmout raised his glass and cocked his head as if entertained by Smith's nervousness.

At last Smith shrugged. His throat was tinder dry from all the running. "What the hell. Bottoms up." He drank deeply.

Chapter
Eleven

Mahmout put down his glass and wiped foam from his mustache. "You should give us more credit, Colonel. This is as safe a house as any that your CIA maintains."

"Who's *us,* and why do you have two names? One Chinese and one something else?"

"Because the Chinese insist the land of my people is in China, so I must therefore be Chinese and have a Han name. *Us* are the Uighers." He pronounced it *weegahs.* "I'm a Uigher from out in Xinjiang. Actually, a half Uigher, but that's a technicality important only to my parents. My real name is Asgar Mahmout. At the metro, they called you Colonel Smith, and you obviously have military training. Do you have other names as well?"

"Jon. Jon Smith. I'm a medical doctor and scientist who happens to be a military officer. And what the hell is a Uigher?"

Mahmout took another gulp of ale and gave a wry smile. "Ah, Americans. You know so little of the world, so little of history, even, sadly, sometimes your own. Charming, energetic, and ignorant — that's you Yanks. Allow me to enlighten you."

It was Smith's turn to smile. He drank. "I'm all ears, as we 'Yanks' say."

"Gentlemanly of you." His voice rose with pride. "The Uighers are an ancient Turkic people. We've lived on the deserts, mountains, and steppes of eastern Central Asia since long, long before your Christ. Long, too, before the Chinese worked up the nerve to escape their eastern river valleys. We're distant cousins of the Mongols and closer cousins of the Turks, Uzbeks, Kirghiz, and Kazakhs. We had grand kingdoms once — empires like you Americans hunger for now." He circled his hand dramatically above his head, an imaginary sword in it. "We rode with the great Khan and with the legendary Timur. We ruled in Kashgar and owned the fabulous Silk Road that Marco Polo raved about on his visit to the Khan's grandson, who by then, of course, had beaten the pompous Hans and taken over China himself."

He drained his ale. His voice was grim as he continued, "Now *we're* the slaves, only worse. The Chinese force us to take Han names, speak Han, and behave like Han. They close our schools and refuse to teach us in anything but Han. They send millions of their own to populate our cities, destroy our way of life, and drive us from our farms into the desert or the high steppes with the Kazakhs, if we wish to survive as a people. They don't let us pray to Allah, and they demolish our historic mosques. They're stamping out our language, customs, and literature. My father was Han. He dazzled my mother with his money, status, and education. But when she refused to abandon

Islam, to raise me and my sister as Han, to leave Kashgar for the pestilence of the Yangtze valley or the swamps of Guangzhou, he abandoned us."

"That must've been rough."

"Ghastly, actually." He went to the refrigerator for another ale. He gestured, silently asking whether Smith wanted one, too.

Smith nodded. "And your Brit accent?"

"I was sent to England." He brought the brown ales to the table and poured. "My mother's father felt a Western-educated man would be useful. My people despair when I'm arrested." He shrugged.

"You studied in London?"

"Eventually, yes. Public schools, then the London School of Economics. My education might seem rather useless here." The microwaves sounded, announcing the food was ready. He brought the steaming platters and bowls and sat down again.

"They want you ready to lead, if they ever get free. I assume you're not the only one sent away to be educated."

"Of course not. There have been several dozen of us over the years, including my sister."

"Does the world know about you Uighers? What about the United Nations?"

Asgar heaped stewed mutton cubes, onions, peppers, ginger slices, carrots, turnips, and tomatoes onto his plate, and Jon did, too. From the large bowl they took handfuls of a thick fried rice dish with more carrots and onions. As Asgar ate, he dipped the cubes of mutton into the dark liquid in the smaller bowl and accompanied it with one of the crisp pancakes, held like a slice of bread.

Jon imitated him and found the food spicy and delicious.

"The U.N.?" Asgar said between mouthfuls. "Of course, they know about us. But we have no standing, while China has an embarrassment of it. We want our land for growing crops and grazing our animals. China wants it because it's rich. Oil. Gas. Minerals. You like the mutton?"

"It's delicious. What do you call the crisp flat fried bread?"

"*Nang.*"

"And the rice?"

Asgar chuckled. He laughed a lot for someone who spoke so bitterly. "It's called 'rice eaten with the hands.' " He shrugged. "It's always been the same for all the peoples of Central Asia. We rode west because we were poor and wanted better land and opportunities. We were fierce, and we had great leaders. Our time passed with the centuries — too much petty bickering, too many small leaders with small kingdoms led by smaller and smaller minds. Eventually the tide flowed back on us in the eighteen hundreds, as it always does with any people, sooner or later." He peered at Jon over his glass. "Remember that, American."

Jon gave a noncommittal nod.

Asgar took a slow drink of the ale. "First there were the Russians with their eyes on India, but glad to pick us up along the way. Then the Chinese came, because they considered our lands their lands. Finally, it was the British, protecting 'their' India. They called it the Great Game, and you're wagering on it again. The only difference for us

169

and most of the world is that it's the Yanks now, not the Brits."

"And you Uighers? What are you doing?"

"Ah, now you're asking the crucial question. We're taking back our country, of course. Or, since we never had a 'country' in the European sense, only a people, we're taking back our land."

"This is your underground?"

"You might say. Not many of us at the moment, but more every day in Xinjiang, across the border in Kazakhstan, and other places. We're only a resistance, a nuisance, alas. Just ambushers, saboteurs, and bandits. We harry the Han. The Han claim there's only some seven or eight million of us. We say we're thirty million. But even thirty million on horses and pickups can accomplish little against a billion with tanks. Nevertheless, we must resist. It's our nature, if nothing else. The result is, we've become an 'autonomous region.' That's meaningless in the larger picture, of course, especially with Urumqi already a Han Chinese city, but it shows we have them worried enough to try to bribe us."

Jon helped himself to seconds. "That's why you told Mondragon about the old man who says he's our president's father, right?"

Asgar nodded. "Who knows whether he is? In any case, he's still an American that the Chinese have held secretly for almost six decades. We hope that will call fresh attention to China's miserable human-rights record and its systematic destruction of its minorities, particularly those of us who are totally non-Chinese. We live a lot closer to Kabul and New Delhi than we do to Beijing."

"Especially if he really is the president's father."

"Especially." Asgar smiled, his white teeth flashing again.

Jon finally pushed his empty plate away and picked up his ale. "Tell me about this old man. Where is he?"

"In a prison near Dazu. That's about seventy of your miles northeast of Chongqing."

"What kind of prison?"

"It's more like a protected farm. It houses mostly political prisoners being 'reeducated,' petty criminals, and old men considered minor escape risks."

"Low security?"

"By Chinese standards, it's low. It's completely fenced and heavily guarded, but the prisoners are in barracks not in cells. There's little interaction with the outside world and few visitors. The old gentleman who says he's David Thayer has some privileges, like a room in the barracks with only one cell mate, some books, the newspapers, and a special diet. But that's about all."

"How did you manage to get his story?"

"As I told you, a lot of the prisoners are political. Some are Uighers. We have an activist network and information grapevine inside for outside news. Thayer heard about the human-rights treaty, knew our people are against the Chinese and could get word out, and so he told them who he was."

Jon nodded. "What information do you have about his history?"

"Not much. Our people say he keeps to himself and talks little, especially about his past. There'd probably be big trouble if he did. But from what he

171

did say, he's been in prisons from maximum to minimum over the years, depending on Beijing's power fights and new theories. It sounds to me as if they moved him around a lot to keep him isolated and hidden."

It sounded logical, and it gave Smith enough to report to Fred Klein as soon as he could get out of the country. But his inability to speak Chinese gave him few options. Without help, he was essentially limited to the usual avenues of foreign visitors entering and leaving the country — international airports, a few passenger ships, and fewer trains. With Public Security looking for him, as well as the mysterious group from the island, those exits would be shut down like vaults.

Asgar had been watching. "What do you think the American government will do about David Thayer?"

"Depends on the president. If I had to guess, I'd say that right now, with the treaty so close to being signed, nothing. He'll tend to wait until the treaty's a reality, then he'll bring up the subject of David Thayer to China's leaders."

"Or maybe leak it to the newspapers to put pressure on Beijing?"

"Possibly," Jon agreed. He considered Asgar. "That's what you want, isn't it — publicity?"

"Absolutely. We need to be on the world's stage along with everyone else. What if the treaty *isn't* signed?"

"What makes you think it won't be?"

"Logic. Mondragon didn't have to sneak off to Liuchiu Island to tell your people about David Thayer. No, he had something he had to deliver,

172

right? You were there to take the delivery. But he was killed and you escaped — and came straight back to Shanghai. That tells me the attackers got what Mondragon had, and you're trying to find it again. The whole thing smells like trouble, and the stench soars when the treaty's figured into it. After all, it's the most important matter between the U.S. and China at the moment."

"Let's say you may be partly right. If so . . . if the president were absolutely sure the treaty was down the drain, he might send a crew to get Thayer out."

"That'd be sure to make the headlines blister. Outraged Chinese *and* Americans."

"But if I don't get word to my people about where Thayer is, none of it's going to happen. It won't help you or your people at all. Can I use my cell phone safely?"

"Bad idea. By now, Public Security must've rigged a way to triangulate wireless in and out of here. There are so few cell phones in the *longtangs* that it'd be worth their while to track every call, especially since they seem hell-bent to find you."

Smith considered. "A pay phone would do, if you can get me out to one. I'll say nothing revealing."

"If I manage it, do you have a plan?"

"The Seventh Fleet's always close to China. That means I'd need your help to get to the coast for a pickup, too."

Asgar stared, pursed his lips, then stood without speaking. He gathered dirty dishes and carried them to the sink.

Jon picked up a load and joined him.

At last, Asgar asked, "Will your government

173

guarantee David Thayer's story is told, one way or another?"

"I doubt it. I expect they'll do what they consider to be in U.S. national interest."

"It's in *international* interest to show what China is . . . for what that means for Hong Kong and Taiwan as well as for Urumqi and Kashgar."

"If that's the case, they'll make sure the world hears, but they'll give no guarantees first. On the other hand, if I can't relay what I've learned to my boss, nothing at all gets out."

Asgar continued to stare. His eyes were hard, black marbles. "I don't think so. You're not that important. No single agent can be, right? But maybe you're important enough that if you don't get back to your chief, they'll be slowed down, looking for you. We wouldn't like that."

Jon met his gaze. "I can see how that would be bad for you."

The Uigher held his stare another moment, as if boring deep into Smith to see what he was made of. Finally, he went to the sink and poured in dishwashing liquid — Palmolive — and turned on the hot water, watching the suds rise. "It won't be easy, Colonel. China is a tight, homogenous country, especially here in the east. In the countryside, it's worse. They seldom see foreigners, Uighers, or even private autos. Just a Land Rover will draw plenty of attention."

"You seem to get around all right."

"That's because we're in Shanghai. Shanghai's not like most of China. It's not even like Beijing. Shanghainese are more Westernized, always have been. Not much makes them stare. But a car full of

174

Uighers out in the boondocks will get plenty of interest. Add Uighers and a Caucasian traveling together, and the police will hear of it. Their interest may be large enough to alert Public Security."

"So what do we do?"

Asgar considered. "We make you a Uigher."

"I'm too tall. My eyes are the wrong color and shape."

"Most Uighers hardly have the Oriental fold at all when we get past our teens. We're Turkic." He studied Jon's features and build critically. "You're definitely large. It's all that healthy American food. But we can darken your skin and add wrinkles. You'll have to squint. Then we'll dress you in some of our traditional clothes, sit you in the middle of a few of us, and scrunch you down. You'll pass, as long as no one examines you too closely."

"Perhaps. Where do you plan to go on the coast?"

"Somewhere south, not too far."

"I'll need to have coordinates for the pickup."

"Understood. But first I'll talk to my people. We must decide how many of us we'll need, what vehicles we'll use, the safest place for you to make contact, and the best route to get there."

"When do we go?"

"Tonight. The sooner the better, while their security people are consulting higher authority and milling around, talking to each other."

"I'm ready."

"Not yet. First, the women will make you a Uigher, while the rest of us make plans. Wait here, Jon. I'll be back."

Left alone, Jon walked around the small,

four-room hideout. There were twelve packed-together sleeping pallets, one bathroom, two more refrigerators, and four microwaves. Large, well provisioned, and comfortable. As he inspected, he realized the voices and boots that had been so close less than an hour ago were gone. The security police had moved on, at least for the time being. There was nothing now but silence . . . silence everywhere, outside and inside the windowless rooms.

He did not like it. Public Security had given up a little too quickly, a little too easily. Why? Either they had been ordered to treat his presence in China as a delicate matter with potential international complications, which meant they were suspicious but not certain he was more than a simple visiting scientist. Or they were waiting outside the *longtangs,* hoping he would show himself. Or . . . they had been making a show with no intention of catching him because they already had him — because Asgar Mahmout and his supposed Uighers were actually working for or with the Public Security Bureau. Which would explain Asgar's casual questions about the human-rights treaty.

If that were the case, was he already trapped in these sealed rooms, or would they continue to string him along in hopes of learning exactly what he was doing? He paused, mulling. He decided they would want to pretend to help him, because arresting him *would* be an international incident if they could not show what he was after. On the other hand, if the whole thing were a cat-and-mouse charade, it gave him a chance.

Chapter Twelve

Friday, September 15

In the cramped office he used in police headquarters at 210 Hankou Lu near the Bund, Major Pan Aitu scowled through his horn-rimmed glasses at a file on his desk. There was nothing especially wrong or unusual about the file of the common street criminal he would testify against later in the day; it was simply that a scowl was Pan's habitual expression when alone. The gentle voice and benign smile were entirely for public use, as were the soothing conservative suits and happy bow ties, all designed to mesmerize the mouse in front of him. His round joviality was a sham, too. There was muscle beneath the fat — hard, trained muscle.

Dressed in a black leather car coat, military brown safari shirt, and black denim jeans, he had the glowering aspect of a menacing dwarf dredged from the depths of the earth. He was still bent over his files, working, when a single knock preceded the entry of his chief, General Chu Kuairong.

"You have located the American scientist?"

"And lost him," the spy said, disgusted. "It is clear we botched the operation. We must have better people, General. The teams I sent covered only the main entrances of his hotel, assuming he was a stranger in our country, unfamiliar with the city, and therefore an idiot. He was obviously leaving and reentering the hotel other ways."

"He's been to Shanghai before?" Chu Kuairong was annoyed. "His records, and ours, did not indicate that."

The major shook his head. "He must have had help."

"Help? By one of *our* people? Impossible."

"It's the only answer," Pan stated flatly. "Someone they've turned, most likely. But despite the help, after we received the authority to pick him up, my fools did finally use some common sense and surveil all entrances and exits. Still, they failed to see him reenter the hotel. Fortunately, they had stationed a man inside in disguise. He's the one who spotted Smith."

The general sighed with frustration, thinking, as he often did, that his budget for recruiting and training effective operatives was far too small. He sat forward on a straight chair, hovering like a giant bird of prey. His bald skull glared under the harsh fluorescent light, and his small, wind-sunk eyes bored into the major.

General Chu growled, "Then they lost Smith again?"

Major Pan related everything that had happened from the time his agents entered Smith's hotel room tonight, discovered he had left everything behind including his clothes, and chased him through the subway and into the *longtangs* of the French Concession.

General Chu listened intently. When the major finished, he thought for a moment. "You still have no idea what this supposed scientist came to Shanghai to find or to do?"

"There's no doubt of his scientific credentials. He is what he purports to be. The problem is what *else* he may be. While we don't know yet why he's here, some possible answers are starting to emerge."

"What answers?"

"A series of events that — to my mind at least — suggests a pattern and direction." Major Pan counted on his short, thick fingers: "One, a certain Avery Mondragon, a well-known American Sinologist who has been working in Shanghai for some years as a general representative of many American business endeavors, has disappeared. His associates report he's been missing since early Wednesday."

Chu hunched further toward Pan. "The day before Colonel Smith arrived in Shanghai?"

Pan inclined his head. "An interesting coincidence, wouldn't you say? Second, a cleaning woman in a downtown business building discovered a dead man in the office of Yu Yongfu, president and chairman of Flying Dragon Enterprises, an international shipping company with connections in Hong Kong and Antwerp. Third, the same Yu Yongfu and his wife also appear to be missing. At least, no one was in his mansion, and no cars were in his garage."

"What do we know of him?"

179

The major indicated the dossier open on his desk. "This is his file. He is a young man who has come far fast and is now wealthy. That he's the son-in-law of Li Aorong may help to explain that. Since Li is a prominent official in Shanghai, and —"

Chu was interested. "I know Li and his daughter personally. He is an old and honored Party member. Surely —"

"Nevertheless, the daughter and son-in-law seem to be missing, and the treasurer of her husband's company is dead. In fact, shot to death. More coincidence?"

Chu sat up. "The dead man in the office was this treasurer? I see. That is interesting. Are we looking for Yu and his wife?"

"Of course."

"And her father?"

"Li Aorong will be questioned in the morning."

Chu nodded. "What else?"

"Another corpse has been found in a car at Hongqiao airport. A young man who was a tourist interpreter and chauffeur. Curiously, he studied for many years in the United States."

"You're suggesting he may have been someone who helped our Colonel Smith?"

"His photo has been identified by Peace Hotel employees. He was seen in the lobby earlier today after Colonel Smith checked in. To summarize: An American resident here disappears. The next day Colonel Smith arrives, the treasurer of a shipping company is murdered, the president of that company and his wife disappear, and an American-educated Shanghainese interpreter and chauffeur is killed the same night and found at an airport."

"You have a theory?"

"Merely a possible scenario," the major cautioned. "Mondragon discovered something about Yu Yongfu's company he considered of importance to the Americans. Smith was sent to find out what Mondragon had discovered and retrieve it. Something went wrong. For whatever reason, the interpreter was assigned or employed to guide and interpret for Smith."

"If you're correct . . . there are those in this country who don't want the Americans to have what Mondragon discovered."

The spy inclined his head. "Indeed."

The general reached into an inner pocket of the civilian Mao suit he wore tonight and removed a long, slender cigar. He bit off a piece of the tip, turned it as he lit it, and puffed one of his smoke rings.

"Did Colonel Smith get what he came for?" he asked.

"That we don't know."

"That is what we *must* know."

"Agreed."

Chu blew another ring. "If Smith did get it, he will attempt to leave the country."

"I've covered all points of departure."

"I doubt it. We have a long coastline, Major."

"He isn't on the coast."

"Then you know what to do." Another smoke ring, this one quicker. "And if he did not get what he wanted?"

"He'll remain in Shanghai until he does."

Chu Kuairong pondered. "No. In that case, he will also try to leave. His cover is blown; he will not be effective if he stays. He sounds too intelligent to try to use public transportation. Instead, he would be clever to arrange a private pickup on the coast. All we have to do is track him, roll up any American agents or assets who help him, stop him at his destination, and — with a measure of good luck — apprehend his rescuers as well as him." The general puffed on his panatela, smiling at last. "Yes, that would be most agreeable. I leave it to you, Pan, to arrange it all."

A piece of the wall moved. Dressed again in his black sweater, black jeans, and black soft-soled shoes, with his light backpack hanging from his shoulders, Jon waited where he could watch the section being pulled out to open the entry into the hidden apartment. He held his Beretta behind him, waiting.

Asgar Mahmout stepped through and turned to help three solemn women who followed. Dressed in typical clothes — slacks and jeans, shirts and blouses, sweaters and sweatshirts, one blazer — two carried makeup kits, the third a bundle of clothes. They were fairly tall and slender and had thick, shining black hair. The one holding the bundle of clothes was taller than the others, with a lean face. Her black hair was pulled back and tied at the nape of her neck. There was a dimple on her chin, a half smile on her lips, and her cheekbones were prominent, sculpted. She was a beauty who knew it and seemed to find it amusing.

Two more men appeared, ducking in through the hole after the women.

Asgar glanced at them and nodded at Smith in

greeting. "I see you put on your work clothes."

"Thought it wise."

The tall, beautiful woman was wearing the blazer over a sweatshirt and jeans. She looked Jon up and down. "Is that the latest fashion for men in Washington?" she asked in clear, American-accented English. The half smile grew broader.

"Only for secret agents on a mission." He smiled back.

One of the men said something to Asgar in a language that sounded somewhat like what Jon had heard among Northern Alliance Uzbeks in Afghanistan.

Asgar answered and translated for Jon. "Toktufan wanted to know where you hid your weapons. I told him you probably had your pistol in your belt at your back under your sweater and your knife on your leg."

"Close."

Asgar smiled. "The other guy back there is Mierkanmilia, and the tall lady who speaks like another Yank is my sister, Alani. She and her friends will turn your face into a Uigher's, if they can. They have Uigher clothes for you to wear, too."

"What will you be doing?"

"Figuring out the best destination, arranging transport, and becoming Uighers again ourselves." He motioned to the two other men. "We'll leave you in Alani's capable hands." The three ducked out through the hole and put the section of brick back into place.

The women held a conference in Uigher. More accurate, the two who had remained nameless asked Alani a torrent of questions.

Finally, she turned to Jon. "Sit there, Colonel Smith." She pointed to a chair. "Take off your sweater."

Jon took off the black sweater, revealing a black cotton turtleneck.

Alani snorted. "A little overdressed, aren't you? Must I lead you by the hand?"

Jon laughed. To his surprise, so did she, and it struck him that she had been imitating some American schoolmaster. A private joke for herself. Under the circumstances, it was remarkable, since she was risking her life for him. He took off the turtleneck and caught a flash of interest in the tall woman's eyes as she contemplated his naked chest.

He offered a smile. "You and your brother are different from the others."

Her full lips gave a quiet laugh as she beckoned the other two women. They had been whispering and laughing behind their hands as they watched him strip. They hurried forward and went to work on his face, first with a pale brown base to darken his skin.

"Why? Are we different to you because we speak English?" Alani stepped back and watched with a critical eye.

"That, and that you're educated abroad. It speaks of a history and a plan."

"You know our father was Han?"

"Yes. It doesn't appear to mean much to either of you."

"It doesn't, except to give us an advantage other Uighers don't have. Also a disadvantage, of course. There is always the chance we could turn. We

184

never have, and they would never suggest it aloud, but it lurks in the backs of their minds."

The two makeup women were in a heated discussion, wielding long narrow-tipped brushes and pointing at his eyes and eyebrows. The brush strokes on his skin were soft, almost tickling.

Alani spoke to them sharply. They retorted, ignored her, and returned to their aesthetic disagreement. Alani shook her head in exasperation and glanced at her wristwatch.

"What advantage does it give you?" Jon wanted to know.

She was still watching the two bickering makeup artists and seemed not to have heard him. "Our mother is the daughter of one of the leaders in our independent government in exile in Kazakhstan. It makes her, and therefore us, important among the Uighers. Our grandfather was the one who made certain we were sent abroad to study."

She barked at the women who had finally begun to work on his eyes. She pointed to her watch. "Because of that, and because our father's Han, Beijing thinks we'd be especially useful as leaders and apologists in convincing our people to accept being part of China. To convince them to give up our heritage and assimilate. This gives us privileges as long as we appear to go along with their plans. It makes good cover, including residence papers that enable us to move around much more freely and even reside for extensive periods in Han territory. They watch us, of course, but as long as they don't catch us, we can go almost anywhere we want."

"Asgar seems to go places he's arrested."

She nodded knowingly. "We despair about Asgar. He's a good man, and he's never been in serious trouble yet. We keep our fingers crossed."

"I'm trying to place your accent. Where did you study in the United States?"

"I lived with a family in New Jersey and went to public schools there, then to the University of Nebraska in Omaha. I'm a mixture of East Coast and Midwest, the perfect blend to study political science and agronomy."

And to be an effective leader of a primarily agricultural people. Her grandfather had been thinking far ahead. "With a minor in guerrilla warfare?"

She smiled. "Asgar again. When the Soviets were in Afghanistan, your CIA was keen to train any Central Asian Muslim ready to fight the Soviets, and he joined the Northern Alliance. They couldn't seem to tell one of us from another, even a Tajik."

The two makeup authorities finally finished, stood back clucking in admiration of their work, and beamed at Alani. She nodded and said something that, since the other women's smiles remained, must have been complimentary. The pair packed up their tubes, bottles, jars, and brushes. They kept turning back to look at his face as one banged on the bricks with the hilt of a dagger she had produced from somewhere under her clothes.

Alani held a hand mirror. "Have a look."

Jon stared, impressed at the results of his new, sticky, and very uncomfortable mask. His eyes had acquired something of the fold, his skin was a light chestnut brown, creased with the wrinkles of sun and wind. If he narrowed his eyes in a squint, he would probably pass in the dark.

"If you're among us, you ought to go unnoticed," Alani decided.

"Let's hope we're not stopped."

"We'll be stopped, of that you can be certain. But with Asgar and my papers, and those we've forged for the rest of us, they should treat us lightly. We'll have to hope they don't make us get out of the Land Rover." She glanced again at her watch. "The others will be back soon. You'd better put on the clothes I brought."

There was a touch of anxiety in her voice, as if time were passing too quickly, and the men were too late.

Her uneasiness infected Jon. As he dressed, he asked, "What are you doing in Shanghai? Officially, I mean."

"We're studying to be teachers of teachers. Well, actually, Asgar and I are. Some of the others are being trained as village leaders or agents for Beijing. The rest are part of our underground network."

He pulled baggy corduroy trousers up over his black jeans. "That's a damned dangerous game, Alani. For all of you."

"We know the risks. They've arrested thousands of us already and executed a hundred or so." She looked him steadily in the eye. "Perhaps it's a game for you and the CIA, Colonel. It's not for us."

The worn, unpressed white dress shirt was tight over his sweater, but the flannel shirt slipped on easily. "I'm not CIA," Jon told her. "And it's never been a game for me."

She considered him. "Yes, I can see that."

"No one's asked me why I'm here, what *I* came for. Not that I intend to tell you."

"What we don't know, they can't get out of us. You're against the Chinese or working to ensure the human-rights accord. That's good enough for us."

The harsh scraping of brick on brick interrupted their conversation. Before the hole was completely open, Asgar climbed through. He was dressed in the rough clothes of a farmer, with the riding boots of a sheepherder. He also wore a decorated white skullcap under a straw sun hat.

He studied Jon from a distance and then closer. "In lousy light, you'll pass." He nodded to Alani. "We're ready."

"Where are we going?" Jon asked.

Asgar motioned to the kitchen table where they had eaten dinner. He spread out a map of the Shanghai Municipal Region and surrounding area and pointed to a spot south of the city. "There's an abandoned pagoda on a hill near the sea in the wider part of Huangzhou Bay, between Jinshan and Zhapu. The shore's a bit of a rock garden there, but there are also a few more inviting beaches. Pebbly, but not bad. One in particular, a little bigger, will suit fine."

"How's the water depth?"

"Not sure, Jon. But Toktufan says a small boat can get close. He's worked the waters around there."

"All right." Jon picked up his backpack, pulled out a black plastic pouch, and extracted a detailed topographic map of the Shanghai area laid over a satellite photograph. He checked the water depths, had Asgar point out exactly where the pagoda and beach were, and wrote down the latitude and longitude coordinates in his small waterproof notebook. When they were finished, he rolled up the maps.

Alani reminded him. "Don't forget your hats."

Jon put on the decorated Uigher skullcap and then a brimmed straw hat. The women started for the hole in the wall. Jon followed.

Asgar stopped him. "We go a different way."

When the others had left, and the brick section had been restored, Asgar led him through the rooms to the farthest bedroom. He pushed a box bed aside, lifted a section of the linoleum-covered floor, and pointed down in the narrow black hole it exposed.

"This way is for us."

Jon was dubious. "Am I going to fit?"

"It widens below. Hope you don't have severe claustrophobia."

"I don't," Jon assured him.

"I'll go first, old boy. Don't worry. Piece of cake." Asgar sat, dangling his legs in the narrow hole. He looked down once and dropped.

Jon followed, barely squeezing past the floor. The tomblike odors of dirt and rock filled his head. He scraped his shoulders all the way down to the bottom of a dark, dank, wood-braced tunnel. A flashlight was alight ahead, where the tunnel narrowed again. He saw Asgar's feet and legs.

Asgar's voice was muffled. "Bigger men than you have passed through fine. Just keep your eyes on my feet and the light. It's about twenty-five of your American yards."

189

Then the light moved, and the feet faded into the dusty shadows ahead. Jon followed, feeling for the first time in his life what claustrophobia was — breathing when it felt as if there were nothing to breathe, certain that in the next second he would be buried alive. His lungs tightened, and blood throbbed at his temples.

Time seemed to stop as he told himself to inhale, to crawl. Inhale. Crawl. Follow the feet, as the dark tunnel seemed to swallow him.

At last the air changed. It stank, fetid and thick. Jon gulped like a dying fish.

"Hurry," Asgar urged and crawled up to his feet.

Quickly, Jon followed. They had emerged into a dark culvert at the end of a stench-filled alley. For Jon at the moment, he could not remember a more beautiful sight.

Asgar trotted ahead, and Jon, still breathing deeply, stumbled after until they passed through an open iron gate and entered a street where two Land Rovers waited at the curb. Hands pulled him into the second vehicle, and he found himself packed into the rear, where the seat had been removed. Three men and two women pressed against him. He recognized Toktufan, Mierkanmilia, and the two makeup artists. The fifth was a stranger, but all were dressed with bits and pieces of traditional Uigher clothing. Alani rode in the front passenger seat, and Asgar drove.

"Why two Land Rovers?" Jon whispered.

"Decoy. In case the police are watching."

The first Land Rover, similarly loaded, headed off.

They waited. Then, five minutes later, they left,

too, turning through dark streets in the early morning hours, until they reached a lighted main road where there was traffic, but not much.

Asgar glanced back. "We're going to take the Huhang Expressway toward Hangzhou. We'll stand out like a sore thumb: Eight country bumpkins from Xinjiang, heading south for Hangzhou, like your Okies in the nineteen-thirties. We'll look like a joke, not a threat — we hope. If the Public Security people aren't already following us, or fell for the decoy, we might just make it."

Chapter Thirteen

Huhang Expressway, China

Under the black night sky, the countryside took on a spectral air of shadows and wavering mists. Jon used a public phone in Gubei New Town in the Changning District to dial a number in Hong Kong. In French, he discussed a proposed business deal that was legitimate, if checked upon. The conversation contained his innocent-seeming code for a rescue by sea, and it related the time and coordinates. As soon as he hung up, the contact would relay the information to Fred Klein.

"The line sounded clear, no sign of being tapped," he told Asgar as the Land Rover resumed its tortuous passage over the bad road that sliced through the rocky, rolling land.

"They were listening," Asgar assured him. "Any long-distance call will be checked, especially to Hong Kong. What's good is that low-level employees do the monitoring, and for them it's routine. They seldom catch anyone unless they're terribly obvious. This time though, the service knows you're here, so they're certain to have ordered a special alert. But if your contact's a solid, long-term cover, you may be all right."

Jon grimaced. "Thanks."

They had been stopped twice at routine checkpoints before they left the city, causing amusement among the police. They had been let through with little trouble. Jon began to relax. Thirty minutes later, they were on the expressway, lightly traveled at this late hour, and more than halfway to Hangzhou. A few kilometers later, they turned off onto a two-lane rural road near Jiaxing, heading southeast toward the coast and the East China Sea.

Even in the darkest hours before sunrise, there continued to be other vehicles — a few passenger cars and an intermittent stream of pickups driven by small farmers, their produce piled perilously high in their truck beds. Smaller entrepreneurs rode bicycles, pulling two-wheeled carts with specialty items to sell in Shanghai.

Asgar drove steadily but slowly, not wanting to attract attention. "If the security police are watching, they'll wait until we hit the beach and the mission's in progress. They'll want to capture the rescue team, too. But we've got time, so there's no sense in taking unnecessary chances by speeding. With luck, they're not following us anyway."

Jon agreed. He settled back and closed his eyes. Everyone but Asgar dozed, awaking occasionally to the clean salt tang of the open sea and the sour odor of mudflats.

At Zhapu, they turned northwest toward Jinshan. Here on the coastal road, the pickups and bicycles flowed in both directions — north to Shanghai and south to Hangzhou. An occasional police car passed, but the officers either paid no attention or grinned broadly at the sight of the unsophisticated rubes.

Finally, the Land Rover pulled off, so Asgar and Alani could check their position. They consulted and used a penlight to scan the map. Alani looked back and said something in Uigher. Toktufan squeezed into the front seat between them. A heated discussion in Uigher began, with Toktufan pointing at the map and then ahead, and Alani trying, apparently, to pin him down to an exact location.

She offered him a pen to mark the map. He shrugged, waved off the pen, and continued to gesture insistently.

Clearly Toktufan was the one who knew exactly where they were going but strictly by visual aids in the dead of night and from the seat of his pants. This did not make Jon feel secure, or apparently Alani or Asgar.

Swearing under his breath in Uigher, Asgar pulled back onto the road and drove on, while Toktufan surveyed the shadowy gloom.

"You sure he can find this beach?" Jon asked.

"He'll find it," Alani said. "The only question is when."

"It'll be dawn in a couple of hours."

She turned in her seat and smiled her small, mocking smile. "You wouldn't want your life to be dull now, would you, Colonel? Excitement and adventure. That's why you became an agent, isn't it? Incidentally, if you aren't CIA, what are you?"

Jon kicked himself for saying that earlier. Damn. "State Department."

"Really?" She seemed to study him, as if she knew what a State agent looked like. Maybe she did.

Asgar's voice was harsh. "Ahead!"

Jon saw the uniforms. A police car blocked half the road. It was a checkpoint.

"Toktufan, in back again!" Asgar ordered.

Toktufan slid out of the front of the slow-moving Land Rover and squeezed in among the others in the rear once more. The Land Rover inched ahead in a snakelike line of pickups, old cars, and bicycles. At the head of the line, drivers and cyclists held up papers. The officer in charge was leaning sleepily back against his car, yawning. Every now and then, he barked an order.

The policemen, however, were busy. They checked identifications and lifted canvases covering loads, whether small or large. When the Land Rover reached the front, the sleepy officer did a double take. He straightened alertly and snapped an order.

The two patrolmen gaped at the eight packed into the Rover. One scanned the papers held out by Alani and Asgar as the second grinned, entertained. The officer barked again, marched forward, and took the papers. He studied them and peered up at Asgar and Alani. Alani smiled. A winning, almost flirtatious smile this time. The officer blinked and stared.

Jon scrunched low to hide his height and build, and the others pressed closer. One of the policemen trained his light across all their faces and said something in Han that included the word Uigher.

The officer, still gazing at Alani, nodded and snapped another order. The policemen turned their attention to the next two cyclists in line. The officer smiled, nodded to Alani, and waved them on.

As Asgar drove away, Jon resisted the urge to look back. Everyone breathed deeply, relieved. The night enclosed the Land Rover with anonymity, and they smiled and whispered among themselves.

But Jon did not smile or whisper. He asked Alani, "Are checkpoints like that common?"

"Sometimes in the city, not usually in rural areas."

"They've been alerted by the Public Security Bureau to look for someone."

Asgar nodded. "But not for Uighers."

"An American like me," Jon agreed.

"It means they don't know where you are, who you're with, or what you're going to do next. If they did, they'd be swarming the coast right now."

"They're obviously thinking I could be trying to leave, or they wouldn't have alerted the police so far from Shanghai."

"That'd be true for any agent whose cover was shattered."

Jon liked none of it. Someone in Public Security suspected he would call for help so had ordered the coastal area around Shanghai on alert. Patrol boats and fighters might be prepared to scramble, too. The patrol boats did not worry him particularly. Jets were another matter.

But he soon had something else to think about. Toktufan leaned forward, spoke in Uigher, and gestured eagerly to the left, away from the sea. Through the press of bodies and heads, Jon caught a glimpse of a narrow building high on the top of an inland hill. Its roof lines were up-curved, in the silhouette of a Chinese pagoda. Excitement rippled through the group.

With a spin of the wheel, Asgar drove the Land Rover abruptly off toward the ocean. The Rover rattled down into a gully hidden from the road. Asgar pulled under the cover of a willow and parked. The sudden quiet of the vehicle made all of them sit still a moment, appreciating it. Shaken by the long, bone-jarring ride, everyone crawled stiffly out and crouched in a circle around Asgar and Toktufan. Trees and bushes surrounded them.

Asgar did the talking in Uigher, with Toktufan throwing in comments and pointing in various directions in the waning moonlight. When they finished, one of the women stood up and vanished among the growth, heading back toward the road above the gully.

Alani turned to Jon. "Asgar sent Fatima to the pagoda with an electric lantern and a shielding sleeve. She'll put it in a window embrasure at the top, with the shield protecting it from being seen from land." She nodded in the opposite direction, toward the water. "The beach is about five hundred meters in a straight line from the pagoda. It's normally deserted, especially at this hour, but there are those who like to fish or crab at night. There's also the chance the police could be watching through night-vision binoculars."

"Then we should avoid the beach as long as possible."

She nodded. "We're armed. We'll go with you as soon as we see the light in the pagoda."

The group stayed together, hunched down in the thick growth, tall trees rising and arching toward an imaginary ceiling overhead. Every second seemed like a minute, every minute an hour. The low whispering from the Uighers was subdued, concerned, and deadly serious. Alani crouched beside him in silence, busy with her thoughts.

A sudden, distant point of light appeared high in the night sky. Asgar materialized among them. He spoke quickly in Uigher and turned to Jon. "Time to move, Jon. I'm not completely certain, but I believe I heard someone near the road while I was crossing. I saw nothing, so I hope I'm wrong. No reason to take chances. We don't know how far offshore your people are, or if they're here at all. Still, we'd best hurry."

"It's time, so they're here," Jon assured him.

Toktufan trotted in the lead, snaking his way through the brush and trees like a phantom. The rest of the Uighers were right behind, weapons in hand. Jon followed with his Beretta ready, while Asgar and Alani brought up the rear. The hushed procession seemed to float among the grasses, wraiths no more substantial than the fog.

At last, Jon heard the splash of breaking waves. A salty breeze stung his face. The trees and brush reached to a low ridge of tufted grass that dropped off perhaps four feet to a narrow, rocky little beach. Jon and the Uighers squatted inside the edge of trees to wait. The moon was nearly down over the black sea, projecting a silvery path toward the horizon. Tall trees swayed, leaves rustling eerily.

There was a flash of light out at sea. Once. Twice. Three times.

Then darkness again — and an abrupt sound. A stumble. A grunt. An angry oath.

"Under the bank!" Jon whispered urgently and rolled.

At the same time, Alani shouted in Uigher.

They slid and dove into the cover of the bank at the edge of the beach nearly simultaneously with a fusillade that exploded in an arc from deep among the trees. The bullets burst into the sand and rained into the surf.

"Wait until you see them!" Jon yelled over the din.

Asgar repeated it for the Uighers. No one panicked. They waited with their backs to the sea, calm, with a sense of cold inevitability.

Another fusillade erupted, and Jon saw movement deep among the trees to his left. He fired. A distant cry. He had hit one, whoever they were. Someone else fired, and then a third shot. There were no cries, no crashing through the undergrowth.

Asgar cursed in Uigher and yelled angrily.

A third volley thundered from ahead, but weaker this time, ragged, and Jon saw to his left that shadows were running from the trees and out into the open swath of tall grass before the beach.

"They're outflanking us!"

Alani repeated his warning, and Jon wondered — were these the same people who had attacked him and Mondragon on Liuchiu Island and then at Yu Yongfu's mansion? Feng Dun once more, using his favorite tactic?

He had no time to analyze further. No matter who they were, they outnumbered the Uighers, and they were closing in. Already Jon could see more movement, visible now, much nearer the front line of trees. So could the Uighers, who opened a careful, lethal fire, sending the approaching attackers to ground.

Asgar crouched beside him. His breath was hot and worried in Jon's ear. "We can hold them for a time, but when those others up the beach move in, they'll trap us if we don't clear out of here soon."

"Right," Jon agreed. "You've done a lot. I'm grateful — you know that. When you have to go, go."

"And you?"

"It's only me they want, whoever they are."

"You don't think they're security?"

"Maybe, maybe not. Doesn't matter."

"It does to us."

Jon understood. "If it's security, I'll try to hold them until you get a good —"

A fresh barrage of automatic fire burst from the left. The Uighers hit the beach and returned fire, but now their front was exposed. Feet ran from among the trees before them, pounding the sand. They were cornered.

"Go!" he snarled to Asgar. "I'll surrender."

Asgar hesitated.

Alani was there. "We can't leave him!"

"Come with us!" Asgar urged.

Before Jon could decide, a withering eruption of automatic weapons fractured the night again, the bullets mowing the stretch of grass between the trees and the low bank. Chilling screams echoed across the dark sea.

Jon and Asgar spun on their heels in time to see eight black shapes rise at the surf line, deployed at equal intervals, still firing over the heads of Jon and the Uighers at the ambushers.

Jon grinned. "I'll be damned. It's our navy. The best of the best — SEALs."

The word spread instantly. The Uighers opened up again on the flanking attackers, who fell back. With shouts and curses, the group above the bank retreated from the assault.

A SEAL loped up from the water and hunkered down. "Orchid." He was broad-shouldered and muscular. His face was covered with black grease.

"Nice of you to drop by."

"Lieutenant Gordon Whelan, sir. Glad we made it in time. We'd better book now. There're patrol boats out there, more than one. They know something's up. Can your people get away on their own?"

Asgar nodded. "If you keep them pinned down a few more minutes."

"Roger. Go."

Asgar called low to the rest of the Uighers. They did not wait for farewells. Crouched low, they crab-walked quickly along the beach to the right and vanished into the darkness. The SEALs provided a steady covering fire, keeping the attackers too busy to notice.

"Get to the raft, sir," the lieutenant ordered. "We have to get out damn quick now."

Jon ran the short distance to the big rubber Zo-

201

diac that had been pulled up onto the beach. White surf churned around it. He clambered aboard. Four of the SEALs fired a final volley before pushing off, jumping in, and paddling swiftly out to sea.

Behind them, the remaining four, including Lieutenant Whelan, continued firing. Then silence. From the raft, Jon watched as the land receded. Shadowy figures had gathered to stare helplessly out to sea, weapons hanging down from their hands.

Jon's heart hammered with leftover adrenaline. He listened to the quiet wash of waves against the raft, felt the gentle rise and fall of it. The Zodiac kept moving farther and farther from the shoreline. The SEALs said nothing. He knew they were thinking about the quartet left behind. Worrying. He was, too.

Finally, at least four hundred yards out, four black shapes suddenly burst out of the water. Hands reached over the side of the raft. The men grabbed the hands and scrambled aboard, one by one.

Lieutenant Whelan was last. He counted heads and nodded. "All accounted for. Nice work, people."

Nothing more was said until they were a half mile at sea. The searing glare of a searchlight suddenly whipped across the dark water to the north. It was sweeping the sea more than two miles away but approaching rapidly.

"They'll spot us soon," the lieutenant said. "Better start the motor, Chief."

One of the SEALs cranked the sealed outboard

motor, and the raft shot ahead, bouncing like a toy across the tops of the swell. Jon held on, enjoying the cold spray on his sweaty face. At the same time, he watched the Chinese patrol boat uneasily. It was approaching through the night, closer and closer, gunfire singing from it, looking for a target. Its searchlight had yet to hone in on them, but when it did —

Then he saw a dark shape, towering ahead like a giant sea monster. It was a submarine. American, thank God. At the same moment that the SEALs raft reached the hulking steel sub, the searchlight on the patrol boat finally found them. Bullets ripped through the rubber as they swarmed up aboard, hauling Jon and the tattered Zodiac after them.

A voice on the bridge bawled, "Get below! Clear the decks!"

The patrol boat caught the submarine in the beam of its searchlight, and its siren shrieked at them. The sub was already submerging as Jon, the SEALs, and the deck crew hurtled down through the open hatches and slammed them closed against the rushing sea. The patrol boat opened fire with a heavy machine gun, but its bullets bounced harmlessly off the steel. As the conning tower sank beneath the surface, the patrol boat moved in aimless, frustrated circles.

Below, as Jon was escorted to a tiny cabin to clean up and rest, he decided whoever had attacked them on the beach had not been national security forces. If they had been, they would have sent more than a lone patrol boat. No, whoever they were, their employer was private.

Beijing

As befitted one of the older members of the Standing Committee, Wei Gaofan's walled compound inside Zhongnanhai had a choice location, near the lotus-carpeted Nanhai — South Lake. In his courtyard stood a manicured willow tree that swayed in the morning breeze, trailing its jade-green branches over thick grass. Small flowering trees and groomed flowers decorated the tiled paths that led to the four small buildings that rimmed the courtyard. Crowned with graceful pagoda roofs, the structures were decorated with columns carved with dragons, clouds, and cranes symbolizing good fortune and longevity. He shared the largest house with his wife, while their daughter, her child, and a babysitter lived across from them. The third building was his office, while the fourth was where the family entertained guests.

The sun had been up more than an hour when Feng Dun was admitted to Wei's office, which was appointed with small treasures from all of China's dynasties since the great Han. Wei, a connoisseur of tea, was sitting at a table, drinking Longjing. Its subtle floral scent perfumed the air. Unlike wine, which was best when aged, tea was most flavorful — as well as most costly — when drunk the year it was picked. This tea was hardly six months old. Grown in Hangzhou, Longjing was the finest, most delicate tea in China.

Wei did not bother to offer any to Feng Dun, nor did he bother to hide his anger. "So the American colonel escaped you."

"He escaped the Public Security Bureau also."

Without an invitation to sit, Feng Dun remained standing, staring down at Wei, who was bald and narrow-eyed, with a bulky torso and spindly legs.

Wei looked at him sharply. "Fortunate for you."

"Fortunate for both of us," Feng said, his gaze unflinching as he matched the hard stare of the immensely powerful member of the Standing Committee.

Wei sipped his tea. "But General Chu and Major Pan suspect something."

"Suspect perhaps, but don't know and never will."

Wei scowled again. "There's Yu Yongfu's wife, who is, I hear, missing."

Feng shrugged. "There's nothing she can do. Her father would be ruined, and she's too intelligent to want that. Your favor can make life very good for him, her, and her children."

"True." But there was still doubt in Wei's eyes. "So, was this American agent really so skilled? How did he get away?"

"He's good, but not good enough to get the manifest. As for his other escapades, he was lucky, and he had help."

"Whose help?"

"First, an interpreter and asset of the CIA, who is now dead. And later, an underground cell of Uighers. They took him to his point of extraction. The stupid police never suspected. They smiled and laughed at the Uighers, and then they let them pass. Imbeciles."

"Can you identify the Uighers?"

"We were never close enough, but they knew the

city and countryside well. Then American SEALs appeared and enabled their escape."

Wei Gaofan nodded, pleased. "A submarine. That means the Americans are very concerned about risking an incident. We are succeeding. You have done well."

Feng Dun inclined his head, acknowledging the compliment, but smarting because he had not been offered the polite gesture of sharing tea. Still, the time to bring up his rewards would come later, when Wei Gaofan assumed his greater role in the destiny of China.

"The manifest is destroyed?" Wei continued.

"Burned."

"You are sure?"

"I was there with Yu Yongfu when he burned it before taking his gun and driving away," Feng said. "Of course I followed."

"The police have found no corpse."

"They may never find it."

"You saw him kill himself? With your own eyes?"

"Which is why I followed. And then he fell into the Yangtze. He wanted it that way."

Wei Gaofan smiled again. "We have nothing left to worry us, while the Americans have much to worry them. Would you care for a cup of tea, Feng?"

PART TWO

Chapter
Fourteen

The Indian Ocean

On the gray ocean, the guided missile frigate USS *John Crowe* slipped into its assigned station. The water was placid, with a gentle southwest swell and a following sea. Dawn glowed low across the sky behind them, while to the west, night still reigned, dark and unfathomable. Radar had raised the *Crowe*'s quarry, *The Dowager Empress*, an hour ago, but the suspect ship was still invisible in the night ahead.

On the *Crowe*'s bridge, Commander James S. Chervenko focused his binoculars on the black horizon and saw nothing. Square and muscular, he had a rugged face with eyes permanently narrowed from years of sea duty.

He spoke to his exec, Lt. Commander Frank Bienas. "Any indication she's not alone, Frank?"

"Nothing on radar or sonar," Bienas reported. Bienas had the fluid grace of a boxer. Young, smart, and handsome, he was something of a ladies' man.

"Okay. When it's light enough to see the freighter, drop back and track by radar alone. I'll be in my quarters."

"Yes, sir."

The commander left the bridge, working his way below. Admiral Brose had impressed on him the importance of this mission, but he needed no one, admiral or anyone else, to do that. He was well aware of the *Yinhe* incident. Today, with China stronger, more stable, and more important to the state of the world, the situation was all the more treacherous. At the same time, allowing Iraq to create a new batch of biological and chemical weapons was no option either.

Once in his quarters, Commander Chervenko opened direct communication with Admiral Brose, as ordered, bypassing task force and fleet HQs.

"Commander Chervenko reporting the USS *Crowe* on station, sir."

"Good, Commander." The admiral sounded as if he had been pulled from his dinner table in Washington, where it was still Thursday night. "How's it look?"

"Routine so far. Radar shows no other vessels, surface or submerged, in the area, and not a peep out of their radio. As soon as it's light, we'll drop back and rely on radar contact."

"Keep monitoring their transmissions and receptions. You have a Chinese interpreter aboard?"

"Yessir."

"All right, Commander. Jim, is it?"

"Jim, yessir."

"Keep me posted on anything that happens out there, the instant it happens, short of endangering the operation or your ship. *Anything,* you understand?"

"Aye-aye, sir."

"Good to have you aboard on this, Jim."

"Thank you, sir."

The transmission over, Commander Chervenko leaned back in his desk chair, his gaze focused on the ceiling of his quarters. This was not the kind of bombshell mission that usually fell to the lot of a frigate commander. He could see a hell of a lot of risk involved, right down to a live engagement that could cost him his ship. He could also see opportunity. In the navy, there were no higher stakes than those that threatened an officer's vessel in combat. And success in the face of high risk was what could make a career. Or break one.

The East China Sea

The pulsing power of the carrier's giant engines reverberated through the hull and into Jon's bones. The sounds and sensations were soothing as he waited in his temporary quarters for the call to Fred Klein to go through to the yacht club back in Washington. He knew Klein's habits. Dinner — if Klein remembered to eat that night — was usually in his cluttered office there, despite the late hour.

The submarine had ferried him to the carrier, which had been running dark north of Taiwan, surrounded by escort vessels. Jon had the distinct impression the captain and the fleet admiral considered being ordered to extract an undercover agent a waste of time for their mighty ship. After a cup of coffee with the lieutenant commander, who had been sent to escort him, he was shown straight to his makeshift quarters. He showered, shaved, and asked to make a call.

211

As he waited, he thought about the Uighers, especially Alani. He hoped they had escaped safely.

When the phone rang, he snatched it up.

"You got out in one piece, Colonel?" Fred Klein's unemotional voice was somehow reassuring.

"Thanks to you, the U.S. Navy, and some local help." He related his escape, from the moment he had ended his call to Klein at the Peace Hotel. "The Uighers want independence from China, but they seem to have no illusions that it's going to happen anytime soon. They'd settle for being able to keep their identity and culture. President Castilla's human-rights treaty might help them do that. Or at least lead to it eventually."

"One more reason to concentrate on getting that agreement signed," Klein said. "So Asgar Mahmout was Mondragon's asset?"

"Thought you'd like to know."

"You're right. Any change with regard to the manifest?"

"It's probably destroyed by now, if they're smart. That copy, at least."

"I agree." Jon could hear Klein puffing on his pipe in the distant office. "Yet you think they tracked you to that beach with the Uighers. If they destroyed the manifest, why would they also want to eliminate you? That seems like overkill. Certainly an unnecessary risk. Are you sure your attackers weren't police or state security?"

"As sure as I can be."

Excited puffing. "Then something else is going on. They don't want the manifest to fall into our hands, that's obvious. But they had plenty of time to make certain *no one* would ever get it. Yet they still tried to kill you, and they did it on their own. Without the police."

Jon's pulse accelerated. He saw what Klein was getting at. "They don't want Chinese government security to know there *was* a manifest, and that an American agent was looking for it. Public Security already knew I was there and was more than I appeared to be, but they couldn't figure out what I was doing. Whoever forced Yu Yongfu to commit suicide doesn't want them to know." He thought rapidly. "Do you think it's some kind of internal power struggle in Beijing?"

"Or maybe the shady deal of some big Shanghai tycoon."

"Isn't that the same thing in New China?"

On the other end of the line, the pipe puffing stopped. The dead air was like a vacuum. Klein said in an awed voice: "The Chinese government doesn't know what *The Dowager Empress* is carrying. That's got to be it!"

"How is that possible? In *China*? Everything's done by committee, by arrangement. Hell, they probably don't even take a leak alone."

"It's the only logical answer, Colonel. Someone, almost certainly very high up, is trying to cause trouble between our nations. It *is* a power struggle, but on an international scale."

Jon swore. "China's got heavy-duty nuclear armaments. A lot heavier than the world knows."

The silence at the far end of the connection was ominous. "Jon, this makes the situation far more dangerous than we'd thought. If we're right, the president *must* have the proof of the *Dowager*'s cargo before he orders any kind of move. I'll have

213

the navy fly you to Taipei right away. You can catch the first flight out to Hong Kong from there."

"What do I use as a legend?"

"We've researched this Donk & LaPierre company. They're a conglomerate with interests in international shipping and electronics. What's perfect for you is they also work in biotechnology."

"I can't go as myself anymore."

"No, you can't. But I've arranged for you to impersonate one of your colleagues at USAMRIID: Major Kenneth St. Germain."

"We look something alike, but what if they check and find he's still there, working?"

"They won't. He's taken an offer to go mountaineering in Chile."

Jon nodded. "An offer Ken would never refuse. Nice work. Now ask your new permanent staff to arrange a meeting between me — or Ken St. Germain — and the head of Donk & LaPierre's Hong Kong office to discuss their work with viruses."

"Consider it done."

"Have you learned anything about the killer I told you about — Feng Dun?"

"Not yet. We're still checking. You get to Taipei, and I'll bring the president up-to-date here. He's not going to be happy."

"You should let him know the latest about the old prisoner who says he's David Thayer, too."

"You have new information?"

Jon repeated what Asgar Mahmout had told him. "The prison farm's outside the city of Dazu, about seventy miles northeast of Chongqing. It's apparently low security, at least by Chinese standards."

"Good. That gives me something to work with,

in case we do have to go in for him. A simple fence won't stop us, and neither will ordinary prison guards. It's helpful that he's got privileges and only one cell mate. If we bring some of the political prisoners out, too, that'll give cover to both Thayer and the mission. I don't like the farm's location — it's a heavily populated area. And I don't like that they move him around. It's possible he could be gone before we get there."

"From what Asgar said, he's been at Dazu awhile. It didn't sound as if there was any hint he was going to be relocated."

Jon heard the slow puffs that indicated Klein was thinking. "Okay, and where the farm is could be worse. At least it's close to the borders of Burma and India."

"Not that close."

"So we'll have to work a little harder. We all have to do that anyway. I want that manifest, Colonel."

The Indian Ocean

In the communications-and-control center of the USS *John Crowe*, Lt. Commander Bienas leaned over the shoulder of the radar man, his gaze fixed on the screen. "How many times has her captain changed course?"

"Counting this time, three, sir." The radar man looked up.

"Describe the changes."

"First he turned forty-five degrees south, then he —"

"For how long? How far did he go?"

"About an hour, maybe twenty miles."

"Okay, go on."

"He went back to his original heading for close to another hour, then went north for maybe another hour, and back to his original course again."

"So he's back where he started?"

"Yessir. Just about."

"And we changed course every time?"

"Sure. I reported the new headings."

"Okay, Billy, good work."

The radar man grinned. "Anytime, sir."

The lieutenant commander did not return the grin. He left the control center and slid down the gangways until he reached the captain's quarters. He knocked.

"Come."

Commander Chervenko looked up from where he sat at his desk doing his paperwork. He immediately saw the concern on Bienas's face. "What's happened, Frank?"

"I think they've spotted us, sir." Bienas reported everything the radar man had told him.

"We changed helm each time?"

" 'Fraid so. Canfield had the bridge. He's too damned new."

Chervenko nodded. "Later would've been better, but we knew they'd spot us eventually. Any increase in radio — ?"

His ship intercom squawked: "Communications, sir. I'm picking up a big increase of radio activity in Chinese."

"Speak of the devil," Commander Chervenko muttered. Then into the intercom: "Get Ensign Wao up there now."

"Aye-aye, sir."

Chervenko remained bent to his communications console. "Chief, crank her up. I need top speed." Then he stood up. "Let's hit the bridge."

By the time the commander and Bienas reached it, Ensign Wao was already there. "They've figured out we're back here, sir, and they're on the horn in a panic to Beijing and Hong Kong."

"A panic?" Chervenko frowned.

"Yessir. That's the funny thing. They know who we are. I mean, they know we're a U.S. Navy frigate."

"They must have a military radar expert on board," Bienas decided, astounded.

Commander Chervenko nodded unhappily. "Tell the chief to give me all he has. No point hiding now. Let's see what they're doing on board." He focused his binoculars on the horizon. It was a clear, sunny day, a calm sea, and visibility was nearly unlimited. Surging forward at twenty-eight knots, the *Crowe* soon raised the *Empress* dead ahead and closed to viewing distance.

Lt. Commander Bienas joined the captain with his binoculars.

"You see what I see, Frank?"

Bienas nodded. The decks of the cargo ship were packed with crew members, everyone pointing astern and waving their arms. An officer stood on the cabin housing, yelling down to them, but the crew members continued to mill around.

"They're worried as hell, Jim," Bienas said.

"I'd say so," Chervenko agreed. "No one told them we were back here, and they were taken by surprise. But someone expected either us or someone like us."

"Or they wouldn't have had that radar expert on board."

"Yeah," Chervenko said. "The bridge is yours, Frank. Keep a close eye on them. The fat's sizzling in the frying pan."

"What do you think the Chinese'll do?"

Chervenko turned away to go below and make his report to Admiral Brose. "I don't know," he said over his shoulder. "I expect a whole lot of people in D.C. are going to be worried about that question real soon, too."

Chapter
Fifteen

Thursday, September 14
Washington, D.C.

President Castilla sat in his Zero-Gravity recliner upstairs in his bedroom in the White House residence, trying to read while worrying about China and the human-rights treaty . . . thinking of the father he had never known and the suffering he must have endured . . . and longing for the first lady.

His mind wandered, and the sentences ran together. He lay the book on his lap and rubbed his eyes. He missed the cutthroat two-handed poker games with Cassie they always played on nights one or the other could not sleep, even if she did win eight of ten. But she was off in Central America, doing good works, surrounded by a gaggle of press, and making friends along the way. He wished she were home, with him. Making friends with him.

His thoughts had begun to drift toward what their lives would be like after he left office, when Jeremy knocked lightly.

"What is it now?" he snapped, hearing his irritation too late.

"Mr. Klein, sir."

Castilla came alert. "Send him in, Jeremy. And sorry, I guess I miss my wife."

"We all do, Mr. President."

Was there a faint smile on Jeremy's face as he avoided any hint of a particular interpretation of why Castilla was missing her? The president hid his own smile with a frown.

Jeremy waited as Fred Klein padded into the bedroom. He closed the door.

Castilla had a sudden image of Klein flowing through the world like fog, silent and impenetrable. What was it Carl Sandburg wrote . . . Yes: *The fog came in on little cat feet. . . .* Klein's feet were far too big for that.

"Have a seat, Fred."

Klein lowered a hip on the edge of an armchair. The Covert-One chief's hands fluttered as if searching for a lost jewel.

"Chew on the damn thing," Castilla growled, "before you drive me to drink."

Klein looked sheepish, took out his battered pipe, and gratefully stuck the stem between his teeth. "Thank you, Mr. President."

"I just hope it doesn't kill you until after I'm out of office," he grumbled. "Okay, what's the bad news this time?"

"I'm not sure if my bulletins are good or bad, sir. You might say it depends on how this *Empress* affair unfolds."

"That's hardly reassuring."

"No, sir." Klein explained the essence of Jon's experiences of the last hours, but not the details. "We're fairly certain that the original invoice manifest must have been destroyed. My people in Iraq have found nothing so far. Colonel Smith is on his way to Hong Kong where we hope the third copy is with Donk & LaPierre."

The president shook his head. "Sometimes I wish all these multinational corporations and holding companies had never been allowed to come into existence."

"So do most governments," Klein agreed.

"What about our other agents in China?"

"Nothing. They haven't caught a hint of the *Empress* and its actual cargo from any of their contacts within the Chinese government or the Communist Party."

Castilla pinched the bridge of his nose, narrowing his eyes. "That's odd, isn't it? Beijing is usually rife with rumor and speculation."

"Colonel Smith and I've come to the conclusion that, in fact, Beijing may not know about the contraband."

The president's eyebrows rose. "You mean . . . it's a *private* venture? A lucrative business deal?"

"With a complication. We think a high Beijing official may be involved, perhaps someone on the Politburo itself."

The president thought rapidly. "Corruption? Another Chen Xitong situation?"

"Possibly, yes. But there also could be a power struggle within the Politburo. Which . . ."

"Isn't necessarily good for us."

"No, sir, it isn't."

The president was quiet, lost in thought. So was Klein as he fiddled with his pipe, absently took out his tobacco pouch, then realized what his hands were doing. He hastily returned the fragrant tobacco to his pocket.

Finally, the president hauled himself out of his comfortable recliner and began to pace, his slippers slapping the carpet. "I doubt it makes a damn bit of difference whether Beijing knows. They'll react the same. They'll defend the rights of their ships to go anywhere on the high seas with any cargo, whether or not they approve of this one. We still have only one way to prevent the chemicals from reaching Iraq without a confrontation and the resulting consequences."

"I know, sir. We have to have that manifest to prove to the world — and to China — that we're not pulling a fast one. But if Beijing *isn't* involved and doesn't know what the *Empress* is carrying, when we do prove what the cargo is, we should get swift cooperation. They'll have no reason to cover up. In fact, they'll want to look as responsible and committed to international peace as everyone else. Or at least we can hope they will." He studied the president, who still paced the bedroom as if he were entangled in an unseen web. "Is this a good time to update you about David Thayer?"

The president stopped and stared at Klein. "Yes, of course it's a good time. What more have you learned?"

"One of Covert-One's assets in China has reported that the prison farm isn't as tightly guarded as it might be. It's possible we'll be able to insert one of my people to make contact and find out what Thayer's condition is and what he wants."

"All right," the president said cautiously. He did not resume pacing.

Klein sensed hesitancy. "Are you reconsidering a rescue incursion, sir?"

"As you said, if Beijing really isn't involved in sending the *Empress* to Iraq, they should be more inclined to cooperate, once they have incontrovertible proof. But a clandestine incursion by us, with a goal that can't help but condemn them before the world, successful or unsuccessful, is going to enrage them."

Klein had to agree. "True."

"I can't risk our nation's safety or the treaty."

"Maybe you won't have to," Klein said. "We can send in nongovernmental, nonmilitary forces. Strictly volunteers. They'd abort at the first sign of discovery. That way, you preserve full deniability."

"You could get that many volunteers with training?"

"As many as I want."

Castilla fell heavily into his armchair. He crossed his legs and rubbed his big chin. "I don't know. History isn't kind to private raids into enemy territory."

"There's risk, sir. I admit it. But far less than with an official operation."

The president seemed to accept that. He mused, "Your first step would be to send someone into China to contact Thayer? Find out if he even wants to be rescued rather than wait for the treaty to free him?"

"That and to report on the military conditions, terrain, locations . . . all the details we'll need if you give the go-ahead."

"All right. Do it. But make no further move until you clear it with me."

"That goes without saying."

"Yes." The president considered Klein, his expression somber. "He probably gave up on coming home years ago. Ever seeing this country again. It'd mean a lot to me to get him out of there. Imagine being able to give him a final few years of peace and comfort here at home." He stared past Klein at the White House wall. "It'd be nice to finally meet my father."

"I know, Sam."

They exchanged a look across the years.

The president sighed and rubbed his eyes again.

Klein stood and quietly left the bedroom.

Friday, September 15
Hong Kong

The Asian headquarters of Donk & LaPierre, S.A., occupied three floors of a new forty-two-story building in the heart of Central, the main business district of Hong Kong Island. Downtown's two other districts were Admiralty and Wanchai, the former red-light quarter but now Hong Kong's third financial district, east of Central. Most skyscrapers in recent years had been built in Central and Admiralty, while new commercial redevelopment projects were under way west of Central. Across the narrowest neck of Victoria Harbor was a fourth section, teeming with activity and humanity — Kowloon, on the mainland.

At exactly noon on Friday, a telephone call came into Donk & LaPierre that bypassed the corporate switchboard and rang in the office of a Mr. Claude Marichal. It did not ring on Marichal's desk phone, nor on a second phone set on a side table next to an armchair for important visitors. Instead, it rang on what appeared to be an interoffice phone — no dial or button pad. It was stored on the top of a three-shelf bookcase under the windows behind his desk.

Startled, Marichal dropped his pen, swore as the ink splashed on his papers, and swiveled to pick up the receiver. "Yes? May I help you?"

"You may, if you're Mr. Jan Donk."

The receiver nearly slipped from Marichal's grasp. He said quickly, "What? Oh, yes. Yes, of course." Keeping his shock under control, he took a deep breath. "Hold on, please. I'll get him." He laid the receiver down on top of the book-case . . . and picked it up again. "It may take a few minutes, so please remain on the line."

"I'll stay as long as I can."

He put the caller on hold, swiveled frantically back to his desk phone, and dialed an extension. "Sir? There's a call that just came in on the private Donk line, asking for him."

"Asking for *him?*"

"Yes, sir."

"It's not Yu Yongfu or Mr. McDermid?"

"Absolutely not."

"Don't let him hang up."

"I'll try." Marichal ended the connection and swung back to the special phone. "I'm sorry, sir. We're having some trouble locating Mr. Donk." He tried to make his voice bright, eager, and helpful. "Perhaps I can help you. If you'll tell me your business with Jan — ?"

"That's all right, but no thanks."

A man came into Marichal's office, tiptoeing, his

finger to his lips, and his eyebrows raised in question. Marichal nodded vigorously while racking his brain for a tactic to stall the caller longer. "It's possible he's already gone to lunch. Mr. Donk, I mean. Left the building. If you'll give me your name and number, or perhaps a message, I'm sure he'll get back to you the moment he comes in. I know he'd hate to miss . . . hello? Hello? Sir? *Hello?*"

"What happened?"

Marichal peered up as he returned the receiver to its cradle. "He's gone. I think he figured it out, Mr. Cruyff."

The man, Charles-Marie Cruyff, nodded. He picked up the receiver of Marichal's desk phone and asked, "Did you get the trace?"

"He called from a public phone booth in Kowloon."

"Give me the number and the location." He wrote it down.

Kowloon

He'd made a mistake. As Jon slammed the phone into the cradle, he knew that. Either the number had been special and unlisted, or Jan Donk did not exist. Or both. Now whoever had answered was alerted that some unauthorized person, speaking American English, knew the number. The only question was whether they had been able to trace his call. That was a question that had only one answer: He must assume they did.

As Major Kenneth St. Germain, Ph.D., wearing a dark-blond wig to match the long hair of the aging hippie and eminent microbiologist, he had landed at Hong Kong International on Lantau Island two hours ago, gone through customs, and taken the Airport Express to the Kowloon Shangri-la Hotel. He wasted no time in his room. After checking the location of Donk & LaPierre, he slid the blond wig into his pocket, donned a new tropical-weight suit, and left the hotel.

The city lay under an oppressive blanket of heat and high humidity that day, unusual for mid-September. Walking out into it was like hitting a wall of diesel fumes and saltwater air, spiced up with the stink of fried meats and fish. He was engulfed by the surging masses of people, cars, and buses that were, if anything, more numerous than in Shanghai. He pushed, dodged, and bumped his way to the Star Ferry terminal, where he had found this public phone.

Now he hurried away, blending into the throngs on the harbor promenade. He looked around for a convenient fast-food kiosk where he could observe the public phone. One thing was to his advantage here — a tall man in Western clothes was only one of thousands walking the Hong Kong streets every day, all of whom must look pretty much alike to the Chinese.

He had eaten only three shrimp by the time the two unmarked black sedans arrived. They were Mercedeses, by the look of them over the distance. Six Chinese men in suits emerged and fanned out. All casually approached the public phone from different directions, scrutinizing everyone. They carried no obvious weapons, but Jon noted telltale buttoned suit jackets and suspicious bulges. There was an anxiety that hovered about them, a touch of angry nervousness.

227

Not national security or even local police. They were something else.

None had looked at the food kiosk yet. That was too good a piece of luck to test. Besides, he had learned all he was going to. He dropped the remainder of the greasy fried shrimp into a trash can and circled away to the ferry terminal. The next departure for Hong Kong Island was in three minutes. He bought a ticket.

Once aboard, he made his way forward to the bow, thinking about the six men, replaying their faces in his mind so he would remember them. Were they from Feng Dun again?

As he considered that possibility, he raised his gaze, remembering his role as a tourist, and looked out across the channel. No one was prepared for the breathtaking view, no matter how many times they had heard about it or studied photos. Ahead, the scene spread so wide it was impossible to take it all in at once. First were the ships, barges, sea-going yachts, green sampans, and ferries, churning across the aqua waters. Then came the piers, docked ships, and waterfront buildings that skirted the island of Hong Kong. Behind them rose skyscrapers of every height, massed like titans readying an attack, with neon advertising signs as their mammoth insignias. Finally, towering over them were cloud-ringed mountains, serene and timeless. Out in the water to the east, islands rose like pyramids. Altogether, the panorama was as large and stunning as New York's.

As the ferry left the terminal, the impact of it all moving toward him was palpable. He caught his breath and turned away — and saw two of the six, their hands sliding up under their suit jackets, as if checking to make certain their weapons were convenient. They were weaving through the throng. Closing in on him.

Chapter Sixteen

Manila, The Philippines

Beneath a glassy blue sky and a blistering sun, the modified C-130 landed at Ninoy Aquino International Airport at 1400 hours. It taxied to a remote hangar far from Manila's commercial terminals, where a camouflaged army command car and armed Humvee were parked inside.

As the hangar door rolled closed, the cargo jet's door opened, and its stairway unfolded. The uniformed driver of the car jumped out, ran around to the side of the car that faced the jet, and opened the rear door.

Concealed inside the hangar, Secretary of the Army Jasper Kott descended the stairway, four aides following. His smooth features were hidden behind black aviator glasses. As he approached the command car, the driver stood at attention. Elegant as usual in a perfectly tailored, three-piece suit, Kott nodded acknowledgment and stepped into the backseat. His aides climbed into the Humvee.

There was already a passenger inside the command car — a uniformed man who wore on his shoulders the single silver star of a brigadier general. Sitting beside the far window, he drew on a thick cigar and exhaled aromatic smoke. "The cigar bother you, Mr. Secretary?" Brigadier General Emmanuel ("Manny") Rose asked.

"Not if you need it to think, General." Kott opened the window as the car pulled away, the Humvee following.

A door the size of an outsized garage door rolled up in the shadowy hangar, and the two vehicles drove through into the sweltering Philippine day.

"On this assignment, I need it for patience." Rose blew another cloud as the tires droned over the tarmac. "You won't believe these people."

"Of course I will. I work in D.C." Secretary Kott glanced out at the palms and tropical vegetation. The hot air did not bother him. Mango trees crowded together in the distance. Birds in violent colors flew from the branches of hibiscus and bottlebrush trees. Ahead, a mirage shimmered on the pavement. It was at least ten degrees hotter here than in Washington — hot, humid, and fecund.

"You've got a point."

The secretary questioned, "You think this al-Sayed prisoner is the real thing? A top leader of the Mindanao Islamic guerrillas?"

"Sure looks like it."

"Why? Because they want to hold on to him, get all the credit?"

"Those who don't want to nail him to a wall and skin him alive, and those who don't want to make a fast deal and cut him loose so he'll keep mum about what they've been doing."

"You've insisted we be present at all interrogations?" the secretary pressed.

General Rose nodded, his jowls quivering, on the verge of outrage. "Damn right. If they neglect our wishes, they don't get any more aid or tech training from us. Just to be sure, I've put my own men on the guard detail."

"Good."

The general paused to smoke and watch the street. He seemed to see nothing that disturbed him. He glanced at the secretary. "You brought a team?"

"A CIA interrogation expert as well as an air force captain who speaks Moro." Kott did not bother to mention he had also brought his chef. "My aide's with them in the Humvee. Tomorrow, we'll have a go at him."

"Yeah. You will if you convince the Filipinos at the dinner tonight to let us."

Kott smiled confidently. "That won't be a problem."

Soon after, both vehicles arrived at the sprawling country estate that was the temporary command headquarters of the American military mission, courtesy of the Manila government. Making small talk for the benefit of anyone who might be eavesdropping, General Rose escorted Secretary Kott to his air-conditioned quarters to rest and freshen up before the all-important dinner meeting tonight with the Filipino politicians and military men.

"This evening then, General." Kott extended his hand.

Rose shook it. He growled around the butt of his cigar, "I'll be ready. Get a good nap. You're going to need it."

As his air conditioner whistled from the corner

of his suite, Kott closed the door and waited five minutes. He opened it and peered in both directions along the hallway. No one was in sight.

Crouched outside beneath a window of the frame building, a slim woman wearing the uniform of a U.S. Air Force captain pressed a contact microphone against the wall. She had arrived on the cargo jet with Secretary Kott.

Inside his suite, Kott's footsteps marched across the floor. There was the click of keys on a keypad being depressed, and the sound of a telephone receiver being lifted.

"I'm here," he said. "Yes. I have to be back by six tonight. In two hours? Fine. Where? The Corregidor Club? Right. I'll be there."

The receiver dropped into its cradle, a wooden chair creaked, footsteps walked away, and finally shoes clattered onto the floor. Bed springs sighed. Kott was relaxing before going to meet whomever he had been talking to. Probably lying on the bed wide awake and looking up at the ceiling where assorted strange insects waited to drop onto the mosquito netting.

The air force captain was also Secretary Kott's Moro interpreter. Her name tag read Captain Vanessa Lim. She left the window. She was not headed off to rest, and her name was not Vanessa Lim.

Hong Kong

The most difficult action for an undercover agent was to do nothing. Jon stood in the bow of the ferry, pretending to feast on the kaleidoscopic cityscape that filled the horizon. Although the skin on the back of his neck puckered, he did not turn again to check the two men who had been moving forward through the press of passengers, studying clothes, faces, and the attitudes of everyone they passed. There was no way they could know what the caller to Donk & LaPierre looked like. In fact, the chance that Feng Dun or anyone else in China knew Lt. Col. Jon Smith was even in Hong Kong was minimal.

But a minimal chance was still a chance. Possible, but not probable. As Damon Runyon once said, "The race isn't always to the swift, nor the battle to the strong. But that's the way to bet." A matter of odds.

Smith remained at the front of the ferry, apparently unworried, no sign he was aware anything unusual was occurring around him. He appeared transfixed by all the exotic sights and sounds, as the ferry drew closer to its terminal on Hong Kong Island.

When the boat slid and thudded along the pilings, dockhands in blue uniforms pulled it in. The crowd moved forward, ready to trample onto land the instant the ferry stopped and the gates opened. Jon joined them. Above them, seagulls circled and cawed, while a wave of impatience rushed through the waiting throngs. Finally, the gates opened. The surge of humanity carried Jon down the wood ramp and up the concrete one. When he looked back, the two hunters had vanished.

Manila

Secretary of the Army Jasper Kott had changed

into a loose-fitting blue shirt, linen sports coat, tan slacks, and bone-colored loafers. He was sitting relaxed, enjoying the stream of cool air from the air conditioner, as he studied a special forces report on a guerrilla force that had made a lightning incursion and strike on a Filipino army garrison in northern Mindanao.

When someone knocked, he marked his place, set the report on a table beside his chair, and went to the door.

The special forces sergeant who had driven him to the headquarters stepped inside. "Good evening, sir."

"All clear, Sergeant?"

"Yessir. Most of their people are taking siestas. Ours are busy with the antiterrorist training. Your car's at the side door. The only sentry is one of my guys."

"I appreciate the help. Very discreet. Thank you."

Sergeant Reno smiled. "We all need a little R and R sometimes, sir."

Kott smiled back, man to man. "Then let's go."

He strode down the silent hallway, the sergeant respectfully three paces behind. Outside, the same camouflage-painted command car waited, its engine on. The secretary nodded approval: A quietly running engine attracted far less notice than one starting suddenly.

He climbed into the backseat, which was empty. The sergeant closed his door, got behind the wheel, and drove the car off. Bored by the poverty-stricken scenery of greater Manila, Jasper Kott settled back, crossed his arms, and considered how he would handle the afternoon's tasks. Once a highly successful executive in private industry, his last position was CEO of Kowalski and Kott — K&K, Inc. — mass supplier of artillery gun mounts to arms manufacturers around the globe. It was true he had grown wealthy and influential, far more wealthy and influential than most of his competitors realized. Still, numbers were useful only in keeping score, not in judging satisfaction.

He was a fastidious man in all ways, from dress to personal habits, from social relations to business deals. He had used his meticulousness as a tool to disarm competitors. In today's rough-and-earthy corporate climate, he simply did not fit the mold. Who would suspect his raging ambition? Who would credit him with a razor-sharp coldness that allowed him to cut his losses without ever looking back? While others ignored him as too prissy to be strong, he rose. By the time they noticed, they were too far behind to hurt or stop him.

He had never had a business opportunity to match the potential of this new one. With pleasure, he contemplated what success would mean . . . untouchable wealth, power beyond the imagination of his colleagues . . . a guaranteed future of more deals, each bigger than the last —

On a quiet street, the sergeant pulled into the driveway of an imposing house on a large lot in one of the better parts of Manila. A high hedge rimmed the property. On the rolling green lawn, palms grew tall against the sky, while tropical flowers in a rainbow of colors spread against the white-plastered walls. It was a hacienda from the Spanish era, stately and secluded.

Kott leaned forward. "Give me a few hours, Sergeant. You have your cell with you?"

"Right here, sir." The sergeant patted the shirt of his uniform. "Take your time."

Secretary Kott marched across terra-cotta tiles up to the long porch. The front door was massive — rich mahogany, while the fittings, including an ornate knocker in the shape of a coiled snake, were polished brass. He knocked and sensed rather than saw a peephole open and close. The door swung open, and a tiny Filipina bowed. She was no more than sixteen and stark naked, except for a pair of high-heeled purple shoes and a purple lace garter as high on her thigh as it could get. Kott's expression did not change.

She ushered him inside to a heavily furnished room where some twenty other women of various ages in various stages of undress stood, sat, and lounged. A well-stocked bar stretched along a wall. The teenager continued on through the room, Kott following, the twenty pairs of eyes assessing him. They climbed a sweeping stairway that could have been in a noble house in Madrid. On the second floor, she led him down a maroon-carpeted hall to the last door. The naked girl opened it, smiled again, and stood aside.

Kott entered. The room was spacious, with gold-flecked maroon wallpaper, gilded woodwork, a comfortable upholstered sitting area, a small bar, and a giant four-poster bed. Still unspeaking, the girl closed the door, and her footsteps faded away.

"Enjoy your usher, Jasper?" Ralph McDermid asked from his easy chair. He was grinning from ear to ear, his joviality on display. His round body and round face looked thoroughly relaxed.

"She's my daughter's age, for God's sake, Ralph," Kott complained. "Did we have to meet in a place like this?"

"It's excellent cover," the chairman and CEO of the Altman Group said, giving not an inch. "I'm known here. They protect me. Besides, I enjoy the company, the merchandise, and the services, eh?"

"Everyone to their own taste," Kott grumbled.

"How broad-minded and egalitarian of you, Jasper," McDermid said. "Sit. Sit down, dammit, and have a drink. Loosen up. We both know you're not the old grandpa you want everyone to think. Tell me about Jon Smith."

"Who?"

"Lieutenant Colonel Jon Smith, M.D." McDermid pressed a button on the table beside the armchair where he sat, and a white-coated Filipino materialized behind the bar.

"An army officer?" Kott shook his head. "Never heard of him. Why? What's he to us?" He called to the barman, "Vodka martini, straight up with a twist."

"He's dangerous, that's what he is. As for why he's important . . ." McDermid related the events from the time Mondragon was killed to Smith's extraction from the Chinese coast.

"He's got a copy of what the ship's actually carrying? Holy —"

"No," McDermid interrupted. "He *nearly* had a copy, but we took it back. I don't know whether he saw it, or understood it if he did. But Mondragon definitely did, which no longer matters since that

238

bastard is dead. However, here we walk a fine line: We want them to know what *The Dowager Empress* is carrying, but not be able to prove it."

The barman arrived with Kott's martini on a sterling tray. Kott sipped appreciatively. "So there's no problem. We're go then?"

"We're all-go, but I wouldn't say there's no problem." McDermid held up his empty highball glass and angled it toward the barkeep, who immediately went to work to replace it. "I doubt Smith, or whoever employs him, is going to give up."

"What do you mean, *whoever employs him?* He's got to be CIA. They recruit army personnel sometimes."

"I meant exactly what I said. As far as my people, and apparently the Chinese secret police, can figure, he doesn't belong to the CIA or to any of the other of our intelligence agencies."

Kott scowled. "You said he works for USAMRIID, and that's the excuse he used to enter China. So he's probably a one-time CIA asset. But he failed to get his job done. So now he's out, and he's probably out of our hair, too."

"Perhaps. But my people say he's very skilled and hardly sounds like a one-time recruit."

Kott drank more deeply. "Some competitor of yours looking to hurt you?"

"That's possible, I suppose. Some renegade agent. FBI maybe, considering how they're getting around these days. But whatever he is, all of us had better be extraordinarily cautious . . . for a multitude of reasons."

"Of course." Kott drained the martini, set the glass down. "But for now, we're on course?"

McDermid nodded. "The frigate *Crowe* is already shadowing the *Empress* in the Indian Ocean."

"Excellent."

"Any more news about military appropriations?"

Kott related the military appropriations meeting in the cabinet room in greater detail. "As I said, Brose and Oda were the only ones willing to give Secretary Stanton full support, and Oda's unimportant. Everyone else has a weapon in development they don't want to lose. It was an edgy meeting."

"And the president?"

"He's worried, and we know why, don't we? It's the *Empress* and a potential blowup with China. If that happens, he's got to have everything activated, whether it's in our arsenal or on the drawing board. If we've got the weapons for a big war in a big area, that'll scare the crap out of the Chinese." Kott sat back, smiling. "I'd say our plan's going smoothly, wouldn't you?"

"But we still have to be careful. If the doves in Zhongnanhai have gotten wind something's up, and if they compare notes with President Castilla, we're as good as dead. That real manifest can't fall into anyone's hands."

Kott was growing impatient. "So eliminate all the copies."

"It's not that easy. We've gotten rid of the one in Shanghai that Flying Dragon had. But there's still one in Basra. The Iraqis think no one can penetrate their security, so they refuse to destroy it, because they don't trust us to deliver if they do.

Anyway, they claim to be fully confident the *Empress* will make it through. There was a third copy in Hong Kong, but I've ordered it destroyed."

"The *Empress* will never pass the Strait of Hormuz. So what's really worrying you?"

"Yu Yongfu — the Flying Dragon president. He was vain, ambitious, unpredictable, nervous, and would never hold up under pressure. You know the type. He had delusions of empire, but a backbone of jelly."

"Had?" Kott asked.

"He's dead. When he learned of this Jon Smith's being in Shanghai, he fell apart. We applied pressure. He committed suicide."

"God dammit, Ralph!" Kott exploded. "That's two more corpses! You can't keep a secret this way. Murder complicates everything!"

McDermid shrugged. "We had no choice. Now we've got no choice with Smith either." He grinned and held up his glass in a toast. "Let's enjoy the pleasures of the house. There's time."

"Damnation, Ralph, they could all be my daughter! Don't you have any civility in you at all?" Kott shuddered.

McDermid laughed loudly. "None the way you define it. I have a couple of daughters around her age, too. I can only hope they're enjoying themselves as much as I plan to."

Kott stood. "You haven't seen your daughters in at least ten years. I have an hour before I can call my driver. Put me in an office somewhere with a phone. I'll get some work done."

McDermid touched the button on the side of the table, signaling the waiter to return. He looked up at Kott, who had stood, eager to leave. There was a wide smile of amusement on the Altman founder's mouth, but his eyes were cold. "Whatever your pleasure."

Chapter
Seventeen

Hong Kong

Constructed of steel, glass, and slate, the building where Donk & LaPierre had its offices was a towering showplace of modernity. Judging by the exacting architectural details and the international renown of its designer, whose name was engraved on black glass beside the front doors, offices here were shockingly expensive and the address coveted.

Wearing his dark-blond wig again, Jon paused outside to check the bustling street. He was back in his cover as Major Kenneth St. Germain. Satisfied he had not been followed, he stepped inside the revolving doors and was deposited into the foyer. He headed across the slate floor toward the stainless-steel elevators. The building's air had been filtered so many times it smelled like a virus-free clean room. But then, the whole place was antiseptic looking.

The thought of viruses brought him back to his cover's latest project, and he began to submerge his own personality into Ken's. As a top USAMRIID researcher, Ken St. Germain, Ph.D., had been galvanized by a virus discovered recently in northern Zimbabwe. The still-unnamed virus resembled the Machupo strain, which came from a distant continent — South America. Ken was using field mice to study his theory that the new virus *was* a form of Machupo, despite thousands of miles and an ocean separating the occurrences.

By the time he left the elevator, reached the glass doors of Donk & LaPierre, and pushed through, he was eager to ask for help with his research from Charles-Marie Cruyff, managing director of Donk & LaPierre's Asian branch. Then, of course, there was his real motive. . . .

"Major Kenneth St. Germain to see Mr. Cruyff," he announced to the woman behind the desk, who looked more like a cover model than a receptionist. "We called ahead."

"Of course, Major. Monsieur Cruyff is expecting you." She had a megawatt smile, perfect golden skin, and just a touch of makeup to enhance her considerable natural assets.

The secretary, or assistant, who came to usher him into the inner sanctum was an entirely different matter. Unsmiling, white-blond hair coiled severely, clothes loose and frumpy . . . she was all Donk and no LaPierre.

"You will please follow me, Major." Her voice was a baritone, and her English was Wagnerian. She led him over a Delft-blue carpet to an ebony door. She knocked and opened it. "Major St. Germain from America, Monsieur Cruyff," she announced.

The man inspiring this deference proved to be

short, broad, and muscular, with the massive thighs of a professional bicyclist. He glided forward from around his desk in his costly beige suit as if he could bend his knees only marginally.

He smiled, holding out a small hand. "Ah, Dr. St. Germain, a pleasure, sir," he said. "You're from USAMRIID, I hear. My people think highly of your work." Which meant he had checked on Ken St. Germain's credentials, no surprise.

They shook hands.

"I'm flattered, Monsieur Cruyff," Jon told him.

"Please sit. Relax a moment."

"Thank you."

Jon chose an ultracontemporary sofa with chrome legs and removable cushions. As he turned toward it, he slipped his pocketknife out of his trousers and concealed it in his right hand. He settled onto the cushions, his right hip next to where two met. He looked up. Cruyff had returned to his desk. He had the sense Cruyff had never taken his gaze from him. His hand tightened around his hidden pocketknife.

"I'm not a scientist, as you may know." Cruyff lowered himself into his chair. "I hope you won't be offended if I tell you honestly I have little free time today." He gestured around his office, which was full of the superficialities of business — photos with important people, plaques from charities, awards from his company — and then at his desk, where file folders were stacked high. "I'm behind in my work, but perhaps there's something I can do for you quickly." He folded his hands over his chest, leaned back, and waited, studying Jon.

Jon needed to plant the knife between the cushions, but until he could get Cruyff to look away, it would be impossible. "Of course, monsieur. I understand. I appreciate any time you can give me." He described Major St. Germain's current research into the new virus. "But my progress at USAMRIID has been slow," he explained. "Far too slow. People are dying in Zimbabwe. With the constant movement between countries and continents these days, who knows where the virus will strike next? Perhaps even here in Hong Kong."

"Hmm. Yes. That could be catastrophic. We are a very dense city. But I don't see what I can do to help." The gaze continued its relentless focus.

Jon hunched forward, his expression deeply concerned. "Your pharmaceutical subsidiary has been working with hantaviruses, and I —"

Cruyff interrupted, losing patience: "BioMed et Cie is located in Belgium, Major. Thousands of miles away. Here in Hong Kong, at least in this office, our dominant assignment is marketing. I'm afraid I have little to offer you —"

It was Jon's turn to interrupt: "I'm aware of that subsidiary. But Donk & LaPierre also has a microbiological research team at a facility on mainland China. Those are the scientists I'm referring to. As I understand it, they're making progress on hantaviruses that have appeared near there. My studies of our new virus lead me to believe it may be carried through mice droppings that dry into dust, become airborne, and infect people, exactly as Machupo does in Bolivia and elsewhere in South America. Of course, hantaviruses like the ones your people are examining are transmitted in the same manner Machupo is. I'm sure you're familiar with those studies." He smiled ingenuously at Cruyff.

"Of course," Cruyff agreed. By doing so, he appeared neither ignorant nor as if he were hiding something. "What exactly do you wish to know? Providing it isn't confidential, naturally."

"Naturally," Jon echoed. "Since Donk & LaPierre is a business, your scientists may have been working on vaccines against the hantaviruses. If they have, I may be able to figure out a new research path based on what they've learned."

"No vaccine, Dr. St. Germain. At least, not that I've heard. On the other hand, they wouldn't report the early stages of something like that to corporate, or even the later stages, until they were sure there was high potential for commercialization. Although it's possible they're pursuing it on an entirely experimental basis, I doubt they'd be working on vaccines for your particular class of viruses."

"Really? Why is that?"

Cruyff smiled indulgently. "Significant outbreaks of hemorrhagic viruses occur only in poor countries. Research and development are astronomically pricey, particularly these days. The Third World simply doesn't have the money to pay for the R and D, much less the vaccines, now do they?"

"Perhaps not. Still —"

"So where would the return on investment be? What would happen to our stock if we pursued such quixotic research and development? We have a fiduciary responsibility to our shareholders."

"Ah, I see. So vaccines are out." He allowed real

247

disappointment to enter his voice. Then he brightened. "Still, you have very good scientists there. They might be doing something fresh and interesting with hantaviruses. I seldom have time to fly to Asia, so I'm going to gamble that you won't be irritated if I ask to visit the facilities anyway. If you would be kind enough to give me permission . . . after all, we scientists learn from each other, you know. I might be able to contribute something to help *them*."

Cruyff's brows raised. "I suppose there's no reason not to. You'll have to secure the proper entry and travel papers on your own, of course, but I'll have my assistant type up a letter of introduction and send it over to your hotel. Just give her the details when you leave. Perhaps with that, China will cooperate and approve your trip."

"Thank you. Your letter will make all the difference."

The pocketknife felt heavy in his hand. The visit was coming to a close, and he still had not had an opportunity to plant it. He fought tension and beamed and nodded toward the two ship models on Cruyff's desk. There were four more in glass cases on the walls.

He said, "I've been admiring your ships, monsieur. Beautiful. Did you make them yourself? A hobby?"

Cruyff laughed and waved his hand. "Hardly. They're the work of professionals, recreations of some of our more successful ships. Donk & LaPierre is primarily a shipping company, you see." He continued to watch Jon. He had not even glanced at the ships.

248

"Do you work mostly with Chinese companies?" Jon asked innocently.

Cruyff was startled. "Chinese companies? No, of course not."

"Oh, I'm sorry. It just seemed logical, and I noticed how many of your ship models have their names in Chinese lettering as well as roman."

Cruyff gave a sudden, involuntary glance, not at his models, but toward a safe in plain sight on the wall to the left of his desk.

That distraction was all Jon needed. With a frisson of relief, he flipped open his fingers and used his thumb to jam the knife down between the cushions.

Cruyff quickly refocused on Jon. "No, not especially. All ships registered in Hong Kong display their names in Chinese as well as in our alphabet."

"Of course," Jon jumped to his feet. "Stupid of me. Well, I won't waste any more of your time. It was gracious of you to see me, and even more to allow me to visit your biomed installation."

"Think nothing of it, Doctor."

Smiling and nodding, Jon backed out and closed the door.

In the outer office, Jon stopped to give the unsmiling Valkyrie the name of the Shangri-la Hotel and his room number. He headed off, smiled at the gorgeous receptionist, and pushed out through the glass doors.

His pulse ratcheted up as a messenger approached. But the messenger did not go into Donk & LaPierre. He passed on down the hall, and as soon as the man was out of sight, Jon made a quick detour into the men's restroom. Locked in a stall, he pulled a tiny listening device from an inner pocket and fitted it into his left ear. It was about the size of a jelly bean, another remarkable invention from intelligence R&D. He paused long enough to change his demeanor.

Radiating agitation, he hurried from the bathroom back into the offices of Donk & LaPierre, rushed past the exotic receptionist as if his return had not only been planned, but demanded, and — with a distracted wave — burst past the startled Brunhilde.

"Must have dropped my pocketknife," he announced as he slammed into Charles-Marie Cruyff's office without breaking step.

Cruyff was leaning back in his desk chair and talking confidentially into the phone. He gazed up, surprised, in midword.

"What!" he demanded of Jon.

Jon grumbled, irritated, "Dammit. *Sorry.* Must've dropped my knife," he repeated. "Let's see, I was standing here, and . . ." He paused before the desk, facing Cruyff, while looking around the airy office as if trying to remember exactly what he had done when he entered.

Cruyff scowled. "I have an important call, Dr. St. Germain. Please be fast." He paused, listening to the voice on the phone.

The cutting-edge directional microphone in Jon's ear picked up Cruyff's end of the conversation loud and clear.

Cruyff cupped his hand around the mouthpiece and whispered, ". . . . *I don't think so. No, sir, he was simply fishing for information about our hantavirus re-*

search, mostly to know if we were working on any vac-cines. He wanted an invitation to visit the lab inside China. What? Yes, absolutely legitimate. Works at USAMRIID, sir, yes. It has to be a simple coincidence. What? Well, yes, as a matter of fact, he did ask an odd question about our working mostly with Chinese firms. He saw my ship models, and . . ."

Jon let his glance fall on the couch. "Ah, that must be it!" He sat down and rummaged between the cushions.

"I'm sure you're mistaken, sir." Frowning, Cruyff continued to watch Jon as he searched. *"Well, per-haps a shade over six feet, yes, and . . ."*

Jon had heard enough. He needed to get out be-fore Cruyff grew too suspicious. Grinning with re-lief, he retrieved his knife from where he had hidden it and held it up. "Here it is. Must've fallen out of my pocket. Sorry for the intrusion, and thanks again, Monsieur Cruyff."

He sped out the door, knocking aside the out-raged Valkyrie, who had arrived to make certain all was well.

Seconds later, Jon trotted along the corridor to the elevators. The door of the only open one was closing. He sprinted, slid through just in time, and punched the button.

As the car started down, he smiled grimly to himself: There was someone who was obviously higher and more important in the company than even the managing director of the Asian branch, so much higher he couldn't be made to wait while Jon searched, and who had wanted to know whether Major Kenneth St. Germain really was from USAMRIID . . . whether he had asked any unusual or unexpected questions . . . and exactly what he had looked like.

And what was the meaning of Cruyff's startled glance at his safe when Jon had asked about Donk & LaPierre's working with Chinese companies?

Manila

Lying under silk sheets on the four-poster bed in the high-ceilinged room that had once entertained Spanish grandees, Ralph McDermid growled into the phone, his languor and good humor long gone. "What else?"

Charles-Marie Cruyff was filling out his description of the man who had come to ask questions that could easily have been asked over the telephone or by e-mail before flying all the way to Hong Kong, and who had also asked about Donk & LaPierre's work with Chinese companies.

"He's in his early forties, I'd guess," Cruyff said. "Trim. Looked as if he worked out a lot or played some vigorous sport."

"Dark hair brushed back?"

"No, sir. What I'd call dark blond, and it was parted on the side. I'm sure —"

"All right. The Shangri-la Hotel, you say? In Kowloon?"

"That's where I'm supposed to send my letter of introduction."

"Wait a few hours first. I want to be back in Hong Kong before then."

"Very well, Mr. McDermid. But I'm sure he was exactly who he said he was. Remember, the appointment was arranged by USAMRIID through our head office in Antwerp."

"Perhaps you're right, Charles-Marie. Perhaps he merely wants to visit your research people. We'll talk further when I get there. Meanwhile, make sure you take care of that urgent matter."

"Of course, Mr. McDermid."

McDermid hung up and lay back, his eyes closed. His joviality did not return, nor did his languor. When the girl emerged from the bathroom, perfumed and glossily nude, he opened his eyes and dismissed her with a curt wave. As she left, he grabbed the phone and dialed.

The polished voice on the other end of the line answered immediately. "Yes?"

"It's me. That problem in Shanghai may not be over after all." McDermid described the USAMRIID scientist and his intrusion at Donk & LaPierre as the other man listened and asked quiet, intelligent questions.

The more McDermid laid out the situation, the more he felt himself calm. This man with the polished voice was the key to his future. The Altman Group had soared high, but it could go even higher, now that he was in his pocket. The future was limitless. As they concluded their conversation, McDermid was smiling again.

Basra, Iraq

Often when he accepted an assignment from the American, Ghassan thought back to that day in Baghdad when, resigned to his death, he had been spared not by Allah but by the vanity of the Republican Guard. Trapped in his shop, defending Dr. Mahuk, he'd had no chance to survive. Suddenly, more Guards burst past, hot on the heels of the un-

253

armed doctor. They had not noticed him, and the others forgot him, as they rushed after, eager to share the credit.

Ghassan had dragged himself outside, leaving a trail of blood. Many hands helped him into hiding. From then on, he had not only walked with a limp, he had abandoned all fear and dedicated his life to freeing his country. Through Dr. Mahuk, he made contact with Colonel Smith again, and he began helping an American voice on the telephone.

Tonight, Ghassan was on such a mission for the Americans. Dressed in black, he crouched on the roof of the building next door to his target — five stories of brick and mortar, pockmarked by the bullets and shells of the Americans and the Republican Guard. Now it housed the local offices of Tigris Export-Import, Ltd., Agricultural Chemicals, one of the few companies allowed to trade in the outside world. In the distance stood the towering bronze statues of the 101 martyrs of the holy war against Iran. They were only a few blocks away, silhouettes lining the boardwalk along the canal. After years of inactivity, the canal was bustling again with ships and fishing boats sailing up and down the Shatt al Arab. Their lights blinked reassuringly in the night.

At last, he heard activity at the street entrance. He peered over the parapet. The cleaning crew was strolling off while the foreman locked the door and followed. It was time. Ghassan hooked a thin cable to his harness, took a deep breath, and lowered himself over the edge. At the first row of windows, he used his suction cup and glass cutter to remove a section of glass. He reached in, unlocked the old-fashioned window, and crawled inside. Concealment of his entry was not important; that he finish his assignment undiscovered was.

Moving with speed and silence, he glided past offices and into the next building. Finally he found the office of the Tigris branch manager. Inside, he switched on his tiny flashlight and searched the rows of filing cabinets until he found the right drawer and the right file — Flying Dragon Enterprises, Shanghai. He searched through the documents more slowly than he liked, as all the letters to and from China were in English.

There it was. The fifth document from the front — an invoice manifest. Laboriously, he compared the English list on the document to the list dictated by the quiet American. When he finally determined they were identical, his spirits soared. The manifest was correct. After a moment of exultation, he slid the document into the plastic envelope strapped under his shirt, returned the file to the cabinet, and hurried through the offices to the window. He rehooked the cable, slipped out, and seconds later stood on the roof. As he stuffed his equipment into his small waist pack, he ran down the staircase. At the street, he fell back into the shadows, scanning all around.

A patrol vehicle packed with Republican Guardsmen drove slowly past.

The moment it was out of sight, Ghassan sprinted away. Twice more on his way home he hid as Guards out on patrol rolled by. Finally he reached his tiny room. His adrenaline still pumping, he removed his special cell phone, which was hidden beneath the planks of his floor, and dialed the American's number. He did not know where the American's office was. He had never asked, and the American had never offered.

"So this is how you get your orders, Ghassan? How efficient of the Americans. But then, they have many advantages we do not."

Ghassan jerked around. The speaker's face was hidden in shadow, while the pistol in his hand showed in the room's gloom. "Hand me the phone and the document."

Discovery was something Ghassan feared every day, and he had practiced well to be prepared. Without allowing himself thought or regret, he bit down on the cyanide pill in his tooth and dropped the cell phone to the floor where his foot crushed it into useless pieces. Pain tore through his body. He felt himself falling into a great darkness. As he collapsed, twisting in pain, rage burned through his mind: Death was nothing. Failure was everything, and he had failed.

Chapter
Eighteen

Washington, D.C.
The president's chief of staff, Charles Ouray, wandered around the deserted sitting room in the White House residence. Dawn was breaking, and pale light flowed in through the windows. From time to time, he reached into his shirt pocket for the pack of cigarettes he had given up carrying nineteen years ago when he signed the pledge. In his early sixties, his triangular face was grim, and his movements erratic with tension.

Every five minutes, he checked his watch. As soon as he heard the door to the president's bedroom open, he turned.

Sam Castilla emerged fully dressed and brisk, his large body svelte in a meticulously tailored suit. "When does the ambassador arrive, Charlie?"

"Twenty minutes, sir. He sounded upset. *Very* upset. He emphasized the matter was extremely serious and said you'd know what he was talking about. He wanted an immediate meeting. In fact, he came close to *demanding* one."

"Did he now?"

Ouray was not going to be put off. "Do you, Mr. President?"

"Do I what, Charlie?"

"Know what's got his tail thumping?"

"Yes," he said simply.

"But I don't?"

The president looked uncomfortable but said nothing.

Ouray kept his gaze steady. Sometimes prying information from the president seemed tougher than breaking into Fort Knox. Ouray said thoughtfully, "The leaks are making all of us paranoid. I found myself not telling my assistant about the defense appropriations meeting. Clarence has been with me twenty years. I know I can trust him with my life."

The president sighed heavily. "You're right. I should've told you." He hesitated as if still unsure. Then he grimaced and nodded, his mind made up. "It's all about a Chinese cargo ship by the name of *The Dowager Empress*. It sailed from Shanghai early this month, bound for Basra. We have an unconfirmed report from a highly reliable source that it's carrying tens of tons of thiodiglycol and thionyl chloride."

Ouray stared. His voice rose. "Blister and nerve weapons? The *Yinhe*."

"In a more ambiguous, more complicated, and more dangerous world than the Cold War. Makes one nostalgic for those awful days when it was just two hairy giants with clubs, circling in a primitive face-off. Not a pretty world, Charlie, but it was simple. Now we've got one really big giant, one sick giant, one sleeping giant, and a thousand wolves biting at our heels and ready at any time to go for our throats."

Ouray nodded. "So what's activated the ambassador?"

"They've probably discovered we've got a navy frigate shadowing their freighter." The president was solemn. "I'd hoped we'd have more time." He paused. "I have reason to think Beijing doesn't, or didn't, know about the cargo. A private deal. But that doesn't matter, does it?"

"Unless we can prove it."

"True."

"Can we prove it?" Ouray asked hopefully.

"Not yet. We're working on it."

The two men stood for a time in silence, staring down at their polished shoes, as the president prepared himself. He was about to start dancing the dance he hated. Posturing, threatening, conciliating, verbally fencing, and flat-out lying. Stalling for time. The dangerous diplomacy ballet that could so easily turn deadly.

Finally the president sighed, opened his suit jacket, and hitched up his trousers. "Well, let's go talk to his excellency." He rubbed his hands together. *"Battle."*

In the Oval Office, the president and his chief of staff stood politely before the president's desk as Ambassador Wu Bangtiao entered. The ambassador of the People's Republic of China was a tiny man with the swift, agile stride of the international soccer forward he had once been. He was dressed in a confrontational dark-blue Mao suit, but the smile on his face, while small, was amiable and possibly friendly.

The president caught the mixed message and looked at Ouray through his peripheral vision. Ouray had a small smile himself, and the president knew his longtime confederate had also understood.

"So good of you to see me on such short notice, Mr. President," Wu Bangtiao said with a moderate Cantonese accent, although the president knew he could speak perfect Oxbridge English. He had studied for years at Christ Church and the University of London. "You are aware, I'm sure, Mr. President, of the reason for my sudden alarm." Despite the positive signs, the ambassador did not extend his hand.

The president gestured. "You know Charles Ouray, my chief of staff, don't you, Mr. Ambassador?"

"We have had the pleasure many times," Wu Bangtiao said, an edge to his voice to show he had noticed the change in subject.

"Then why don't we sit down?" Castilla said cordially.

He gestured to one of the comfortable leather armchairs that faced his desk. As the ambassador settled in, the president returned to his large desk chair. Ouray took a straight chair against the wall some distance to the side. Ambassador Wu's feet barely touched the floor; the chair was designed for far taller New Mexican ranchers, which, of course, was why the president had sat him there.

Hiding a smile, the president leaned back and said pleasantly, "As for why you're here, Ambassador Wu, I haven't a clue. Why don't you fill me in?"

Wu's eyes and smile narrowed. "One of our cargo ships on the high seas reports that your frigate, the USS *John Crowe*, has been keeping it under surveillance."

Charles Ouray said, "Are they sure the frigate isn't simply on the same course, Mr. Ambassador?"

Wu's gaze grew icy. He turned it onto Ouray. "Since your warship is far faster than a simple cargo ship but has maintained its current position behind it many hours, the conclusion can be only that the *Crowe* is shadowing the *Empress*."

"I wouldn't say that's the only conclusion," the president said evenly. "May I ask exactly where this ship of yours is?"

"The Indian Ocean." He glanced at the clock. "Or possibly the Arabian Sea by now."

"Ah. And its destination is — ?"

"With all due respect, Mr. President . . . that's hardly relevant. The ship is on the high seas where the right of passage to any port belongs to every sovereign nation in the world."

"Now, Mr. Ambassador, we both know that's hogwash. Nations protect their interests. Yours does. Mine does."

"And what interest is the United States protecting by harassing an unarmed commercial vessel in international waters, sir?"

"That's what I've been trying to tell you, Ambassador Wu. Since I haven't been informed about the *Crowe*, I have no details, not even that your freighter is anywhere near our frigate. But I assume that if you're correct, the situation's the result of some well-known, routine operation by our navy."

"America routinely shadows Chinese ships?"

The president exploded, "That's horseshit, and you damn well know it! Whatever the reason for this alleged shadowing is, I'll find out. Is that all, Mr. Ambassador?"

Wu Bangtiao did not blink. He stood. "Yes, Mr. President. Except that my government has instructed me to inform you that we will protect our right of free passage anywhere and everywhere on the high seas. Including against interference or attack by the United States."

The president stood even more quickly. "Tell your government that if your freighter is violating international laws, regulations, or accepted limitations, we reserve the right to intervene to stop such a violation."

"I will present your view to my government." Wu inclined his head to Castilla, nodded to Ouray, turned gracefully, and stalked out of the Oval Office.

The president studied the door that had closed behind Wu Bangtiao without really seeing it. Charlie Ouray was doing the same thing.

Finally, the president decided, "They don't know what the *Empress* is carrying."

"No. But does that change anything?"

"Normally, I'd say no." Castilla rubbed his jaw. "Only there was more restraint there than I would've expected. You agree?"

Ouray clasped his hands between his legs and leaned forward, frowning. "I'm not sure. That last sounded a lot like the standard warning, the same posturing as usual."

"Pro forma. To be expected. But Wu's a consummate master of the nuance, and I had the impression his delivery this time suggested that the warning was, indeed, pro forma. In fact, he intended it as a hint that he *was* posturing."

"Maybe so. But he knows we were lying about the *Crowe*."

"Of course he does, but there again he let me get away with it. Didn't challenge me, and didn't deliver the formal warning until I'd dismissed him, which forced him to make it or get the hell out with empty hands."

"He didn't come in firing all guns either, that's for sure. But he was definitely wearing the Mao armor."

"His presentation was ambiguous," the president decided. "Yes, that was the message. Beijing, or at least a majority of the Standing Committee, is in the dark. Still, they can't let China be pushed around with the world watching, no matter what the circumstances. On the other hand, I read it that they're not looking for a confrontation. They won't make the situation public, at least not yet. They're giving us a little leeway and some time."

"Yeah, but how *much?*"

"With luck, at least until the *Empress* gets so close to Basra that we have to make a move." The president shook his head unhappily. "Or until the whole thing is leaked, blows up, or falls apart."

"Then we'd damn well better keep it under wraps."

"And get our proof."

"Yeah," Ouray said. "But I have a suggestion."

"What?"

Ouray remained hunched forward as if he had a

sharp pain somewhere in his gut. His aging face seemed brittle. "After listening to you and Wu, I understand even more why this demands tight secrecy. Nevertheless, it's time to bring in Defense Secretary Stanton, Secretary of State Padgett, and Vice President Erikson, because the Chinese government's on to us. That means Stanton and Padgett need to be prepared. And if — God forbid — anything were to happen to you, the vice president will have to deal with this situation. We'd have to bring him up to speed instantly. There might not be time."

Castilla considered. "What about the joint chiefs?"

"For now, it's probably enough that Brose knows. The others could get trigger-happy and complicate things."

"Okay, Charlie. I agree. Set up a meeting. Include Brose."

"Yes, sir. Thank you, sir."

Alone, the president swiveled to the high windows behind his desk. For a few seconds, he saw a little boy in his mind, and he smiled. The boy was like he had been, oversized for his age and with messy straw-blond hair. He was raising his arms up eagerly to a man. The man bent low to pick him up, but the man's face was hazy, out of focus. The child could not see the face, could not see his father.

Hong Kong

Outside Donk & LaPierre's building, Jon dodged through the crowds and traffic and crossed Stanley Street to a Dairy Farm ice cream parlor.

264

Blaring horns and Chinese curses punctuated the air. He ordered a cup of coffee and watched the entrance to the showcase building. When no uniformed guards or civilians came rushing out as if looking for someone, he finished his coffee and hailed a taxi to take him to his hotel.

Still vigilant, he watched all around as the cab wove through the congestion, turned into the tunnel that dove under the harbor to Kowloon, and at last pulled up to the Shangri-la. Once in his room, he dropped onto his bed and used his scrambled cell phone to report to Fred Klein. As usual, Klein was at his desk in the Anacostia marina.

"Do you ever go home, Fred?" Jon pictured the dim office, the shutters and drapes closed, turning day into perpetual night.

Klein ignored the question. "You got there safely, I take it."

"So far, yes." He hesitated, a sour taste in his mouth. "But I've made a mistake."

"How bad?"

"Hard to say." He explained the phone call to Donk & LaPierre. "Obviously, Jan Donk doesn't exist, or the phone number was unlisted, or both. Maybe it was a special number for Yu Yongfu that only he'd know, and it didn't sound like a Chinese entrepreneur."

"It could be a number specifically for the *Empress* deal."

"Whatever, Donk & LaPierre knows someone unauthorized has the number now, is in Hong Kong, and could be interested in the *Empress*. They were worried enough to send armed thugs to the phone booth. Which brings me to the next problem."

"I can't wait." Klein's voice was tired, irritable. "You're sure you're up to this assignment, Colonel?"

"Anytime you want to bring me home, be my guest," Jon growled.

There was a surprised silence. "All right, Jon. Sorry. Merely trying to lighten the situation, which is grim enough back here."

"Trouble on your end?"

"The Chinese have spotted our surveilling frigate. Their ambassador is making waves, if you'll pardon the nautical metaphor."

"Is it out of control?"

"The president thinks not yet. They appear interested only in dancing so far. We both know that won't last. Give me some good news before you depress me even more with the next problem. Did you get anything from your appointment with Donk & LaPierre?"

"Three things. Managing director Cruyff has something in his safe he's worried about, and he's antsy about being questioned over connections to Chinese companies."

"That's two."

"Three is the big one. Someone a lot higher is involved — someone Cruyff reports to, who knows I was in Shanghai and what I look like." He described the meeting and his trip back into the office to eavesdrop.

"It should be simple enough to identify Cruyff's boss in Antwerp."

"Since Cruyff spoke English to him — not

French or Flemish — I don't think he was reporting to Antwerp. No, whoever the boss is, he's here in Hong Kong. My blond wig left Cruyff and him with just enough doubt to move slowly, but sooner or later, they'll send people here to the hotel. I need information about the man on top, so I can gauge what to do."

"In these days of international corporate conglomerates and holding companies, we can't rule out that his Belgium bosses aren't English or American. But all right, I'll get right on it. What will you do now?"

"Food. Something decent for a change. And sleep. A whole night's sleep would be a novelty."

"I'm not sleeping, and neither is the president."

"It's morning there."

"A mere technicality. Take your cell with you, and sleep with it and your pistol under your pillow. I'll get back to you, Colonel. Sweet dreams."

Aloft, En Route to Hong Kong

Ralph McDermid considered the company's top jet — a retrofitted 757 with a gourmet kitchen, cherry-paneled conference room, and sleeping suite — to be his personal transport. In fact, its free use was written into his forty-page employment contract, which, of course, included the usual stock options, monetary incentives, golden severance package, insurance, and use of company cars, cleaning services, club memberships, and houses and apartments around the globe.

He was sitting back, his feet up, lulled toward sleep by the jet's purring engines, when his phone rang. It was Feng Dun.

McDermid was instantly awake. "Where the devil have you been?" he demanded. "I've tried three times to reach you!"

Feng's voice turned cold. "I've been looking and making calls, Taipan."

McDermid was never quite certain whether Feng's use of the old honorific was insulting. He suspected so. In the 1800s, the Chinese had used *taipan* to describe European and American freebooters who took fortunes out of Hong Kong and China and gave little back.

But McDermid needed Feng, so he said only, "What have you learned?"

"Li Kuonyi has disappeared. She was at her father's house, now she's gone. No one knows where. Not her staff, and, of course, no one at Flying Dragon."

That worried McDermid. Now that Yu Yongfu had killed himself, his wife might turn into a loose cannon. It would depend on her level of grief and her concern about their children.

McDermid asked, "Her father doesn't know where she is?"

"So he says. Her children are with him. I'll watch them closely."

"No. Assign your best people instead. I've got something else I want you to handle personally."

"And that is . . . ?"

"Jon Smith. He may be in Hong Kong."

In the distance, Feng clicked his teeth, interested. "This man is like the snake at midnight. He keeps appearing where least expected. You didn't warn me he had such talent."

McDermid bit off a retort. "I suspect he's

looking for the third copy of the invoice manifest. I know the cover he's using and where he's staying. How long will it take you to get to Hong Kong and kill him?"

Chapter Nineteen

Saturday, September 16
Hong Kong

It was an hour before sunrise when the slender Chinese man took the master key from the apron pocket of the night housekeeper and dragged her slack body into the hotel linen closet. The soft, limp flesh was sickening in its inertness, like a sack of rice that had leaked half its contents. He closed the door and locked it.

His name was Cho. He was in his early twenties, looked far younger, and his heart was pounding. Although he was experienced, a professional, the fear never relented, but his adolescent appearance enabled him to go where older men could not. That secured him many well-rewarded assignments, and he always delivered.

Cho ran along the hallway until he found the room number. He inserted the key into the lock and pressed open the door until it caught on the night chain. He listened.

When he heard nothing and no light turned on, he closed the door an inch, inserted a slim home-made instrument, and deftly slipped the chain free.

Returning the instrument to a special pocket in his black jeans, he crept inside the dark room, shut the door soundlessly, and slid to the left.

Motionless, he stood with his back against the wall, waiting for his eyes to adjust. He could feel the warm moisture in the dark air — his prey was in the room somewhere, breathing deeply, asleep. The muffled sounds of night traffic far below penetrated the closed drapes. Otherwise, there was no sound, no movement.

The young killer crept forward. Encased in flexible slippers, his feet made no noise on the plush carpet. He found the bed. The man lay on his back, breathing rhythmically, unaware that in seconds there would be no more rise and fall of his chest, no more breath.

There was a problem: The man was covered by sheets and a blanket. Cho hesitated. Should he strike through the blankets even though he was unsure of the exact position of the man's body, or should he try to pull the covers down as far as the naked and vulnerable chest?

Then he saw the hand. It was the right one, and it dangled out of the sheets and blanket, over the edge of the bed. It was as slack as the corpse of the housekeeper. As he stared, it twitched. He followed the movement up the arm, under the covers, down the shoulders and chest. Smiling to himself, he withdrew a dagger from inside the waistband of his American jeans, held it point down in his fist, and raised it.

Jon had been watching Charles-Marie Cruyff glide closer to him through a viscous mist, a wicked smile on his face, and a sharp dagger between his teeth. An American frigate sailed after Cruyff, but Jon saw it would arrive too late to help. Besides the pirate dagger, the grinning Cruyff had a red bandanna covering his head and forehead and tied at the nape of his neck. He reached the bed, and . . .

. . . Jon opened his eyes a fraction of an inch. He moved nothing else, only his eyelids. He had been dreaming of Cruyff, but the shadow hovering over his bed was not Cruyff. This was no dream. The faint glow of light that seeped under the corridor door showed the shadow as a lean shape, now not two feet away. A hand rose. Jon saw a glimmer of reflected light. A dagger. Saw it suddenly flash down.

His right hand shot up and caught the wrist. The wrist was so thin he thought it might snap in his grip. Then he felt the strength in it. The shadow reared back like a wild animal in terror. In a convulsion of retreat, the whole body attached to the wrist pulled madly back from Jon's grip.

Jon tightened his hand and jerked the wrist toward him to shake the dagger free.

But the dagger did not drop. The hand would not release it. Jon hurled himself up, and the rearing shadow fell to the rear, dragging Jon with him, twisting to be free. His momentum fully backward, the man toppled to the floor.

Jon landed on top with his full weight. Abruptly, the man stopped moving. Panting, naked except for his shorts, Jon suddenly felt the chill of the dark room. He heard the muted noises of distant traffic. His attacker did not move.

Jon kept his grip on the killer's wrist but reached over with his other hand to take the knife. There was no knife. Quickly he felt the carpet around the wrist. No knife there either. But he felt something hot and liquid on his bare chest. There was a faint, metallic stench of fresh blood. Instantly he felt for a pulse in the wrist. There was none.

He jumped up, switched on the light, and drew a sharp breath. The hilt of the dagger protruded from the side of the man's chest, where it must have been jammed as the man twisted when they fell. A small amount of blood seeped into his black shirt.

Jon took a deep breath. And walked toward the phone on the bed table . . . and stopped. There was no way he could call the Hong Kong police. Questions would be asked.

He returned to the corpse and saw that the blood had not yet oozed to the carpet. He lifted the thin body in his arms. It was light as a baby's. He carried it to the bathroom, laid it in the tub, and stood back, considering.

The harsh buzz of his cell phone made him whirl. He hurried from the bathroom and pulled the phone out from his bedcovers.

"Fred? I —" he began.

Fred Klein interrupted, his voice bristling with news: "I have two possible candidates for your mystery man — the one who appears to be more important to Donk & LaPierre than Charles-Marie Cruyff. One is a routine guess, the other quite a different pot of fish."

Jon barely heard. "I just killed a man. He was so small, he looked like an undernourished thirteen-year-old. If I hadn't turned on the light, I never would've guessed he was an adult. He . . ."

The shock was a split second. Then: "Why? Where?"

"He was sent to murder me. Chinese. Here in the hotel."

Klein's shock became alarm. "The body's still there?"

"In the bathtub. No blood on the carpet. We got lucky, didn't we? I got lucky. He nearly had me. Some hungry guy needed their money, whoever the bastards behind all this are, and I got lucky, and he didn't."

"Calm down, Colonel," Klein snapped. Then, almost gently, "I'm sorry, Jon."

Jon took a deep breath and steadied himself. For a moment, he felt disgust for being so eager for an "adventure" to break up the monotony of the biomed conference in Taiwan. "Okay, I'll move the body somewhere. They won't find a trace here."

As he spoke, he heard Klein's opening words in his mind: *I have two possible candidates for your mystery man — the one who appears to be more important to Donk & LaPierre than Charles-Marie Cruyff. One is a routine guess, the other quite a different pot of fish.*

Somewhere deep inside, he felt himself rally. A wave of rage swept through him, and then dull acceptance. For the first time, he saw how crucial it was to him that he believed he was working for something good. How could anyone do this job otherwise?

He asked briskly, "Tell me about the 'routine' candidate for Cruyff's big boss."

"That'd be Louis LaPierre," Fred Klein said.

"He's the chairman and managing director of Donk & LaPierre worldwide. He's in Antwerp, speaks English, but at the same time is a thorough-going Belgian Walloon. His first language would certainly be French, and his second Flemish. It's highly unlikely he and Cruyff would converse in English."

"Of course, in Hong Kong almost everyone speaks English. It might've been because Cruyff and LaPierre didn't want lesser mortals in Antwerp to overhear."

"The possibility occurred to me, too."

"Who's the second candidate?" Jon asked.

"That's where it gets interesting. As it turns out, my financial and corporate experts found a maze of fronts, subsidiaries, and offshore companies masking who ultimately owned Donk & LaPierre itself. Finally, they were able to discover that — big as it is — Donk & LaPierre is a wholly owned subsidiary of a far larger entity, which turns out to be the source of my second candidate: the Altman Group."

"Never heard of it."

"You probably have," Klein assured him, "but you had no reason to pay attention. Most people don't. Altman employs expensive publicity people to keep it off the front pages. However, Altman's famous . . . almost mythical . . . in global business circles."

"I'm listening."

"It's a multiproduct, multinational conglomerate . . . but it's also the planet's largest private equity firm. We're talking about making and breaking enormous fortunes daily. Now figure in

Altman's executives — insiders from the past four presidential administrations, including a former president, a former secretary of defense, and a former CIA chief. That's not all. Altman Europe is run by a former British prime minister, with a former German finance minister as second in command. Altman Asia is led by a former Philippine president."

Jon whistled. "Talk about a golden Rolodex."

"I've never heard of another company with so many political stars on the payroll. Altman's global headquarters is in Washington, which isn't particularly unusual. However, its address is more gold — on Pennsylvania Avenue, midway between the White House and the Capitol. Only a fifteen-minute walk either direction."

"And a stone's throw from the Hoover building," Jon decided, seeing the geography in his mind. "Hell, it's at the very center of the Washington establishment in all ways."

"Exactly."

"How could I *not* know about Altman?"

"As I said, an iron hand when it comes to general publicity."

"Impressive. Where did it come from?"

"What I'm about to tell you is public information. Anyone could find it, but since Altman keeps such a low profile, few people care. The company started in 1987, when an ambitious federal employee quit his job, borrowed a hundred thousand dollars, and brought in his first political celebrity — a retired senator. With that marquee name, Altman started growing. It bought up companies, held some, and sold others, always for decent

276

profits, sometimes for obscene ones. At the same time, it attracted bigger and bigger names for its letterhead. Today, its political clout and door-opening ability is impressive, to say the least. It's a thirteen-billion-dollar empire, with investments of all sorts around the world. Hell, they've probably got something going in Antarctica, too."

"So what you're saying is Altman's basically a giant financial holding company." Jon considered where it fit into his assignment. "Are the Asian headquarters here in Hong Kong?"

"They are."

"Does the Philippine ex-president speak nothing but Tagalog and English?"

"No, he's fluent in at least six languages, including French and Dutch. But he's not in residence there now. Hasn't been for months. He's at a health spa in Sweden. We checked, and he hasn't had any calls from Hong Kong in weeks."

"Then who *is* the second candidate for Cruyff's boss?"

"Ralph McDermid, the investment guru who founded the company."

"McDermid? Then where did 'Altman' come from?"

"It was his father's first name," Klein explained. "Altman McDermid. He was a failed businessman — lost his drugstore in the Depression when he was just starting out, rebuilt it, but lost it again in the 1960s when a big Walgreen store came into the little town in Tennessee where they lived. He never worked again. His wife supported the family by cleaning houses."

Jon nodded. "Could be Ralph McDermid's

trying to make up for what happened to his father. Or he's scared to death it'll happen to him, so he's building a stockpile against disaster."

"Or he's such a financial genius he can't help himself." Klein paused. "Ralph McDermid is in Hong Kong right now. He's an American, speaks nothing but English."

Jon let that sink in. "All right, I get the picture, but what the hell would Ralph McDermid care about the *Empress*? It's just one ship. It seems damn small potatoes for that kind of powerhouse megalith he's running."

"True. But our information is solid: The Altman Group owns Donk & LaPierre, and Donk & LaPierre are equal owners with Flying Dragon of the *Empress* and its cargo. What I need from you — instantly, if not sooner — is that third copy of the manifest. Check into Ralph McDermid. See if you can tie him to the *Empress,* and see if he has the third copy."

Friday, September 15
Washington, D.C.

President Castilla paused to find the exact words to convey both the gravity of what he was about to reveal and the justification for holding back as long as he had. He gazed around the highly secure situation room in the basement of the White House, at the five men who sat on either side of him at the conference table. Three looked mildly puzzled.

"Obviously, since we're meeting here," he told them, "you know there must be some kind of serious situation. Before I describe it, I'm going to apologize to three of you for not bringing you into the loop sooner, and then I'm going to explain why I don't have to apologize."

"We're at your disposal, Mr. President," Vice President Brandon Erikson said. He added sincerely, "As always." Wiry and muscular, Erikson had sable-black hair, regular features, and a casual, Kennedyesque air that voters found disarming. A youthful forty years old, he was renowned for his dynamic personality and energy, but his true strength was his brisk intelligence, which hid political acumen far beyond his years of experience.

"What situation?" Secretary of Defense Stanton wanted to know, suspicion in his voice. He turned to stare around the table, the overhead light making his bald head gleam.

Secretary of State Abner Padgett asked, "Do I gather Admiral Brose and Mr. Ouray already know what you intend to tell us?" His voice was deceptively quiet, but his eyes flashed at the insult. His meaty frame lounged in his armchair, unconsciously displaying his natural self-confidence, the same self-confidence that Castilla relied on over and over again to send into hot spots around the world to cut hard deals and soften hard hearts. Padgett was the best man to dispatch on a touchy diplomatic mission. Contrarily, he had a short fuse at home.

"Admiral Brose had to know," the president snapped and glared at them. "I told Charlie only this morning, so he could call this meeting. Your reactions are precisely why I don't have to apologize. There are entirely too many overblown egos and personal agendas in this cabinet and administration. Worse — and all of you know this is the un-varnished truth — some folks are talking to people they shouldn't, about subjects they shouldn't. Do I make myself clear?"

Henry Stanton flushed. "You're referring to the leaks? I hope that isn't intended to apply to *me*, sir."

"I *am* referring to the leaks, and what I said applies to everyone." He fixed his glare on Stanton. "I decided that in this situation no one would be told, except on a need-to-know basis. *My* need for them to know. Not yours. Not anyone else's either. I stand by that." His jaw was rock hard. His mouth was grim. His gaze was so flinty as it swept over them that, at that moment, his face could have been carved out of Monument Valley stone.

The vice president was conciliatory. "I'm sure we understand, Mr. President. Decisions like that are difficult, but that's why we elected you. We knew we could trust you." He turned to Stanton and Padgett. "Don't you agree, gentlemen?"

The secretary of defense cleared his throat, chastened. "Of course, Mr. President."

"Absolutely," the secretary of state said quickly. "He has the facts."

"Yes, Abner, I do, such as they are. And now I've made the decision that it's time to bring you in." He leaned across the table, his hands clasped. "We have a possible repeat of the *Yinhe* debacle with China."

As they stared, riveted, their alarm growing, he described what had happened so far, leaving out any specific reference to Covert-One and to the man who claimed to be his father. As he talked, he could see they were already considering how the situation might impact their departments and responsibilities.

When he finished, he nodded to the vice president. "I do apologize to you, Brandon. I should've brought you in sooner, in case anything happened to me."

"It would've been better, sir. But I understand. These leaks have made us all leery. Under the circumstances, with secrecy so vital, I probably would've acted similarly."

The president nodded. "Thank you. I appreciate that. Now, let's discuss what each of us must do to prepare in case this does escalate and we're forced to go public without proof and stop the *Empress* on the high seas."

Admiral Brose spoke up. "We need to assess what China will do next, now that they've spotted our frigate. We should also figure the size of a conflict like this into our military plans and appropriations."

Secretary of State Padgett agreed. "We must think about not only conflict with China, but what we can do to take a strong posture of deterrence."

"The Cold War all over again?" the vice president wondered. "That'd be a tragedy." He shrugged unhappily. "But at the moment, I see no alternatives."

Charles Ouray said, "We've got to keep this information confined to those of us here. Is that understood? If the *Empress* problem leaks, we'll know it's one of us."

Around the table, heads nodded solemnly, and the discussion resumed. As the president listened, a part of his mind began counting — two, four, one, two, two, and one. Among the six men there, they had twelve children. He was surprised that he was aware how many children each had. Surprised, too, that, when he thought about it, he remembered their names. Abner's youngest had him stumped.

But then, he could recall the children of most of the other people he had worked with over the years. Knew their names a lot of the time, too. For only an instant he wondered what that meant. Then he knew. . . . In his mind, he could see that little boy again, reaching up to the faceless stranger.

There was a pause in the conversation, and he realized they were waiting for him to say something. "State needs to get ready to go into high diplomatic gear. Defense needs to figure out what we've got that we can use to scare the shit out of China. The navy needs to come up with alternate plans to board and inspect the *Empress*." He slammed his hands on the table and stood up. "End of discussion. That's all, gentlemen. Thanks for coming."

Chapter
Twenty

Saturday, September 16
Kowloon

In his hotel room, Jon put on gloves, searched the young man's pockets, and found a master key, a few coins, and a pack of gum. He put everything back, including the key, and checked the corridor. Deserted. He carried the corpse to the fire stairs landing. The steps reached far up and far down in silence. He climbed two flights and propped the body against the wall of the stairwell.

The dagger still protruded from the emaciated chest. He pulled it out. With the wound open, blood flowed like the Yangtze. Sighing, he left the knife beside the killer and returned downstairs.

Once more in his room, he propped a chair against the door, in case someone else with a master key and a way to flip the chain lock had ideas. Last, he scrubbed the tub and scrutinized the floors and furniture, including the bed. There was no trace of blood, and nothing had been dropped.

With relief, he took a shower. In the steaming

water, he scrubbed until his skin glowed, forcing his mind away from the dead man and into the future. As he toweled off, he made plans.

At last, he returned to bed. He lay awake for some time, trying to calm his disquiet as he listened to the occasional night sounds of the hotel, the scattered noise of traffic, and the mournful horns of ships and boats in the harbor. All the sounds of life in a busy city on a busy planet in a busy galaxy in a busy universe. An indifferent universe, and galaxy, and planet, and city.

He listened to the beating of his own heart. To the imagined sound of blood flowing through his veins and arteries. To sounds heard nowhere but in his own mind. Sometime before daybreak, he fell asleep again.

And jerked awake once more. He sat bolt upright. Out in the corridor, the wheels of a room-service cart ferried an early breakfast to someone. The first rays of morning showed around the drapes, while city noises rose and crescendoed. He jumped out of bed and dressed. When the assassin did not report in, and he did not reappear — whether or not the body had been found and the police called — another assassin would eventually be sent.

Fully dressed in the same suit, fresh shirt, and new tie, he selected items from his suitcase — his backpack, a pair of gray slacks, a gaudy Hawaiian shirt, a seersucker sport jacket, canvas running shoes, and a collapsible Panama hat. His black working clothes were already in the backpack. He packed everything else in, too, including his folding attaché case.

Finally, he put on his dirty-blond wig and adjusted it in the mirror. He was Major Kenneth St. Germain again.

After a final survey of the room, he left, carrying the suitcase and wearing the backpack. The carpeted corridor was still empty, but behind the doors, televisions had been turned on, and people were moving.

Jon rode the elevator down to the floor above the lobby and took the stairs the rest of the way. From the doorway, he scanned the lobby east to west, north to south. He saw no police, no one who acted like police, and none of the killers from yesterday. There was no one he recognized from Shanghai. Still, none of his precautions guaranteed no one was waiting.

He stood out of sight another ten minutes. At last, he crossed to the registration desk. If he left without checking out, the hotel might notify the police, especially since it was only a matter of time until the corpse upstairs was discovered. While he waited for the bill, he asked the bell captain to call a taxi with an English-speaking driver, to take him to the airport.

The cab was barely out of sight of the hotel when Jon leaned forward from the backseat: "Change of plan. Take me to Eighty-eight Queensway in Central. The Conrad International Hotel."

Dazu, China

A thousand years ago, religious artists carved and painted stone sculptures into the mountains, caves, and grottos that surrounded the rural village of Dazu. Now a metropolis of more than eight

285

hundred thousand, Dazu had terraces of well-maintained rice paddies as well as high-rise buildings, small farmhouses nestled among trees, and mansions surrounded by formal landscapes. The soil and climate of the green, rolling land were favorable for city gardeners and suburban farmers, who grew as many as three crops a year, most still using the methods of their ancestors.

The prison farm was less than five miles from the giant Sleeping Buddha, carved at Baodingshan. Secluded and isolated, the prison was a sprawl of frame buildings and walkways, locked behind a tall, chain-link fence that had raised platforms at each corner for the armed sentries. The dirt road that led to it was never traveled by tourists or city people. Inmates, who worked in fields and paddies operated by the distant Beijing government, were marched to and from work by armed guards. They had little contact with locals. Light as the confinement and security appeared, China did not coddle those it branded criminals.

The old man was one of the few inmates excused from the fields and morning march. He was even allowed some privileges, such as the cell — almost a normal room — he shared in the barrack with only one other prisoner. His offense was so long ago that neither the guards nor the farm's governor remembered what it was. This ignorance left them nothing specific to condemn him for, nothing easy to cause hate or fear, nothing long-standing to punish and feel righteous about. Because of this and his advanced age, they often treated him like a grandfather. He was given treats and a hot plate, books and newspapers, pens and writing paper. All illicit, but known to and ignored by the usually stern governor, a former PLA colonel.

This made it more disconcerting to the prisoner when very early in the morning, even before breakfast, his Chinese cell mate vanished to be replaced by a younger, non-Chinese man. He had been brought in at dawn, and since then he had been lying on his sleeping pallet. His eyes were usually closed. Occasionally, he stared up at the unpainted barrack ceiling. He said nothing.

Frowning, the old man went about his activities, refusing to let this abnormality interfere with his routine. He was tall and rangy, although on the thin side. He had a rugged face that was once handsome. Now it was heavily lined, the cheeks sunken, the eyes set in hollows. The eyes were intelligent, so he kept them downcast. It was safer that way.

That morning, he went to his clerical assignment in the governor's office as usual, and, when lunchtime arrived, he returned to his cell and opened a can of Western lentil soup, heated it on the hot plate, and sat alone at his plank table to eat.

The new prisoner, who was perhaps fifty, had apparently not moved from his pallet. His eyes were closed. Still, there was nothing restful about him. He had a tough-looking, muscular body that never seemed completely at rest.

Suddenly he jumped lightly to his feet and seemed to flow to the door. His face had a gray stubble that matched his iron-gray hair. He opened the door and scanned the barrack, which was empty because most of the inmates ate beside the fields.

He closed the door, returned to his pallet, and lay down again as if he had never moved.

The old man had watched with a kind of envy mixed with admiration and regret, as if he had once been as athletic as that and knew he could never be again.

"Your son can't believe you're alive. He wants to see you."

The longtime prisoner dropped his spoon into his soup. The younger man's voice had been soft and low, yet somehow carried clearly to his ears. The newcomer stared calmly up at the ceiling. His lips had not moved.

"Wha . . . what?"

"Keep eating," the motionless man said. "He wants you to come home."

David Thayer remembered his training. He bent to his soup, lifted a spoonful, and spoke with his head down. "Who are you?"

"An emissary."

He sipped. "How do I know that? I've been tricked before. They do it every time they want to add to my sentence. They'll keep me here until I die. Then they can pretend nothing ever happened . . . I never existed."

"The last gift you gave him was a stuffed dog with floppy ears named Paddy."

Thayer felt tears well up in his eyes. But it had been so long now, and they had lied to him so many times. "The dog had a last name."

"Reilly," the man on the pallet said

Thayer laid down his dented soup spoon. Rubbed his sleeve across his face. Sat for a moment.

The man on the floor remained silent.

Thayer bent his head again, hiding his lips from anyone who might be watching. "How did you get in here? Do you have a name?"

"Money works miracles. I'm Captain Dennis Chiavelli. Call me Dennis."

He forced himself to resume eating. "Would you like some soup?"

"Soon. Tell me the situation. They're still not aware of who you are?"

"How could they be? I didn't know Marian had remarried. I didn't even know whether she and Sam were alive. Now I understand she's dead. Terrible."

"How did you find out?"

"Sam's visit to Beijing last year. I get the newspapers here. I . . ."

"You read Mandarin?"

"Washington wouldn't have sent me if I weren't fluent." Thayer smiled thinly. "In nearly sixty years, I've become expert. In many of the dialects, too, especially Cantonese."

"Sorry, Dr. Thayer," Captain Chiavelli said.

"When I read about Sam's visit, his name jumped out, because Serge Castilla had been my closest friend at State. I knew he'd been helping in the search for me, too. So I did some calculations. President Castilla was exactly the right age, and the paper said his father was Serge and his mother Marian. He had to be my son."

Chiavelli gave an almost invisible shake of his head. "No, he didn't. It could've been a coincidence."

"What did I have to lose?"

The Covert-One agent thought about that. "So why did you keep quiet until now? You've waited a full year."

"There was no chance I'd ever get out, so why embarrass him? And why risk Beijing's finding out and vanishing me completely?"

"Then you read about the human-rights treaty."

"No. It won't be announced in the Chinese papers until it's signed. The Uigher political prisoners told me." Thayer pushed the soup bowl away. "At that point, I allowed myself to hope. Maybe there was a chance I'd be overlooked among the crush of releases and accidentally let go." He stood up and walked to his hot plate.

Chiavelli watched with half-closed eyes. Despite Thayer's advanced age — he had to be at least eighty-two, according to Klein — he walked energetically, steady and firm. His posture was erect but relaxed. There was a spring to his step, now, too, as if he had shed years in the fifteen minutes they had been talking. All of this was important.

Routine had saved Thayer's sanity. He picked up a chipped enamel kettle, carried it to the scarred sink, filled it, and put it on the hot plate. From a little cupboard, he brought out two chipped cups and a tin canister of black tea. His method of making tea was an unusual mixture of traditional English and traditional Chinese. He poured the boiling water into the earthenware pot, rinsed it, poured it away, then measured in four teaspoons of tea. He immediately poured more boiling water onto it and let it steep less than a minute. The result was a pale, golden-brown liquid. The pungent aroma filled the cell.

"We drink this without milk or sugar." He gave Chiavelli a cup.

The undercover agent sat up and leaned back against the wall, cradling it.

Thayer sat at the table with his. He sighed. "Now I'm beginning to believe getting out because of the treaty is just the pipe dream of a man at the end of his years. They've held me in secret far too long to admit that they've held me at all. It'd make their human-rights record look even more despicable."

Chiavelli drank. The tea was light-bodied and mild for his Italian-American palate, but it was hot, a welcome improvement to the underheated barrack. "Tell me what happened, Dr. Thayer. Why were you arrested in the first place?"

Thayer set down his cup and stared into it as if he could see the past. When he looked up, he said, "I was working as a liaison with Chiang Kaishek's organization. My job supposedly was to bring about some kind of detente between his Nationalists and Mao's Communists, so I thought it'd help the process along if I personally went to Mao and reasoned with him." He gave a smile that was half grimace. "How ludicrous. How *naive*. Of course, what I didn't see was that my real mission was to keep Chiang in power. I was supposed to make deals, hold talks, and stall until Chiang could destroy Mao and the Communists. Going to Mao was the quixotic notion of an inexperienced intellectual who believed people could talk rationally together even when power, values, cultures, ideas, classes, haves, have-nots, and geopolitical spheres of influence were in conflict."

"So you really did it? You actually went to see

Mao *alone?*" He sounded both amazed and horrified.

Thayer gave a thin smile. "I tried. Never got to him. His army decided I was an agent of the West, or of Chiang, or both. Of course, they arrested me. I would've been shot by the soldiers, if Mao's politicians hadn't intervened because I had diplomatic status. Over the years, I often wished I had been shot on the spot."

"Why did they report you dead and then hold you like the Soviets held Wallenberg?"

"Raoul Wallenberg? You mean the Soviets *did* have him?"

"Denied they did, never released him, and for fifty years continued denying they ever had held him. He died early on, in custody."

Thayer seemed to sag. "I expect what happened to me was what happened to him. They couldn't believe he was nothing more than he appeared. That's the direct result of paranoia, the kind that happens when anyone who speaks out is ruthlessly suppressed. At the time I was captured, the Communist revolution was sweeping China. There was such chaos . . . endlessly changing commanders, new civilian orders, confounding proclamations, and bureaucrats who had no idea what was going on. I think I must've been simply lost in the machinery. By the time Zhongnanhai stabilized, it was too late to send me home without creating an international incident and losing face." He turned the warm cup between his gnarled fingers. "And here they intend for me to stay. Until I die."

"No," Chiavelli said firmly. "What happened to Wallenberg isn't going to happen to you. You won't die in captivity. When the treaty's signed, China will release all political prisoners. The president will make a point of bringing you to the attention of Niu Jianxing and the rest of the Standing Committee. I've heard he's called the Owl, because he's a wise man."

David Thayer shook his head. "No, Captain Chiavelli. When that treaty is signed by the general secretary and my son, I will have been conveniently 'lost' again. If my son pushes too hard and makes an issue at this late date, no one will ever find me. Instead, a hundred old men will appear and claim to have witnessed my death a half century ago. There'll be assorted proofs. Probably pictures of my grave that is now, alas, deep underwater behind some new dam." He shrugged, resigned.

Chiavelli studied him. The Covert-One agent was a former special forces captain who had operated in Somalia and the Sudan. Recently, he was called back into action in the valleys, caves, and mountains of eastern and northern Afghanistan. Now his new assignment was David Thayer. His first question was whether Thayer could be extracted.

He had surveyed the immediate area and found it encouraging. It was sufficiently rural and remote, if not sparsely populated — nowhere in China, except for Xinjiang, Gansu, and the Mongolias, was sparsely populated. Outside Chongqing, the roads were bad, military installations scattered, and airfields primitive. Fortunately for his assignment, outside Dazu, they were largely nonexistent.

The camp guards were well armed, but they lacked sharp discipline. Their resistance to a swift, heavily armed, and well-planned raid would likely be minimal. With some help from inside, which he planned to provide, and a certain amount of good luck . . . experienced raiders could be in and out within ten minutes, back in the air within twenty, and more than halfway to the border and safety before significant military force could be assembled.

The big question now was Thayer's stamina. So far, Chiavelli liked what he saw. Despite his age, he seemed in decent condition.

"How's your general health, Dr. Thayer?"

"As good as could be expected. The usual aches, pains, discomforts, and annoyances. I'm not going to leap tall buildings or climb Mount Everest, but they keep us in shape here. After all, there are fields to be plowed."

"Calisthenics, jogging, walking, working out?"

"Morning and evening calisthenics and jogging, when the weather's good. Minimal calisthenics in the barracks, when it isn't. The governor likes to keep everyone busy when we're not working. I do clerical work, of course. He doesn't want us to sit around and plot or get into arguments. Inactivity leads to thinking and restlessness — a dangerous combination in a prisoner." Thayer hesitated. He sat up straighter. His faded eyes narrowed as he turned to stare at Chiavelli. "You're thinking about getting me out of here somehow?"

"There are considerations. Constraints. Not just your health, but what my boss thinks and what the president can and can't do. You understand?"

"Yes. That was my life. Politics. Interests. Diplo-

294

macy. Those forces are always at work, aren't they? The same 'considerations' that made State keep me ignorant about what we were really doing back in 'forty-eight. That and my naïveté got me into this mess."

"The Chinese won't keep you here much longer, if I have my way. And I think I will."

David Thayer nodded and stood. "I have to go to work. They'll leave you alone for now. Tomorrow, you'll go to the fields."

"So my friendly guards tell me."

"What's your next move?"

"I make my report."

Hong Kong

In a pricey boutique in the Conrad International Hotel, Jon bought a white Stetson hat, using the credit card for one of his covers — Mr. Ross Sidor from Tucson, Arizona. He put on the hat, checked into the hotel, and overtipped the bellman so he would remember Mr. Ross Sidor. As soon as Jon was alone in his room, he went to work: He changed into the gray slacks and neon-bright Hawaiian shirt from his backpack. Over the shirt and slacks, he put on the suit he had worn yesterday to Donk & LaPierre. It was tight but manageable. Finally, he added the blond wig again and shoved his Beretta into his belt at the small of his back.

Ready to go, he packed the blue seersucker sport jacket, canvas running shoes, folded Panama hat, and backpack into his black attaché case. He picked it up and left the room.

He saw no one suspicious in the lobby. Outside on Queensway, he walked deeper into Central, carried along by the mob of pedestrians that seemed to live their entire lives on the streets of the city. He had gone a block when he spotted three of the armed men who had searched for him around the public phone in Kowloon yesterday. As soon as they saw him, they spread out through the traffic and pedestrians. They made no attempt to close in; he made no effort to lose them.

He also did not try to disguise his destination. If they recognized him as Major Kenneth St. Germain, they might be surprised and, he hoped, confused to see him return to the high-rise that housed Donk & LaPierre.

When he spotted the building, he shoved through the crowds to the entrance. As he went inside, his three tails took up posts across the street, one talking urgently into a cell phone. Jon smiled to himself.

Altman Asia occupied the top ten floors of the building. The head of Altman Asia was Ferdinand Aguinaldo, the former president of the Philippines. His office was even higher — the penthouse. Jon took the elevator up.

The waiting area was decorated with green bamboo, tall carved tables, and high-backed chairs and sofas.

The Filipina receptionist smiled politely. "May I help you?"

"Dr. Kenneth St. Germain. I'd like to see Mr. Aguinaldo."

"His excellency is not in Hong Kong at this time, sir. May I inquire why you want to see him?"

"I'm here on behalf of the surgeon general of the United States to consult with Donk &

LaPierre's biomedical subsidiary on mainland China and its research into hantaviruses." He showed his USAMRIID credentials and flashed a fake letter from the surgeon general's office. "Mr. Cruyff downstairs sent me up to talk to Mr. Aguinaldo."

The receptionist's eyebrows raised, impressed. She studied the surgeon general's signature and looked up. "I'm sorry that Mr. Aguinaldo isn't here to receive you, sir. Perhaps Mr. McDermid can help. He's chairman and CEO of the Altman Group worldwide. He's a very important man. Perhaps you could speak with him?"

"McDermid is here?" Jon said, as if he knew the CEO and chairman personally.

"On his annual visit," she said proudly.

"McDermid will do. Yes, I'll see him."

The woman smiled again and opened her interoffice line.

Lawrence Wood stepped inside the elegant penthouse office of Ferdinand Aguinaldo, head of Altman Asia.

"What is it, Lawrence?" Behind the big desk, Ralph McDermid stretched and yawned.

"The receptionist says a Dr. Kenneth St. Germain has arrived with a letter from the U.S. Surgeon General. He wants to see Aguinaldo. He says Cruyff down at Donk & LaPierre sent him up, and she wonders if you'd care to meet the man, since he has such good credentials."

McDermid said, "Tell her I'll be free in fifteen minutes."

Wood hesitated. "Cruyff couldn't have sent him."

"I know. Just give her the message. On the other hand, I'll do it myself."

"As you wish." Wood frowned and returned to his outer office.

McDermid touched his intercom button. He was feeling more cheerful. With the strange arrival of Jon Smith, things were looking up. "I'd be delighted to see Dr. St. Germain," he told the receptionist. "Ask him to give me fifteen minutes, and then I'll be down." As she gave her usual pert reply, he severed the connection and dialed his man, Feng Dun. "Where are you, Feng?"

"Outside." Again Feng cursed Cho, the assassin chosen for the night. He had failed to eliminate Smith, and his corpse had not been discovered in time to send a replacement. "My men saw him go in. Did he return to Donk & LaPierre?"

"No. He's up here in the penthouse lobby. He wants to see me."

"*You?*" A moment of shock. "How does he know you're even in Hong Kong?"

"One wonders. I'm fascinated. I think we're lucky he survived your killers. I want to learn more about this unusual doctor's sources."

Chapter
Twenty-One

Beijing

To Major Pan Aitu, the small office of Niu Jianxing — the legendary Owl — was intriguing. As ascetic as a monk's cell, it had unadorned walls, shuttered windows, a worn wood floor with no rug, a simple student desk and chair for the master himself, and two wood chairs for visitors. At the same time, the desk and the floor were clogged with haphazard piles of files and documents, ashtrays stinking with masses of half-inch butts of the English cigarettes that were Niu's one indulgence, stained tea mugs, food-encrusted paper plates, and other detritus that indicated his days were long and intense. It was a contradiction that mirrored the man himself.

As a longtime intelligence agent, Major Pan was an astute reader of the intricate maze of individual psychologies, and so he enjoyed himself while Master Niu continued to read the report he had been bent over when Pan arrived. The only sound was of Niu's turning over sheets of paper.

Major Pan decided the office displayed the serenity of the solitary thinker, as well as the cluttered turmoil of the man of action, fused together in the same person. Yes, the Owl was a throwback to those giants who had founded and led the revolution. Poets and teachers who became generals. Thinkers who were forced by the necessity of history to brawl and kill. Pan had known only one of those revered ones — Deng Xiaoping himself, in his extreme old age. Deng had been but a young general back in the idealistic years between the Shanghai Massacre and the Long March. Major Pan did not like many people. He found it a waste of time. But there was something about Niu Jianxing that appealed to him.

Niu, true to form, broke the silence without looking up, a hint of rush in his voice. "General Chu tells me you have a report he would have you give me directly."

"Yes, sir. We thought it best, considering your request for information on the cargo ship."

"*The Dowager Empress*, yes." Niu nodded down toward his paperwork. "You have what I want?"

"I may have some of it," Pan said, cautiously. He had learned to use extreme care when making claims or promises to leaders of the government, especially to those on the Standing Committee.

Niu Jianxing looked up sharply. His decidedly unsleepy eyes were hard points of coal behind his tortoiseshell glasses. His sunken cheeks and delicate features showed displeasure. "You don't *know* whether you have it, Major?"

The intelligence agent felt a moment of emptiness. Then: "I know, Master Niu."

The Owl sat back. He studied the small, pudgy Major Pan, his little hands, his appeasing voice, his benevolent smile. As usual, Pan was dressed in a conservative Western suit. He was the perfect operative — slippery, anonymous, clever, and dedicated. Still, for all that, Pan was also a product of the Cultural Revolution, Tiananmen Square, and a too-rigid system that left little room for the individual. Plus, there was the five-thousand-year history of China that valued the individual even less. If Niu continued to push for a yes-or-no answer, the spycatcher would say no rather than give a positive statement that could be construed as a declaration of success. If he were to know everything Major Pan had learned about the *Empress* before the Standing Committee met later today, he would have to let him tell it his own way.

Niu repressed a sigh of frustration. "Make your report, Major."

"Thank you, master." Pan explained who Avery Mondragon was and described his disappearance the day before Jon Smith arrived in Shanghai.

"You believe this Mondragon is, or was, an American intelligence agent?"

Pan nodded. "I do, but not an ordinary one. There's something unusual about the Americans involved in this case. They act like undercover spies, yet they're not spies. Or at least not affiliated with any of the intelligence agencies we know of in the United States."

"That would apply to Colonel Smith — the doctor and scientist — also?"

"I believe so. His scientific work isn't a cover. He really is a medical doctor and scientist. At the same time, he appears to be using his specialty as a cover."

"Interesting. Are these American operatives private? Perhaps working for a business or an individual?"

"It's possible. I will continue to seek an answer."

Niu nodded. "It may be of little practical significance. We shall see. Go on, Major."

Pan warmed to his report. "A cleaning woman discovered the body of a man named Zhao Yanji in the office of the president of Flying Dragon Enterprises in downtown Shanghai. Flying Dragon is an international shipping company with connections in Hong Kong and Antwerp."

"Who was Zhao?"

"Flying Dragon's treasurer. Not only is he dead, the company president is missing, as is his wife. The president's name is Yu Yongfu. His wife is Li Kuonyi."

"The beautiful actress?"

"Yes, sir." The major related the rapid rise of her husband into wealth and power with the apparent help of her father, the influential Li Aorong.

The Owl did not know Li Aorong personally but by reputation. "Yes, of course. Li is high up in Shanghai's municipal government." What he did not say was that Li was also the protégé of Wei Gaofan, one of his hard-line colleagues on the Standing Committee. All things considered, Wei was the most powerful of all the hard-liners, and Li Aorong's politics were identical to Wei's.

"Yes," Pan acknowledged. "We spoke with Li. He has no explanation for the murder of Zhao or the disappearances of his daughter and her husband. But —" Pan moved forward, perching on the edge of the straight chair, as he explained about An

("Andy") Jingshe, the young interpreter who had studied in the United States and who was seen in Colonel Smith's company. Later, Andy was found shot to death in his car. "That is, so far, what we know."

The Owl's expression was somber behind his large glasses. "An American in Shanghai disappears. Colonel Smith arrives the next day. The treasurer of a shipping company is murdered. The president of that company and his wife vanish. And an American-educated Shanghainese interpreter is killed that night. Is that your report?"

"With the addition that when we finally located Colonel Smith again, he evaded us, fled, and has apparently gotten out of China altogether."

"We can speak of that later. When does my request for information about the cargo ship, *The Dowager Empress*, appear in your report?"

Pan sat back, chastised. "Flying Dragon Enterprises is the owner of the *Empress*." He should have said that earlier.

"Ah." Niu's chest tightened. So that was the connection. "You have formed an opinion of these events?"

"I think that after Yu Yongfu acquired Flying Dragon, his treasurer discovered something he didn't like, something that concerned the United States. He leaked it to Mondragon, who took the information to the Americans. Or tried to. Something went wrong. Mondragon was most probably killed and the information lost. Smith was sent in to retrieve it. Also, it seems to us that Andy Jingshe was an American asset assigned to guide and interpret for Smith."

The minister pursed his lips, thinking. "There-fore . . . people in our country — not our security forces — are willing to go to extremes to stop the Americans in their quest, whatever that quest is. The information the treasurer discovered, and Smith's attempts to find it again, led to the death of the treasurer, the disappearances of Yu Yongfu and his wife, and the murder of the interpreter."

"Something along those lines, sir. Yes."

Niu's sense of foreboding increased. "What do you think the treasurer found at Flying Dragon that has ignited this dangerous uproar?" He reached for a cigarette.

"I had no thoughts about that until you asked for information about the *Empress*. That was when I learned she was part of Flying Dragon's fleet. I don't know what prompted your inquiry, but the connection to the case of Colonel Smith can't be a coincidence."

"I asked for information about the freighter, its destination, and its cargo. Which is everything there is to know of such a ship."

"Yes, sir."

He lit his cigarette and inhaled uneasily. "What have you found?"

"The destination is Basra. It's scheduled to ar-rive in the gulf in approximately three days."

"Iraq." Niu shook his head. He did not like that news. "What's the cargo?"

"According to the manifest on file, it's carrying DVDs, clothing, industrial products of various types, farm implements, agricultural supplies — the usual load one would expect to be going to Iraq. Nothing special. Certainly nothing that should interest the Americans." As the counter-intelligence agent concluded, he watched the Owl with a question in his eyes.

"Yet the Americans are interested. Very interested," Niu said, turning the question back on Pan. He was not about to inform the major of the emergency that was brewing about the freighter. Thus far, only the Standing Committee and Ambassador Wu in Washington knew. He hoped to resolve it before it exploded into a crisis. "You have a thought about all of this, Major Pan?"

"If, as I now suspect, the *Empress* is involved, it can be only because of the cargo."

"Therefore, you think the official manifest filed by Flying Dragon is false, and the Americans know this."

"What other conclusion could there be?"

The Owl inhaled. He blew out smoke. "Did Colonel Smith get what he came for?"

"That we don't know."

"That is what I *must* know, Major. *Immediately.*"

"We will find Yu Yongfu, question his father-in-law, and investigate Flying Dragon."

Niu nodded. "Now tell me how Colonel Smith evaded you a second time, without speaking our language or having been in China before, and then escaped the country . . . after his interpreter was killed?"

"We think he had help from a cell of the Uigher resistance. My people are searching for them now, but they hide among the old *longtangs,* as hard to catch as rats in a sewer. The police don't take them seriously enough, largely because they're so few. Consequently, they've gone unregulated. Like the

305

rat, they're smart, adaptable, and determined."

"Obviously there aren't as few as we'd like," Niu said. "How did they help Smith?"

"They took him into the *longtangs* and hid him, and then they managed somehow to get him out again. After that, we have only hints. A police roadblock recalls letting a party of Uighers in a Land Rover pass through. Two of the Uighers had long-standing residence papers for Shanghai, and anyone with official passes like that, of course, can move about freely. Later, many shots were heard on a Huangzhou Bay beach between Jinshan and Zhapu. And this morning, one of our patrol boats reported a submarine identified as American surfaced offshore soon after the gunfire ceased."

Niu was silent. He smoked. At last, he nodded. "Thank you, Major Pan. Continue the investigation as a top priority."

Major Pan looked reluctant to leave, as if he wanted to resolve all of these questions here and now, but he was also a well-trained government man. He stood up, his stubby body erect.

He straightened his European suit jacket. "Yes, sir."

Niu put out his cigarette as the agent closed the door behind him. He leaned back and rocked on the back legs of his chair. He contemplated the question of what was so important that the Americans would risk not only sending a submarine within a few thousand yards of China's coast, but dispatching a guided-missile frigate to shadow the *Empress*. The situation had a sour taste.

Shaking his head with worry, he thought about the gunfire on the beach and about the ambitious

Li Aorong, who apparently had helped his son-in-law to great business success. Then Niu contemplated what he could not tell Major Pan, or General Chu Kuairong, or anyone else in the government or the Party: He was secretly making every effort to open up China to all of the opportunities the world offered.

Melancholy swept over him. He remembered how, when he was a young man, Chairman Mao had spoken eloquently of his yearning for the open, simple days before 1949, when all he had to do was write poetry and fight the enemies of China. After that, he was trapped in the hidden, dirty, and convoluted machinations of governmental interests and power.

What Niu wanted at the moment — the signed human-rights agreement — could lead to a better life for everyone. Still, he suspected the treaty had far more opponents in the public sector than it did supporters. But then, that was because so many high officials were opposed . . . on both sides of the ocean.

Hong Kong

A polite smile on his face, Jon Smith settled into one of the high-backed chairs in the penthouse lobby outside the Altman office suite. He had heard Ralph McDermid tell the receptionist he would see him. As he waited, he clicked open his attaché case as if to check his notes.

Abruptly, he slammed the lid closed and jumped up. "Damnation! I'm sorry. Didn't mean to swear, miss. I must've left my notebook down at Donk & LaPierre." He glanced at his watch and then at the polished grandfather clock that stood in a corner. "McDermid's coming to meet me in fifteen minutes. I'll be back in ten."

Before she could protest, he ran, carrying his attaché case to the elevators. He punched the button and stepped into the car, which was empty. As the doors closed, he smiled and waved back at the startled woman. He had little time and silently urged the elevator to hurry. He got off two floors below and rushed along the corridor until he found a public restroom. Once inside a stall, he peeled off his outer suit and put on the light-blue seersucker sport jacket, the blue canvas running shoes, and the collapsible Panama hat from his attaché case. With his gray slacks and Hawaiian shirt, he had the gaudy appearance of an American tourist with more money than taste. He packed the suit into the attaché case, and the attaché case into his backpack. He put on the backpack and slipped out the door.

Thinking about what he suspected he would find, he stepped onto a different elevator and faded into the rear as businesspeople entered and left at several of the floors, heading down. When the car at last reached the mezzanine, he pushed his way through the packed passengers, who were continuing down to the lobby.

He got off the elevator. The inner wall of the mezzanine was lined with glass doors into expensive boutiques, travel agencies, and office shops. The outer wall was no wall. It was a marble parapet that rose to waist height, interspersed with thick pillars supporting the floor above. The parapet overlooked the vast lobby. Jon stood in the cover of a pillar, where he could see the marble stairs that swept up to the mezzanine, the bank of elevators, and the building's entrance.

Jon waited impatiently. Suddenly the man he had hoped to see was there — the big Chinese who had led the attack in Shanghai. *Feng Dun.* He was pushing in through the lobby's glass doors, followed by three men Jon also recognized. For the first time, he got a good look at Feng: He was so pale his skin seemed to be bloodless. His close-cropped hair was a light red with patches of stark white. He was shorter than Jon had thought when he saw him in the dark. Still, he was tall for a Han, maybe six-foot-three, and muscular — not an ounce more than two hundred pounds. He paused just inside the doors and surveyed the lobby as if searching for something — or some-one.

Ralph McDermid put his patented genial smile on his face and walked out of the private pent-house elevator. He paused to gaze around the re-ception area for Dr. Kenneth St. Germain.

Except for the receptionist, the luxurious room was empty. She stared in awe.

He frowned at her. "Where is he?"

"Er, Mr. McDermid. I'm very sorry, sir, but Dr. St. Germain rushed downstairs to pick up his notebook at Donk & LaPierre. He'll be right back." She glanced at the clock. "Oh, my. He said he'd be gone just ten minutes, but it's fifteen al-ready. Should I call to see what happened?"

"Yes. But ask only whether he's there now or was there. That's all. Don't speak to him or have him sent up." It was possible the man could have gone to Donk & LaPierre for some reason.

She called, asked her questions, and ended the connection. She looked at McDermid in confusion. "They say he's not there and never was. Not even earlier."

Behind McDermid, the elevator doors opened. As McDermid turned, Feng Dun stepped out. Feng held a 9mm Glock that looked small in his big hand.

The receptionist's eyes grew large and frightened as she took in his appearance. Her gaze froze on the Glock.

Feng's whispery voice asked, "Where is he?"

"Gone," McDermid said, disgusted. "He left fifteen minutes ago."

"He's still in the building," Feng said flatly. "We've been watching. He can't leave. He's trapped."

Jon was on edge, his shoulders tight, his muscles aching to fight. Still, he remained hidden behind the mezzanine pillar, studying the lobby below.

After Feng Dun had instructed his three gunmen, he entered an elevator. The numbers above the door indicated it had shot straight up to the penthouse. Even though Jon had already guessed, he was still shaken: It looked increasingly probable that Ralph McDermid had stalled Jon upstairs so he could summon these killers. Which meant the chairman and CEO of the mighty Altman Group was likely not only a player in the *Empress* crisis but was intimately involved in the bloody aspects of it.

Beneath Jon, the three hunters took up unobtrusive positions, where they could cover all exits. When Feng Dun returned, he did not so much stride from the elevator as appear as if by magic, suddenly there on the lobby floor. He made a subtle gesture close to his hip, and the four converged on a corner behind potted palms. As they conferred, they observed everyone who passed through. Feng glanced up at the mezzanine once and seemed to fix his gaze on where Jon stood in the shadow of the column.

Jon stepped slowly back. He checked his disguise, from the Hawaiian shirt to his blue tennis shoes. He tugged the Panama hat lower over his forehead and slipped his Beretta into the small of his back under the seersucker jacket. As he headed for the staircase, he bent his knees a fraction of an inch and aimed his toes inward, giving him a faintly prissy walk.

He did not look at the killers, although each glanced at him. He found himself stiffen with tension, waiting for one to decide he was worth stopping. As he passed them and closed in on the glass doors that opened onto the street and safety, he could feel someone's gaze hot on his back. He pushed through the glass doors, waiting to be stopped.

When he was not, he felt a moment of surprise, then relief. As he walked out of the building and crossed the street, the daylight seemed particularly bright and welcoming. He took up a position in the shadows and waited.

Chapter
Twenty-Two

It was nearly dark when Ralph McDermid finally left the building through a side door, although Feng Dun and his hunters had emerged hours before, one at a time, and scattered as if on assignments. Because the Hong Kong crowds had swollen with the evening rush to go home, Jon did not hang back. During the afternoon, the humidity had broken, and the struggle through the mass of pedestrians was easier.

Frustrated and worried, he hurried to keep the CEO in sight. McDermid walked only as far as the Central station of the M.T.R., the subway. Jon waited twenty seconds, bought a ticket, and followed. There were fewer people on the platform, and Jon paused, making certain no one else surveilled the CEO — either surreptitiously or as a hidden bodyguard.

When the train came, McDermid entered a car, and Jon slipped on behind, through a second door. McDermid wove forward until he found a space he liked on one of the stainless steel benches. He sat and stared into space, making eye contact with none of his silent, weary fellow passengers and ignoring the colorful advertisements, all of which were in Chinese, very different from the days before the island returned to mainland China's control and commercials appeared in English as well.

Jon moved in the opposite direction and grabbed a pole, his back half turned, where he could catch McDermid in a window reflection. He found himself wondering why anyone of McDermid's position and wealth was riding the subway. Not going far? Not wanting to use company cars or personnel in another man's empire? Tired of the pandemonium and pressure of the streets? Cheap? Or, more likely, he wanted no one, not even a chauffeur or taxi driver, to know where he was going.

The ride was remarkably quiet and smooth. McDermid never bothered to gaze around, apparently unconcerned that he might have picked up a tail. He got off a couple of stops later, at the Wanchai station. Jon waited until the last moment again, when the CEO was already some forty feet away, to squeeze out through the closing doors. He hurried out to Hennessy Road, where McDermid was ambling along, looking relaxed. McDermid led him through Wanchai, Hong Kong's former red-light district. Once notorious for sex and drugs, the area had fallen on hard times. The result was that the city's booming financial district had invaded. New high-rises clustered together, and the newest and best hotels asked and received more than three thousand dollars a night for rooms.

Hands in his pockets, McDermid strolled down neon-lighted Lockhart Road, where most of the remaining sex trade was. Here, Wanchai still lived down to its tawdry reputation. Wanchai girls loitered at bar doors and gave a well-rehearsed *pssst* to any man who looked as if he could pay. There were gaudy hostess clubs, topless bars, discos, and raucous English and Irish pubs. The signs and the spielers, the neon and the come-ons were still loud and bright here, broadcasting the delights inside for the hungry and the lonely.

But the beat was gone. Neither he nor McDermid gave more than a glance at the tarnished pleasure shacks, while Jon again wondered where McDermid was headed — and why.

At last, the CEO turned into a side street and then into a brick office building in the shadow of a spanking new higher-and-shinier, glass-and-steel monolith of offices. The street was narrow. Vendors assembled their gear. A few stores offered peep shows and porn, tattoos and adult toys. At the same time, a steady stream of middle-class office workers and executive types left the brick building on their way home to the darkening hills and suburbs, a reflection of the cultural schizophrenia that Wanchai had become.

His curiosity growing, Jon used the exiting stream as cover and slipped inside. In the marble-lined lobby, Ralph McDermid stood facing a row of filigreed elevators. When a car emptied a small river of people, he walked inside, the only passenger, since everyone else was leaving. Again Jon watched the numbers of the floors light up on the indicator above the door. McDermid's car stopped on the tenth then returned down.

Jon stepped into another car and pressed the

button. At the eleventh floor, he rushed off and ran down the fire stairs two at a time. Finally on the tenth, he peered out into a twin of the empty, marble-lined corridor above. Where had McDermid gone?

Jon jerked back when three women left one of the offices and headed toward the elevators, chattering in Chinese. Flattened against the stairwell, he listened, mystified, wishing he had learned the language.

Before he could look out again, other footsteps clattered along the marble floor and stopped at the elevator, where the three women were still talking. More doors opened and closed, and the unseen corridor was silent again . . . except for a rustling that passed directly outside his door.

Jon cracked it open and peered out. Dressed in the black pajamas and conical straw hat of a rural peasant, a Chinese woman disappeared through the door at the very end of the hall. *But where was McDermid?* As he was about to go looking, he heard what he thought was the CEO's voice from somewhere to the right, beyond the elevators. He gave a grim smile, pulled out his Beretta, and padded into the corridor.

He listened at each door. All were identical — cheap and hollow-core, with steel mail slots and name plaques that announced the businesses housed inside, everything from accountants to start-up Web site companies, dentists to secretarial services. Muted voices sounded from behind several, and a radio station from one. He was beginning to worry that he had somehow lost McDermid when he heard him again.

He slowed. The muffled tones were coming from the other side of a door that proclaimed in Chinese and English: DR. JAMES CHOU, ACUPUNCTURE & SHIATSU. It appeared that Ralph McDermid indulged in acupuncture or shiatsu massage or both. But why did he go to the trouble of taking the subway here and then the long walk? McDermid was a physically soft man. Or was he here for a different purpose? Perhaps this was a front for an old-fashioned "massage parlor."

As Jon thought that, he dropped low and peered in through the mail slot. The reception area was sparsely furnished, with cheap molded-plastic chairs and tables. The couch was overstuffed and had bamboo arms and braces. Magazines in both Chinese and English lay on the tables and couch. The waiting room was deserted. So where was the voice coming from? Had he been wrong?

Weapon in hand, he turned the knob and crept inside. That was when he saw the second door. McDermid said something from the room on the other side of it.

Jon had begun to smile to himself when suddenly there was complete silence. The talk had stopped in the inner office. Two people — McDermid and the doctor or the masseur — should make some sound . . .

Jon's chest tightened as a new answer occurred to him. There was another reason McDermid might take the subway and walk. McDermid could have expected to be followed. He could have expected Jon. The unpleasant truth was . . . McDermid could have lured him into an ambush.

Jon spun, dove to the floor, and skidded behind the couch, his Beretta ready.

The hall door flew open, latch and hinges ripping, and crashed to the floor in a shower of splinters. Two of his earlier tails slammed through the opening, pistols preceding them.

Jon squeezed off two rounds. One of the men fell onto his face and slid across the linoleum floor, leaving a slash of red blood. The other flung himself backward out of harm's way, into the hall again. Jon's bullet had missed him.

Jon snaked forward on his elbows. The second man darted into view again, gun aimed at the couch. Jon was halfway toward the door, where the gunman had not expected him to be. Jon fired once. This time there was a grunt of pain, a curse, and the man fell back.

Warily, Jon reached the shattered doorway and positioned himself low but where he could rise to see along the hall toward the elevators and where anyone trying to enter the reception room through the second door would have to be fully inside before they could focus on him and shoot. Ahead in the hall, two men bent over a third, who sat against the wall. Blood pooled at his side, where Jon's shot had connected. They glanced angrily back at the office where Jon hid and watched.

Jon scrambled up, ran to the couch, laid it on its cloth side, and pushed it to the doorway. He positioned it to cover his flank and dropped to the floor again.

He could hear the sounds of feet outside in the corridor, trying to be quiet. His hunters were moving in. He made himself stay down. He counted off ten seconds, raised up, and dropped one with a single shot as he burst in, low to the floor.

As the cry of pain echoed against the marble walls, the office's other door blasted open and shots slammed into the couch's bamboo and stuffing. Jon fell flat, waiting. His heart ticked into his ears. Finally, a man jumped through the door and into the room, a tiny submachine gun in his hands. Jon fired off a bullet. The man catapulted back against a large window and crashed through, his scream receding as he dropped from sight.

Jon raised above the couch again to check the hall. They were closing in — three this time. He fired twice, and they scurried back, but for how long? They would try again from the inner room, too. He had another clip, but eventually they would coordinate better, attack simultaneously from both doors, and that would end it. He would be killed or captured. He was unsure which they wanted.

Sweat broke out on his forehead. On one knee, he waited for the next assault from the inner office. Without warning, they barreled through. There were two now. They moved faster and were cleverer, diving to either side, while he had to remain alert in case those in the hall attacked simultaneously. He emptied his gun, spraying the chairs, tables, walls. He slammed in his last clip — and they were gone.

Or were they? Abruptly, more shots exploded, shook the walls. But from where? The hall or the inner office? And where were the bullets? Nothing hit the couch where he crouched, and nothing slammed into the waiting room. Should he drop or remain kneeling? As another fusillade erupted, he realized the noise came from out in the hall. Oddly, they were not shooting at him.

He raised up and looked. There were four of them, including the two from the inner office. The fifth and sixth — both injured — lay in one of the elevators, the doors jammed open. The remaining four hunters were firing *away* from him, toward the opposite end of the corridor. Abruptly, one turned and shot back, trying to keep him pinned down.

He returned fire, rising and dropping. Suddenly there was swearing, scrambling, and the slam of a door as heavy feet raced away. He listened. An elevator door closed. There was silence from both the corridor and the inner room. *Were they really gone? Or was this another damn trick?*

Cautiously, he leaned out to look. The hall was empty in both directions. The old building creaked. Somewhere on another floor, a toilet flushed. Jon inhaled. He wiped his sleeve across his forehead as he studied the motionless man he had shot, who still lay sprawled on the floor of the waiting room. He crab-walked to him. The man was dead, and his pockets carried nothing that would identify him.

Disappointed, Jon jumped up and sped into the inner office. There was a massage table, a cabinet, a chair, and a portable radio-and-CD player. Everything had been riddled with gunfire. Wind whistled through the broken window through which one of the men he had shot had crashed. Below, sirens screamed. The Hong Kong police were on their way.

There was a second door in here, too. It stood open into the hall. He sprinted toward it and gazed carefully out. The corridor was still deserted, blood and bullet casings making a trail to the elevator. Beretta in both hands, he moved toward the elevators, too, swinging the pistol front and back, covering the passageway, as he continued past and reached the last door in the hall, the only other one that was open. It faced the length of the corridor.

Beretta up, he rolled around the doorjamb and pointed. In his sights was the Chinese peasant woman he had seen earlier from his hiding place in the stairwell. Still dressed in her black pajamas and conical straw hat, she sat cross-legged on the floor, her back against a rolltop desk. There was a cell phone at her side. Both hands aimed a thoroughly nonpeasant 9mm Glock at him.

"Who are you?" he demanded.

Still keeping her Glock aimed at him, her voice was irritated as she said in perfect American English, "So this is the answer. Your goal in life is to screw up my operations. Your timing stinks." But she smiled.

"Randi?"

"Hi, soldier." She lowered her weapon.

He stared as he put his away. "Unbelievable. The CIA just keeps getting better at their disguises." So this was where the other gunfire had originated. Randi had created the diversion that had saved him.

She uncoiled from the floor and rose to her feet in a single motion. "Do I hear sirens?"

"You do. We'd better get the hell out of here."

Beijing

The scent of camellias floated in from the lush garden at Zhongnanhai as Niu Jianxing — the Owl — leaned back, listening angrily to the discussion at tonight's special Standing Committee meeting. All of his intellect was being required to keep his program on track in the face of the *Empress* crisis. He could not allow his bad temper to show.

"First the American spy, who has, it seems, been allowed to escape," Wei Gaofan complained. His fierce, temple-dog scowl made his usually unsmiling face seem almost kindly. "Now this American warship — what is it? the *John Crowe?* — invading our rights on the high seas! It's an *outrage!*" It was the hawk party line.

"Exactly how did Colonel Smith escape?" Song Riuyu, one of the younger members of the Standing Committee, asked.

Niu said calmly, "That is being investigated as we speak."

"How is it being investigated?" Wei Gaofan demanded. "Are you forming one of those endless, pointless committees like the Europeans do?"

Niu's voice was suddenly sharp. "Are you volunteering for that committee? If so, I can certainly form one and would be honored to add your name . . ."

"You have the confidence of us all, Jianxing," corpulent Shi Jingnu purred in his smooth, silk-merchant's voice.

The general secretary intervened: "These matters concern all of us. I, for one, need answers to both questions. Are the Americans just waving the

321

Roosevelt big stick, or are they actually sharpening their Kennedy swords?"

"A full report on the escape of Colonel Smith will be in your hands tomorrow," Niu promised.

"And their frigate shadowing our cargo ship?" The secretary glanced down at the papers before him on the long table. "*The Dowager Empress,* is it?"

Niu nodded. "That's her name. She's owned by Flying Dragon Enterprises."

He cast a swift glance toward Wei Gaofan, because the son-in-law of one of his closest protétgés was the president of Flying Dragon. Still, Wei showed no particular interest — or even a reaction — to Niu's statement.

Niu continued, "She's registered in Hong Kong. I have completed an investigation of Flying Dragon and learned it's operated by one Yu Yongfu in Shanghai, and that the *Empress* is en route to Basra, Iraq." There was still no reaction from Wei. At the least, he should be offering his observations if not the information that he knew Yu Yongfu.

"Iraq?" questioned Pao Peng, the secretary's old Shanghai partner, suddenly becoming alert.

"What is its cargo?" Han Mengsu, another of the younger men, demanded.

"The actual cargo seems to be in dispute," Niu said. He explained the possible connection of Lieutenant Colonel Smith to the *Empress.* "Smith came to Shanghai looking for something."

"What does the manifest say the cargo is?" Wei Gaofan questioned.

Niu recounted the innocent cargo listed on the official manifest.

"Well, there you are," Wei Gaofan said angrily. "As usual, the American bullies are throwing their weight around to impress their own people, as well as Europe and the weaker nations. It damn well is another *Yinhe*, and this time we absolutely can't permit them to board. We're a strong, independent nation, far larger than the United States, and we must put a stop to their warmonger politics."

"This time," Niu insisted, "there really could be contraband material aboard the *Empress*. Do *we* want such material to reach Iraq, especially without our knowledge or permission?" From the corners of his eyes, he continued to carefully observe Wei, not wanting him to become suspicious that he knew about Wei's connection to Flying Dragon. The information would prove useful at some point. But not yet. As far as the Owl was concerned, patience and knowing when to act were the keys to success in all things.

"On what is that conjecture based?" Shi Jingnu demanded, his unctuous tone uncharacteristically absent.

"Colonel Dr. Smith is an unusual man to send as an agent. The only reason I can think is that he was in Taiwan and was that rare American who could get into China immediately by invitation. Whatever he actually came for had to be vital *and* time urgent."

The general secretary pondered. "And you suggest that his mission could be to discover the truth about the *Empress*'s cargo?"

"That would qualify."

"Which," Wei Gaofan declared, "makes it all the more imperative the Americans are not allowed to interfere with it. If the charges are true, we would be exposed to the world."

"Even if we had no knowledge and were innocent?" Niu asked.

Shi Jingnu said, "Who would believe that of China? And if they did, would we not appear weak and vulnerable? Not able to control our own people and in need of American oversight?"

Song Riuyu looked grave. "We may have to show our power this time, Secretary."

Pao Peng nodded, one eye directed at the general secretary. "At least, we should plan to match them threat for threat."

"A standoff?" the secretary mused. "You may be right. Who agrees?"

From behind his half-closed eyes, Niu Jianxing counted the hands. Seven. Two were raised a little lower and less certain than those of Wei Gaofan, Shi Jingnu, and Pao Peng. The secretary did not raise his hand, but that was irrelevant. He would not have called for a vote had he been opposed.

Niu had a formidable task ahead if he were to save the human-rights accord. He did not like to think what else might need to be saved, if, during the standoff, someone pulled a trigger.

Chapter
Twenty-Three

The Arabian Sea

In the clear air of late morning in the southern Arabian Sea, the day's heat was beginning to build as Lieutenant (jg) Moses Canfield leaned on the aft rail enjoying the fresh air before he went below for his watch in the communications-and-control nerve center of the *John Crowe*. The *Empress*, which they had been shadowing for close to twenty-four hours, was hull up on the horizon, still making a steady course for Basra. Only the officers knew where the *Empress* was heading and what she was supposed to be carrying, and they had been ordered to tell no one. The secrecy somehow made Canfield's nerves worse. He had found it difficult to sleep last night.

Now he was reluctant to go below. He had always been a little claustrophobic, which had prevented him from considering the submarine service, and his imagination was working overtime. He imagined himself trapped belowdecks as the *Crowe* absorbed a direct missile hit and plunged to the bottom within seconds, taking everyone with it. He shivered in the day's growing heat and told himself to get a grip.

His nervousness had not been helped by the firm lecture from Commander Chervenko about waiting patiently and alertly when shadowing a ship until one was sure it was really changing course and not simply going on a brief side venture.

"Never jump to conclusions about the actions of the enemy, Lieutenant," Chervenko had told him. "Get information before committing your ship. Put yourself in the other man's position and consider what he would do. Finally, always be sure of your identifications."

"Aye-aye, sir," Canfield had answered. He was mortified and a shade angry at the commander.

The touch of anger, as it so often did, refocused Canfield's mind and, at least temporarily, chased away his claustrophobia as he looked at his watch, turned from the rail, and hurried below to his post in the cramped communications-and-control center.

Radar man OS2 Fred Baum was leaning back in his chair, drinking a Diet Coke. There had been nothing on the screen except the *Empress* since late yesterday. The *Crowe* was in action, and the excitement of pursuit, which had sustained Canfield's people for most of the last twenty-four hours, was exhausted. Now they faced another day with only a blip on the radar or, when on deck, a distant silhouette. Boredom was becoming a danger.

Canfield decided to give them a version of the captain's lecture. "All right, people, let's shape it up. The *Empress* skipper could make a move any damn time. Don't jump to conclusions about the

326

actions of another ship. It all may look routine, but she can turn on you in a second. We can't be sure what the Chinese have aboard or what they have in mind. They might have a big gun or missiles, too. Always think every second about what could be in the mind of the enemy skipper."

"Aye-aye, sir."

"Sorry, Lieutenant. You're right."

"Wish they'd do some damn thing."

"You can say that again."

"I mean —"

"Hold it!"

The shout came from OS2 Baum at his radar monitor. For a long moment, no one reacted. At first, the warning seemed nothing more than another comment in the stream of weary complaints about inaction.

Almost in unison, they turned to look.

"Report, Petty Officer!" Canfield snapped.

"I've got something!" Too excited to remember to say sir when talking to Canfield. "I think it's a *new bogey!*"

"Take it easy, Baum." Canfield leaned over his shoulder. "You *think?*"

Baum pointed to a tiny dot that appeared and then disappeared at the edge of the screen, astern of the *Crowe*. "It's damn low in the water, Lieutenant. A real small profile."

"Where?"

"Dead astern."

"How far?"

"Maybe fifteen miles."

Canfield turned his head. "Radio?"

"Nothing, sir."

Canfield bent again. The blip had vanished. "Where's it gone?"

"It's still there, Lieutenant. Like I said, it's low, so it gets obscured by the running sea. Trust me, it's there and coming closer."

Canfield was having difficulty spotting it as the radar arm swept around. "You sure it's not some weather anomaly? Maybe a surface disturbance?"

"Yessir, I'm sure." Still, Baum craned, not quite as certain as he claimed. "It's just damn small."

"But coming closer?"

"Yessir. I mean, we're hanging back, matching that tub up ahead."

Canfield knew the *Empress* could do only fifteen knots at top speed, and that was pushing it.

"Damn!" Baum peered at the sweeping screen. "Now it's out of sight again." He looked up at Lieutenant Canfield. "But I know I saw it, sir. It was there, and moving —"

"Lieutenant!" Sonar Technician First Class Matthew Hastings bellowed.

"What, Hastings?"

"I've got it, too. Dead astern!" Hastings held up earphones.

Canfield clapped one phone to his ear. "How far astern?"

"Right where Freddy's bogey was."

Canfield turned his head. "Baum?"

"Still nothing on radar yet, sir."

Canfield glared at Hastings. "How fast?"

"Twenty knots, maybe twenty-two."

"Whale?" It was a possibility. A big whale, logging on the surface.

Hastings shrugged. "Could be, but they don't usually swim so fast unless they're scared. Wait!" The sonar technician cocked his head as if the motion could make him hear more clearly. "Propellers, sir. It's got an engine."

Canfield's voice rose. "You're sure?"

"Shit, Lieutenant. It's a *sub*. Closing in on us!"

All talk was cut off as if someone had pressed the mute on a TV remote. Silence enveloped communications-and-control like a cocoon. Canfield hesitated. It had to be the same bogey as the one Baum had spotted on the radar — a sub running with only its conning tower above the surface. Now it had dropped off the radar screen because it had submerged. Would it have dived if it did not intend to attack? Commander Chervenko's words reverberated inside his head — *be sure before you act, be very sure*.

"Can you identify the sub, Petty Officer?"

"No, sir." ST1 Hastings sounded uneasy. "Single screw, I'm sure of that. The engine's quiet, but kind of ragged. I'm getting a resistance signature I never heard before." He listened for a time. "It's not ours. I can guarantee that."

"Conventional or nuclear?"

"Nuclear for sure, but not Soviet. I mean, not Russian. I know what those suckers sound like. A small sub, attack type, nuclear."

"British, maybe?"

Hastings shook his head. "Too small. Doesn't sound right for that." He glanced up at the lieutenant again. "If I had to guess, from what I learned in training, I'd say it's an old Chinese Han class. They got new ones in the works, but I ain't

329

heard they launched any. Besides, it's got the burred sound of an old design."

The silence hung heavier as Hastings continued to listen. "It's closing in, Lieutenant."

"How far."

"Ten miles."

Canfield nodded. His lungs felt squeezed. Still, he shouted, "Sparks? Call the bridge! *Pronto!*"

On the bridge, Commander Chervenko said quietly to Lt. Commander Bienas, "You have the bridge, Frank. Better clear for action. Everyone to their posts. I'm going below."

"Aye-aye, sir."

Chervenko slid down the gangway, entered communications-and-control, and nodded to Lieutenant Canfield. "Tell me, Mose."

Canfield filled him in on everything that had happened from the moment OS2 Baum had spotted the small blip on his radar.

"All right. Are we sure it's Chinese?"

"Hastings can't identify it as anything else so far."

"I've had some experience with a Han class, maybe —"

ST1 Hastings looked up. "Captain! She's slowing down!"

Commander Chervenko moved in to stand behind the sonar technician. "How far back, Hastings?"

"Five, six miles, sir." The first-class petty officer's eyes stared into some empty, distant place as he concentrated all his senses on his hearing. "Yeah, definitely slowing, sir."

"You hear any activity?"

Hastings concentrated. "No, sir. Just the screw. It's at a way lower speed."

"Matching us?"

He looked up, impressed by the commander's accurate prediction. "Yessir, I'd say that's exactly what she's doing."

Chervenko nodded. "Shadowing the shadower."

The technicians glanced uneasily at one another.

Chervenko turned to Canfield. "Keep on top of it here, Mose. Report any change, no matter how small. I want to know if they hiccough back there."

"Aye-aye, sir."

"I'll be in my quarters. Tell Frank on the bridge."

Chervenko left the electronics-crammed center and hurried to his cabin. He dialed his secure phone again.

The big voice on the far end of the line boomed, "Brose."

"This is Commander Chervenko on the *Crowe*, Admiral. We've got some company out here. You're not going to like it."

Hong Kong

When Jon thought back over the past few years to how much his life had changed since the Hades virus had killed his fiancée and had been on the verge of a world pandemic, one of his few pleasant constants had been her sister, Randi Russell. Although he seldom saw Randi, since she was usually in the field, they sometimes found themselves in the Washington area at the same time. They had a standing arrangement to leave a message on the other's answering machine. When they connected, they would have drinks, dinner, and dancing — but their dancing was almost entirely verbal, because neither could divulge their espionage activities.

Covert-One was such a highly secret organization that he could not mention its name, much less that it existed. At the same time, she usually could say nothing about her Langley missions, which took her around the world. Occasionally, they found themselves involved in similar assignments, such as when Jon had convinced her, Peter Howell, and Marty Zellerbach to help him stop the terrifying geopolitical threat caused by Émil Chambord's futuristic DNA computer.

Instead of returning to the corridor where so much shooting had happened only moments before, Randi opened a side door in the office. They ran across a storage area to another door that opened into another corridor. Their first priority was to get out before the police arrived. The sirens in the distance were growing louder, closer.

"Thanks for the diversion," he told her. "They were closing in on me."

"Always glad to help a pal." Her American voice from the Chinese face was unnerving. The CIA had done a remarkable job of turning a citified blond Caucasian into a black-haired Chinese peasant.

"Where are we?"

"Same building," she told him, "but a different wing. It's the old English style of office construction. It kept the 'lifts' and corridors from being too crowded."

This wing was quiet after quitting time, too. They rushed into an elevator and headed down to the ground floor — and then down one more level toward the basement.

As the elevator clattered, Jon said, "Impressive how well you know this building."

She glanced at him. "Research."

"So my problem upstairs was impacting your assignment."

She said innocently, "Ralph McDermid not only likes acupuncture, he's been panting after the girl who gives the shiatsu massage. This time, he seemed to have more than needles and flirtation in mind. You must've activated him somehow. Could there be something not on the up-and-up in the Altman Group's China installation?"

"How do you know those gunmen were here for me? Maybe I bumbled into a trap set for you. The CIA doesn't tail private American citizens for the fun of it. Langley must suspect McDermid's up to something against our interests."

The dance had begun. They looked away from each other as the elevator stopped and the door opened onto a storage basement, complete with the stink of dampness and the scurrying noises of rats.

"Why in the devil were you tailing McDermid?" Her voice was half aggravation, half resignation. The perfect Chinese mask of her face remained impassive.

To reveal his investigation into the *Empress* would encourage her suspicions about his Covert-One activities. He needed to tell her something plausible. She might not believe him, but she would be in no position to accuse him of lying. He decided the same story he had given Charles-Marie Cruyff would have to do.

As she led him through a dim maze of cellar rooms, he explained, "I was at a biomedical convention in Taiwan for Fort Detrick when I ran into a fellow from Donk & LaPierre's field lab in China. What he described was intriguing, so I caught a flight to Hong Kong, hoping to get permission to take a look at his work. The lab's honcho, Cruyff, sent me to McDermid, who I guess is his boss. McDermid's been impossible to pin down, so I tailed him and stumbled into this hornet's nest."

"Right." Randi shook her head. "And I'm here for the noodles."

He thought he heard her chuckle. He said, "Far be it for a humble scientist to inquire into a CIA field operation."

"You always hang around office mezzanines in a Hawaiian shirt, straw hat, and running shoes, when you want a professional, scientific favor? Probably for the same reason you carry a Beretta and extra ammo. Oh, gosh, wait a minute. I'll bet you planned to put a gun on him to convince him to be nice."

So she had either been watching him deliberately, or they had crossed paths because of the similarity of their missions. "In case you haven't noticed," he said blithely, "Hong Kong's miserably hot. Of course I wear Hawaiian shirts. As for the Beretta . . . remember, my final destination was mainland China. I arranged with the Pentagon for

334

permission to carry, because the field lab's in a remote area — bandits and all."

He had managed to turn her suspicions into an innocent story. In fact, all of it could be true. But he knew her well; she would not drop this. She would find harder, more probing questions. It was time to distract her and to get out of the building.

He nodded at cement stairs ahead. "Those for us?"

"Clever of you."

Again, she led the way, bending so her tall hat did not catch on the low ceiling as she climbed. At the top, she pushed open a slanting door and slid out. He followed, lowering it quietly behind. She was already moving away. He fell in beside her. They were in a narrow alley that smelled of urine and charcoal. Moonlight reflected off the grimy brick-and-stone walls.

Five minutes later, they were in a taxi heading back toward Central.

"Where do I drop you?" Randi asked. She pulled off the hat, shook out her black wig, and sat back.

"The Conrad International," Jon said. "Listen, everything I told you was true, but there's a little more —"

"What a surprise, dearie."

He shot her a look. "USAMRIID thinks there's something fishy going on at Donk & LaPierre's Chinese lab. Maybe they're conducting research, doing experiments that'd be illegal in the States, and putting government grant money intended for basic research into applied research to develop commercial pharmaceutical products."

"I expected something like that. So you're here investigating?"

Jon nodded. "I won't ask exactly what the CIA's interest in McDermid is, but maybe we could share anything we find not directly related to our own assignments."

Randi turned away, looking out the window. She was smiling. Despite all the baggage between them since her sister's death, she liked Jon. She enjoyed working with him. She turned back, still smiling. "Sounds like a good thing. Okay, soldier. Whatever I turn up that I can't use, I'll tell you. And vice versa."

"Deal."

The taxi stopped at his hotel on Queensway. As he got out, he turned back to ask, "Where do I contact you?"

"You don't. I know where you are. If anything changes, leave a message at your hotel's front desk addressed to Joyce Ray."

Despite the proposition he had offered her, he wanted very much to know what the CIA's connection to McDermid and the Altman Group was. He would ask Klein to check into what Langley was up to, which meant he would have to let Randi go her own way for now.

"Fine," he said. "Keep in touch."

She was still smiling as the taxi pulled away into traffic.

Chapter
Twenty-Four

Washington, D.C.

In his bedroom, the president was still buttoning his shirt when Jeremy knocked and spoke through the door, "Director Debo, sir. She says it's urgent. Would you like to take the call?"

One more emergency was not what he needed. "Of course. Put her through." The Director of Central Intelligence, Arlene Debo, had been appointed to the position by the previous administration, and he had kept her on, despite her affiliation with the opposition party, because he trusted her. She was very good at the job.

Her voice was just below strident, her natural tone. "Mr. President, my people ran the statistics on the leaks. The vast majority of them are related one way or another to defense and military matters. Did you know that?"

"Yes, why?"

"Because I instructed our agents to concentrate most heavily on the area on and around the joint chiefs, and it's paid off with our first hit."

The president sat down on the edge of his bed. "Who?"

"Secretary of the Army Jasper Kott."

"Kott? Kott himself? Are you sure?" He was shocked.

"He went to Manila on somewhat questionable army business, so we put an agent with him. Sure enough, he slipped away in civvies and went into the city to what appeared to be a pleasure trip to a brothel where our agent was unable to follow. However, she'd had the foresight to contact our station chief, and he had a man there quickly, who went in as a customer. He learned Kott had insulted the house by not being there for 'fun.' He was meeting a man and reporting on your recent military budget session."

The president frowned. "What man?"

"Ralph McDermid, CEO of the Altman Group."

"*McDermid?* My God. He was telling him about our budget discussion?"

"Indeed, Mr. President."

"Insider trading?"

"We don't know yet, but we'll find out. Our agent and her team are shadowing McDermid now, too, as we speak."

"Keep briefing me, Arlene. Thanks."

"My job, sir."

After hanging up, he finished dressing, his forthcoming breakfast with the vice president far from his mind as he pondered the possible motives for Secretary Kott's deceit and McDermid's involvement. Was it simply extremely bold economic espionage to gain a business advantage . . . or something else?

Few people knew the White House had two

family dining rooms — one in the northwest corner of the main floor and the other upstairs in the private quarters, remodeled with a small kitchen originally for Jack and Jackie Kennedy in 1961. Like Jack Kennedy, Sam Castilla preferred to keep the upstairs one private for his family, too. He and Cassie could sit around with uncombed hair, still in their bathrobes, drink coffee, and read the Sunday papers without worrying about being disturbed except under the most unusual emergencies.

Still, he liked this family dining room on the first floor, too. Although it had a vaulted ceiling and was furnished with solemn Hepplewhite and Sheraton pieces, it was small relative to other White House rooms, and the fireplace and yellow walls gave it warmth and intimacy. This morning, it smelled pungently of chiles and cheese. He had invited Vice President Brandon Erikson for breakfast to discuss his coming trip to Asia.

The vice president forked a mouthful of scrambled eggs, New Mexico style, and nodded with appreciation. "What do you call them, sir?"

"*Huevos jalapeños,* one of Celedoño's best recipes," President Castilla said. "And you don't have to be so damned formal here, Brandon. This is us having breakfast so we can talk about your trip east, not some official briefing."

"Being in the White House tends to make things formal." The vice president had an easy smile and a smooth voice.

"Some think that and worse. I remember Harry Truman called it the big white jail, and William Howard Taft said it was the loneliest place in the world. But I tend to agree with Jerry Ford. He claimed it was the best public housing he'd ever seen. I like that."

"The place does inspire awe."

The president examined the vice president's handsome face, the perfectly barbered cheeks, the thick black hair that made him look a good ten years younger than his forty. He had the kind of manly Hollywood good looks that attracted women and encouraged trust in men. A valuable political combination.

Since this was their last term, and the party was increasingly focused on Erikson as its next presidential candidate, Castilla decided to have a moment of fun. "You planning to live here, too, Brandon?"

Erikson chewed, his eyes closed. When he opened them, he sighed with appreciation. "These are some fine eggs. Please give my compliments to Celedoño. Of course, Sam, I'd be a fool to be working my tail off if I didn't have a few ideas. Might be pleasant to have a shot at seeing what I can accomplish."

"You did plenty in the congressional elections. You were everywhere at once. We appreciated that. You'll have a lot of IOUs to call in."

Erikson smiled wider. "Especially since so many of our candidates won. I'm proud of that."

Brandon Erikson knew the political score. It was one of the prime reasons Castilla had wanted him on his ticket. Now it was Erikson's chance, and Castilla figured he had earned it. "You have enough money? You know the opposition's been filling their war chest for eight years, just waiting to make a roaring comeback. They'll throw everything at you, including the sidewalks of New York. And if I'm right about who your opponent's going to be, you're facing one of the nation's largest family fortunes."

For the first time, the vice president showed uncertainty. The cost of not just running but winning a national campaign had become obscene. Candidates spent more than half their time on the telephone or at fund-raisers, convincing donors to empty their pockets, instead of working on issues.

"I'll be ready," the vice president vowed. Ravenous ambition was naked on his face, then vanished.

For a moment, Sam Castilla was sent back into the past, to his beginnings as a young congressman in New Mexico, with no money, no name, and no connections. Serge Castilla had said, "Be careful what you dream, son. No one's going to give it to you. If your dream's expensive, plan on paying for it yourself."

He saw Serge — the man he had always called Dad — smile knowingly, his desert-bleached eyes amused, his dark skin a cobweb of wrinkles. Serge had understood him well. He wondered what kind of advice David Thayer would have given. Whether he was as wise and kind. What kind of man he had aged into. For an instant, he was furious at being cheated of his biological father, and then he felt the deep sadness that must be David Thayer's. To have been in captivity for a half century, kept from everyone and everything he loved, from his own dreams and ambitions. . . . What kind of personal hell had Thayer been through?

He pulled himself back to the present. "You know you have my complete backing, Brandon. Now I'd like your input. As I recall, you're visiting Afghanistan, Pakistan, and India."

"We're trying to keep it flexible, of course. The political situation is so dicey in those areas that I might stop in Hong Kong and Saudi Arabia, too. With all the terrorist threats, the State Department has some arm-twisting in mind for me."

"Sounds good. We have to keep working on this on all fronts."

"Exactly —"

The door of the dining room opened, and Jeremy's head appeared around it. The president's personal assistant would never have interrupted a breakfast with the vice president unless the matter was urgent. "Admiral Brose, sir. He needs to see you immediately."

Castilla shot a rueful smile at the vice president. "Okay, Jeremy, send him in."

The vice president took a final mouthful of eggs. "If you don't mind, Sam, I'd like to stay. Keep myself informed, although I'm sure I'm not going to be needed."

Castilla hesitated. There was still part of him that wanted to hold the situation under wraps. He nodded. "Tactful and accurate. Stay put and pour yourself some coffee."

The door opened all the way, this time to admit the imposing bulk of Admiral Stevens Brose in full uniform. He saw the vice president and stopped.

"It's all right, Stevens. The vice president's feet are already wet. I'm guessing the situation with the *Empress* must be what's brought you here so early."

"It is, Mr. President. I'm afraid —"

Castilla waved to a chair at the table. "Sit. Have some coffee before we plunge into the quagmire."

"Thank you, sir." The chair creaked as the outsized chairman of the joint chiefs sat, poured, and drank. Then: "The *Crowe*'s got a Chinese sub on its tail."

"Hell and damnation!" the vice president breathed.

The president simply nodded. "We expected something, Stevens."

"Yessir, we did. But this is bolder than I figured from what I heard of your meeting with the ambassador."

"I agree," Castilla said. "A submarine threatening a frigate that's threatening a cargo ship doesn't leave a great deal of wiggle room for anyone."

Erikson asked, "How powerful is a Chinese submarine, Admiral?"

Brose's brow furrowed. "That'd depend on its class. Commander Chervenko on the *Crowe* has some experience with Chinese subs from when he served in Seventh Fleet's Task Force 75 around the Taiwan Strait. He and his sonar technician think the sub's an old Han class. That'd be logical, since the majority of their operational subs *are* Hans. But it could be the more powerful Xia back at sea once again. It'd almost certainly be modified and updated . . . or even a new class, launched in secret. We know they've been working on a better boat for years."

Erikson pressed, "But what's their power like?"

"The *Crowe* should be able to handle a Han on

343

its own, although you never know for sure what upgrades there could be. With the Xia, it's hard to say. We know little about it except that the design's had problems and that it's definitely stronger than the Han class. If it's a new class, then the *Crowe*'s in a bad way, playing Russian roulette."

Erikson looked worried as the president asked the admiral, "You have some ideas about why the Chinese's reaction is so big?"

"Beyond muscle flexing for internal consumption, no, sir. They could be trying to show us they're stronger now than at the time of the *Yinhe* and eager to challenge us in the international arena."

The president frowned. "Demanding respect, you might say."

"That's it, sir," Brose said. "Maybe it's a hint to our allies to beware, too."

"Probably an effective hint," the president added grimly. He drank coffee. "Of course, it could be that someone there overreacted."

"A mistake?" Erikson considered. "That's really frightening, Sam."

"What if it's deliberate? What if it's some Standing Committee hard-liner who wants to scare his own people by escalating the confrontation?"

Brose exhaled. "That'd mean there's a power struggle inside the walls of Zhongnanhai."

The president nodded. "If that's so, the *Empress* could become the line in the sand between the factions. With us in the middle, too, the situation could turn catastrophic."

"With fingers on the buttons, the world would

end up in the middle." Brandon Erikson shook his head worriedly. "In the Cuban missile crisis, you remember, the Soviets sent subs to shadow our blockade ships. One of their skippers was so furious he gave the order to prepare to fire a torpedo into us. The other Soviet commanders had to talk him out of it. That was far too close for anyone's comfort, on either side of the Cold War."

"It can happen," Brose admitted. "Chervenko's a steady man, but you never know what strain will do. Truthfully, I'm more worried about the Chinese sub commander. God knows what in hell's going on in his mind."

The trio lapsed into anxious silence.

At last, Brose grunted and heaved a sigh. "What do you want to do, Mr. President?"

"Is the Chinese sub making any aggressive moves?"

"Chervenko says not."

"Then we continue exactly what we're doing."

"There's not a lot of time left, sir."

"I know."

Vice President Erikson said, "It's getting to the brink, Sam. Isn't it time to inform the country? The cabinet. Congress. The people? They should know what we're facing and against whom. We have to be prepared for the worst. We have to prepare *them*."

The vice president and admiral studied the president where he sat at the table, his eyes staring at something only he could see.

At last, he nodded unhappily. "I suppose you're right. But we'll bring in only the cabinet and Congress for now. Brandon, talk to our key people on the Hill. I'll convene the cabinet. When it's time to alert the public, I'll let you know. But not right now. Not yet."

The vice president said, "Are you sure it's wise to leave them uninformed? If this thing blows up in our faces, it won't look good for you."

"There'll be a war of words before anyone shoots."

"And if there isn't?" Erikson pressed.

"That's why I get paid to stay up all night with a bellyache, Brandon. To take the risk. I won't cry wolf until I see an actual one. That's a dangerous game that wears people down so that after a while they no longer listen to warnings. When I cry wolf, it's because there's a real damn wolf, dripping fangs and all. That way I know people will listen."

Admiral Brose agreed. "That's how I'd play it, Mr. President. Better we concentrate on facts and evidence."

Antwerp, Belgium

The worldwide headquarters of Donk & LaPierre was a four-story brick building built in 1610 in the usual Flemish step style. Because it was convenient to her apartment — just north of the Meir and not far from the Grote Markt, the Kathedrale, and the Schelde River — Dianne Kerr decided to walk to her appointment with Louis LaPierre, chairman and managing director. The receptionist immediately sent her up to the top floor.

There an excited young man hurried to greet her. "Mademoiselle Kerr, what an honor. I read your novel *Marionette* with great interest. I'm

Monsieur LaPierre's private secretary, and he is eager to speak with you. Please come this way."

The corridors of the old building were narrow, but the ceilings were high, graced by tall windows. The same was true of Louis LaPierre's private office. It was relatively small — heating was a problem in the seventeenth century — but high-ceilinged, with tall windows, a handsome fireplace, and a view across Antwerp's vast docks.

The managing director himself was small and slender, with an Old World elegance in dress and manner. "Ah, Mademoiselle Kerr," he said in meticulous English with only the slightest French accent. "I have, of course, read your books. They are, shall we say, most exciting. Such adventures, such intrigue, such deviousness, and so vivid. I particularly enjoyed *The Monday Men*. How could you know so much about assassins? Surely you were a covert operator yourself?"

"No, Monsieur Director," Kerr said modestly and completely inaccurately. One did not talk about being MI6. That credo had been broken in recent years, even by some of those whom she had thought trustworthy. Fortunately, most still adhered to the code. Besides, for an adventure novelist, it was probably wise not to invite speculation as to the possible truth of her plots.

LaPierre laughed. "I doubt that, Mademoiselle Kerr, but please sit and tell me the purpose of this visit."

Kerr chose a wood-and-brocade Flemish chair. It was thoroughly uncomfortable. "In a single word, research."

"Research?" LaPierre arched an eyebrow. "You

are planning a thriller about Donk & LaPierre?"

"An adventure novel concerning the eighteenth- and nineteenth-century China trade. I thought it would be interesting to do something historical for a change. Your company's renowned, of course. I believe the original Jan Donk Importers had their start even before then. Correct?"

"Quite true. You wish, then, to examine our archives?"

"With your permission."

"Of course, of course. Our directors enjoy the right kind of publicity. They will be delighted." LaPierre smiled and then appeared to have a sudden thought that concerned him. "But are you aware that our archives — in fact, all of our records up to today — are here in this building?"

Kerr acted startled as she lied smoothly, "No, I didn't. You mean . . . they're *still active?* All of them, back to the sixteenth century?"

LaPierre nodded. "Of course, early records were few, and trade was far simpler then. Those from the twentieth century prior to the last five years are on microfilm."

Kerr frowned. "That creates a bit of a problem. I mean, you can't very well have me bumbling around in your files during business hours, can you?"

"Actually, the archives are set off by themselves, so that is not the problem. No, the trouble comes from another direction. We no longer let independent researchers in. In fact, the last time we did officially was a decade ago, and of course, he had lied to us. He was actually searching for the company's collusion with the Nazis —"

"And, of course, there was none," Kerr echoed. "Not a shred of evidence."

"Exactly. But as soon as the world learned he suspected that there was . . ." He did not finish the sentence.

"It must have been very bad for business. So the problem is that you're willing to let me do my research, but you'd rather not let anyone know of it until I can credit the company generously in the novel?"

"Yes, yes. I am pleased you understand. We have had success in the past with allowing a few select researchers in at night to work after hours. Would you be willing to do that?"

"Well . . ." Kerr considered. "I suppose I can change my schedule. I *am* excited about the early history of Donk & LaPierre."

"Very well. Then it is done. Our security will be alerted. I, myself, often work late. You must take no documents from the building though. Our archivist will show you around so you can orient yourself and learn how to properly handle the oldest papers."

Kerr smiled. "Very gracious of you. How can I do anything but accept gladly?"

"When would you care to start?"

"Would tonight be too soon?"

"Tonight?" For a moment, there was a flicker of doubt in LaPierre's face. "Of course. I will instruct my assistant to give you a letter and a badge. He will introduce you to the archivist, too."

Dianne Kerr stood. "You're most kind. I promise to not get in your way."

"I trust you completely."

Chapter
Twenty-Five

Dianne Kerr presented herself at the locked front doors of Donk & LaPierre precisely at eight P.M., casually dressed in black jeans, a black turtleneck, black cotton socks, navy-blue running shoes, and a tan leather jacket. She carried a briefcase.

The guard at the door nodded. "Good evening. Mevrouw Kerr, is it?" His English had a heavy Dutch accent.

"That I am." She showed the letter and her badge.

"You will hang the badge around your neck, please, and open your briefcase."

She opened it, revealing yellow writing pads, Post-it notes, a French dictionary, a Dutch-Flemish dictionary, current world almanac, and ballpoint pens.

The guard nodded. "A writer's tools, *ja?*"

"Nothing changes." Kerr smiled.

Once inside, she climbed to the top floor, where the archives were housed. Besides the chairman's office, the archives were the only other occupant. Cavernous, filled with filing cabinets, the room smelled faintly antiseptic. The ventilation and temperature-control system burred softly in the background. According to the archivist, the system was oversized and had special filters to keep the air clean, which helped to preserve the documents.

Kerr took out a yellow writing pad and carried the very first handwritten file of Jan Donk Imports to a narrow table lined with rows of tall wood chairs. The documents were grayed and fragile. Handling them carefully, she read and made notes.

Four hours later, Monsieur LaPierre himself was finally gone, security had finished its midnight rounds, and the building was as silent as a vault. Kerr opened her briefcase once more and pressed a brass fitting. A hidden compartment opened, and she extracted a miniature camera and a pair of thin, latex gloves. As she pulled on the gloves, she strode to the other end of the archives, to the last file cabinet, which housed current correspondence and reports.

It was fastened with a combination lock.

Kerr pressed her ear to the lock and turned the dial. She could feel its guts through her fingers . . . the faint click as a tumbler fell, then another, and another. Her heart rate accelerated, and the lock opened. She thumbed through the folders until she found her target: Flying Dragon Enterprises, Shanghai. Looking quickly around, she removed the file. As she examined each paper inside, every tiny sound in the old building made her pause.

When she found the right document, a ship's manifest, she allowed herself a quick smile of relief. She had no idea why it was wanted, but she was often able to uncover the reasons for her assignments eventually. Perhaps this one would give her the basis for another thriller. She photographed it, put it back into the file exactly where it had been, returned the file to the cabinet, and relocked it. Removing her gloves, she hurried back to her briefcase.

She packed it quickly and studied the archive room one last time to be sure she had left not the slightest trace. At last, she turned off the lights and headed for the door.

On the first floor, she made enough noise to alert the dozing security guard.

"You are finished, Mevrouw Kerr?"

"For tonight. There's only so much reading and scribbling one can do."

The guard chuckled and crooked his finger. Kerr opened her briefcase, and he leafed through her voluminous notes, made sure there were no original documents, nodded, and shut the lid. "You go home now?"

"I think an ale or two and then to bed."

"Ja, goede nacht."

Outside, Dianne Kerr smiled to herself. She would, of course, return at least twice more, to make certain her legend was believed. She did not stop for the two ales. Instead, she went straight home to her darkroom, where she developed the microfilm, made an eight-by-ten print, and faxed it to Washington. A fine night's work for a desk-bound novelist, extremely well paid, and without a trace. With the possibility of further adventure to-morrow night, to steal the actual document and leave behind a meticulous copy so difficult to dis-cern from the original it could pass for years undis-covered.

As usual, Fred Klein slipped into the West Wing through the kitchen staff entrance, from where the secret service whisked him straight up to the residence.

In the Treaty Room, President Castilla sat on a sofa, morosely contemplating his coffee. He looked up as soon as Klein entered. "You look as bad as I feel. Didn't the fax come?"

Klein closed and locked the door. "Worse. It came. It's not what we need. Antwerp has the fake manifest on file, too."

Castilla swore. "I'd really hoped . . ." He shook his head. "So we have nothing from Baghdad, Basra, *or* Antwerp." He paused, thinking. "Maybe there's been a mistake. Why would your operative bother to send the fake? Didn't he know it was fake?"

"She. No, sir, she didn't. I couldn't tell her exactly what was in it, or why we wanted it, because she's European operating in a European city. If something went wrong, if she were caught or said something . . . there was too much risk someone would find out about the *Empress* crisis. In Iraq, it didn't matter. They already know why we want the manifest, and they're not going to leak what we're up to, because they want the chemicals."

The president sighed. "Some days staying in bed sounds like an attractive idea. The news seems to be getting worse and worse. Sit and have some coffee with me, Fred."

As Klein settled in next to him, the president poured and handed him a steaming cup. "Over at Bethesda, they tell me I have to cut down on my coffee. Even Cassie's getting on me about it. But to hell with all of them. They don't have this job."

"No," Klein said, chewing on the mouthpiece of his empty pipe. "They don't. You said something's happened." He removed the pipe long enough to drink.

Castilla took a defiant gulp. "The Chinese have upped the ante. This time they've sent force, not words — one of their submarines to chase the *Crowe*."

Klein's eyebrows rose above his wire-rimmed glasses. "But they haven't attacked?"

"No, and neither have we."

Klein took out his pipe and turned it in his hands, ignoring the coffee. "Where did they get the sub, Mr. President? Where did it come from so quickly? Not the Taiwan Strait, or Hong Kong, or even Hainan Island. That's too much distance from the *Crowe*. The sub had to have been on station in the Indian Ocean, more likely the Arabian Sea itself."

The president straightened. He swore. "You're right. They must have subs watching the Fifth Fleet."

Klein nodded. "And now, one's been sent to let us know someone in Beijing wants to crank up the confrontation, escalate the threat."

"Agreed. My take is that it's a power struggle inside the walls of Zhongnanhai."

"Makes sense. But is it the whole Standing Committee? Maybe even the Politburo itself?"

"It'd help to know."

"Nothing any Covert-One associate or asset has turned up indicates it," Klein said. "Of course, the

Chinese are keeping the situation under wraps, just as we are. There hasn't been a mention of the *Empress* by their press."

"So is your advice to prod, watch, and wait? Continue our threat and pretend theirs isn't there?"

"For now, yes. Later, you'll have the proof, or you'll have my resignation."

The president's eyes grew icy. "That's not good enough, Fred. What progress *have* your people made?"

"Sorry, Mr. President. Must be getting old. This one's wearing me down. Too many intangibles." Klein crossed his arms, the stem of his pipe sticking out from his fist. "First, we're certain the Belgian co-owner of the *Empress* knows there's contraband in the cargo. Second and probably even more important" — he paused to make certain the president saw that he saw how important this was — "the Belgian company is wholly owned by the Altman Group. It looks as if their chair and CEO, Ralph McDermid, might have his fingers stuck deep into the affair."

"Ralph McDermid again?" The president's voice rose. "McDermid isn't just chair and CEO, he *is* the Altman Group. He founded it, built it into one of the largest financial empires the earth's seen, and he did it in less than two decades. My God, he's got one of my predecessors working for him plus cabinet secretaries from the last four administrations, former FBI and CIA directors, congressmen, senators, and a few ex-governors."

Klein knew all of this. He controlled his patience until the president finished. "Yes, sir. You said

355

'again.' Is McDermid involved in something else?"

The president took off his glasses and pinched the bridge of his nose as if fighting off a headache. "The White House leaks." He repeated Arlene Debo's report about the secret meeting in Manila between McDermid and Secretary of the Army Jasper Kott. "You think there may be a connection between the leaks and the *Empress* situation?"

"We'd better find out. What I don't understand is why McDermid would involve himself in something like the *Empress*'s cargo. He's making a fortune already. His company's filthy rich. So why risk so much for one shipment of chemicals? He'll make an obscene profit, but that's nothing new. It makes damn little sense to me."

"One load of contraband hardly seems worth it," the president agreed. "Maybe McDermid's been conducting various illegal operations for a while. He could be one of those types who's always looking for the next thrill, and the more outside the law he goes, the higher the emotional payoff."

"Or maybe some of his companies are in trouble, and he's figured out a way to ease debt by backing illegal ventures like the *Empress*. He sure won't have to pay taxes on it."

They sat in worried silence, trying to see an answer. Finally, the president decided, "I don't recall any company that approaches Altman's success in the wholesale conversion of former high government rank to gigantic profits. But then, business and politics have always gone hand in hand. Throw in the military, and doesn't that remind you of Dwight Eisenhower's warning about allowing the military-industrial complex to grow too influential, that there was a danger it'd run amok?"

"It reminds me, yes, and not happily," Klein agreed. "A former Altman employee told my researcher that the company's code is: *Mix business and politics correctly, and they pay exceptionally well.*"

"Sounds like an understatement. But maybe that's the answer. That could be what McDermid's up to. For him, there's no ceiling to wealth. He can never have enough. He'll make a quick financial killing on the *Empress* and go looking for his next conquest."

Hong Kong

Randi Russell told the taxi driver to circle the block, and when they again drew abreast of the entrance to the Conrad International, she told the driver in fluent Mandarin, "Stop here."

Jon had been looking all around casually, as if checking for a tail or stakeout. As she watched, he turned on his heel, apparently satisfied he was clean, and walked into the hotel's glittering lobby. She continued to survey the area until she spotted the Chinese street vendor standing behind his cart in a shadow, a cell phone in his hands, speaking urgently as he, too, observed Jon disappear.

Just what she had suspected. McDermid's troops were continuing to surveil Jon. She did not believe Jon's story for a second, but at least he was out of her way for the night. As she told the driver to take her back to the building that housed the Altman offices, she dialed her cell.

"Savage," the voice answered.

"Did you pick up McDermid?" she asked, her hand cupped around the cell's mouthpiece.

"Sure did. Tailed him around the daisy chain and right back to his office building. He's gone up to the penthouse."

"Is our team in place?"

"Affirmative."

"I'm on my way."

When they reached it, she paid the driver and walked up to a black Buick sedan, carrying her conical hat. She opened the door and dropped into the front passenger seat. "I'll take it from here, Allan. You get indoors and watch for McDermid's chief shark. When you see him, tail him."

Short and heavyset, Allan Savage was no one's image of a CIA agent, but that was to his advantage. He nodded, climbed out of the car, and crossed the traffic to the high-rise. Randi slid over and settled behind the wheel to wait.

Her phone beeped. It was Allan. "Already?" she asked.

"McDermid must've forgotten something. He's on his way back out."

Randi clicked off and watched as the CEO hurried from the building. As he arrived at the curb, so did his black limousine. The chauffeur ran around to open the rear door. As the limo drove away, Randi made sure she and the Buick were close behind.

The limo wound up into the dark hills toward Victoria Peak. Here the houses were large and impressive, and the city's lights spread out below in a shimmering minuet across the great harbor, the outlying islands, and the dazzling Kowloon peninsula. The glitter dimmed farther north in the New Territories but continued even into mainland

China, where Guangzhou glowed on the horizon.

The limo pulled into the driveway of an older, Chinese-style mansion that overlooked Repulse Bay. As Randi watched, Ralph McDermid dismissed the limo, and a slim young woman ran out of the mansion to greet him. Arm in arm, they strolled into the house.

Randi clicked on her cell phone. "Looks as if he's gone to roost. If we're lucky, we've got a couple of hours. Put Berger on. Ham, you have the equipment?"

"In our hot little black bags," electronics expert Hamilton Berger said cheerfully. "As soon as the honcho assistant trots away, we're in the phone-bug-planting business."

"Be careful. We're not dealing with some dumb embassy this time."

"He'll never find a thing."

"Good. I'll hang on to McDermid. He's a busy boy."

"Call you when the bug's in, and we're out."

"Can't wait." Randi ended the call and took a thoroughly American turkey-and-cheese sandwich from inside her clothes. As shadows did a ballet of lust on the other side of McDermid's drawn drapes, she ate and wondered what Jon really wanted from McDermid.

From the corridor outside Donk & LaPierre, bright light fell across the dark, empty desk in the company's lobby, where the exotic Chinese receptionist had sat. Jon relocked the door behind him and stepped lightly past the shadowy desk to the inner doors. After he had slipped out of his hotel through the back way, he had hailed another taxi that had brought him back here. Dressed again in his dark work clothes, he listened. There were no sounds inside, and he saw no light. The offices appeared as deserted as he had hoped.

The door was unlocked. He stepped inside and padded along the Delft-blue carpeting, pausing to listen at each office, until he reached the ebony door of managing director Charles-Marie Cruyff. This sanctum was defended by a pair of heavyweight locks. After five attempts with different picklocks, Jon finally opened both and pushed the black door into the office.

Enveloped in murky silence, he switched on his pocket flashlight. His gaze swept over the ultramodern sofa, Cruyff's mahogany desk and ship models, the ship models on the walls, to the wall safe to the left of the desk. He crossed quickly to it. Cruyff had glanced involuntarily at the safe when Jon had mentioned working with Chinese companies. He hoped that meant there was something important in there about the *Empress*. Particularly, he hoped it was the real manifest.

The safe was compact, with a simple combination lock — just what he remembered. Klein had supplied him with a small electric drill. It made a low, steady whirr as the state-of-the-art bit bored into the steel. When he had drilled four holes, he packed tiny amounts of plastic explosive into each and connected them across the knob of the lock to a miniature blasting cap. Working quickly but carefully, he covered the safe with a sound-deadening pad, moved back behind the desk, and paused, listening to the pounding of his heart.

He turned the handle on the miniature detonator. The explosion was muffled but loud enough to be heard as far away as the reception area.

His Beretta ready, he listened. When five minutes passed, he holstered the Beretta and returned to the safe. The door had swung open an inch. He pulled it farther open, removed all the documents, and carried them to Cruyff's desk, where he quickly examined them.

And stopped at the fifth. It was the letter that must be the one that had prompted the reply he had found in Yu Yongfu's safe in his Shanghai mansion. A letter addressed not to Jan Donk, but to Managing Director Charles-Marie Cruyff of Hong Kong. It was signed by Yu Yongfu, president and chairman of Flying Dragon Enterprises. More important . . . it was cc'd to Ralph McDermid, president and CEO of the Altman Group.

Riveted, he continued to read to the bottom of the page. Nothing interesting . . . although an envelope had been stapled to the corner. He checked it — a Donk & LaPierre business envelope with a handwritten notation:

Basra invoice
The Dowager Empress

After all this time . . . all the deaths. . . . This was it! Fingers trembling with eagerness, he pulled open the envelope, yanked out a single sheet of stationery, and unfolded it.

On it was writing that matched the writing on the envelope, but there was no manifest. As a hot bolt of rage shot through him, he stared at the note:

361

You've wasted your time, Smith. You didn't really believe I'd leave anything so important somewhere you could find it so easily? I've destroyed the manifest. You're next.

It was signed with the initials RM. Ralph McDermid. Arrogant bastard. He had known! How — ?

As he thought that, Jon froze and looked up. *You're next.*

"Good evening, Colonel Smith." The whispering voice came from the open office door.

The office's overhead light flashed on. Feng Dun stood just inside the doorway, his mottled red hair shining in the light. His expression was grim, but a small smile of genuine satisfaction played at the corners of his mouth. He held a mini Uzi aimed at Jon. As they stared at each other, Feng gestured behind him. Four armed men ran past and spread out across the office.

Chapter
Twenty-Six

Sunday, September 17
Beijing

The faint click of the Westminster wall clock sounded in Niu Jianxing's ears before it struck the half hour. His alert gaze darted around his study in the courtyard house at the edge of the old Xicheng district, mirroring the churning of his mind. Dispatching the submarine *Zhou Enlai* to menace the American frigate was a move of such colossal stupidity, so criminally dangerous, so completely counterproductive to China's interests and the very existence of the People's Republic that he was beside himself with disgust and fury.

The fire in his eyes would have shocked his colleagues, whom he had taught to expect the sleepy Owl of Party and government meetings. This alert, energetic man was the unleashed Niu. Like a tiger, he prowled his study, grappling with what he was beginning to understand. Although Wei Gaofan had covered himself well, now there was little doubt in Niu's mind that it was Wei who was behind the decision to send the sub.

This stupid move not only revealed to the Americans that the Chinese navy had been shadowing their Fifth Fleet, it astronomically increased the danger of a disastrous confrontation over the *Empress*.

When Major Pan had first reported his suspicions about Jon Smith, Li Aorong's connection to the *Empress* had made the Owl suspect Wei Gaofan might be guilty of corruption, since Li was Wei's protégé, and Li did not go to bed without Wei's blessings. It seemed both men planned to make a small fortune on the cargo. Wei would not be the first Zhongnanhai official to succumb to private greed.

But the *Zhou Enlai*'s new assignment had turned that assumption inside out. It was too easy an answer, too obvious.

Hands clasped behind his back, the Owl turned on his heel and marched across his study again, each foot hammering home his revulsion and rage. Now he knew it must be that snake Wei who had turned against the human-rights accord. Wei was sabotaging it, and — worse — it was only part of his infidelity. In fact, Wei intended to cause an incident with the United States of such magnitude that it would turn the clock back to the Cold War . . . to the building of new weapons of mass destruction . . . to societal controls that would lead to catastrophes like the Cultural Revolution . . . to an isolated China putrefying in its own recycled bitterness.

That was what Wei was after, Niu decided, disgusted and afraid. Not greed for money; greed for power.

When a tap sounded at the private rear door of his study, the Owl hurried to it with an alacrity that was in sharp contrast to his sixty years. He unlocked the door to admit Major Pan.

"Come in. Come in." He impatiently motioned the agent to sit facing his desk.

Nervous, the major lowered his pudgy body onto the wood chair and perched like a wary bird, ready to fly. Summonses to drive to Beijing from Shanghai in the middle of the night always made Pan nervous. Especially a summons from a member of the Standing Committee.

Niu resumed pacing. "What progress have you made in the matter of the American agent and *The Dowager Empress*?"

"Not much, master." Pan craned his neck, watching Niu's progress around the room. "The storm has passed, leaving little sign behind. We've had to release Li Aorong. He continues to insist he knows nothing about his son-in-law's business activities, or where he and his daughter have disappeared."

Niu stopped and stared. "You *had* to release him? Why? If it were some legal technicality, I can —"

"No legal technicality."

"Then *what?*"

Pan chose his words carefully. "I believe the question was raised to General Chu as to the propriety of holding Li without arresting him."

"A routine policy in a national security matter was questioned? Of General Chu? Absurd. Who asked such a question?"

"I believe the Central Committee."

Niu frowned. General Chu had run up against the Central Committee, a bad position. Still, the general should have informed him of the order. Now Niu would have to watch the general carefully, too, to make certain where his loyalties lay.

Niu returned his thoughts to the major, repressing his anger and frustration. He had momentarily forgotten Pan's reluctance to reveal anything that could indicate a definite view of a subject not directly connected to his official duties. Pan protected himself, which was one reason he had held his position in Public Security so long.

But Niu no longer had time for such niceties. The *Empress* would arrive in Iraqi waters Wednesday morning. It was already after midnight Sunday. "Meaning Wei Gaofan?" he asked bluntly. "I know my colleagues, Pan. Tell me. It will go no farther than this room."

Pan hesitated. At last he said cautiously, "I believe that could be the name General Chu indicated." A hint of hope crept into his voice as he continued, "Should I rearrest Li Aorong, sir? I could put him under house arrest. At least we would know where he was."

"No!" Niu said instantly. Then he tempered his tones. "That would not be productive."

The last thing Niu wanted was to alert Wei to his suspicions, or to suggest to Pan that there was more here than a simple counterintelligence investigation. "For now, Major Pan, continue to keep him under surveillance. You are still watching him, are you not?"

Pan gave a slow nod, his gaze warily on Niu.

The nod was so small that Niu had the impression the major hoped it might be overlooked. Niu interpreted it to mean that Wei Gaofan had leaned harder on General Chu than Pan had suggested, which meant Pan was continuing to watch Li Aorong on his own initiative. General Chu did not want to know what Pan was doing, but at the same time, he wanted Pan to make progress.

Niu had believed for many years that this was the way Pan operated and why he was unusually successful — careful not to actually break orders, but bending them to get results. It was what Niu needed now, and one of the reasons Pan was valuable.

"Good," he told him, resuming his pacing. "Continue exactly as you're doing."

"Yes, sir." Major Pan nodded sagely, well aware that Niu was telling him to keep his name out of it also.

"What else do you have for me?" Niu asked.

"We've been examining Yu Yongfu's business operations, but there seems to be nothing revealing there about Colonel Smith."

"What about Yu and his actress wife? Do you have any leads?"

"Not as yet."

Niu returned to his desk chair and sat. "I've had the pleasure of meeting Li Kuonyi several times. She's a clever woman and a good mother. If she can't be found, I'd suggest that perhaps she doesn't want to be. Which would mean she and her husband might be, how do you say it, 'on the run'?"

"That had occurred to me," Pan acknowledged.

"If not, could her father have spirited her away

so she'd be unavailable to discuss her husband's affairs?"

"That, too, master."

"Or maybe she's being hidden by powerful forces?"

Pan did not want to discuss that possibility, but at the same time he did not deny it was an option.

"Have you found evidence of anyone else being part of the *Empress* venture?" the Owl continued.

"Only the Belgian company I spoke of — Donk & LaPierre."

"Nothing else?"

"No."

"But you wouldn't rule it out, Major?"

"I rule nothing out in an investigation."

"An admirable trait in a counterintelligence officer," Niu said.

From the moment Pan had entered his office, Niu had been assessing the spycatcher's position on everything they discussed, but had found it, as always, nearly impossible to be certain. His gaze remained impassive, and his soft face neutral and unsmiling. Still, Niu had no choice but to use Pan, if he wanted to uncover what he needed.

"Continue your investigation as you see fit, but from now on report to me first. I must know all there is concerning the voyage of the *Empress*, particularly its cargo, and about everyone involved in the transaction. Within the country or abroad."

"First? In case General Chu should ask questions at some point, may I have that in writing, sir?"

There it was. The agent was covering his back again. Niu almost smiled. On the other hand, such caution had enabled Pan to survive in a job that was perilous for many reasons and from many directions. The difference between an excellent technician like Pan and a leader was exactly the willingness to take large risks. Pan was no gambler.

At the same time, the Owl was beginning to believe that his lifetime of work for China . . . his stubborn commitment to his country's growing into an important and friendly world power . . . was in jeopardy. To save both his vision and his nation, he would chance anything he must.

"Of course, Major," Niu said smoothly, "but you must not reveal it unless absolutely necessary. Is that understood?"

"Completely, sir."

Without another word, Niu wrote a letter authorizing Major Pan Aitu to be his official agent, who must report first to him and to no other.

With a quiet thrill and a moment of nervousness, the spycatcher watched. As soon as the paper was in his hand and then into his pocket, he slipped out the way he had arrived — through the back door.

It was after one o'clock. He paused in the dark and shivered. Winter's early chill was beginning to touch Beijing. He was puzzled. For some reason, Niu Jianxing suspected Wei Gaofan of at least corruption . . . possibly more. He himself suspected Wei of some connection to the *Empress* and was relieved to be under orders from Niu Jianxing at last. But not too far under.

He hurried to his car. He must return quickly to Shanghai. There was much to be done.

Hong Kong

His eyes snapped open to a pitch-black room. The air stank of droppings and dirt. Somewhere, a rat scurried away. Jon involuntarily shuddered as he listened for the high-pitched chatter and the sharp-clawed click of the horde of rats he imagined circling in the dark. But there was no noise. No rats, voices, traffic, cries of night birds . . .

A pinpoint of light appeared ahead. He had to look up to see the tiny beam. It felt warm, even hot, on his face, but he knew that was an illusion built on hope. An illusion and a spatial delusion caused by the absolute darkness, with no point of reference, no sense of dimension, everything flat black. Except the tiny beam that was real, and by concentrating on it hard enough, moving his head, and opening and closing his eyes, he finally brought it and the room into focus.

He was in a chair, his legs bound at the ankles. Someone was tying his hands behind him, roughly. Nylon rope burned through his skin. The point of light was not a crack in the walls or ceiling, but a reflection from a corner off a small metallic silver box attached high on the wall. A reflection of light from around the corner, in front of Jon and to his left. This room was L-shaped, and Jon was tied to the chair at the rear of the L's long arm.

Oriented now, he felt better. A wave of something close to euphoria washed over him as if he were on solid ground again, a part of the world — and then it all came back . . . his excitement that he had finally found the invoice manifest, the note from "RM" that not only showed that the manifest

370

was gone but revealed the dangerous depths of the Altman founder's arrogance . . . the lights flashing on, Feng Dun and his killers. . . .

He had been guilty of one of the oldest mistakes in the world — so involved he had dropped his guard. Now it was not the knowledge that he would likely die that bothered him, because that was always there in black work. You knew it could happen. It would not, of course, you told yourself. But it could. What shook him was the failure. The president was left to face a deadly confrontation with no acceptable options.

Jon hardly heard the door open around the corner of the L. A light flared on overhead, momentarily blinding him. Someone left, and someone else arrived. When his eyes adjusted, Feng Dun stood alone in front of him, scowling.

"You've caused us a lot of trouble, Colonel Smith. I don't like people who cause me trouble." His whispery voice was measured, his manner unhurried. As he stepped closer, his movement was fluid.

"That's strange hair," Jon said. "Especially for a Han. The white makes it even odder."

The blow smashed into his face, spinning him and the chair over backward. His head slammed against the floor. In the split second between the impact and the pain, he realized Feng had been so fast he had not seen his hand move. Then violent pain overtook him, and he felt blood run hot and sticky down the side of his face. For a few disorienting seconds, it seemed as if he had floated out of the room.

When his vision cleared, and the pain receded,

two men he had not seen were lifting his chair back onto its legs. Feng Dun's face was inches away, staring at him. His eyes were such a pale brown they appeared to be empty sockets.

Feng said, "That gentle tap was to focus your attention, Colonel. You've been skilled and intelligent. Don't be stupid now. We won't waste time discussing who and what you are. The question that interests me now is who do you work for?"

Jon swallowed. "Lieutenant Colonel Jon Smith, M.D., United States Army Medical Research Institute . . ."

The blow was little more than a slap this time, snapping his head sideways, but drawing blood again, and leaving his ears ringing.

"You appear on no American intelligence roster we've found. Why is that? Some secret section of the CIA? NSA? Maybe the NRO?"

His lips were swelling, making his speech thick. "Take your pick."

The hand crushed the other side of his face, the room disappeared again, but the chair did not move. Dimly he realized the job of the two other men was to keep him upright as Feng beat him.

"You're not a conventional agent," Feng told him. "Who do you report to?"

He could not feel his lips move and did not recognize his voice. "Who are *you?* You're not Public Security Bureau. Who thinks I'm not CIA, NSA? McDermid? Someone inside . . . ?"

The two fists struck seconds apart, a perfect combination, and as searing, crushing, swelling pain overwhelmed him and merciful blackness washed toward him, his brain told him the man had been a prizefighter, a professional, and he hit much too hard . . . hit too hard . . . hit too . . . hard . . .

Ralph McDermid stood behind Feng Dun. "Damnation, Feng. He's not going to tell us anything if he's unconscious, now is he?"

"He's strong. A big man. If we don't hurt him, make him afraid not only of pain and death, but of me, he'll tell us nothing."

"He'll tell us nothing if he's dead."

Feng smiled his wooden smile. "That's the fine print, Taipan. If he doesn't believe we'll kill him, he'll say nothing. But if he's dead, he can't say anything. One must find the balance. My job is to convince him I'm so savage and reckless that I'll kill him by accident, not realize my own brutality, and get carried away on a euphoria of inflicting pain. Yes?"

McDermid flinched, as if suddenly afraid of Feng himself. "You're the expert."

Feng noted the fear and smiled again. "You see? That's the reaction I need from him. We'll find out nothing until he can hardly move his mouth to talk. Just enough pain so he can barely think, but not so much that he *can't* think."

"Possibly less physical methods?" McDermid said uneasily.

"Oh, there'll be those, too. Don't worry. I won't kill him yet, and he'll tell us whatever you want to know."

McDermid nodded. Besides being a shade afraid of Feng's unpredictability, he was concerned about Feng in other ways. He had a feeling the big ex-soldier was sneering at him the same way he had sneered at his other employer — Yu Yongfu. At the time, Feng's insults had not been noteworthy, since he was reporting on Yu to McDermid. But later, when Feng demonstrated the clout necessary to have a submarine sent to shadow the USS *John Crowe*, McDermid started to worry.

At that point, what had been murky became clear: Feng had serious military or national government connections far above what appeared to be his station in life. As long as those resources were doing McDermid's bidding, McDermid was more than happy to pay Feng a fortune and overlook his rudeness. Still, McDermid had not risen to be one of the most powerful money men in the world by missing the obvious. Feng was connected. Feng was dangerous. McDermid still had him under control, but for how long, and what would be the price to keep him there?

Chapter
Twenty-Seven

Saturday, September 16
Washington, D.C.

The cabinet meeting was behind him, and Congress had been alerted to the brewing crisis with China. Carrying a mug of coffee, the president again sat at the head of the long table in the windowless situation room. The joint chiefs and his top civilian advisers had found their chairs, shuffling papers and conversing in hushed voices with their aides.

The president barely registered their presence. Instead, he was thinking about the millions across the country innocently going about their business who, if the new situation leaked, would hear about a possible war with China. Not a sportsmanlike excursion watched on TV, like *Monday Night Football*. Not an undercover battle against terrorists or a small conflict in a small country where fewer Americans would die fighting than died in traffic accidents on a holiday weekend. Not just any war. A real war . . . a *big* war . . . one that would detonate like a volcano and continue night and day, day in and day out. The dead would be their sons and daughters, or their neighbors or themselves, all returning home in body bags. *China.*

"Sir?" It was Charlie Ouray.

The president blinked and noted all the solemn and stern, or angry and anxious faces on both sides of the long table. They were watching him.

"Sorry," he told the room. "I was seeing the ghosts of war past and war future. I didn't see war present. Can any of you?"

The river of faces reacted each according to who and what he and she was. Shock that he, their commander in chief, would be defeatist. Fear of what could be coming. Resolve . . . neither afraid nor fierce but quietly determined. Solemnity at the magnitude of the unknown, near and far. A few with the gleam of "great" things in their eyes, of honor and awards and a place in history.

"No, sir, not really," Admiral Brose said quietly. "No one can, and I hope no one ever has to."

"Amen," Secretary of Defense Stanton intoned. Then his eyes glittered. "That said, now we prepare. War with China, people. Are we ready?"

The deafening silence was an answer no one in the hushed room could mistake. The president looked at his coffee and had no taste for it.

"If I may speak for my colleagues with the navy and air force," Army Chief-of-Staff Lieutenant General Tomás Guerrero declared, "the answer is, not really. We've been planning, training, and preparing for the exact opposite. We need —"

Air Force General Bruce Kelly broke in, "With all respect, I disagree. With some exceptions, the bomber force is prepared for any war. We do need to rethink our advanced fighter force, but for the immediate future, I see little problem."

"Well, dammit, *we're* not ready," Guerrero countered. "I've said it before, and I say it now, the army's been stripped of the bone and muscle it needs for a long, tough, nose-to-nose war over a vast area against a giant population, a mammoth army, and a national will to fight."

"The navy —" Admiral Brose began.

"Gentlemen!" National Security Adviser Powell-Hill protested from her seat at the opposite end of the table, facing the president. "This isn't the time to bicker about details. The first action we have to take is to prepare the complete readiness of what we *do* have. The second is to get cracking on what we need."

"The first action," the grave voice of the president brought instant silence, "is to prevent this confrontation from happening at all." He moved his adamant glare from face to face, one by one, until he had circled the table. "There will be no war. Period. None. That's the bottom line. We do *not* fight China. I'm convinced that cooler heads over there don't want war. I know *we* don't, and we have to give those cooler heads a chance."

His gaze arced around the table in the opposite direction, as if telling them, one by one again, that he knew damn well some of them — and a lot of their high-paying constituents — would like nothing more than an expensive, thrilling hostility, and telling them, and their special constituents, to forget it.

"This confrontation has a solution." His tone

left no room for argument. "Now, what are your ideas about what that solution is?"

Their blank faces reminded him of a roomful of New Mexican ranch barons who had just been told to find ways to double the water allotments for the Navajo and Hopi reservations.

"I suppose," Secretary of State Padgett offered, "we could ask for a secret, top-level summit to discuss the matter face to face."

The president shook his head. "A meeting with whom, Abner? The Zhongnanhai leadership will likely not want it to seem as if there's anything to talk about — not without calling the whole Central Committee into session and then getting at least an eight-to-one majority on the Standing Committee to approve it."

"Then send them a message they can't miss," Guerrero suggested. "Approve the appropriations for the air force's new fighter, a bigger and longer-range bomber, and the army's Protector artillery system. That will get their attention. Probably scare the shit out of them and get them to a summit, too. Yes, with that threat hanging over them, I'd think they'd jump for a summit in a nanosecond."

A murmur of approval flowed around the room. Even Secretary Stanton failed to object. He looked concerned, his face ashen, as if his resolve for the smaller, quicker military had been shaken badly.

Vice President Erikson demurred, "I'm not sure that's the right message to be sending, General. It could escalate matters rather than pacifying them."

Stanton regained some of his confidence. "Whatever we do will in all probability heighten the problem, Brandon, even if we do nothing. Too little could be construed as weakness; too much as threatening. I think some show of force, resolve, and readiness could make them hesitate to push us too hard."

Erikson nodded reluctantly. "You could be right, Harry. Perhaps a simple approval of already existing weapons systems wouldn't be too strong."

"Do we really want to return to a policy of mutual deterrence? Something that could drag on for years and drain both national economies?" the president asked. "Make China hunker down behind its Great Wall again with its missiles bristling just when we're making progress?"

Admiral Brose's voice boomed out over the geopolitical debate. "I think what the president might find most effective is a smaller solution to the immediate tactical problem. How do we prove what the *Empress* is carrying?"

The blank looks reappeared on the faces of the gathered military and civilian brains.

"That'd be nice," President Castilla agreed mildly. "You have an idea how to accomplish that, Stevens?"

"Send a crack team of SEALs from the *Crowe* to perform a clandestine recon of the *Empress*'s cargo."

"Can that be done?" Vice President Erikson wanted to know. "On the high seas? From and to moving ships?"

"It can," Brose assured him. "We have special equipment and trained teams."

"Safely?" Secretary Stanton worried.

"There'd be risk, naturally."

"Of failure? With casualties?" Abner Padgett of State asked.

"Yes."

"Of discovery?" Erikson pressed.

"Yes."

Secretary of State Padgett shook his head violently. "An overt act of invasion, even aggression, against Chinese territory on the high seas? At that point, we're inviting war."

Everybody nodded, solemnly or vigorously, in agreement, while the president took off his glasses and pinched the bridge of his nose. "How much risk of discovery are you talking about, Admiral?"

"Minimal, I'd say. With the right team, under the right leader who'd understand that his people could not — under any circumstances — be discovered. To abort first no matter what the danger to the team."

The president sat silently, his eyes distant, thinking again about the millions of people across the country who might soon be nervously watching TV or listening to the radio with one eye and one ear on the alert as they went about their daily lives, which most were rightly loathe to sacrifice for an unnecessary war.

His military and civilian advisers turned their collective gaze on Chief of Staff Charlie Ouray as if he could read what was happening inside President Castilla's mind.

"Sir?" Ouray said.

Castilla gave a small nod, more to himself than anyone else. "I'll take that under consideration, Stevens. It offers a possible solution. Meanwhile, I need to inform all of you that for some days we've been pursuing an intelligence operation that could solve the entire situation." He stood. "Thank you all. We'll meet again soon. Until then, I want everyone to get your sectors ready. Send me a report about how you envision handling China and how and when you'll be completely ready for a full-scale conflict."

Sunday, September 17
Shanghai

In the passenger compartment of his private Mercedes limousine, Wei Gaofan savored both his Cuban Cohiba and his recent success over Niu Jianxing. With the *Zhou Enlai* flexing its torpedoes, and the American frigate *Crowe* polishing its missiles, Niu, the reformer — in Wei's mind, "reformer" meant appeaser, revisionist, and capitalist — was going to find few on the Central Committee receptive to his demeaning "human-rights" treaty, or, in the end, the disastrous direction Niu intended to take China.

The Mercedes was parked on a side street in the Changning district. Separated from his bodyguard in the front seat by a panel of bulletproof glass, Wei studied the area, where lights showed from windows, the street's only illumination. He was waiting for his chauffeur and second bodyguard to return from their assignment.

Wei did not like loose threads or unresolved issues. Li Aorong and his daughter were both, and they needed to be swept up and disposed of. Until they were, he would not feel secure. His plan had risks, and while Niu Jianxing was many things Wei disliked, a fool was not among them.

The other members of the Standing Committee could be brought back to their senses once the Owl was silenced.

Abruptly he straightened. There were footsteps in the night, approaching the limousine. The front door of the Mercedes opened, and his chauffeur and chief bodyguard slid in behind the wheel next to the other bodyguard. Wei watched his chauffeur pick up the intercom.

His voice sounded clearly from the rear speaker as he reported: "Master Li is in his house, as he said, but I saw no evidence of the daughter having been there recently, master. Her children were asleep with their nanny in a separate cottage."

"You searched everywhere?"

"The potion knocked the old man into deep sleep. The children and the woman were already asleep. The grounds and buildings were otherwise deserted. I was able to investigate thoroughly, as you instructed." The chauffeur turned his head to look back through the one-way glass as if he could see Wei. He was frowning. "There was something else."

"What?" Wei tensed.

"Public Security Bureau people. Major Pan Aitu himself and a team."

"Where?"

"Lurking outside. Some in cars. Very discreet."

"Watching the house?"

"Or Li Aorong."

Probably both, Wei Gaofan thought to himself. He shifted uneasily in his seat. Pan would never dare act against his interests . . . unless someone else were backing him. Niu? It was possible Niu had discovered that Wei had used pressure to have Li Aorong released from Public Security custody. He shook his head angrily, thinking. Yes, this smacked of further interference from the dangerously liberal Niu.

His cell phone buzzed so loudly he ducked below the windows as if he had been fired upon, forgetting his bulletproof safety. He recovered at once and straightened, annoyed at how tense he was.

He jammed his cell phone button and barked, "Wei here."

"We have Jon Smith," Feng Dun said.

Wei's anger evaporated. "Where?"

"In Hong Kong."

"Who does he work for?"

"He hasn't told us — yet."

"Did he get proof of the cargo and send it to Washington?"

"There's no more proof, so nothing could be sent." Feng described the American's capture and the note McDermid had left in the envelope in the safe after he had shredded the manifest.

Wei's mood improved dramatically. He did not approve of McDermid's theatrical insult, but it did no harm to Wei. "Be quick with your questioning. Find out from Smith what the Americans know and eliminate him."

"Of course."

Wei could see Feng's smile that was like no human smile, but one pasted on a wooden dummy. Feng was his man. Still, he repressed a shiver, clicked off, and sat back to consider this new information: Now Niu Jianxing would have no proof of the *Empress*'s cargo. Niu's cooperation with the Americans would be impossible, and he had nothing at all to take to the Standing Committee.

Yes, the *Empress* would sail on to Wei's profit, as other ships with other illicit cargo had before . . . or the situation might still explode to his even greater profit. He laced his fingers across his stomach, pleased, as if he had just feasted on pheasant and honey.

Saturday, September 16
Washington, D.C.

In the upstairs Treaty Room, the door was locked, and President Castilla and Fred Klein were standing shoulder to shoulder at one of the windows, gazing down at the White House grounds. The president described the day's meeting with his military and civilian advisers.

Klein said, "You may have to use Admiral Brose's suggestion for a SEAL recon mission."

The president glanced at the Covert-One chief. A great black cloud seemed to hover over him like a thunderstorm gathering over White Sands. "What's happened?" There was a heaviness to the words, a weariness that carried the entire weight of the last four days. Resigned. Expecting the worst.

"We may have lost Colonel Smith."

"No." The president inhaled sharply. "How?"

"Have no idea yet. The last time we talked, he was heading off to break into Donk & LaPierre in Hong Kong." Klein related Jon's earlier activities — surveilling Ralph McDermid as he took the subway

384

to the Wanchai district, the trap inside the office building, and Jon's escape with Randi Russell.

"Agent Russell?"

"Yes. Remember, she's the one Arlene assigned to follow Kott to Manila, where he had that clandestine meeting with Ralph McDermid."

"Of course. Then what happened?"

"Jon asked for additional supplies and equipment to help him search Donk & LaPierre's offices. The entire operation there should've taken less than an hour. Ninety minutes, tops. And now he's missing."

"If there was a last copy of the manifest at Donk & LaPierre, Fred — it's gone?"

"If Jon's gone or caught, the manifest is, too."

The president looked at his watch. "How much longer do you give him?"

"I've got local Covert-One people out looking. Two . . . three hours, then I send out a dragnet. It's always possible he was captured and is being interrogated. That he'll be able to hold out. That the locals will find and free him. But . . ."

"But the manifest might still be gone."

"Yes, Sam. Probably is gone."

"And Colonel Smith might be dead."

Klein gazed down at his shoes. His voice was tight. "Yes. God, I hope not. But yes."

The president nodded. He heaved a sigh. "All right, we'll find another way. There's always a way, Fred."

"Yes, of course."

Neither said more, their silence acknowledging the lie in their optimism.

At last Klein said, "I'd like to know everything

the CIA has learned from Agent Russell and her people."

"I'll call Arlene."

Klein nodded, almost to himself. "Perhaps it *is* time to attempt that SEAL mission. If it's successful . . . if they find the chemicals, take over the ship, and dump it all overboard without the submarine's knowing . . . that solves the whole problem, and it wouldn't matter —"

"That the manifest was gone and Smith was dead? Is that what happens to all men who have to do your job?"

Klein seemed to deflate. Then his head raised, and his gaze was steady. "I had in mind the total loss of the manifest, Mr. President, not Jon's death. But, yes, I expect that, sooner or later, it does happen to all of us."

"Spymasters," the president said quietly. "It must be horrible."

"I've brought you very bad news. I'm sorry, Sam."

"So am I. So am I. Thank you, old friend. Good-bye."

After Klein left, the president continued to stand in silence. He knew what he had to do, but he neither wanted to nor was comfortable with it. He had never been at ease ordering people to risk their lives for their country, as much as he knew that was what they expected to do, what they had signed up to do, what he had done when it was his turn long ago. He had fought in his own war, and he knew no one signed up to die.

His sigh was more like a deep breath. He picked up the phone again. "Mrs. Pike? Get me Admiral Brose."

Moments later, his phone rang.

The admiral's deep voice appeared in his ear. "Yessir, Mr. President."

"How soon can you put that SEAL team on the *Crowe*?"

"They're on the *Crowe* now, sir. I took the liberty."

"Did you? Well, I expect you're not the first field commander who's done that to a president who hasn't made up his mind."

"No, sir, I wouldn't think so. May I ask if you *have* made up your mind?"

"That's why I called."

"Are we go, sir?"

"Yes. We're go."

"I'll transmit the order."

"Don't you want to know why, Stevens?"

"That's not my job, Mr. President."

The president hesitated. "Right again, Admiral. Keep me posted."

"What I know, you'll know."

As the president hung up, a quote he had read once years ago in a biography of Otto von Bismarck came to mind. Something like . . . a person's moral worth begins only at the point he is willing to die for his principles. He was not risking his life for his principles, but he was risking his future, which was not all that important, and the future of his country, which was. That might not be a full commitment for those stern and demanding old Prussian squires, but it weighed heavily enough for him.

Chapter
Twenty-Eight

Sunday, September 17
The Arabian Sea

Tension was wearing on the small cadre of officers of the USS *John Crowe*. This was far from an ordinary military emergency, which often turned out to be a false bogey, a lost craft, or a mechanical failure. One mistake, and they could cause not only their own deaths but war.

In the communications-and-control center, the calm commander, James Chervenko, broke the radio connection with Admiral Brose back in Washington. His eyes, narrowed by decades at sea, had become laserlike slits of intensity as he had listened to Brose's orders.

He removed his headset and turned to Lt. Commander Gary Kozloff. "You're go."

"Right," Kozloff acknowledged. No surprise. He had guessed. "Chopper prepared?" Kozloff was one of those extraordinary SEALs who was all muscle and brains. Long, lean, and fiercely proud of his work, he crackled with purpose. His presence seemed to fill communications-and-control, giving momentary reassurance to everyone around.

"Ten minutes."

"We'll be ready."

Chervenko nodded as if to say that was to be expected. "Remember, Commander, the overriding mission protocol is total secrecy — you were never there. The first hint you might be discovered, you're gone."

"Yessir."

"We'll keep close tabs on the sub and the *Empress*. If anything looks hinky, I'll radio to abort. Keep your communications on at all times."

"Will do, sir."

"Good luck, Gary."

"Thanks, Jim." Gary Kozloff gave a short smile. "Nice night for a swim."

On the shadowy deck, Kozloff's team of four SEALs were suited and ready, waiting for the order. When Kozloff reappeared, they jumped expectantly to their feet. He nodded, and they did a final check of their equipment.

"You have your magnetic climbing gear?" It would be critical tonight. When the air resonated with "aye, sir," he said, "Let's hit the chopper."

They made their way aft to the SH-60 Seahawk. Silhouetted against the starry horizon, it looked like a giant, menacing bird. The wind was light, carrying the scents of diesel and salt water. Inside the Seahawk, attached to its lowering rig, was a special Combat Rubber Raiding Craft (CRRC) Zodiac, already loaded for the operation.

The five SEALs climbed aboard the chopper, the rotors erupted into full power, and the great craft rose into the night and banked left. No lights showing, it quickly melded with the darkness as it circled out of sight toward the *Empress*, ten miles ahead. The air around them thundered with the chopping blades.

As his ears grew accustomed to the noise, Lt. Commander Kozloff watched the reflections of the moon and stars off the rippled sea below. He was worried, and that was unlike him. If you prepared properly, you knew you and your team would execute well. That was the only guarantee anyone got. But this time, they were using the new, small Zodiac and the new climbing equipment designed specifically for a helicopter-delivered, clandestine boarding operation on a fully moving ship at sea. They knew their equipment, but there had been no time to practice the usual varied and complicated scenarios.

He had the highest confidence in himself and his people. You could not be a SEAL otherwise. Still —

Abruptly, Kozloff brought his concentration back to the scene below. They had reached the *Empress* and were hovering over it, as planned. The freighter was going about ten knots. Kozloff could see cargo, a partially lighted deck, and the usual ropes, gear, and hold covers. There were three Chinese sailors — impossible to tell on this commercial freighter which one or ones were officers, if any — on the open bridge. The trio were gazing up at the helicopter, expressions angry, and he worried again. Would they dive for cover while their ship fired?

The plan was for the chopper to appear to be doing recon and then close-up surveillance. Innocent, not deadly. He waited, aware his men were also studying the bridge below, concerned about how the Chinese would react.

As two continued to glare up, the other got on the horn. In response, the helicopter swung left and right, as if waving . . . or doing a nautical nose-thumbing. The Chinese sailor broke his communications link, threw back his head, bellowed what was probably a string of obscenities, and shook his fist at the chopper.

Kozloff liked that — the sailors had bought the surveillance ruse and expected nothing more dangerous from the Seahawk. As his SEALs chuckled, his spirits lifted. The Seahawk resumed full speed and banked in such a wide arc away that they lost sight of the freighter.

"Ready?" the pilot called into Kozloff's ear receiver.

Kozloff looked at his men. They gave him a thumbs-up. He barked into his pinpoint mike, "Ready. Take us down."

The Seahawk swept low to the swell of the open sea and hung there, vibrating. The SEALs pushed the Zodiac out the side hatch, and the lift operator lowered it to the surface. The SEALs hooked to the lift and went over the edge, one by one, and dropped into the water. For an instant, Kozloff had the usual double reaction — shock at the feeling of suspension that the water gave, and relief to be where he felt so at home.

As the Zodiac bounced on the undulating sea two dozen feet away, Kozloff struck out in a crawl, pulling the water. It was black, impenetrable, but he did not notice. Focused on the operation, he clambered aboard, the others following. He started the electric outboard, and soon they were speeding toward the oncoming *Empress.* This was the safest direction to approach, where they ran less risk of being sucked into the ship. It was also faster, since the *Empress* was headed directly toward them.

When the *Empress* came into view, the chopper was sweeping over it again, a noisy diversion. Kozloff studied the cargo ship, calculating and adjusting the Zodiac's direction so that it would run parallel, not dead on. At just the right moment, he would turn hard to the right. Protected by the darkness and the aerial insult of the helicopter, he would pilot the Zodiac to the *Empress*'s side, where his people would hook silently to the hull with the magnetic mooring. If all continued to go well, they would use the magnetic climbing gear to swarm up to the dark forward deck, where they would begin their critical search.

On the USS *John Crowe,* Commander Chervenko watched the Seahawk settle down onto its helipad in a perfect landing. He ducked under the still-turning rotors and ran toward the door. "Everything go okay?" he shouted to the pilot.

"Great, sir! They're there."

Chervenko gave a brisk nod and hurried back down to communications-and-control. As he entered, his gaze instantly went to OS2 Fred Baum, who was concentrating on the radar screen. "Can you pick up the Zodiac, Baum?"

"No, sir. Way too small."

"Hastings? You hearing anything?"

"Only the *Empress*'s screws and that sub that's dogging us, sir," Sonar Technician First-Class

Matthew Hastings said. "No one can pick up that electric motor behind the noise of the freighter."

Chervenko pursed his lips with satisfaction. "Good. Maybe our boys will pull it off." He turned to leave and thought better of it. "Keep alert. Watch for anything funny the *Empress* does, and —"

"Sir?" Hastings at sonar was listening intently. His voice rose. "The *sub.* That Chinese sub is moving in fast! *Real fast!* She's closing in on us!"

Chervenko grabbed an earphone and listened. The submarine was definitely approaching at full speed. "Anyone got anything else?"

Another technician called out, "They're arming torpedoes, sir! Running them in!"

Chervenko whirled to the radioman. "Call the abort! Abort!"

The communications technician bent to his mike and yelled, *"Abort! Abort! Abort!"*

The Zodiac pounded through the sea to within only a few feet of the towering steel side of the *Empress.* For the SEALs, it was like looking up at a skyscraper, except that the skyscraper was moving at a fast clip, while they were moving toward it and trying not to be sucked in, caught in the turbulence, or slammed against the side. Disorientation and surprise twists from the sea killed many. Still, Kozloff was accustomed to disorientation, and his brain was well trained to calculate exactly how to approach the looming freighter most safely, without cracking up against it.

He inched the Zodiac closer. Cold spray hit his face. The stink of oil and metal was oppressive. Without needing an order, the SEAL who was responsible leaned far out and clamped the magnetic docking device to the *Empress* on the first try. Water surged up over the Zodiac's sides, drenching them. At the same time, the point SEAL activated his magnetic hooks and began to climb, a spider scaling a monolith. Soon the next SEAL climbed, then the next.

Kozloff watched proudly. The safety of night . . . the diversion by the chopper . . . the nearly perfect anchoring . . . everything told him that this vital operation was going to be successful.

He allowed himself a smile as he activated his magnetic climbers and attached them to the hull. Instantly he felt the pull, the sense of safety. The damn things really worked. He launched upward, just as the first SEAL reached the ship's deck.

Suddenly his minireceiver screamed in his ear, *"Abort! Abort! Abort!"*

With a wrench of his gut, he forced himself to reverse his drive to push onward. He made himself believe the incomprehensible: Success was withdrawal.

He flipped the switch, opening the line to his men. *"Abort! Come back! Abort, dammit. Abort! Get your asses back down here on the double!"*

The men dropped down the wall, sliding quickly by reducing the magnetism in their hand-hold and foot-hold units. He worried about the top man, who had disappeared onto the ship. From the Zodiac, he stared upward, unconsciously holding his breath. *Where was his point man?*

When the point SEAL appeared, he was like a fireman on a greased pole, dropping straight down the hull, his expression pissed and trying to hide it.

As soon as his feet touched the Zodiac's side, one SEAL yanked him aboard, while another released the magnetic anchor. Kozloff turned the boat away from the freighter, fighting waves and the drag of the sea that tried to suck the Zodiac into the ship's screws.

His people watched the hulking *Empress* without talking. They could still be seen.

When no searchlight appeared, Kozloff took a deep breath of relief. The only good thing as far as he was concerned was at least that part of their mission was successful — *The Dowager Empress* had not spotted them.

As he accelerated back toward the *Crowe*, the *Empress* thundered onward, leaving the Zodiac to pitch and yaw in the rough wake. Now that they were safe, his men began grumbling.

"What in hell happened?" asked the point man.

"We could've made it!" complained the anchor man.

Kozloff silently agreed, but he was also commander. "Orders, people," he said sternly. "We had orders to abort. We don't question orders."

Commander Chervenko leaned over the shoulder of Hastings, listening to the submarine. He stiffened as he heard the enemy vessel slow. Had he heard right?

Hastings swallowed. "The sub's easing up, sir. Falling back."

The radioman called, "Bridge says the Zodiac's home. It's signaling off the starboard bow. Commander Bienas says he's slowing to pick up the SEALs."

His voice radiating relief, Hastings added, "Looks like the sub's dropping back to its original position behind us, sir."

Chervenko inhaled. It was the most emotion he allowed himself in front of his men. He was drained by the last few hours. As he looked around at the tight faces, he knew they were even more so. At least he had years of experience under his belt buckle. "All right, let's figure out how in hell that sub knew to threaten us just when our SEALs were about to board the *Empress*. Hastings?"

"No way they picked up the Zodiac or the Seahawk on sonar, sir."

"The *Empress* saw the Seahawk hovering," OS2 Fred Baum suggested. "They put two and two together."

"That could've been it," Chervenko agreed. "Good work everyone. Keep your eyes and ears open. Call me if there's anything else."

As Chervenko hurried down to his quarters to report to Washington, he knew there was no way *The Dowager Empress* could have detected the unloading of the SEAL team far ahead in the nighttime ocean. The *Empress* knew they had been hassled by the Seahawk, but that was all. The only way the Chinese sub would have known to move ahead to threaten the *Crowe* so the SEAL raid was stopped was if they had been warned in advance. Someone had warned the Chinese submarine. Someone in Washington.

Saturday, September 16
Washington, D.C.
The president stood at the windows of the Oval

396

Office, looking out over the Rose Garden, his back to the distraught Admiral Brose. "They failed?"

"The Chinese sub moved in." Brose's voice was wooden. "It loaded and armed torpedoes. Commander Chervenko thinks they knew the raid was coming and guessed the chopper overfly was the start."

"Someone here warned them?"

"That's how it looks." The admiral's remark suggested the president might know more than he did. The admiral had not been included in the recent information about the leaks. No one but the DCI and Fred Klein were tight in the loop.

"All right, thank you, Stevens."

The admiral stood, but he did not leave. "What now, sir?"

The president turned, his hands clasped behind, his tall figure framed in the window. "We go on as before. Make sure all the services are ready and that we have a strong presence in Asian waters on a war footing."

"Then, Mr. President?"

"Then we wait for China's move."

"The *Empress* should reach Iraqi waters Monday evening our time. Tuesday morning theirs." Brose's hard gaze fixed on the president. "Today's Saturday, so we're talking just one and, maybe, a half days. Things were bad enough when we still had almost a full week."

"I know, Admiral. I know."

The admiral heard the unspoken criticism and nodded slowly. "My apologies, Mr. President."

"No apology needed, Stevens. Go see that your

people are taken care of. Were any hurt?"

"We don't know yet. When I talked with Chervenko, the *Crowe* hadn't picked them up yet. I thought you'd want to know about the abort as soon as possible."

"Yes. I did. Thank you."

When the admiral left, President Castilla remained standing. At last he let out an agonized sigh. He picked up his blue phone, the direct, scrambled line to Covert-One headquarters.

Fred Klein answered immediately. "Yes, Mr. President?"

"The SEALs had to abort." The president repeated Brose's report. "The Chinese were warned. Commander Chervenko is sure."

"Was it Secretary Kott?"

"No. I sent him on a special mission to Mexico to keep him out of Washington. He's completely off the page, and the CIA's watching him, just to be sure."

The president paused, feeling again his outrage and disgust at Kott's misuse of power. His leaks had caused devastating damage, and the president intended to hold him accountable. But not yet. It was too early to tip his hand.

He continued, "I'll tell Arlene Debo that a leak here in Washington may be the source for the sub's aggression on the *Crowe*. Obviously, we can't lay that one on Kott. Have you heard from Jon Smith?"

"Afraid not," Klein told him. "Another hour, I activate my people."

"We'd better both pray they find him and the manifest. He's our last chance."

"What does Arlene say about McDermid? Any news from Agent Russell?"

"More bad news. Russell has disappeared, too."

PART THREE

Chapter
Twenty-Nine

Hong Kong

Two Chinese men dragged a struggling peasant woman into the L-shaped room and flung her to the floor near where the man slumped in a chair, his hands tied behind, his face bloodied, his feet naked. The room was airless.

"Take a good look," one told her in Cantonese. "When you're questioned, remember — that'll be you if you don't answer."

Dressed in loose pajama trousers and shirt, the peasant woman cowered on the floor and blinked in the way of someone who has not understood a word. The man shook his head, beginning to worry. He looked at his partner, and they left.

Randi heard the door lock behind them. Her black eyes flashed angrily, and her gaze swept over the room, analyzing it. The two wide windows, one front and one back, were covered by drapes. The morning light penetrated only in thin lines around them. She did not move, concerned she was being observed from somewhere. She studied Jon and the knots that tied him to the chair. Silently, she swore. *Damn.* They had him, too, and they had been tuning him.

She had stumbled into more than she or Langley had expected. Whatever Jon was working on this time, clearly Ralph McDermid was part of it. Experience had taught her that when her almost brother-in-law showed up, something significant was likely involved.

Langley was rarely in the loop of whatever exactly Jon was doing. His employer must operate at the highest levels of the federal government, no matter how much he denied it. That meant the leaks McDermid had somehow orchestrated might be only the tip of some political or military iceberg. If she were right, her assignment took on a new dimension she would, for the moment, keep to herself.

Meanwhile, she had to hope her local team had realized by now she had been taken while staking out Ralph McDermid and his latest girl novelty, and that they were already mounting a rescue. On the other hand, she could not count on it.

She crumpled back against the floor as if overcome by fear. What she had to figure out was some way to escape so she could contact them. At the same time, she could not let them realize she and Jon knew each other or that she was a Langley spy, no matter what they did to Jon or to her.

As if hearing her thoughts, the door to the L-shaped room opened, and Ralph McDermid entered. The Altman CEO was followed by Feng Dun, but it was McDermid who stood over her.

He asked harshly in English, "Why are you following me? *Spying* on me? You'd better talk, if you

404

don't want to rot in one of your government prisons."

She forced her body to do nothing. She lay on the floor in her peasant disguise without moving a muscle, as if she understood no English and had no idea what he said or even that he was speaking to her.

Feng Dun kicked her in the ribs. She howled in protesting Mandarin and twisted to look up at the two men, an innocent peon cringing with fear.

"She's not from this area," Feng Dun told McDermid in English. "She's speaking Mandarin from around Beijing or farther north." He casually kicked her again and switched back to Mandarin to demand, "What are you doing so far from home, peasant? Why are you in Hong Kong?"

Randi howled once more, a small, aggrieved nobody being picked on by the powerful. "There is no work on the land of my father!" she screamed. Then, weeping: "So I left for Guangzhou, but the money is better here."

"What the hell is she saying?" McDermid said.

Feng repeated it. "It's a common story. Millions leave the country to look for any kind of job in the cities."

"Millions don't end up following me. Why was she spying? For whom?"

Feng translated the question with a few twists of his own: "You were following Mr. McDermid most of the day. Did you think we didn't see you? Mr. McDermid is a very important man. Unless you want to be given to the police, who will put you in prison for the rest of your life, you'll tell us who paid you and what he wanted you to find out."

Ever since Feng and the two other men had surprised her, listening at the bedroom window in the garden of Ralph McDermid's mansion, Randi had been thinking of what she could say that they would believe. A lot would depend on their level of paranoia. On how much McDermid had to hide, on how many enemies he had, and on how well he and Feng Dun knew those enemies.

She decided to try to evade a little longer. She would continue to act like a frightened, unsophisticated country woman, then give them the "mystery man" story. "I was only looking for money," she whimpered. "The gate to the garden was open. I heard voices, and I went in to ask the rich foreigner for help."

Feng Dun's foot kicked so fast she did not see it move until it exploded in pain against her ribs.

She shrieked like a pig being dragged to slaughter. As she writhed on the floor, she managed to gasp, "My family *must* have money. I don't earn enough in the factories to send to the village. I have to have more. And . . . and sometimes I have to steal. It was such a fine house . . . there'd be much money in such a house. There'd be beautiful things to take and sell. . . ."

"Stupid peasant!" Feng's pale face flushed pink and contorted in rage. "You followed him *all day*. You were *spying* on him. Probably for far longer!"

Randi gave her best cunning, groveling, pleading, terrified-nobody performance. She grabbed at McDermid's ankles and blubbered up into his repulsed face.

Feng cursed in Mandarin, grabbed her by her pajama top, and dragged her away from McDermid. "Peasants! They pretend they're being skinned alive if you bump into them. I'll give her something real to howl about." He spun around. In his soft voice, he spoke rapidly to the other two men. "Get the electrodes and the blowtorch."

His words were in Shanghainese, but Randi understood the dialect. Her mind reeled. She could stand torture as well as most, but resistance would almost certainly end up incapacitating her even if she were rescued or managed to escape. Still, there was one story they might believe completely: She would give them Jon.

He was already hurt. For all she knew, it could be serious. She steeled herself as she glanced at him. He sagged against his bindings, unconscious, not even moaning. She could do nothing for either of them if she, too, were badly injured. And she could do nothing for the Company and certainly nothing for America.

She would let them get their blowtorch, their electric devices, or whatever other horrors Feng Dun had in his torture arsenal. If they chose the electrodes, they would apply a nasty stun to her first, which she knew would leave no serious damage. She would not break and give them Jon until the second or third jolt. The longer she held out, the more they would believe what she told them. If they started with the blowtorch, she would have to gamble and give him up sooner. Blowtorches frightened her.

The two grinning men returned with their persecution tools. Reflex was a physical reaction beyond control of the mind. Only a split second after she had reacted did Randi realize Feng Dun had been watching.

He smiled again. "Light the blowtorch," he told one of the men. To the other, he ordered, "Bring another chair. Take off her sandals."

Ralph McDermid swallowed hard. "Is that really necessary —"

"Yes, Taipan," Feng Dun's voice had a harsh, irritated edge. "In matters of this importance, hands must get dirty. Even bloody."

The second man grabbed a chair from a corner. Feng Dun picked her up by the shoulders. She sagged, but he lifted her as easily as if she were a straw doll. He dumped her onto the chair. The first man lit the blowtorch, while the second pulled off her sandals.

She shrieked again in Mandarin. "No! No! I'll tell you. *He* hired me." She pointed at Jon, who still did not move against his ropes. "I was afraid to say it. You would hurt me as you've hurt him. But . . . *that's the man who did it.* He paid me, told me to follow the gentleman there, and remember where he went, what he did, and who he talked to. Everything the foreign gentleman did. I needed the money. My father and mother are old. They need medicine and food. Their house is old. It must be repaired. *Please! Don't hurt me!*"

She chattered on as if terror had unleashed a flood of words. McDermid and the other men turned to study Jon as Feng translated. A look of understanding came over McDermid's face. Randi could see belief in his eyes, saying to himself, *Yes, of course. Why didn't I guess that from the start?*

408

Feng was not looking at McDermid. He was staring at Randi's feet. He stepped closer, grabbed her hands, and turned them over to peer at the palms.

Distracted by Feng's movements, and relieved that the blowtorch was not going to be necessary, McDermid said, "Feng? What is it?"

Feng dropped Randi's hands, grabbed her chin, and tilted it up. He stared at her face, her eyes, her hair. His long fingers felt like steel nails against her forehead and scalp, and her stomach plunged.

She pulled back. "Owww! *You're hurting me!*"

"Stay still."

Abruptly, the fingers dug into her forehead below the hairline. Her flesh-colored scalp and black wig peeled off in his hand, revealing the tight skullcap that held down her own hair.

"Feng!" McDermid's broad face looked stunned.

Feng pulled off the skullcap, and her blond hair tumbled out.

His two musclemen gaped as if they had seen a miracle.

McDermid announced stupidly, "She's not Chinese!"

"No," Feng said, without taking his gaze from Randi's face, "she's not Chinese."

"But how did you — ?"

"Her feet," Feng said. "Rural people wear sandals most of their lives. She doesn't have the gap between her large toe and the others." He studied her with a kind of admiration. "Her hands have been artificially coarsened and aged, probably with latex skin. The same kind of product gave her eyes an Oriental fold and shape. She's probably wearing contact lenses, and there's a subtle pigmentation on her skin from some kind of long-lasting skin dye. It's a remarkable piece of intelligence tradecraft, the work of experts."

Everyone in the room, except the unconscious Jon, stared at Randi the way they would at an exotic zoo animal.

Fear rushed through her. She thought fast. They would no longer believe her story that Jon had hired her. Feng had deduced that she worked for an intelligence agency. Nothing would change his mind about that now. Whatever new lie she told must contain that admission. Sweating, she considered possibilities . . . what Feng and McDermid might believe . . . what legend she had the skills to make credible.

"So," Feng said in that ghostly voice that seldom varied, which made it all the more intimidating. "You aren't Chinese, but you speak Mandarin as well or better than I do, and I'd guess Cantonese and Shanghainese, too, yes? Certainly English. You've understood every word we've said. You've been ahead of us from the start. You're highly trained by a large organization with global interests and the need for operatives who can speak foreign languages. Even our American friend there can't speak Chinese. But he isn't CIA, is he? A special person, perhaps, recruited for a special mission, but with a real Langley agent to work with him, yes? And, of course, that Langley agent would be you."

Randi made a decision. She curled her lip and said in disgusted Russian, "Don't insult me."

Ralph McDermid took a half step back, his eyes wide as if he had been slapped across the face.

Feng Dun blinked.

"And you're right about Colonel Smith," she continued in perfect Russian. "He's not CIA. What or who he is precisely, I know as little as you." Give them a small confirmation. It could distract them. "But I'd like to know, too. It could prove useful to us later."

McDermid demanded, "What did she say?" When Feng translated, McDermid frowned angrily. "Why is a Russian agent following *me?*"

Randi switched to Russian-accented English. "The Altman Group isn't the only arms dealer."

"Russian intelligence is interested in doing business?" McDermid sensed profit. "Does the Kremlin want to work with us?" He had done good deals with Russia in the past, but recently Moscow had grown greedy, demanding a larger cut.

"In Russia today, life is good for few."

McDermid studied Randi. He decided, "You're not working for the government. You're moonlighting for yourself or others. For one of your capitalist oligarchs, perhaps. Someone who wants to know what the Altman Group is doing for reasons of business utility."

Randi gave a slow nod, as if reluctant to admit it. "We do what we must. My father was GRU. One becomes accustomed to living well."

GRU was the old Soviet military intelligence. Feng said, "Does this oligarch have a name?"

"Possibly." She cocked an eyebrow and looked at McDermid.

Feng turned his head toward McDermid, too.

411

Then he glared at her. "I don't believe you. What weapons deal is Mr. McDermid making in Hong Kong that brought you here?"

"Stop, Feng." McDermid saw dollar signs. Russia still had weapons many people wanted, particularly in the Third World. Although those dictators and self-appointed kings cried poverty, they managed to come up with the cash when it came to guns and ammunition. If this woman had access to a private store, which had probably been looted from the government's dwindling supplies . . . "We need to talk."

Feng remained focused on Randi's face, searching it for something he could not quite pinpoint but seemed sure was there. Then he looked at Jon Smith. He had still not moved. Feng again considered Randi.

"Feng," McDermid repeated.

The enforcer glanced at him, turned, and walked toward the door.

McDermid followed, after a reassuring smile at the moonlighting Russian agent with the business connections.

Chapter Thirty

In an inner office, Ralph McDermid's cell phone rang. He took it from his pocket. "This is McDermid."

The polished voice said, "We need to talk."

McDermid covered the mouthpiece. "I'd better take this," he told Feng Dun.

"Very well. My people must eat anyway."

McDermid nodded. "It's been a long night. Get something downstairs. I want white toast and coffee. Cream and sugar. A Danish, if you can find one. Then we'll talk more about the Russian."

The footsteps of Feng and his men thumped down the wood stairs, while McDermid found a seat on a packing box that held adult toys for a sex shop on the street floor.

He returned to the phone. "I have good news for you."

"What news?"

McDermid related the capture of Smith and the Russian agent. "This is the end of our major problem. All of the copies of the manifest are destroyed."

The voice on the other end said with relief, "Ex-

413

cellent. And did you give my information about the SEAL operation to Feng Dun to pass on?"

"Yes, it's over. He made the connection to one of his people, who got the information to the sub's captain. You hadn't heard?"

"Not yet. It will be a pleasure to act surprised. The White House won't try again, now that they know the Chinese will be watching for more attempts. Tell me about the Russian woman. You say she was spying on you? I don't like the sound of that."

McDermid filled him in. "We can make use of her perhaps. I'll know more soon."

"It's interesting, but let's keep our focus. I'm out on a limb on this. We'd better bring it home."

"*You're* out on a limb? Consider my position. If I'm not worried, you don't have to be."

"What will you do with Smith?"

"Whatever we need to. That's Feng's province. But first, I want to find out for whom he works."

"If anything happens, I know nothing about this."

"Naturally. Neither do I."

Cheered by their progress, McDermid hung up and remained sitting on the packing box, thinking about the new good fortune the Russian woman might have brought. Depending on what she was offering, it could be another billion in the long run.

As soon as she heard the door close, Randi bent to put on her sandals. Her whisper was so low, so directed only toward Jon, that it would be inaudible from the door around the corner.

"Jon? Jon? I'm going to get you out of this. Can you hear me? Jon?"

"Of course, I can hear you. I'm not deaf, you know. At least not yet." His speech was thick through his swollen lips. A hint of pain in the cheerful whisper. "Terrific work. I'm impressed."

Relief rushed through her, mixed with annoyance. "You've been awake the whole time, damn you."

"Now, now." He tried to raise his head. "Only most of the time. I —"

Randi put a finger to her lips, shook her head, and signaled him to slump again. She stood up and walked around the bare room. She examined the floor, walls, and ceiling, as if searching for another way out. What she expected to find were listening devices and closed-circuit cameras, but there were no cameras and no recent changes in the walls that could conceal bugs. Nothing hung on the walls, and there were no wall fixtures and no furniture other than the two straight chairs. She could not be completely certain there were no listening devices, but she did know there were no cameras.

She returned to her chair and said in a low voice, "Okay, they can't see us, and I can't find any mikes, but let's keep it down, just in case. How much did you hear?"

"Most of it. Giving me to them was masterly, probably the only story they would've believed. The Russian bit was positively brilliant. The peasant howling and crawling wasn't bad either. I had no idea you had so much talent as a groveler."

"Your approval warms my heart. But we're still

415

trapped here. Unless you want your feet fried to a cinder on your way to a shallow grave, we'd better figure out what to do when they come back."

"I'm ahead of you. You were doing fine, so I had plenty of time to think. What do you know about the big guy with the crazy hair?"

"Feng Dun?"

"Yes, that's the name I have for him, too."

"He's from Shanghai. A former soldier, guerrilla, and adventurer. Very undercover. Now he's an enforcer for high-level businessmen."

"Where'd he get that hair?"

"There are plenty of redheaded Han, probably from some long-ago minority they assimilated. I'd guess the white's just an odd sign of his aging. Now it's your turn. While I was crawling around on the dirty floor, saving your bacon, what did you come up with to get us loose?"

"We jump 'em and split."

She was speechless at the inadequacy of that. "You're kidding."

"Think about it," he said, the pain in the voice intensifying the more he spoke through his sore lips. "What else do we have? Are there more of them out there on the other side of that door?"

"They blindfolded me. Probably, but we don't even know where we are."

"Yes, we do. Or at least, I do. I've been listening, and even though I was blindfolded, too, I was able to figure out a few things. It's morning now, probably late morning. I heard vendors' voices, awnings being opened, and boat horns and whistles from the harbor. Plus, I think there was a rumble from underneath us, as if the subway runs somewhere

416

near. I figure we're in Wanchai again, in some back street not so far from the harbor."

"From the look of this room, we're in an old building," Randi decided. "And that means probably only one staircase — only one way out."

Jon nodded. "Right, so our best shot really is to jump them. You can handle McDermid, right?"

"With one hand."

"Use two. Just to be sure, not to mention fast."

"Consider it done. We'll need to be out of here in a hurry, before the others know what's happening. But can you do it? You look seriously banged up."

"I've felt better. The good thing is nothing's broken, and I'll rise to the occasion. The threat of death is a fine motivator to get a fellow off his duff."

She studied him and nodded. He had that determined look she had seen in him before. "You're the doctor."

"Get me loose, but leave the ropes on so it looks as if I'm still tied."

She undid the knots, her fingers fumbling as she hurried.

As she worked, he said, "They'll ask you a lot more questions about your Russian contacts. What you're after. What your arms dealer has to sell and wants to buy . . . all that. You've got to keep their attention, especially Feng's."

She left the ropes entwined, so they would look tight. "Thanks for the advice. I never would've figured it out by myself."

Jon ignored her sarcasm. "He'll have his gun, of course. I intend to blindside him."

417

"Then you make damn sure you get him the first time."

"I know. I —"

They heard the key turn in the lock. Jon instantly slumped in the chair, careful not to move the nylon ropes. Randi resumed her nonchalant posture in the other chair, ready to do business with McDermid, if the price was right.

McDermid appeared first. Feng Dun walked behind, not hurrying, his expression a mixture of suspicion and disapproval. He did not like the way McDermid was handling the Russian woman. He cared nothing about McDermid's business, and, besides, he did not trust her. She was too glib. No one had yet asked her to prove that she was who she claimed to be. It was an oversight he intended to correct now.

From under his nearly closed eyelids, Jon saw the questions on Feng's face. And although the killer was distracted, he was watching Jon.

McDermid walked directly to Randi. "All right, let's talk about your people. We're going to —"

"Hold it," Feng announced. "First I'll check the American."

He pulled Jon's head up by his hair. Jon groaned, and he drooled saliva from his slack mouth. Without warning, Feng slapped him across the face. Jon gave a feeble flinch and collapsed so heavily Feng had to support his head with one hand while he used the other to tug on the nylon cords across Jon's chest.

Randi felt her muscles tense with fear as she tried to maintain her casual slouch on the chair. Jon's cords held. She had looped them several places, and Jon had expanded his chest to make them tight. When he relaxed, the loops would slip. Then he could work free unseen.

"Finished?" McDermid said impatiently. The Altman CEO did not wait for an answer. He returned his attention to Randi. "We . . . What's your name, I can't just call you the Russian."

"Ludmilla Sakkov." She nodded toward Feng Dun. "What's his name?"

"You don't need to know my name, Russian. *If* you *are* Russian," Feng said, observing her closely from head to toe. "I once fought for the Russians —"

At that moment, Jon leaped from his chair far more quickly than he had thought possible. Relaxing, feeling the cords slip, then lunging. The loops fell away, the chair clattered backward, and his right fist caught Feng Dun on the point of his jaw. The blow snapped Feng's neck back and sideways, pinched his spinal column, and knocked him sideways where he would have pitched into McDermid, if McDermid had still been standing there.

He was not. Two powerful karate chops to the throat and the side of the head from the suddenly standing "Russian" had knocked McDermid to the floor, unconscious. Feng's legs tripped on McDermid's legs, and Feng slammed down onto his shoulder.

"Jon!" Randi shouted.

As Feng landed, he shook his head to clear it and reached under his jacket. They could see his pistol, but he had sprawled too far away for them to reach it with a kick. He rolled over onto his back, the gun

419

in both hands, preparing for a target. At the same time, shouts erupted outside the room. Feet pounded to the door. Feng's men.

They were trapped again, and they had fewer options.

"The window!" Jon said.

He spun, nearly fell over from a wave of pain, and ran straight at the drapes that covered the big window. He slammed through in a loud shattering of glass and splintering of old wood, and was gone, carrying the protective drapes with him. Without letting herself think, Randi followed.

The room had been on the third floor of a building from the thirties. A scream escaped Randi's throat as she and Jon plunged down.

Jon and Randi flailed through the air, desperately grabbing at anything they could see as they plummeted. They smashed onto a heavy canvas awning. Safe, they gazed with relief at each other, collecting their wits. The awning groaned. They scrambled toward the frame, trying to grab it. The steel supports resisted and bent.

As shouts sounded from the window above, the canvas ripped, dumping them toward the street again. But there was a second, shorter awning, shielding a window. They landed, slid off, and landed again — this time on the umbrella of an omelette vendor. Instantly, it collapsed, too.

They fell hard to the street, barely missing the omelette cart. As the vendor yelled, they lay stunned, reeling. Around them, businesspeople were preparing for the new day. Delivery trucks rumbled along the narrow street, parking on the curb, blocking the traffic so that only one lane could pass. Pedestrians stopped to stare at the European couple who had crashed into their midst, especially since the blond woman wore rustic country clothes. A babel of languages filled the air as they gathered, some pointing upward as they explained the unusual event.

Jon's mouth and face were bleeding again, and there was a ragged tear in his trousers where fresh blood oozed up. He moved his arms and legs. He hurt everywhere, but nothing seemed broken.

Randi had landed on her back. Gasping, trying to breathe normally, she checked herself for injuries, for broken bones, for blood. Remarkably, she appeared to be unhurt.

They sat up, almost at the same moment. As the circle of the curious closed in, they exchanged another look of relief, this time mixed with exhaustion. Still, it was not over. Feng Dun and his men were probably already chasing down the stairs after them.

As they struggled to their feet, she told him, "There's an alley."

Jon nodded, unable to talk. They limped toward it, pushing people out of their way.

"Randi! Here!" CIA operative Allan Savage waved his arms from where he stood on the fender of a black Buick. His nondescript face was worried. Two more members of Randi's team were shoving their way toward them.

"Who's this guy?" Agent Baxter wanted to know as he slung Jon's arm over his shoulder and supported him toward the car.

"Don't ask. Get him inside. Fast!"

With his peripheral vision, Jon saw Feng Dun burst through to the street next to an adult shop, his head swiveling as he looked everywhere. Three other men crowded out behind. All aimed weapons. When the crowd saw them, they screamed and ran.

Jon's legs moved weakly, unable to hold him up. Randi tumbled into the back of the Buick. Agent Baxter threw Jon in after her.

Shots ripped the street. People continued to scatter, finding cover where they could. From the car, Allan Savage in the driver's seat and a female agent in the back returned a withering fire from minisubmachine guns.

As Feng Dun and his killers dove back into the doorway, Savage ground the Buick's gears and drove away, screeched around the first corner, and was gone.

The CIA safe house occupied a four-story building on Lower Albert Road in Central. The Buick drove into an alley behind the building, a cement wall slid open, and the car disappeared inside. The first floor had been gutted, the hidden garage installed, and the front area turned into an insurance office where people came and went all day, doing legitimate business. The insurance agency made a small profit, which pleased the DCI in Langley as well as the congressmen and senators on the oversight committees.

On the second floor was the safe house's first-aid room. An American-born Hong Kong doctor on Langley's payroll examined their wounds and bruises and took X rays with a portable unit.

He declared Randi "one lucky little girl."

Allan Savage and the others on the rescue team winced as they saw the scowl that appeared on Randi's face, expecting the worst for the doctor. But to their astonishment, she merely glared. The doctor, who had expected at least a smile of appreciation, was confused.

He turned hastily to Jon, who was a different matter. "That's a nasty battering your face took, and you're bruised around the ribs." He muttered to himself as he took X rays of Jon's injuries and was amazed to find nothing more than the severe bruising. "Still, you're well beat up. I'd say you were out of action for a week . . . at least three or four days. You could get an infection from those facial wounds and the lacerations in your mouth."

"Sorry, Doc," Jon told him. "Work to do. Clean me up and shoot me full of antibiotics. Painkillers sound like an attractive idea, too."

After the doctor left, the crew provided lunch. Soup only for Jon.

Allan Savage apologized to Randi. "Sorry we were late, but Tommie tailed you fine until they got you to the street. That's where she lost you. She never saw exactly where they took you. We were combing the area building by building when you came flying out those windows. That was a damned risky way to escape. How'd you know how high you were and what was under the windows?"

"Don't ask me." Randi gave a toss of her head toward Jon. "It was his idea. I just followed." She wolfed down eggs and bacon.

Jon shrugged. "I figured it was an older, lower building. Anyway, without weapons, and Feng Dun's going for his gun and the rest of the gang damn near into the room, we didn't have time to even grab our chairs and swing them. It was out the window or dead."

There were awed looks all around.

The other female agent, Tommie Parker, said to Randi, "Who *is* this guy?"

"Meet Lieutenant Colonel Jon Smith, M.D. That's Jon without an *h*. He's a researcher for USAMRIID. What else he is remains open for speculation, right, Jon?"

"Randi sees conspiracies everywhere." Jon grinned innocently. The painkillers were taking effect. Between them and the soup, he was beginning to feel much better. There were flesh-covered Band-Aids on his face, and his fat lip was hardly a pretty sight. Still, he figured he could look a lot worse. Now what he wanted was a few uninterrupted hours of sleep.

"So do we," Allan Savage said, studying Jon.

Jon sighed. "I'm a doctor, a microbiological scientist, and I work at Fort Detrick for USAMRIID. Sometimes they send me on special assignments. Especially in cases of emerging viruses. Why don't we leave it at that?"

Tommie frowned, her dark eyes suspicious. She had shoulder-length brown hair and a sweet, gamin's face that Jon had decided hid shrewd intellect and a daring spirit. "What virus is emerging in Hong Kong, Colonel?"

"None. But there's one inside China," he lied, "and Donk & LaPierre's medical division is inves-

424

tigating it. The government wants to know more."

"Which government?" Tommie probed suspiciously.

Randi interrupted, "That's the only thing about Jon I'm sure of — he works for our side."

Jon had a retort ready to fling when the last agent from the Buick, Baxter, leaned into the first-aid room through an open door. "We're picking up something on the phone bug we installed in McDermid's office last night. A call just came in."

They jumped up and ran out along the hallway and into a rear room crammed with electronic gear, machines, and instruments. Randi and Jon pushed through to stand close to a notebook computer from which a woman's voice spoke with a slight accent. "You're Ralph McDermid?"

Chapter
Thirty-One

Ever since he returned to his penthouse office, Ralph McDermid had been alternately worried and angry. As he worked on a new agreement to acquire a troubled Asian investment firm in Hong Kong, his mind returned to the morning's debacle with Jon Smith and the woman. He was angry with himself for allowing the woman, who might not have been Russian after all, certainly not someone looking for a business deal, to play him so easily, and at Feng Dun, for underestimating Smith.

Still, the situation was hardly lost. It was true the pair was on the loose, and Jon Smith was dangerous, but little harm had actually been done. Smith still had no way to prove the *Empress* carried illicit chemicals. Feng would eventually find and kill him — he had the resources, even here in Hong Kong.

These thoughts reassured him. When his phone rang, he answered with his usual well-honed civility. "Yes, Lawrence?"

"A lady, sir. On line two. She sounds rather young, and . . . ah . . . attractive."

426

"A lady? And possibly attractive? Well, well." He was expecting no calls from any "lady," and this made him feel even more optimistic. "Put her on, Lawrence. Put her on."

He was straightening his tie as if she could see him when her voice appeared in his ear in slightly stilted English. "You're Ralph McDermid?"

"Guilty as charged, my dear. Do we know each other?"

"Perhaps. You're chairman and CEO of the Altman Group?"

"Yes, yes. That I am."

"Your corporation is the owner of Donk & LaPierre?"

"We're a financial group, and we hold many companies. But what — ?"

"We've never met, Mr. McDermid, but I believe we'll soon have occasion for that. At least figuratively."

McDermid felt his bad temper returning. This sounded like no woman suggesting a tryst. "If this is business, madame, you'll need to call my office, state what that business is, and make an appointment. If your concern is with Donk & LaPierre, I suggest you call them directly. Good day to you —"

"Our business is with *The Dowager Empress*, Mr. McDermid. Believe me, you are wise to deal with us directly."

McDermid's eyebrows rose. "What?"

"The *Empress* is a ship, in case you've forgotten. A Chinese cargo vessel en route to Basra. Its cargo is, we believe, of great interest to the Americans. Possibly to the Chinese also."

"Tell me what you want, and we might be able to benefit both of us."

"We're delighted you're ready to talk of mutual benefit."

He lost his temper. "Stop speaking in riddles! You'll have to tell me far more to convince me I need to listen. Otherwise, stop wasting my time!" Attack, as he had learned personally over the years, was often the best defense.

"The *Empress* sailed from Shanghai in early September for Basra. In its holds are many tons of thiodiglycol for Iraq to produce blister weapons as well as thionyl chloride to produce both blister and nerve weapons." The woman's quiet voice took on a sinister edge. "Is that sufficient, Mr. Ralph McDermid, CEO, founder of the Altman Group?"

McDermid found it difficult to speak. He pressed the recording button on the phone, signaled for Lawrence, and said carefully, "Precisely whom do you represent, and what do you want?"

"We represent only ourselves. Are you ready to hear our price and terms?"

Lawrence entered the office. McDermid gestured for him to have the call traced. At the end of his patience, he snapped, "Who the hell are you, and why shouldn't I hang up immediately?"

"My name is Li Kuonyi, Mr. McDermid. My husband is Yu Yongfu. As you no doubt recall, he's the president and chairman of Flying Dragon Enterprises. He's an intelligent man. So intelligent and farseeing, in fact, that he saved his company's copy of the *Empress*'s invoice manifest. We have it with us."

★ ★ ★

In the CIA safe house, the exclamation burst from Jon before he could stop himself, "Holy hell!"

All eyes turned to look.

Randi said, "Jon? You know what this is about?"

"Later," he said, waving his hand. "Quiet. *Listen*."

McDermid's shocked silence had ended. He'd had enough. "Your husband burned the manifest and committed suicide. A tragedy, as we say. I don't know what *your* game is, but —"

"You were told my husband had killed himself to save his family on the orders of my father and those far higher politically. You were also told he burned the manifest and shot himself in the head and fell into the river. All of that's a lie. He burned a useless paper and fired his pistol, yes. He fell into the river, yes. But the bullets in the weapon weren't real. What Feng saw was a charade. I know, because I staged it."

"Impossible!"

"Has the body of my husband been found?"

"Many bodies are never found in the Yangtze delta."

"Do you know my husband's voice, Mr. McDermid?"

"No."

"Feng Dun does."

"He isn't here."

"You are, of course, recording this conversation?"

There was a pause. "Yes."

"Then listen."

429

A male voice came onto the line. "I'm Yu Yongfu, McDermid. Tell that traitor Feng that the last time we spoke I offered him a bonus. He told me of the death of the American spy, Mondragon, on Liuchiu Island and about a second American who escaped and was seen in Shanghai. Tell him that, unfortunately for him, my wife is my business partner, and I never withhold information from her. Never. It was she who advised me to keep the manifest safe, and she's the one who orchestrated my 'suicide.' Everyone believes she's the smarter of us in all ways, but that's not true. I'm rather intelligent myself — after all, I convinced her to marry me."

Then the man was gone, and the woman returned. "Play that for Feng. Now you and I need to talk business."

"Why doesn't your husband do the talking, madame?"

"Because he knows that in this area, I am smarter and stronger."

McDermid appeared to think about that. "Or he's dead, and you played a recording."

"You know better than that. Still, in the end, does it matter? I have the manifest, and you want it."

"And what do *you* want, Madame Li?"

"Money for a new life far from China for my children, my husband, and myself, but not such an enormous amount that it would sting you more than a mosquito bite. I'm reasonable. Two million American dollars should be good for all of us."

"That's it?" He let sarcasm fill his voice.

She ignored it. "We'll need travel and identity

papers, as well as an exit visa. The best papers."

He paused, rethinking his objections. "For that I get the manifest?"

"That's what I said."

"And if you don't get what you want?"

"The Americans and Chinese will receive the manifest instead. I'll arrange for it to be put into their hands myself, just as I arranged Yongfu's 'suicide.' The original will go to Washington, and a copy will be sent to Beijing."

McDermid laughed. "If Yu Yongfu is truly alive, he will know that's impossible. It can't happen. If by some chance it *did* happen, he'd be dead, and so would you."

There was no humor in the woman's steady tones. "That's a risk we're willing to take. Are you willing to risk the White House and Zhongnanhai receiving the manifest and what we know of the entire *Empress* story?"

Again McDermid hesitated. Life was full of surprises, many of them unpleasant. This was such a surprise and fraught with so many dangerous repercussions that he could not afford to dismiss this woman, whoever she might be. "And how do you propose we consummate this negotiation?"

"You or your representative will bring the money and the identity papers to us. We'll give the manifest to you in return, once we have our payment."

McDermid laughed again. "You think I'm a fool, Madame Li? What guarantee do I have the manifest will actually be turned over to me, or even that it still exists?"

"We're not fools either. If we attempted such a

deception, you'd indeed hunt us down. But you're not a criminal who succeeds by fear. Once you have the manifest and we're gone, your incentive to kill us will be far less. In fact, probably not worth the money, time, and trouble. Bad money after good, as they say."

"That'd require considerable thought."

"Again, what does it matter? You have to do it."

"Where would this exchange take place?"

"At the site of the Sleeping Buddha near Dazu. That's in Sichuan Province."

"When?"

"Tomorrow at dawn."

"You're in Dazu now?"

"Did you think I'd tell you so easily? Where we are is unimportant. You're undoubtedly having this call traced and will soon know anyway. Develop patience. It's a characteristic of the East that the West should adopt."

McDermid needed to stall. First, to play Feng the tape and make sure these people were whom they claimed. Second, if they were bona fide, to give Feng a chance to find and eliminate them before any meeting. "Do you know what time it is, madame? If you're as smart as you say, and if your husband truly is Yu Yongfu, then you'll know I can't possibly put together two million American dollars in cash *and* get to Dazu from Hong Kong so quickly. In addition, I'll need to confirm your story with Feng."

There was what sounded like whispered consultation. These people were less assured than they sounded.

"You'll come yourself? To China?" she asked.

He did not plan any such thing. "Madame, you can't know Feng Dun very well if you think I'd trust him with two million dollars in cash."

A momentary silence. "Very well. *Two million dollars in cash, new identity papers, travel papers, and an exit visa. The Sleeping Buddha at dawn the day after tomorrow.*" She hung up.

Lawrence popped his head around the door. He was grinning. "Got them. They're in Urumqi."

Saturday, September 16
Washington, D.C.

It was deep into the night, and the marina on the Anacostia was mostly deserted. In his cloistered office, Fred Klein looked up at his ship's clock for the tenth time in the last hour. He made a quick calculation: Midnight here would be noon tomorrow in Hong Kong.

Where the devil *was* Jon? He rocked in his desk chair, restless despite his exhaustion. From his years of experience, he knew there could be a thousand possible explanations for Jon's disappearance — anything from clogged traffic to a subway breakdown or some bizarre natural occurrence. There was also the possibility that Jon had been discovered and shot to death. He did not want to think about it, but he could not stop himself.

He looked at the clock again. Where . . .

His phone rang. The blue phone on the shelf behind his desk. Klein grabbed it. "Jon . . . ?"

"I'm not Jon. I hope he's not missing, whoever he may be."

"Sorry, Viktor."

Klein tried to keep the disappointment from his

voice. He refocused. Viktor Agajemian was a former Soviet hydraulics engineer, now officially Armenian but still living and working in Moscow. His firm was helping to build the mammoth Yangtze Gorges Dam project, and he had papers to travel anywhere in China. He was also one of Klein's first recruits to perform occasional tasks for Covert-One in Asia, particularly in China.

"You made contact?" Klein asked.

"I did. Chiavelli says, and I quote, 'Old prisoner appears authentic. Physical condition is good. General area rural, infrastructure bad, military installations few and scattered, and airfields primitive. Potential resistance average-to-minimal. Estimated time: ten to twenty minutes, total. Escape is promising.' That's it, Fred. You planning to break the old boy out?"

"What do you think about an operation like that?"

"From what I saw, Captain Chiavelli may be right. On the other hand, I didn't actually see the prisoner."

"Thanks, Viktor."

"Anytime. The money will arrive in the usual manner?"

"You'd be told of any change." Klein's mind was already back on Jon Smith.

"Sorry to be crass, but times are not the best in Russia or Armenia."

"I understand, Viktor, and thank you. You are, as always, the professional in everything." Klein hung up, thinking that they might possibly have to use Captain Chiavelli's report if . . . Where the devil *was* Jon?

He studied the clock. At last, he took off his glasses, rubbed his eyes, and sat staring at the blue telephone, willing it to ring.

Sunday, September 17
Hong Kong

In the CIA safe house, Jon turned on his heel. "I have to go."

"Whoa, soldier," Randi said. "You go nowhere until you tell us what this is all about."

Jon hesitated. If he did not explain, they would report to Langley and start digging. But how much could he reveal without disclosing everything? Not much, and this time there was no clever story to throw them off track. The resurrected wife of Yu Yongfu had supplied too many details, including the freighter's illegal haul. He could say nothing more without hinting at what Li Kuonyi had not described — his mission.

"All right, I'll level with you," he said, "but I can't reveal exactly what's going on. The need-to-know is off the scale, and I have my orders. But I can tell you this much: I'm working for the White House. They sent me because I happened to be in Taiwan at a scientific meeting and had the opportunity to get into China right away. It was a matter of convenience for them. The woman you just heard is the wife of someone who's vital to the situation. Both she and her husband had disappeared. We'd heard nothing about his being dead. I've got to get this new information to my chief immediately."

"What was all that about a ship and a manifest?" Randi wanted to know.

"That's what I can't tell you."

Randi stared into his eyes, searching for deception, but this time she could find none — just worry, which worried her. "Does what you're working on have any connection to leaks of information from the White House?"

"Leaks? Is that your assignment? Is that why you've been following McDermid?"

"Yes. Your operation turned up McDermid, too?"

"Yeah," Jon said. "I've got a lot to report."

"I'd say we both do."

Tommie, who had left the room, rushed back inside, swearing. "We were tailed. If you're thinking of leaving, Jon, you'd better go out the side way, through the next building and the next. That will put you on a cross street."

"Who is it?"

"Feng Dun and his people. They're watching the street and the alley. The only good thing is they don't seem to know exactly where we are."

"Is that exit clear?" Jon asked. No safe house could exist unless it had two or three ways to escape.

"Not yet. You'd better wait."

"You have a back room I can borrow? I need to report in."

Randi said witheringly, "You sure you want to risk it? The room might be bugged. We might hear something."

Jon did not like keeping her in the dark any more than she liked being in it. He looked around at the CIA agents and offered his most ingenuous smile. "I trust all of you. Hell, you saved my butt. And I sure do appreciate the doctor and the food and the help getting out of here. With luck, I'll be able to return the favor."

Randi glowered and shook her head. At last she heaved a dramatic sigh. She hated it when he was being charmingly right. "You're such a pain, Jon. Oh, very well. I'll find you a place myself."

Chapter
Thirty-Two

The two men were alone in McDermid's luxurious penthouse office, surrounded by museum-quality paintings and Ming Dynasty vases. Feng sat with his thick arms crossed, his broad face emotionless, in the chair opposite McDermid's desk. "Smith and the woman have gone to ground." Feng had ordered most of his men to pursue the pair after their escape, while others had stayed behind to question the crowd. That was how Feng had learned an American voice had shouted to the woman from the escape car. The voice had called her Sandy or Mandy or Randy.

"What the hell does *that* mean?" McDermid asked, barely able to contain his anger as he waited to play the tape of his conversation with Li Kuonyi.

"It means my men were able to track them to Lower Albert Road, where they disappeared into an alley."

"*Disappeared?* What are they, shamans?"

"There's obviously some kind of safe house on the street, and it has hidden entrances. My men are watching."

"Are they CIA after all?"

"We still can't find any affiliation to a known intelligence agency for him. We have only a partial name for her, not heard clearly. It could be a first or a last name. We're checking our sources to see whether we can identify her. But provisionally, I suspect she's CIA. What or whoever they are, they'll reappear."

McDermid had not counted on so many problems. Give him a sick company or an underperforming portfolio, and he was in his element. Better yet, show him a politician at loose ends or a defeated senator growing bored, and he would use them to pull in investment funds or to lobby a piece of legislation until it passed. For him, that was child's play. The *Empress* cargo was something else. It was a deal so big it would crown all others.

Inwardly, he sighed. It was worth any amount of trouble. "Maybe. Forget Smith and the woman for now. Listen to this." When the tape finished playing, McDermid's usually smiling face was flushed with outrage. "Is that Li Kuonyi and Yu Yongfu?"

Feng Dun glanced uneasily around the penthouse aerie and nodded. "They fooled me."

"They fooled you!" he exploded. "That's *all* you have to say? You *idiot*. Yu's alive, and *he still has the manifest!* They switched documents so you'd see him burn something else, and his suicide was smoke and mirrors. That's why he had to fall into the river, so you wouldn't have a corpse. He used blanks, dammit. *How could you be so stupid!*"

Feng Dun was silent. Disgust for McDermid glinted in his eyes and then was gone. "It was the woman. I should've suspected. She's the man in that family."

"That's *all* you have to say!" McDermid raged.

Feng shrugged and offered one of his marionette smiles to the outraged CEO. "What do you want, Taipan? Li Kuonyi tricked me. I'd guess she's fooled many, including her own father. He believed Yu died, just as I did. We must see she doesn't fool any of us again."

"What we need is to get that manifest before the Americans do!"

"And we will. She called you first. That's a good sign. She either doesn't think the Americans will pay as much or she doesn't trust them. She won't contact them unless she has no other choice."

"How can you be so damn sure!"

"The Americans want good relations with China. Once they have the manifest, the crisis will be over, and she's smart enough to know that if Beijing wants her husband and her returned so they can be punished, the Americans will hand them over. She'd rather have your money than rely on Washington to treat her kindly."

McDermid's anger cooled as he reflected on Feng's explanation. "You may be correct. It'd be a greater risk for her and Yu. All right, I bought some time for you. Go to Urumqi and find them."

Feng's expression was close to a sneer. "I wouldn't count on that, Taipan. Do you know where Urumqi is?"

"Shanghai, Beijing, Hong Kong, and Chongqing. For all I care, the rest of your benighted country is a desert."

"You aren't far wrong." Feng's wooden expression had an edge of both mockery and admiration. "I told you Li Kuonyi was smart. Urumqi is in Xinjiang, at the northern edge of the Taklamakan Desert. There's little in China farther from Hong Kong, and it'd be impossible for you or me to get there before late tomorrow. But inside China, they can go almost anywhere from Urumqi in a few hours. There are two major cities near Dazu — Chongqing and Chengdu. They can fly into either, but so can I. Still, they've made it twice as hard for anyone, even me, to find them."

"But you'll do it anyway, won't you, Feng." It was an order.

"I'll fly to Chongqing immediately. Find them first or not, I'll be at the Sleeping Buddha hours before the dawn meeting."

"You intend an ambush?"

"Naturally."

McDermid flared up again. "The woman will expect an ambush!"

"To expect is one thing. To prevent is another. I'll plan well and make them wait for what they guess will come, or perhaps I will surprise them first."

"Why would they bother to meet you at all?"

"If I'm right, they're afraid of both Washington and Beijing. Sooner or later, Major Pan and his secret police will track them down. You and your money are the best chance for them and their children to survive in the manner they want. So yes, they'll suspect. Which means they'll try to safeguard themselves and whoever's with them. But as Li Kuonyi said on the tape, they have no choice."

"I hope you're right this time."

"They won't trick me again." His eyes seemed to darken.

"The woman's been a step ahead of you since Shanghai."

"That will make her overconfident."

McDermid considered. He was not a physical man, but he was not weak either. He could hike to wherever this Sleeping Buddha was, and he could shoot. He had survived as a lieutenant in Vietnam, where lieutenants were food for pigs, and he had beaten Washington at its own game, becoming the ultimate insider. As he weighed everything, he decided the manifest was far too important to trust to Feng alone.

"We'll both go," he decided. "You leave tonight, and I'll follow tomorrow night. Who's your contact in Beijing?" Increasingly, McDermid wanted to know the identity of who had the clout not only to order a submarine to follow the *John Crowe*, but who could convince the sub's captain to act upon unconfirmed information that SEALs were planning secretly to board the *Empress*.

Feng raised one eyebrow. "You don't pay me for names. You pay me to get the job done."

"I pay you to do whatever I damn well say!"

"No one pays me that much, Taipan." There was scorn in Feng's voice.

McDermid glared, while Feng's expression was impassive. The Feng Duns of the world were minor players in McDermid's mind — necessary but of limited use. He had employed such men on various projects for two decades, finding them among the globe's underground of mercenaries, agents extraordinary, and assassins, who survived not only by wits and skill but by connections. If they wanted the next job, they avoided burning the last.

"The Altman Group has holdings in Chongqing," McDermid said at last, dropping the subject for the time being. "Get me permission from your friend in Beijing to fly there on business. I'll need the papers immediately, of course."

"And the money?"

"I'll arrange for it."

"You'd give them two million?" Feng sounded almost impressed.

McDermid nodded. "We won't fool Li Kuonyi without it. Besides, two million is nothing compared to what I'll gain from success."

"Aren't you worried the cash will tempt me or my men?"

"Should I be?" McDermid studied him. "You'll get a substantial bonus when this is over."

"Your generosity is well known." Feng's soft voice was almost ghostly. "I'll prepare my team and arrange for your passage, Taipan."

McDermid watched him leave the office. He had again heard the contempt in the use of the old honorific *taipan*.

Dazu

Dennis Chiavelli sweated in the unseasonal heat of the early September afternoon as he chopped green heads of bok choy from their roots and tossed them into wheelbarrows that were being pushed up and down the long rows of vegetable fields by older inmates. The work was exhausting but mindless, and it gave him time to reflect on how fortunate he was to be a soldier behind enemy lines instead of a field hand breaking his back.

The light whisper seemed to carry on the breeze. Except there was no breeze. "They're transferring the old man."

"When?"

"Tomorrow," the guard said as he passed along the rows. "Early."

"Where to?"

"Didn't hear," the guard said and was out of earshot, walking ahead, his old Type 56 assault rifle slung muzzle down from his shoulder.

What had happened? Had he made a mistake? Chiavelli chopped angrily at a bok choy. Had one of the guards betrayed Thayer? No, if that were the case, the old man would be gone already, and he, Chiavelli, would have been interrogated or killed. He remembered what Thayer had said: *They've held me too long to admit they ever held me at all.* With the human-rights accord actually possible, someone might have realized they still had at least one American prisoner. They were probably moving to isolate Thayer once more, storing him where he would never be found.

He must alert Klein. When the lunch signal sounded, the prisoners fell into line, and the guards marched the ranks to the dirt road where a pickup truck waited to feed them. Chiavelli stalled and fussed until he was able to drop in beside one of the Uigher political prisoners.

"I need to get word out," he whispered.

The Uigher nodded without looking at him.

"Tell your contact they're moving Thayer tomorrow morning. Ask for instructions."

Without acknowledging the request, the Uigher got his food and joined the other Uighers at the side of the road. Chiavelli took his meal to the shade of a stubby oak tree. As one of only two Westerners in the prison complex, no one wanted to eat with him. The risk of suspected contamination by outside political ideas was too great.

His mind in a turmoil of rotten possibilities, he forced himself to eat. He doubted Klein would have time to set a rescue operation in motion, which left him with no choice but to bust Thayer out before morning himself. At which point, he and Thayer would have to take their chances in the open country with the Chinese army after them and everyone else too frightened to help. He did not like those odds.

Hong Kong

Alone in a back room of the CIA safe house, Jon called Fred Klein on a borrowed cell phone.

"Jesus, Jon! Is that you?" The relief in the Covert-One chief's voice was palpable.

"Yes, alive, with quite a bit to report."

"I'll bet." There was something different about Klein's breathing. It was slightly uneven, ragged, as if emotion were interfering with the spymaster's ability to talk. And then the moment was gone. He demanded with his usual brusqueness, "Tell me everything, from the beginning."

Jon reported finding the arrogant note from "RM" at Donk & LaPierre, Feng's capture of him, and Randi's arrival in Feng's interrogation chamber. "Ralph McDermid was there with Feng. Our escape was more flamboyant than I liked." He

445

described Randi's investigation of the White House leaks, which was why she had been following McDermid, and the conversation between McDermid and Li Kuonyi and Yu Yongfu that all of them had heard over the CIA phone bug.

Klein bellowed, "They're *alive?*"

"And with Flying Dragon's original invoice manifest."

Excitement pulsed in the Covert-One chief's voice. "Dawn two days from now in Dazu?"

"Yes. McDermid pushed the meet back a day. I think he hopes Feng Dun can locate Li and Yu before then and grab the manifest."

"Remind me to thank McDermid when we lock him up in Leavenworth. His time's coming, believe me," Klein vowed in his lowest growl.

"Can you get me to Dazu by then?"

"I'll get you there. As for Ralph McDermid and the leaks, I was just recently informed about his role. Disgusting and apparently true."

"How do you figure to get me back into China?"

"When was the last time you made a parachute jump?"

Jon was not sure he liked that question. "Four or five years."

"What about a high-altitude jump?"

"Depends on how high."

"As high as I can get you."

"You're going to whistle up a nice big plane for me?"

"If I can land it somewhere and not draw attention. Meanwhile, since McDermid's there in Hong Kong, see whether you can turn up anything about him and the leaks and why he's involved in a smuggling deal like the *Empress*. On your own *and* from the CIA. Might as well use them if we can."

"You're all cooperation."

That earned a hoarse chuckle. "Glad to have you back, Jon. I missed our amusing repartee." Klein broke the connection.

Jon went looking for Randi. Now that McDermid and Feng Dun were focused on retrieving the last invoice manifest, their interest in Randi and him would plummet. After all, what could he do without it? If he were careful, that meant he could return to his hotel, change his appearance, and pick up McDermid's trail again until he had to head off to a refresher course in jumping.

He found Randi sitting in an office with Tommie Parker. "I have to leave now," he told them.

"What about Feng Dun and his crew?"

"My bet is they're gone."

"Gone?" Tommie frowned.

Randi said, "He means to Dazu. They won't care about us all that much now. Whatever the leaks were all about, whatever Jon is really working on, is in Dazu. Right, soldier?"

Jon refused to dance. "Close enough. I owe all of you, and Randi three times over. It isn't the first time, probably won't be the last, and I wish I could reveal more. But orders is orders."

Randi smiled reluctantly. "If there's anything we can do to help, give us a jingle, and to hell with the DCI." She looked him straight in the eyes. "Take care of yourself. I know you think you feel fine, but you look like you connected with a Mack truck."

"Nice image." Jon made his thick lips smile. "You, on the other hand, are untouched."

She sat there in an office chair, lounging back, long legs crossed, blond hair a wild wreath around her sculpted face. He saw questions in her eyes, but worry for him, too.

"My job," she said dryly. "Gotta keep the face malleable and primed to be disguised."

"That's the CIA for you. Ready to rock. Where's this side exit?"

Tommie, who had been watching the exchange with amusement, said, "You won't need it. You were right. They're gone."

"I'll use it anyway. No sense pushing my luck."

Washington, D.C.

Fred Klein's eyes snapped open. Instantly awake, he lay on the hidden Murphy bed in his dark office. The night in the marina outside was deathly still, the last boat, a battered seagoing trawler that had arrived at eleven P.M. from Bermuda, was snugged down, and its crew gone home.

The jangle of the phone sounded again. That was what had awakened him. He had talked to Jon and fallen instantly asleep. He sat bolt upright, swung his legs over the edge, and lurched to his desk chair, still drugged with his first nap in thirty hours.

It was his blue phone. He grabbed the receiver. "Klein."

"Your new office must be sumptuous for you to be so soundly asleep," Viktor Agajemian said. The former Soviet engineer chuckled. "I've been ringing for two minutes, but I knew you'd be some-where there, yes?"

"What does Chiavelli want, Viktor?"

"Ah, yes. We don't exchange social calls any-more, do we?"

"Not at three A.M."

"Good point. Very well, Captain Chiavelli tells me the merchandise is to be moved tomorrow morning. He doesn't know where or why, but all indications are it's not related to his mission."

"Damn!" Klein exploded, fully awake now. "That's the message?"

"Word for word."

"Thank you, Viktor. The money will be in your account."

"I never doubted it."

Klein ended the connection, but he continued to hold the receiver, considering. So Chiavelli thought the order to move Thayer was either rou-tine or connected to the human-rights treaty. Pos-sibly, it was related to the *Empress*. In any case, it was a disaster. He could never have a civilian team, or even a military team, in place quickly enough. He looked up at his ship's clock. Yes, there still might be time for an alternate plan. He depressed the cradle of the blue phone and dialed again.

Hong Kong

Jon had been right. He had observed the hotel long enough to know no one was watching him from outside — except, of course, the CIA agent Randi thought he had not seen at the safe house. You had to hand it to her. She was a bulldog when she was on assignment.

Smiling conspiratorially about his all-night absence and battered appearance, the hotel staff welcomed him back. He left them to speculate and rode up to his room. Once alone, he went to the bathroom mirror, where he pulled off the Band-Aids from his face and studied his wounds. He winced when he touched them, but they were all relatively superficial. He yearned for a shower, but settled for using the Jacuzzi in the bathtub.

He was soaking peacefully when his cell phone buzzed. It was in the pocket of the hotel robe, hanging within arm's reach. He had left it behind when he had broken into Donk & LaPierre.

"Yes?"

"You leave tonight," Fred Klein told him.

"What do I do in Dazu for a day and a half? Pretend I'm a tourist? I thought we decided I'd be better off here, digging into what McDermid's up to."

"That was three hours ago. There's been a serious development." He told Jon about Viktor Agajemian's call.

"Can you get the extraction team ready that soon?"

"That's where you come in, Colonel. You're going to have to help Chiavelli get David Thayer out of prison."

"Only two of us? How do we do that? Have you forgotten I don't even speak Chinese?"

"Chiavelli does. There's not time for me to explain it all. You'll find out the details when you land. Can you leave now?"

"I'm in the bathtub. Give me twenty minutes."

"Don't bother to pack. I'll send someone in to

do that and check you out after you're gone. A car will be waiting downstairs to take you to the airport. There'll be gear and clothes inside. A navy jet will fly you to the carrier. Good luck."

"What about . . . ?"

But Klein had already broken the connection. With a groan, Jon rinsed off, climbed out, and dried himself carefully, avoiding the injuries on his face and the ugly contusions and welts on his body. The hot water and Jacuzzi jets had soothed the bruises, and he felt better. He dressed and left the room. All the way down on the elevator, his uneasiness grew. What was Klein sending him into now?

Chapter
Thirty-Three

In her shortest, tightest, lowest-cut black sheath, Randi Russell turned every male eye at the British Consul's party, and most of the female eyes, too, as she entered the glitzy throng. For a change, she wore no facial disguise, only a light touch of glamor-queen makeup. Still, her pale blond hair was swept elegantly upward, and her physical attributes tended to focus an audience's attention, so she hoped her target — Ralph McDermid — would be sufficiently distracted to not recognize her.

She picked a glass of champagne from a passing tray and joined the only person she knew — an executive from a British firm that was an MI6 front.

He smiled at her. "Working or playing?"

"Is there a difference, Mal?"

"Worlds. If you're playing, I can make a pass."

"How sweet," she smiled back. "Another time."

He gave a sad sigh. "So I'm only your pimp tonight. Pity. All right, whom would you like to meet? And what's your cover, by the way?"

She told him, and he took her around the room, the eyes following. Soon, McDermid spotted her.

He stared. She gave him a bold smile and continued her conversation with an older Chinese woman high in the local government.

"Would you kindly introduce me to your charming friend, Madame Sun?"

McDermid had come up silently behind Randi and touched her on the arm as he passed to address Madame Sun.

The older woman favored him with an indulgent smile while she advised Randi, "Be careful of this one, child. He's a renowned charmer."

"Mr. McDermid's reputation precedes him," Randi said.

"Then I'll leave you to become acquainted."

McDermid inclined his head to Madame Sun in a polite good-bye. When he focused again on Randi, she saw a momentary cloud pass before his eyes, as if he sensed something was not quite right.

She pouted, altering the structure of her face. "Your reputation does precede you, Ralph McDermid. May I call you Ralph?"

The cloud passed, and the lecher returned. Possibly a combination of her clear American English, the revealing dress, and the thoroughly Caucasian face.

He smiled. "What reputation would that be, my dear?"

"That Ralph McDermid is a powerful man in all ways."

The flirtatiousness of that from a stunning woman made even McDermid raise an eyebrow, if not very far. "Exactly who are you, dear?"

"Joyce Ray. I work for Imperial Import-Export, San Francisco."

"Or they work for you?"

"Not yet."

McDermid laughed. "An ambitious woman. Well, Joyce Ray. I like you. Shall we pass along the food tables and find seats? Perhaps outside?"

"I *am* hungry." Randi gave it the double meaning, and she could see a pink flush rise an inch above his collar. He had bitten.

"Then off we go." He gave her his arm.

They walked to the buffet table and carried their plates to a secluded corner of the patio. He told her a few carefully selected anecdotes about the Altman Group and learned in return that Imperial was a wholesaler with clients in major cities across America and branches in most countries. Also, that she was a vice president.

They got along famously, and she was working her way toward prying information from him, when he stiffened. There was a faint vibration beneath his dinner jacket. His cell phone.

"Excuse me a moment." No smile. No endearment.

She made no attempt to follow as he walked out past hibiscus and frangipani into the garden. Far too risky and obvious. In any case, it would not matter.

He was gone less than thirty seconds. "I have to leave. Rain check, okay? I'll call your company."

Before she could respond, he marched off. She waited until he was out the door.

She followed, first on foot and then by car, always at a discreet distance. She was still tailing him when he drove down into the parking garage of his office building.

She waited then parked six cars away and watched him stand in front of the elevator, foot tapping. As soon as a car arrived, he stalked inside, and the doors closed. She climbed out and rushed to the elevator. The indicator went all the way to the top. The penthouse. What had brought McDermid here at such a late hour? She did not like it. On the other hand, perhaps she would learn something useful.

She sprinted back to her car, skirt riding up on her thighs. Inside, she switched on the portable link to the wiretap bug. She heard McDermid's voice: *"Okay, I'm in my office."*

"What's so important that we had to talk?" A man's voice. She did not recognize it. *"Please don't tell me you allowed Smith to escape."*

"I allowed nothing," McDermid snapped, *"but, yes, they escaped."*

"What do you mean, 'they'?" The voice was not young, not old. Calm, well modulated, and forceful. A certain projection to it.

"He was helped by another agent. We think she's CIA."

"Think? Charming."

"Don't get sarcastic. We need each other. You're a valuable member of the team."

"I'll stay that way only as long as I'm behind the scenes."

"It's not as bad as you think. In the end, neither Smith nor the CIA woman damaged us or our project."

"That the CIA may have you under surveillance doesn't concern you?" the voice demanded uneasily. *"Even if it's not related to our deal, they've traced at*

least some of the White House leaks to you. That should bother you one hell of a lot."

"Realistically, the leaks are of little consequence to either of us. Until someone figures out exactly which ones I'm interested in and why, I'm not going to worry. Besides, we have far larger problems."

"Such as?"

McDermid hesitated. Then he delivered the bad news: "Yu Yongfu's alive. So is his wife. Worse, they still have the Flying Dragon manifest."

There was a bellow of outrage. "This is your fault, McDermid. Where are they? Where's the damn manifest!"

"China."

A lengthy pause, as if he were controlling his shock. "How? You assured me the manifest had been burned!"

McDermid sighed and explained the details. "The two million isn't much, just coffee money, but I won't pay it unless I have to."

"It wouldn't end there anyway, and there's no guarantee we'd get the document." The shock was gone, replaced by an even inflection that was almost soothing. Definitely the man was a polished speaker and on-his-feet thinker. Probably accustomed to public appearances. She was beginning to believe he was a politician, someone accustomed to the necessity of diplomatic discourse that said nothing and revealed less. But it was definitely not Secretary of the Army Jasper Kott, on whom she had eavesdropped in Manila. "How will you handle it?"

"The way they instructed, with a few surprises. Feng should be nearly in Dazu by now."

"If Li Kuonyi is as intelligent as you say, she'll expect

him." There was a thoughtful pause, and when the stranger spoke again, Randi realized she'd had an eerie feeling about him since she first heard his voice. She had heard him somewhere, perhaps not long ago. *"I'm not at all sure you're well advised to continue to use Feng."*

"There's no time to replace him. Besides, he not only knows all the players now, he spent time in Dazu on some kind of operation. He has the kind of free movement in China that's hard to find for a Westerner."

The voice said nothing, but its familiarity continued to resonate in Randi's mind. Where? When? Who was he?

McDermid continued, *"There may be another problem with Feng. An unfortunately large one."*

"What?"

"He may not be working only for us."

"Explain."

"Just as I paid him to work for Yu Yongfu so he could report on his activities to me . . . I'm beginning to wonder whether he's reporting on our activities to someone else. Someone in Beijing perhaps. Whoever it is must have either a lot of money or a lot of power. Otherwise, Feng wouldn't bother."

The voice was grim, alarmed. *"You had him checked."* It was a statement not a question, and Randi realized one of her problems. This was the man's private voice, sarcastic, dry. What lingered in her mind was a public voice, but she'd had contact with so many men in high government posts that her memory was overloaded with them.

"Thoroughly," McDermid said. *"We know he isn't Public Security or the military. No, it'd be a private party."*

"One with an interest in the Empress?"

"That's how I read it."

"Very well. Do whatever you have to. I don't want to know the details. Just make sure the president doesn't get the manifest."

"You want the profit not the problems."

"That's our arrangement."

McDermid's words were sharp, a warning: *"Your hands are as dirty as mine. If I go down, you do, too."* The phone slammed into its cradle.

In the Buick, Randi sat back and closed her eyes, running the voice through her mind. She attached faces to it. She tried it out in different environments. After a half hour, she gave up. The answer would come to her at some unexpected moment, she told herself. She could only hope it would be soon.

She dialed her cell. "Allan? You heard the new call?"

"Sure did," Allan Savage said.

She told him about the familiarity of the voice. "Did anyone there recognize him?"

"I've heard him before, too. But I can't place him, and no one here can either. But then, most of our guys are electronic geeks with atrophied recall systems who don't know who the DCI is and think the Gipper's still president."

"Okay. I get the picture. See that the tape gets sent to Langley in the next pouch. Have the lab boys check it against other voice prints."

"You want me to make our report?"

"No. I'm coming in." She would talk to the DCI directly.

Beijing

The night enclosed Wei Gaofan's office in Zhongnanhai in soft darkness, with the lights of Beijing glowing above his walls, turning the starry sky a shining pewter gray. He stood in his doorway, staring out at his courtyard and the graceful willow tree and the groomed flower beds that usually gave him a sense of tranquility. Still, tonight he was heavy with distrust.

He was called the ultimate hard-liner, as if it were an insult, but his was the vision that was pure. The Owl and his fellow liberals were politically blind. They were incapable of seeing what he saw. He pitied them, but at the same time, they were his ideological enemies. China's enemies. They were forcing the country on an unnatural path that would do more than expose it to the world. Their way invited in the three contagions — capitalism, religion, and individuality.

When his phone rang, he returned inside to his desk. The call had come in on his private line, known only to his network of cronies, protégés, and spies.

He had a premonition of bad news. "Yes?"

Feng Dun's tones were corpselike, confirming the premonition: "Yu is alive. It was the woman. She tricked me."

Wei inhaled sharply. "And the Flying Dragon manifest?"

"Li and Yu still have it. Yu never burned it." He reported in detail.

Wei fell heavily into his chair. His stomach knotted, but he kept his voice steady. "Where are they?"

"Dazu. I'm on the road now. Heading there from Chongqing."

"What are they doing?"

Feng explained the call from Li Kuonyi to Ralph McDermid and the deal they made. "I'll have Yu, Li, and the manifest in less than forty-eight hours."

"You're positive?"

"It's hardly to our benefit for me to be unrealistic."

Feng's voice had returned to its normal, whispery timbre. This turn of events had shaken him, but already he was showing renewed confidence. In all the years Wei had employed Feng, he had never known him to lack self-assurance. If anything, the former soldier of fortune had an overabundance of it. But this was no small problem, and the political complexity of it would be beyond the grasp of most security experts.

Feng had always been loyal to him, even when sent off to work for others so he could bring back information. But then, Wei had taken Feng with him as he had risen in government. Yu Yongfu would never have been able to do for Feng what Wei could. Likewise, neither could an American, even Ralph McDermid. For a former mercenary like Feng, it was an honor to work so intimately for a member of the Standing Committee, and the income was more than generous, especially when others paid him as well. When Wei became general secretary, Feng's future would be secure, too. They were locked together, two ambitious talents who each had need of the other.

"Do you want help in Dazu?" Wei asked. "Now

isn't the time to go off like a solitary desert wolf."

Feng hesitated. "If you have a trusted army commander in the area, his presence with a unit of troops could prove useful, if by some accident we're detained by the local authorities."

"I'll arrange it. And Feng? Remember, Li Kuonyi is cunning. A dangerous adversary."

"There's no need to insult me, master."

Those were apparently harsh words from an underling, but Wei accepted them with a smile of understanding as he hung up. Feng had definitely returned to normal. Like the wolf, hunger drove him, and he was ravenous for the two people who had made him look like an amateur. Now he was even more determined to bring home the wayward manifest.

Wei gazed out his window at his garden again. The premonition of bad news persisted. He had begun to suspect that Major Pan's investigation into Colonel Smith and the family of Li Aorong had turned up more about the *Empress* than the major had written in his report to General Chu or that Niu Jianxing had communicated to the general secretary or the Standing Committee. At the same time, Wei was quietly lining up support on the Politburo and the Central Committee.

It was an unfortunate possibility that he would have to eliminate Feng Dun and Ralph McDermid, as well as Li Aorong and his daughter and son-in-law to cover all trace of hard-line involvement in the *Empress* scheme.

When Feng initially alerted him to McDermid's plan, it had seemed a stroke of good fortune. But now he sensed danger. For a lifetime, he had survived and prospered by acting quickly and ruthlessly on what he sensed.

At the top of a ladder set against a courtyard wall inside Zhongnanhai, a maintenance mechanic completed his repair of one of the floodlights that illuminated Wei Gaofan's garden. As he worked, he muttered under his breath at Wei Gaofan's paranoia. Wei's fear of assassination meant he would allow no shadows in his garden.

His impatience with the eminent member of the Standing Committee was at a higher level than usual, because he was not only a maintenance worker, he was a spy. He had used the directional microphone hidden in his toolbox to record the recent phone conversation inside Wei's office and was now anxious to deliver the tape to his superior in the counterintelligence section of the Public Security Bureau. Besides, his replacement had arrived and was already raking dirt near Wei's office. His listening device was in his toolbox, too, which was sitting on a granite boulder, aimed at the office window.

The spy climbed down and carried his ladder and toolbox to a shed hidden by dense shrubbery so as not to detract from the manicured park. Once inside, he opened a compartment in the bottom of the toolbox and removed the miniature audiotape.

He put everything away and dialed his cell phone. "I have a recording." He listened. "Ten minutes, yes. I'll be there."

He switched off the cell, locked the shed, and hurried through the lush lakeside grounds to a guarded side door in the outer wall. It was used only by service workers.

The guard, who passed him out every night at the end of his shift, still insisted on seeing his ID. "You're leaving late."

"Command-performance repair for Master Wei. One of his damned lights went out, and he nearly had a stroke. Couldn't possibly wait for morning." It was only a partial lie. He himself had knocked out the floodlight so he would have a reason to sit up there for a couple of hours, recording conversations. There was a lot of political turmoil right now, according to his handler, and every phone call to and from Wei must be recorded. His job was to find excuses to be in a position to make the recordings.

The guard rolled his eyes. Wei Gaofan's demands were well known. The guard stepped aside, and the worker walked into the street, turning away from Tiananmen Square. He pushed through tourists still strolling around the Forbidden City. Finally, he entered an old-fashioned tea shop, where he paused in the doorway. There was his handler. He was reading a newspaper at a table in the middle of the shop.

The maintenance man ordered a pot of low-grade Wu Yi and a packet of English biscuits. With them in hand, he walked to a table toward the rear. As he passed the man, he dropped his biscuits, bent, and picked them up. He continued on and sat.

Major Pan Aitu was in a hurry. Still, he finished his tea first and folded his newspaper before he left. The spycatcher walked two blocks to his car.

Once in the car, he picked the tiny cassette from inside his shoe and inserted it into a mini tape player. He listened to the entire conversation, stopping at points to rewind and listen again.

Then he leaned back against the headrest, frowning. The meaning was clear: Li Kuonyi and Yu Yongfu were not only alive, they had the invoice manifest of the *Empress*'s cargo that Colonel Jon Smith had come to China to find. The Shanghai couple were probably already on their way to Dazu, preparing to sell the document to Feng Dun on behalf of Ralph McDermid. But in truth, Feng would take back the document and kill the couple for Wei Gaofan.

The implications of Feng's report to Wei Gaofan were also clear. Implications the Owl would be most interested to know. Wei Gaofan was personally involved in the *Empress* and its cargo.

Events had progressed to the point that he must come to a decision as to where his best interests lay. On one hand, Wei Gaofan already employed Feng Dun, had clearly been involved in the *Empress* and its cargo from the start, and would not likely welcome a counterintelligence agent such as himself, who knew too much.

On the other hand, the Owl — Niu Jianxing — who was obviously opposed to Wei Gaofan and his hard-line stance, knew nothing of these developments. He would be most grateful.

Now Pan must go to Dazu, which was a considerable distance. When he got there, he would have to make the decision. He had done well in the new China, had no desire to return to the old, and all in all his best interests might indeed lie with the Owl.

Chapter
Thirty-Four

Aloft over Sichuan Province
Jon sat against the bulkhead of a high-flying Navy E-2C Hawkeye AWACS jet, his head resting back. It was nearly eleven P.M. The vibration of the aircraft's engines hummed into his ears. The plane was totally blacked out, as it always was on a reconnaissance mission. But this was no ordinary recon.

Edgy with nerves, he wore his usual black working clothes, with his Beretta holstered at the small of his back. A black insulated jumpsuit lay ready beside him. Since he would leave the plane at thirty thousand feet, he would need it. He had made hundreds of jumps, but never from such a height, and the truth was . . . it had been a long time since his last one. The navy personnel on the carrier had gone over the basics with him and thrown in a couple of tips.

He had oxygen equipment because he would free-fall to ten thousand feet before opening the chute. There was no war down there, at least not a shooting one, and no one would be watching and waiting . . . theoretically. The drop zone had been calculated carefully — created from satellite photos that were less than twenty-four hours old. Cloud cover was expected to be adequate. Winds were relatively mild.

Every technical precaution and preparation had been made. Now it was up to him to ready himself psychologically. He went over each step in his mind, looking for human error and unforeseen problems. He shook out his arms and legs periodically to keep his muscles loose.

A crewman came back. "Time, Colonel. Suit up."

"How long?"

"Ten minutes. Skipper said to tell you everything looks on the button. Moon won't be up for a couple of hours, weather's holding, and no one's locked onto us. All's quiet, as they say. I'll be back to test your equipment and give you the heads up. Remember, when you jump, make sure you don't fall upward. That wild-and-crazy tail assembly of ours can chop you like salad greens."

The crewman went away, chuckling at his own bad joke. Jon did not laugh. He hooked his Heckler & Koch MP5K to three rings on the special harness that crossed his chest to hold it in place. He dabbed blacking onto his face, avoiding his wounds. He struggled into the insulated oversuit and gloves and zipped the suit closed. After buckling on the outer harness, he hooked on his two parachutes and attached his oxygen, altimeter, GPS unit, and other equipment.

Getting hot, he felt as if he weighed a half ton. He wondered briefly how troops dressed for full combat could even move and answered his own unspoken question: Because they had to. He remembered. He had been there himself.

Ready, he waited, overloaded and overheated, hoping it would not be long. He was sufficiently uncomfortable that all he wanted was to get it over with. Jump, fall, and land. Almost anything was better than this . . . even facing the black void outside the AWACS.

"Here we go." The same crewman was back, tugging and checking his equipment for proper attachment and functioning. At last, he slapped Jon on the back. "Start breathing your oxygen. Watch that light up ahead. When it flashes, slide open the door. Good luck."

Jon nodded and did what he was told. As he fixed his gaze on the light, he felt the compartment depressurize. When the light flashed, he slid back the door. As the inky air sucked at him, he had one moment of indecision. Then he remembered something his father had told him a long time ago: Everyone dies, so you're one hell of a lot better off to live your life now than to look back and wonder what you missed.

He jumped.

Washington, D.C.

It was nearly noon in the nation's capital, and the president was working at his table desk in the Oval Office. He had received and discussed the contingency war plans of the joint chiefs, from a mere show of force against Taiwan by the Chinese to full-scale invasion of the island nation and the unthinkable — a nuclear strike aimed by mainland China at the United States.

President Castilla leaned back in his chair and closed his eyes. Under his glasses, he rubbed the eyelids, then he clasped his hands behind his head. He thought about war, about trying to fight a nation of 1.3 billion, give or take a few million the Chinese had probably lost or never counted. He thought about nuclear weapons and felt as if he were losing control. It was one thing to face off against small, poorly armed nations and terrorists, homegrown or foreign, whose limit was to kill thousands, and quite another against China, which had unlimited capacity for mass devastation. He doubted China wanted war any more than he did, but what was the difference between a submarine commander so angry he was ready to fire a torpedo and an outraged hard-liner in a high place with his finger on the nuclear trigger?

A light knock on his door preceded the head of Jeremy. "Fred Klein, sir."

"Send him in, Jeremy."

Klein came in like a nervous suitor, eager but apprehensive. Both men waited for Jeremy to leave.

"Why do I think you've brought me good news and bad news," the president said.

"Probably because I have."

"All right, start with the good. It's been a long day."

Klein hunched in his chair, sorting everything in his mind. "Colonel Smith is alive and well, and the original copy of the invoice manifest Mondragon tried to deliver to us has reappeared."

The president sat up like a shot. "You *have* the manifest? How soon can you get it here?"

468

"That's the bad part. It's still in China." He detailed Jon's report from the time he was captured, his escape, and the phone call from Li Kuonyi. "He had to tell the CIA team he was working for the White House, but that's all. Covert-One was never mentioned. A special, one-time assignment again."

"All right," Castilla said grudgingly and scowled. "Now we know Ralph McDermid is definitely in the middle of the whole thing. But it changes nothing about the danger presented by the *Empress.*"

"No, sir."

"Without the Flying Dragon manifest, we're facing war. Li Kuonyi and McDermid's people are meeting in Dazu tomorrow morning?"

"No, sir. Tuesday morning. Before dawn probably."

"That's cutting it even closer, Fred." The president looked at his clock. "Brose says we're down to hours. Our military's standing poised for trouble. What are you doing now to get the manifest?"

"At this moment, Colonel Smith is on his way back into China. He knows Li Kuonyi by sight, and she knows who and what he is. She might deal with him for asylum in the States."

"He's gone? I thought you said two mornings from now in China."

"Something else came up. I sent him a day early."

The president nearly exploded. "Something *else!* What in hell could've happened that's so critical that it's taken your focus from the manifest!"

Fred remained calm. "It's your father, Sam. And

469

I haven't shifted my focus. A problem has appeared, and I think Colonel Smith can handle both it and the manifest."

"My father." The president felt his stomach plummet. "What problem?"

"I've had a report from the prison that they're moving him tomorrow morning, their time. Our man inside doesn't know why, but once Thayer's moved, our chances of freeing him anytime soon get very slim. My team can't possibly arrive early enough, so I came up with another plan. The trouble is, it's riskier. The only good thing in this mess is that Li Kuonyi's choice of location has handed us an opportunity to make rescuing Dr. Thayer less risky. By sending Colonel Smith in early, I increase our chances of success."

The president was alarmed. "Not at the expense of our main goal, Fred."

"No, Sam. Never. You know us better than that."

"You, yes. Smith I'm not so sure about. He went in alone?"

"He won't be alone, sir, but I don't think you want to know more. There's likely to be a lot of deniability needed."

"Tell me what you can."

"We've got Chiavelli and a network of political prisoners inside the prison, Smith outside, and some imported private help I mentioned that you don't want to know about, especially since they helped him earlier. I've poured considerable U.S. greenbacks around, so — barring any more disasters — we've got a good chance to break out Thayer successfully. Then Captain Chiavelli will spirit him to the nearest border. At the same time, Smith and the others will go to the Sleeping Buddha and lie in wait."

The president still seemed dubious. "All right. Smith has a place to hide all day tomorrow?"

"Yes, sir."

The president sat for a moment nodding, his mind somewhere else. "What if the whole thing's been a fraud? A trap? What if there are no illicit chemicals?"

"Given everything we've learned, that's improbable."

"But not impossible?"

"In intelligence and international politics, nothing's impossible. Not as long as human beings are running things."

The president was still focused somewhere far from the Oval Office. "Why does anyone take this job? There's a certain blind hubris in wanting it." Then his gaze returned to Klein. "I appreciate all you and Smith are doing. This hasn't been easy, and I doubt it's going to get easy. Hours, at the outside, and China so far away."

"I know. We'll do it."

Absentmindedly the president's hand pressed against his suit jacket. Through the expensive cloth, he could feel his wallet. The smiling man with the cocky fedora appeared in his mind. There seemed to be a question in his eyes. He longed to ask him what it was. Instead, he banished him.

Aloft over Sichuan Province

The E-2C's slipstream blasted Jon clear of the Hawkeye in seconds, and, except for the brush of air against his cheeks, he had the sensation that he was floating motionless in space. Not moving at all. Still, he was falling at an incredible rate — more than one hundred miles an hour. In the nearly windless sky, he needed to know his altitude and what his course toward the drop zone was. Battling the forces of air and gravity, he raised his right wrist to look at the LED displays of his altimeter and GPS unit. He was still twenty thousand feet up, directly on course. The lack of wind was his best ally.

Fortunately, this was no precision jump, although there were mountains no more than a few miles away. To know when to open the chute, he needed to keep his eyes on the altimeter. As long as the wind remained calm, he should be falling at the proper angle to hit the field dead center. *Bad use of words,* he told himself. *Call it "on target."*

He was feeling almost euphoric as he planed on his air cushion. Abruptly, the GPS unit began to blink. It was a warning that he was off course. Jaw tight, he maneuvered his falling body to alter the shape of the air cushion, and he made a slow turn. The GPS unit stopped blinking.

Relieved, he was about to check the altimeter again when his wrist began to vibrate. It was the alarm that warned he was nearing the vertical point of no return. Once he dropped to that height, it would be too late to open his canopy. His heart began to pound. He forced his body upright and pulled the ripcord handle.

There was a momentary whispering of air above as the tightly packed parachute unfolded. He looked up, hoping . . . and his body suddenly lurched against the harness straps. The canopy was open, the harness had held, and he was back on schedule.

All noise vanished. He threw the ripcord handle away. He swung gently and floated downward, the black canopy flaring above. The GPS unit reported he was slightly off course, and he corrected by pulling on the steering lines. The one thing he must not do was collapse the canopy by steering too wildly. Once steady on course again, he looked down and saw lights closer than he expected. That always happened. The ground seemed to rush up faster than you anticipated, because as you drifted, you had no idea of your descending speed.

He looked down again. The lights came from windows in scattered clusters of houses and villages. In the middle was darkness — a wide, black space. That had to be his target area, at last.

He silently thanked the satellite photos of the Dazu area, all those navy people who had calculated the drop, and the windless weather. He jettisoned everything he could — oxygen tank, gloves, insulated flight cap. But as the ground sped up toward him, it was still invisible. Worriedly, he checked his altimeter. Still one hundred feet. A matter of just a few seconds to impact.

When he saw the ground clearly — a plowed field as advertised — he felt suddenly comfortable. He knew exactly what to do. He relaxed, spread his feet apart, bent his knees, and hit. As his shoes sank into the soft, broken earth, a dull wave of pain rolled through him, a legacy from the beating this morning. He pushed the pain from his mind. He bounced up slightly, settled back, caught his balance, and heaved himself upright. The rich scent of the dark soil filled his mind. The canopy flowed silently to the earth behind.

Alone in the night in almost the middle of the field, he listened. He heard quiet insect sounds but not the distant noise of motors. The Chengyu Expressway from Chongqing to Chengdu was somewhere close, but at this late hour on a Sunday night, few cars would be traveling. Shadowy in the distance, black stands of trees stood like sentries. Quickly, he removed all his instruments and harnesses, stripped off the insulated jumpsuit, gathered up the black chute, and used his entrenching tool to bury everything, except the GPS unit.

He had finished covering the cache when he heard a faint noise, distant and metallic. As if two small pieces of metal had bumped into each other.

He waited. Tense, straining to hear in the night. A minute. Two. The faint noise did not occur again.

He unhooked his MP5K minisubmachine gun, removed the harness that had held it stationary during his jump, and slung the weapon over his shoulder. Next he dug a shallower opening and laid the entrenching tool and harness inside. He used his hands to pile soil over it.

Brushing the dirt from his hands, he unslung the MP5K, read the GPS unit to find his directions, and hooked it to his gun belt. At last, he headed across the field toward the line of trees. They were a darker, more ragged black against the lighter black of the night sky. As always, he scanned around, watching the horizon, the distant lights, and the tree line.

Within two minutes, he thought he saw movement at the edge of the trees. Thirty seconds later, he dove onto his stomach, his submachine gun grasped in both hands. He picked night binoculars from his gun belt, snapped them over his eyes, and examined the row of timber. There was a small structure inside the trees that could be a shed, a cottage, or a house. It was too vague in the binoculars' greenish light for him to be certain. He thought he saw a farm wagon and a two-wheeled cart, too. None of it moved. Nothing. Not even a cow or a dog.

Still, he had seen something. Whatever it was, it appeared to be gone. He waited another two minutes. At last, he hooked the binoculars back onto his gun belt. He checked the luminous dial of the GPS unit again, climbed to his feet, and moved off.

Once more, he heard the noise. His throat tightened. Now he knew exactly what it was: A pistol hammer had been cocked. As he hurried on, the shapes seemed to rise from the field itself, as if from mythical dragon's teeth. Shadows encircled him. Shadows with weapons, all trained on him.

Crouched in the dark field, his MP5K ready in his hands, Jon tensed to make a move, any move.

"I wouldn't, if I were you. The lads are rather nervous."

He saw a stir in the dark ranks around him. They had blackened faces but no uniforms. Instead, they wore baggy clothes and close-fitting wool caps. In the same instant, he also realized that the voice that had cautioned him in good British English was familiar. Even as he thought all this, the ragged troops parted, and the speaker walked through.

"Someone named Fred Klein said you might care for help." There was a flash of white teeth as Asgar Mahmout smiled briefly and continued forward, the same old AK-47 slung muzzle down over his shoulder. He held out his hand.

"Good to see you again." Jon shook it, and the Uighers closed in protectively, watching over their shoulders for trouble.

"Christ, man," Asgar said, staring. "Your face looks like dog vomit. What the devil happened to you?"

Chapter Thirty-Five

Monday, September 18
Dazu

After Jon gave him a brief rundown of his escape from Feng Dun and his killers, Asgar Mahmout shook his hand again in admiration. Meanwhile, Jon counted twenty Uighers, including Asgar. They wore that same odd mixture of colorful, baggy Uigher clothes and loose Western garb as in Shanghai. Most were cleanly shaved, while a few had thin, drooping mustaches like Asgar's. They said nothing. Asgar explained they spoke bad Chinese and no English.

Jon surveyed the field. The dark eyes of Asgar's men were looking nervously all around. "We'd better get out of here."

Asgar spoke to them in Uigher. With Jon shielded in the center, the group moved off. To the left were fields of rice paddies, their watery surfaces reflecting like black mirrors in the starlight. Farther off were low mountains — purple inkblots against the night. That would be where the Buddha Grottos were carved, including the

477

Sleeping Buddha, where Li Kuonyi would meet McDermid's representative — probably Feng Dun.

Asgar was beside Jon. "There's an ancient legend about those mountains. The Han believed the peaks were goddesses who came down to earth and fell so deeply in love with it they refused to return to heaven. The Han have moments when they aren't so bad. But don't tell anyone I said that."

Jon asked Asgar, as the two kept pace through the quiet night, "How do you know Fred Klein?"

"I don't, chum, but it seems I know people who do. They relayed his message, along with considerable welcome cash in payment for said aid."

"Who do you know who knows Klein?"

"A certain Russian engineer named Viktor."

"He contacted you for Klein?" Jon asked.

"At first, yes. But this recent collaboration came about when I sent him a message from Captain Chiavelli, in the prison."

Now Jon understood. "You have contact with Uighers inside."

"The Chinese call them criminals. We call them political prisoners. In any case, they're minor criminals with disproportionate sentences as compared to equally minor Chinese criminals."

"One man's patriot is another man's terrorist."

"Not quite that simple," Asgar said, still making Jon feel the universe was slightly askew with the clipped Brit voice coming out of a Turkic-bandit mouth. "The crux of the matter is, does the action of the freedom fighter or terrorist benefit his cause and his people? If it doesn't, then he's simply an egomaniac, a fanatic for whom the 'cause' matters more than its goal. It's a question I often ask myself, and I'm not always as sure of the answer as I'd like to be, especially about others who've worked across the border for a free East Turkestan their entire lives."

"I thought it depended on what was in the self-interest of the powerful nations."

"Ah, well. That, too, eh?"

Directly ahead was the stand of trees, thicker and deeper than Jon had been able to perceive. As soon as the band reached the grove, they skirted to the left, alongside the rice paddies. The men turned on small flashlights. As always, Jon scanned everywhere. When he gazed up, he almost stopped. In the murky tree limbs were clumps that looked like gigantic nests of wasps or bees.

"What are they?" he asked Asgar.

"Bundles of unthreshed rice. The farmers store rice up there to protect it from mice and rats."

As they left the soft, plowed field, they broke into a lope and headed into what appeared to be the beginning of an arm of a forest. There were birch and pine and low bushes struggling to grow under a high, thick ceiling of leaves and needles.

A few hundred yards inside, Asgar gave a whispered command, and three of the men turned back, heading for the edge of the trees where the crew had entered. Mahmout was setting up a perimeter defense. The rest rounded a rock cropping into a protected dell, where they settled into resting spots as if they had used this as a stopping place before. As three more split off to vanish among the dark trees, the rest leaned back, cradling their weapons, and closed their eyes.

Asgar motioned Jon to join him. They sat near the remains of a fire.

"After you left China," Asgar told him, "we slipped away from the beach safely, too, but it was inevitable whoever was chasing us would figure out about the Land Rover full of crazy Uighers. We sent several of the ones with residence in Shanghai back to hide in the *longtangs,* and I brought the rest west, to lie low until things settled down again. It's our longtime pattern, you see."

"So you were near here when you got the message about Viktor?"

"Yes. My contact in the prison camp had sent word that this Russian engineer, Viktor, wanted to get an American agent named Chiavelli into the camp to talk to David Thayer."

Jon nodded. "Fred's planning a lightning raid to rescue David Thayer."

"Not anymore," Asgar said. "We inserted Captain Chiavelli with the help of some excessive bribes. His report about Thayer and the situation was favorable. However — we don't know whether the prison governor got wind of the rescue, or it's just incredibly bad luck — Thayer's being transferred out tomorrow morning. Captain Chiavelli gave the news to our prisoners, and they got it out to me. I sent word to Viktor, who reported it to Klein. I know that, because Viktor gave me a return message from Klein."

"To meet me, right? That was why the sudden change of plans."

"Right. He wants you to help break out Thayer

480

and Chiavelli. A great deal can go wrong, and he seems to feel your skills could be immensely helpful inside the farm."

"*Inside?*"

"Exactly. If it's necessary, we'll have to sneak in. Then you, Chiavelli, and I will bring Thayer out. Of course," he added cheerfully, "if it goes bad, you may have to shoot your way out, which is probably the main reason Klein wants you there. You're the backup gun."

"Swell," Jon said. "What could go wrong?"

"For one thing, a guard or two could decide to become unbribed."

Jon sighed. "Even better."

"Cheer up. This will be a cupcake compared to the assignment of some of my fighters. You see, once you're out of the prison — without, one hopes, their knowing Chiavelli and Thayer are gone until morning roll call — the real trouble begins."

"Getting Thayer and Chiavelli out of China?"

"That's our job, and a doozy it is. There's an old Chinese adage that says it all: 'Close your eyes, spin in a circle, and no matter where you are or what time it is, when you look again, you'll see a Han.' The population's so enormous that Westerners stand out like fish in the Taklamakan Desert."

"Then there'd better be no gunfire. It could play hell with my primary assignment."

"Klein's aware of that. He said you should skip the diversion if you thought it'd damage your chances for the main mission."

"You'll be with me on that operation, too?"

"That we will," Asgar said. "In force. We'll get Thayer to the border, too."

"You have a place to stash me tomorrow?"

He nodded. "You'll be safe as a temple mouse."

"When do they want us at the prison?"

"Our people inside should be ready now. The timing's up to us. They're waiting for our signal."

"Then let's go. How far?"

"Less than ten miles."

"Any other instructions from Klein?"

"Other than making sure I knew your principal mission was to save the human-rights treaty and that we're assured money and influence in Washington in exchange . . . no." The expression on Asgar's stoic face darkened. "Your White House wears blinders. All they're thinking about is getting Zhongnanhai's cooperation with the treaty. We won't get anything more from them after that. We're expendable, which doesn't give us a lot of reason to help. But at the same time, your Klein realizes we have to, because of our own interests."

"I wouldn't count Fred's goodwill short. He won't forget you, and geopolitics change."

Asgar nodded without much conviction. "After the prison, where's the second operation?"

"The Sleeping Buddha."

Asgar was dubious. "That'll be crowded damn soon after dawn any day. Tourists and vendors, you know."

"With luck, we'll be in and out long before they arrive."

"You care to give me a hint what we should prepare for?"

"An ambush and a different sort of rescue mission."

"What are we rescuing?"

"The same document I failed to get in Shanghai."

"Which is important to the human-rights treaty?"

"Yes," Jon said. "Now I have a question. . . . Do you have an escape route set up out of China that I can use to get the document out, too?"

"More than one. You never know what the contingencies are going to be. Dissidents and revolutionaries without exit plans are fools. Fortunately for us, resistance is very un-Chinese, so the Han aren't good at handling it. Are we going to need a fast bunk?"

"Probably, yes."

"I'll alert my contacts." He looked around at his men. Some were already snoring. Smart guerrillas, they slept when they could. "Let's move."

He circulated, waking them, speaking softly. They checked their weapons, took bandoliers of extra ammunition from boxes hidden among the rocks, and waited, prepared. A low whistle from Asgar brought the six pickets in with reports of everything quiet.

A gibbous moon hung just above the treetops. Asgar sent out his point men, nodded to Jon, and the remainder broke into two columns and moved deeper into the timber. Ten minutes later, the forest thinned, and they emerged onto a dirt road where a Land Rover, an ancient Lincoln Continental limousine, and a battered U.S. Army Humvee waited.

Jon raised his eyebrows in question. "That's a lot

of foreign horsepower for rural China."

Asgar smiled. "One's a reluctant gift from a Tajik journalist, and the other two were midnight 'requisitions' in Afghanistan. Amazing what you Yanks give to various warlords in and out of the Northern Alliance, and how careless they can be with their ill-gotten swag. Shall we saddle up?"

They climbed into the three vehicles, which cruised out in a caravan on the rough road, one after the other, beneath the broad, starlit sky. Although the Uighers did not look like it, they behaved like a trained and highly disciplined unit, which encouraged Jon. They drove along a series of dirt roads past farmers, fields, and animals. In this part of China, Asgar explained, even a bicycle was a luxury. Most people walked long distances to see family and barter for goods. Consequently, there were few vehicles on the road or parked beside buildings. Still, there was evidence of people everywhere. The farmhouses came in clusters, in small villages, and in larger villages. Shacks offering barbering, food, and tea appeared periodically beside the road. Still, no one came out to see who was passing by so late. Whether in rural or urban China, it did not pay to be too curious.

"They probably wouldn't report us if they did look," Asgar told him. "It's not wise to attract attention from officials, even out here."

Less than a half hour later, Jon saw the outlines of a chain-link fence and two guard towers in the distance. The drivers turned off their headlights. Asgar gave an order, and the vehicles rolled off into a stand of timber.

"The government won't allow houses to be built

484

any closer than a mile to the prison. We don't want to be seen or heard by the guards, so we'll park here."

"And then?"

"It's just like any military anywhere. We wait."

Sunday, September 17
Washington, D.C.

The Chinese ambassador had demanded to speak with the president immediately. The matter was urgent, or so he said. Chief-of-staff Charlie Ouray took the request upstairs to the president, who was working on a bill in his overstuffed recliner, his reading glasses perched on the end of his nose.

Charlie noted that the president had moved a framed family portrait to the lamp table beside him. It was lying faceup. He must have been looking at it. Charlie had never seen the photo before. It showed the president as a gangly teenager in a football uniform, standing between his proud parents, Serge and Marian Castilla. All three were smiling, arms wrapped around one another. They had been a close family, and now Serge and Marian were both dead.

Charlie focused on the president. "Shall I tell the ambassador that he doesn't get to make demands? I can soften it by saying you might be able to squeeze him in for a few minutes tomorrow. Maybe in the late afternoon."

President Castilla considered the pros and cons. "No. Tell him, as it happens, I want to see him, too. Let him worry about what that could mean."

"You're sure, sir?"

"It won't set a precedent, Charlie. We can let him cool his heels some other time to make the point. Right now, I want to hammer at the *Empress* and at the same time give a strong hint of willingness to work with the doves in Zhongnanhai to defuse the confrontation. We want that human-rights accord for a lot of good reasons."

"Still, Mr. President, we can't let him think —"

"That we don't want an incident? Why not? If my theory's correct, there are at least some on the Standing Committee who feel the same as we do. Maybe we can pry confirmation out of our eminent ambassador."

"Well —"

"Make the phone call, Charlie. He won't browbeat me, you know that. Besides, I've got some brickbats of my own. If what we believe is true — that there's a power struggle going on over there — he'll be just as uneasy and cautious about the whole situation as we are."

Chapter
Thirty-Six

Half an hour later, Ambassador Wu Bangtiao walked into the Oval Office. This time he wore a simple Western business suit, but his face was neutral, as if he were delivering a recorded message. The same mixed signals, but with more weight on the outrage this time.

"These intrusions into Chinese sovereignty are becoming intolerable!" the tiny ambassador snapped, speaking this time in his perfect Oxbridge English. His tones held barely suppressed fury.

The president remained seated behind his desk. "You might care to go back out of the Oval Office, Ambassador Wu, and make a fresh entrance."

Castilla caught a faint hint of a smile as Wu said, "My apologies, sir. I fear I am so upset I forgot myself."

The president refrained from saying Wu Bangtiao never forgot himself. Bluntness had to be used judiciously. "I'm sorry to hear that, Ambassador. What is it that's so upset you?"

"An hour ago, I received a communication from my government that our military in Sichuan Province reported a high-flying aircraft, identified by our experts as an E-2C Hawkeye AWACS of the type flown by your navy, had violated Chinese airspace two hours before. In light of your navy's continued harassment of our cargo ship on the high seas, my government sees a pattern and strongly protests these incursions on our sovereign rights."

The president fixed his hard stare on Wu. "First, Mr. Ambassador, the matter of the *Empress* violates no Chinese sovereign rights."

"And the flyover? Would you know anything about that?"

"No, because I'm sure it never happened."

"Sure, sir? But no categorical denial?"

"I'd be stupid to categorically deny what I know nothing about and which could have a perfectly reasonable explanation should it actually have happened. You say your military identified the aircraft as an AWACS? The area you speak of is quite close to northern Burma, where we have drug interdiction operations with, I believe, China's full support."

Wu inclined his head in acknowledgment. "A reasonable theory, Mr. President. However, we've also had a report there was a possible parachutist into Sichuan at nearly the same time. Near Dazu. Local authorities are investigating as we speak."

"Interesting. I wish them success."

"Thank you, sir. Then I'll bother you no more." Wu, who had not been invited to sit, started to turn toward the door.

"Not so fast, Ambassador. Please have a chair." The president made his expression as stern as possible. But underneath the severity he felt a surge of optimism for the risk he was about to take. Wu Bangtiao had said not a word about the abortive SEAL raid on the *Empress*. That could mean only one thing — the Standing Committee knew nothing about the SEALs' attempt. The warning to the Chinese sub had been delivered by one member or faction on the Standing Committee, while the rest were ignorant.

Wu hesitated, unsure of what the unexpected request signified, then smiled and sat. "You have another matter to discuss, Mr. President?"

"The matter of a Chinese submarine taking up a position perilously close to the frigate *Crowe*. A warship threatening the warship of another nation on the high seas? I believe that'd be considered an 'incident' by any standards of international law."

"A simple precaution. Balancing the power, you might say. All vessels have a right to be where they are. Under the circumstances, my government considered it had no choice. After all" — the faint smile appeared again — "we're merely shadowing the shadower. A routine matter."

"Now, of course, because of all this, you've revealed one of your secrets — China has subs monitoring our Fifth Fleet. The Indian Ocean is the only place it could have come from so quickly." A flat statement.

Wu's careful eyes flickered. Perhaps it was annoyance that his overall negotiating position had been undercut by someone in Beijing. Still, he said nothing.

"We, of course, had always considered such surveillance a possibility, but now we have concrete confirmation. But be that as it may" — the president waved his hand — "I'm going to do something unusual. Something, I might say, not all my advisers agree with. I'm going to tell you why the *Crowe* is there. A few days ago, we received incontrovertible information that the *Empress* is carrying substantial quantities of thiodiglycol and thionyl chloride. I doubt I need to tell you what those chemicals can be used for."

The president waited.

When the ambassador's expression did not change and he made no comment, the president continued, "The quantities are substantial. In fact, so substantial that they could have no other purpose but weapons manufacture."

Wu stiffened. "Another *Yinhe*? Really, sir, wasn't once —"

The president shook his head. "That time, you knew for certain we were wrong. That allowed you to stonewall to the end and make us look like louts. It was a win-win situation for you. If we didn't board, you appeared to have made us back down, scoring major points. If we *did* board, we'd be seen as reckless and arrogant. Since we boarded, you scored a coup on the international stage."

Wu appeared stunned. "I'm shocked, Mr. President. We were simply supporting international law, then and now."

"Bullshit," the president said pleasantly. "However, I've told you this for a reason — this time we believe Zhongnanhai *doesn't* know what the *Empress* is really carrying and never has known. We think Zhongnanhai is totally uninvolved in the venture and was surprised by the appearance of the *Crowe*. Which means that when we do board, whatever else happens, your nation is going to look very bad at a time when trade with the rest of the world is one of your long-term, paramount goals."

For a time, Wu Bangtiao sat silently, his steady gaze fixed on the president, obviously assembling his thoughts. When the words came, once more what they did *not* say carried the real meaning: "We could not permit such a gross violation as boarding a Chinese flag vessel in the open sea."

No protest, no denial, no hedging, no bluster.

The president heard the unsaid. "Neither the United States, nor the world — including China — can risk chemical weapons of mass destruction in the hands of irresponsible regimes."

Wu nodded. "Then, sir, we have an impasse. What do you suggest?"

"Perhaps concrete proof could break the impasse. The actual manifest."

"Proof would be impossible, since no such cargo could come from China. However, could such proof exist, my government would, in the interest of international law, have to consider it."

"If it exists."

"Which it cannot."

The president smiled. "Thank you, Mr. Ambassador. That, I think, concludes our meeting."

Ambassador Wu stood, inclined his head again, and walked from the Oval Office.

The president watched him go. Then he pressed his intercom button. "Mrs. Pike? Ask the chief of my secret service detail to come to the Oval Office."

President Castilla sat in the shaded Covert-One office of Fred Klein. "Your AWACS and Jon Smith

491

were spotted outside Dazu. The local authorities are looking for him. At least that was what Ambassador Wu said."

"Damn," Klein swore. "I'd hoped that wouldn't happen. Colonel Smith's got a tough enough job as it is."

"Why didn't you use a B-2? The stealth properties would've been useful."

"No time to get one from Whiteman. We had to go with what the navy had available. I'd have used a higher flying fighter, but we didn't want to risk an ejection seat being found. How much did they spot?"

"All the ambassador said was the plane had been detected and a parachutist might have been seen coming down."

"Good. That probably means they're not even sure about the chute, and they haven't come close to pinpointing his landing or found his equipment. With any luck, he's on schedule."

"With the help you had waiting that I don't want to know about?"

"That's the plan, and let's say the Chinese wouldn't like our 'help' any more than they would an all-American operation."

The president related the rest of his meeting with Ambassador Wu. "We were right. Beijing knew nothing about the *Empress* until the *Crowe* showed up, which clued them in that something was wrong. I think when I named the chemicals, Wu was shocked. He'll report to Zhongnanhai. How close are we to having that manifest?"

"I haven't heard from Smith, but I didn't expect to yet. Any word about the new leaker?"

"No, dammit. We're looking. I've cut back every piece of information to only those who must know."

Monday, September 18
Dazu

From where they waited deep inside the small grove of trees, Jon could hear an occasional car or truck roar past on the distant toll expressway. A mile or more away in three directions, a few farmhouses still showed light. The tense breathing of the Uighers was a nervous rhythm in his ears, along with the slow beat of his own heart. A Uigher grunted as he shifted position. Jon moved, too, loosening his joints. But from the prison camp itself, there was nothing. No sound, no movement.

Asgar peered at his watch. "Our two chaps should've been here by now. Something's not right."

"You're sure they were ready to leave?"

"Should've been. We'd better go in and take a check."

"That sounds like trouble."

"Should we abort?"

Jon mulled. He wanted to get David Thayer out of prison, but he was concerned about bringing hordes of police and military down on the area and frightening Li Kuonyi away from the meeting. Still, Asgar, Chiavelli, and he — working together — increased the chances of success. Three armed professionals. Otherwise, it was just Chiavelli and Thayer, and Thayer had probably not fired a gun in a half century, if even then. One way or another, the pair would attempt to escape tonight. If they got out but alerted prison authorities in the process, they would bring armed troops to the area.

The safest outcome was to help Thayer escape undetected.

Jon said, "Let's find them."

Asgar circulated among his people, telling them in a quiet voice what was happening and what he planned. He tapped three to accompany him and Jon, and the five slipped out of the woods. Bent and silent, they trotted across a newly planted field, where Jon's bruised body ached from running on such soft soil, then through a shadowy orchard of ripening apple trees, where the firmer soil helped him recover.

With a signal from Asgar, they came to an abrupt halt and went to ground. Before them, to the left and right, extended an open space that had been cleared around the perimeter of the prison's chain-link fence. Rolled razor wire topped the fence. About ten yards deep, the open area was littered with dry clods of dirt. It was unplanted, unwatered, untrampled — a sterile no-man's-land.

"I'm going to the fence," Asgar whispered. "I'll take —"

"You'll take me," Jon said. "I want to let Chiavelli and Thayer know I'm here, and I can't communicate with your men anyway. They can stay back and cover us."

"All right then. Come along."

Crouched, they tore toward the fence. Jon sweated from the strain on his sore muscles. Just as they reached it, a searchlight blazed on from the guard tower to their left. They dove to the dirt, their bodies pressed tight against the fence. Dust from the dry earth filled Jon's nostrils. He fought a sneeze, at last swallowing it.

Asgar's whisper was little more than a vibration as the searchlight beam probed, passed over, and passed over again. "What the devil's going on? I've never seen them this alert."

"Something's spooked them."

"Right. When that light gives up, we crawl west."

In the darkened barrack room, David Thayer was seated at his plank table, packing a few keepsakes and papers into a waistpack.

Dennis Chiavelli held a small flashlight so Thayer could see what he was doing. The light illuminated Thayer's thatch of white hair from beneath, making it glow like fresh snow.

"You okay to do this?" Chiavelli asked. "This could turn out to be a lot harder than we expect. You could be hurt or die. It's not too late to change your mind."

Thayer looked up. His faded eyes danced. "Are you insane? I've been waiting a lifetime. Literally. I'm going to see America again. I'm going to see *my son* again. Impossible! I feel like an old fool, but I can hardly believe this is happening." Unembarrassed joy radiated from his wrinkled face.

Chiavelli jerked around toward the window. "What's that?"

"I didn't hear anything."

But the old man's hearing was bad. Chiavelli crossed to the window. "Damn!" He peered out and cursed softly again.

"What is it?"

"The governor. He's got a squad with him.

495

They're doing a barrack check. Now they're heading for the Uighers. My guess is our barrack is next."

Thayer's parchment skin paled. "What do we do?"

"Return everything to where it was." Chiavelli sprinted back from the window. "Undress again and pretend to sleep. Hurry."

Moving with amazing speed for a man of his years, David Thayer put the few keepsakes and papers back where they belonged, stripped off his outer clothes, and pulled his nightshirt down over his head. At the same time, Chiavelli yanked off his clothes and, wearing his underwear, slid into his pallet.

The noise of a door banging open into the barrack silenced them. Moments later, two guards entered the room, ordering, "On your feet."

Both feigned sleepiness, and the guards pulled them roughly up from their pallets.

As the governor entered, he glared at Chiavelli and chided the guards, "Don't be so rough on the old one." He studied Thayer for a sign he had not been in his pallet. "You were asleep, prisoner Thayer?"

"I was having good dreams," he said irritably, his eyes half-closed.

"We need to search."

"Of course."

The guards investigated the cupboard, moved the pallets, and looked out the windows to see whether anyone was hiding. There was nowhere else to look in the bare room. The governor walked slowly around.

At last, he told Thayer, "You may return to sleep."

As he left, the guards close behind, they heard him order, "Post a guard at each barrack. Conduct a pallet check every hour. The prison is locked down. There'll be no work tomorrow, and no one enters or leaves. No one, until further notice."

The governor marched out of sight. As the guards followed, someone closed the door.

Chiavelli hurried to the window. He stood there for some time. "He's going back to his office, but he's short a guard. He must've left one at the barrack door."

"That won't matter."

"The bed check and lock-down will. We can't leave tonight. Even if we managed to escape the farm, they'd be on us before we got five miles."

David Thayer collapsed on a chair. "No." His bony shoulders slumped. His face was a mask of despair. "Of course, you're right."

"The only good thing is they don't seem to have connected it to us, and you won't be transferred tomorrow. The lock-down's saved you from that."

Thayer looked up. "Now we wait. And hope. I'm used to that. Still . . . this time, it all seems much harder."

Chapter
Thirty-Seven

Between occasional, seemingly random sweeps by the searchlight beam, Jon and Asgar worked their way around the fence, sometimes crawling, sometimes trotting, always hunched over. Asgar knew where they were going, when to crawl, and when to chance moving faster. Suddenly, he dropped to his heels.

Jon pulled in beside him, squatting, too, and followed his line of sight through the fence to a low, square building set ten yards inside the chain-link enclosure. There was a double door in its rear wall, but no windows. From the big door, an unpaved drive ran to the fence and out to a road.

Asgar said, "This is where they'll come out."

"What's the building?"

"The kitchen and mess. We'll stay here and hope like bloody hell we don't have to cut our way inside. Those rear doors are for loading and unloading supplies. The important aspect of this piece of real estate is that there's a blind spot between the doors and the fence — about ten feet wide — out of sight of the guard towers."

"That's a damn useful discovery."

They settled in to wait, again lying close to the fence. Jon focused on the double doors. Time seemed to stand still, and the night closed in. The noise of booted feet marching across wood walkways broke the silence. It was a heavy sound, threatening.

Jon frowned at Asgar. "What does that mean?"

"They're marching away from the barracks toward the governor's building and the guardhouse." Asgar's voice was barely audible. "There must've been an alarm, or perhaps the governor made a snap inspection. It doesn't look good, Jon."

"A lock-down?"

"We'll know soon," Asgar said grimly. He found a loose pebble and lobbed it over the fence. It struck the ground with a tiny, nearly inaudible *thikkk*.

Jon still saw nothing move inside the prison, not even a shadow. Then he felt a sharp sting on his cheek. He had been hit by a return pebble. He picked it up.

Asgar nodded. "That's the signal. They're locked down. We'll have to wait. With luck, twenty-four hours from now, everything will be normal again. The only good thing is they won't transfer Thayer in the morning. Of course, it's possible the lock-down will last longer, maybe even a week."

"I hope not, for all our sakes. Especially for Thayer's."

Sunday, September 17
Washington, D.C.

Charles Ouray entered the Oval Office quietly. "Mr. President? Sorry to disturb you."

Late afternoon sunlight warmed the room and the back of the president's neck. Castilla glanced up from the *President's Daily Brief.* "Yes?"

"The DCI would like a word."

The president took off his reading glasses. "By all means, bring her in, Charlie."

Ouray returned with a woman in her early sixties. Not tall, she was on the heavy side, with short, efficient gray hair. Compact, she had a formidable chest and walked with a purposeful stride. Some who had faced her questions compared her to a light tank — quick, fast, and powerful.

"Have a chair, Arlene," the president told her. "It's always good to see you. What's up?"

She glanced toward Ouray, who had taken his usual spot, leaning against the wall to the president's right.

"It's all right, Arlene. Charlie knows everything now."

"Very well then." She sat, crossed her ankles under her chair, and paused to compose what she was going to say. "Would you first bring me up to date about Jasper Kott and Ralph McDermid? Where do we stand with them? When do you want to reveal what we know?"

"Besides your people, the FBI's watching, collecting information. Part of the problem is, what have they done that's really illegal? Leaks of unclassified information aren't. But once we can document their roles in the *Empress* mess, we may be able to get them on aiding illegal contraband. Or maybe Kott *has* leaked classified information to McDermid. An investigation takes time, as you know. In any case, we'll need strong evidence to convict them, so we don't want to alert either yet. Now I've told you what I know. What about you? Have you learned something new?"

She nodded somberly. "A big clue to the new leaker's identity. McDermid has been consulting someone else here in Washington. Another associate, we'll say. Perhaps a partner. A man. Probably highly placed. Anonymous, so far."

The president absorbed that. He repressed an outraged curse. "How do you know this?"

"We have a tap in McDermid's Hong Kong office."

For the first time in days, the president smiled. "There are times when I thoroughly enjoy the deviousness of the CIA. Thank you, Arlene. A sincere thanks. Your problem, I take it, is you haven't been able to identify him yet?"

"Right. One of our agents in Hong Kong believes she recognizes the voice, but she hasn't been able to place him."

"Have you heard it?"

"The tape's not good enough over the phone, but it's on its way to Langley via courier."

"When you place him, let me know. If none of your people can put a name to him, bring the tape here. Maybe someone in the White House will recognize him."

"Yes, Mr. President." She started to stand.

The president stopped her. "How are you doing otherwise with your investigation of McDermid?"

"We've found nothing yet for why he or Altman is involved in the *Empress* affair, except of course the obvious reason — financial profit from the sale of the chemicals."

"All right, Arlene, thank you. I appreciate your work."

"It's my job, sir. Let's hope this is over soon. It's like a firecracker that's on the verge of turning into a nuclear missile."

"Amen to that," Ouray said from his wall.

"Good hunting," the president said. "Keep me up to date."

"Certainly, Mr. President."

"See the DCI out, Charlie," Castilla said. "I'll talk to you later."

When both had left, the president reached for the blue telephone to ask Fred Klein to drive over. He needed to let him know what the CIA had discovered — and what it had not. And he, too, wanted to take no chances with another leak.

Monday, September 18
Dazu

A lemon-colored haze rested on the eastern horizon, signaling dawn. The aged limousine, Humvee, and Land Rover drove in a caravan five miles past rolling farmlands and wooded hills. The thin morning light grew warmer, sunnier. At last they pulled into a dark courtyard, draped in moist shadows. In the distance, the violet hills of Baoding Shan were beginning to transform into pale green. That was where the Sleeping Buddha was carved, where the all-important meeting with Li Kuonyi and her husband was scheduled. Jon studied the hills, wondering what the night would bring.

An old Soviet-made bus was parked in the courtyard, its motor running.

"What's that for?" Jon asked as Asgar parked. The other vehicles pulled in alongside, and the drivers turned off their motors.

"Alani and her group expected to use it to transport David Thayer and Captain Chiavelli to the border. Their cover was as a group of Uighers heading home to Kashgar."

"Sounds risky. Even with your makeup team, they'd never pass in daylight."

"Wait here. I'll show you."

He crossed the dusty yard and spoke to the old Uigher behind the wheel of the bus, who immediately turned off the engine. He got out stiffly and followed Asgar's men into the house.

Asgar beckoned Jon. "Come along."

Inside, Asgar pointed to a pair of voluminous women's garments like Afghan burkas, lying on a rustic wood table, one black and one brown. "In Xinjiang, many of our women wear veils, but some go even more extreme and wear these monstrosities. We'll dress Thayer and Chiavelli in them and sit them next to Alani because she's tall. If they keep their knees bent, they should pass."

"At least weapons can be hidden underneath."

The farmhouse looked old, with a worn wood floor and exposed timbers as beams. It was furnished with homespun tables, chairs, sideboards, and bureaus for hanging clothes. Through an archway stood a bedstead and a wood washstand, on which were a clay bowl and jug. He saw no sign of the Uighers, but the old bus driver sat at a bare table in a kitchen through another narrow arch.

"Where do I sleep?" Now that he knew he had to wait until tonight, he was abruptly exhausted.

Every muscle ached. The wounds on his face itched. He wanted to wash off the blackout cream, eat, and fall into any kind of bed he could find.

"There's a hidden cellar. Plus, the barn has secret rooms behind the stalls. You want to sleep now or eat?"

"Eat. Then sleep."

Jon followed him into the kitchen where fourteen of his guerrillas were seated at another table, wolfing food, and women were cooking and putting full platters on both tables. Among the women was the pair of giggling makeup artists from the Shanghai *longtang,* who started giggling the instant they saw his face. They pointed him to the sink, where he used cool water and homemade soap that smelled of tallow to get the blackout goop off his skin.

Feeling better, he sat at the table with the old man, who stared up from his food as if to ask, "What *are* you?" Then he shrugged and resumed eating.

Asgar joined him, carrying a bowl of the same rice laced with mutton scraps, carrots, onions, and some kind of shelled bean, all held together by melted sheep-tail fat, which they had eaten in the *longtang.* He put it on the table with the other dishes. Famished from the long night and unrelenting tension, Jon took generous portions of everything. The thin-skinned dumplings and thick filling were delicious. The mutton kebabs were crisp on the outside, tender on the inside, and without any of the odor many Americans found unpleasant.

As Jon ate, Asgar watched and shoveled food

into his mouth, too. The moment seemed to bring out nostalgia in Asgar. He said ruminatively, "Uighers were nomadic sheepherders long before we settled into farming. Mutton is to us what seafood is to Japan, beef to the Argentine and States, and beef and mutton to the Brits. That was one thing I liked about England. I could get good mutton, and if I were lucky enough to find the rare English-raised Southdown, ahhh . . . that was the best mutton I'd had since leaving home."

Jon used the bread to wipe his plate. "Not many people like English food as much as you do."

"I loved it, old boy. *Real* English food. Lots of suet in the puddings and dumplings plus all the roasts, thick gravies, organ meats, and mutton. Maybe that's why when so many Brits came here in the old days they seemed to understand us far better than the Chinese and Russians ever did or ever have."

When they finished, Asgar led him back out across the courtyard's hard-packed dirt to a small house against the left wall. Inside, a solitary Uigher stood at a window overlooking the courtyard, his assault rifle resting on the sill.

"We have sentries on all the walls, too," Asgar explained as they passed.

"What happens if you get a visit from Chinese authorities?"

"There's an extended Uigher family that lives here and farms. We take cover, and they do the meet and greet. Everyone knows the family."

Jon followed Asgar down a cleverly hidden narrow staircase into a cellar illuminated by bare lightbulbs. Rows of pallets held sleeping men and women. Asgar pointed to the empty one next to his, lay down, and was snoring instantly.

Jon stretched out, tensing and relaxing his muscles. He told himself he felt better. In any case, he was certain he would feel better when he awoke. As he tried to drift off, his mind kept returning to the problem of David Thayer. The potential for trouble and failure at the Sleeping Buddha less than twenty-four hours away was enormous enough. Any glitch in the attempt to free Thayer could ruin the entire mission. He rolled over, tried one side then the other. At last, he fell into a restless sleep.

Beijing

It was late morning, and usually the Owl would have been in his office at Zhongnanhai for hours by now. Instead, he worked at his desk in his home study. He was smoking one of his favorite Players cigarettes and putting his chop to security documents when his wife ushered in Ambassador Wu Bangtiao. The Owl immediately put down his cigarette and stood to greet him. For once, there was a broad smile on his face. The ambassador was an ally and friend, who owed his post in Washington, D.C. to the Owl's influence and discreet lobbying.

As his wife disappeared out the door and closed it, Niu said, "Welcome, my good friend." He grasped Ambassador Wu's small hand. "This is a surprise, especially considering the difficulties between us and the United States." A slight rebuke in his tones: "Until I received your message this morning, I'd no idea you were returning."

The ambassador acknowledged the admonition with a flicker of his eyes. "I slipped into the country quietly, leader, because of the difficulties. I needed to consult with you privately about your wishes. Naturally, I came directly from the airport, and I'll return directly to the airport."

Niu's shoulders tightened at the enormity of what would bring the ambassador here so covertly over such a long distance, but again he offered a rare smile. "Of course. Sit. Relax."

Wu sat, his back barely touching the chair. He made no effort to relax, and Niu had not expected him to.

"Thank you," Wu said. "May I speak frankly, leader?"

"I insist. Whatever we say will remain here." Niu picked up his ashtray and walked around to sit in the chair beside the ambassador, again in an act of friendship. Still, he did not offer Wu a cigarette. That would be going too far. "Tell me." He smoked.

"I believe I've been delivering the messages to the American president exactly as you wanted . . . which was, and I'm sure still is . . . that China must stand firm against any invasion of our sovereign rights. At the same time, China doesn't seek an incident or confrontation that might escalate beyond anyone's control."

Niu simply nodded. With even the closest ally, verbal commitment was not the way until absolutely necessary.

Wu gave his tiny smile in return. "The American president indicates he understands that. As I've said before, he's unusually subtle for a Westerner. He reads nuances. I detect sincere concern that the standoff could escalate into war. Unlike others, when he says he doesn't want war, I believe he means it. He confirms that with word choice, emphasis, and etiquette."

"Impressive." Niu controlled his impatience.

"As unusual as that is for a Western head of government, he's done something even more unusual: He's revealed what he's doing and why."

The Owl's eyebrows rose. "Explain."

As the ambassador recounted the most recent conversation in the Oval Office about *The Dowager Empress*, Niu listened in silence, mulling uneasily. Suddenly he realized what was disturbing him: The U.S. president had unwittingly given him the correct question to ask. If the United States did not want the confrontation, and China did not want it, who did? Why did it continue? At the moment, the crisis seemed completely unnecessary, almost as if it had not only been staged, but its escalation orchestrated.

He considered what he had learned from Major Pan, and he recalled the discussions of the Standing Committee. Among the hawks, Wei Gaofan again stood out. It was true that through the alliance with Li Aorong and Li's son-in-law, Wei could expect to make a profit from the shipment. Perhaps he had been making profits from such shipments for quite a while. But was that Wei's ultimate goal now that news of it had reached the upper levels of government in both China and the United States?

No. The Owl was certain Wei would sacrifice profit instantly if he could take China back into the past. At heart, Wei was an ideologue, a true hard-line Communist who had never gotten over

Mao, Chu The, or Tiananmen Square. To go back to those days was his dream. His sending the *Zhao Enlai* submarine to threaten the *Crowe* proved that. He would encourage the confrontation to escalate into violence to force his point. To win, he might even go to war.

The Owl remembered Confucius's two definitions of disaster: One was "catastrophe," the other "opportunity." Wei had seen the discovery of the *Empress*'s true cargo not as a catastrophe but as an opportunity to achieve something far more important to him than money.

"The president asks," Ambassador Wu continued, breaking into the Owl's thoughts, "whether concrete proof, in the form of the actual invoice manifest, would be enough for you to defuse the situation with the Standing Committee. Would the committee allow Americans to board, perhaps in conjunction with our submarine crew, or, alternately, would the committee end the situation by ordering the cargo destroyed in such a way that the Americans could confirm it? In short, would you be willing to work with our people as President Castilla works with his, to end this dangerous problem?"

Niu inhaled his cigarette thoughtfully. While Wei saw the past as the future, Niu was comfortable with the unknown, with a future based on ideals like democracy and openness. The choice was stark: If he did not risk all, Wei would win. On the other hand, if he risked all and won, Wei — the preeminent hawk on the Standing Committee — would be brought down by his own deeds.

"Leader?" the ambassador asked, his face concerned at the long silence.

"Would you like a cigarette, Ambassador?"

"Thank you. Yes, I'd like one very much." A moment of gratitude softened the ambassador's worried face.

The two men smoked companionably. Crucial decisions must not be rushed.

"Thank you for bringing me this news," Niu said at last. "I haven't been wrong in my choice of ambassador. Return immediately to Washington and tell President Castilla I consider myself a reasonable man, while, of course, continuing to warn of the dire consequences should any Americans attempt to board."

Wu put out his cigarette and stood. "He'll understand. I'll convey your exact words." They exchanged a determined look. With a rustle of his long coat, Wu left.

Smoking furiously, Niu jumped to his feet and resumed pacing. The Americans clearly did not have proof of the cargo yet. That was most disquieting. Proof was essential. He stopped in the middle of the floor, wheeled on his heel, and marched back to his phone.

Standing over his desk, he dialed.

As soon as Major Pan answered, the Owl demanded, "Tell me what you've learned."

Without prompting, Pan revealed the taped telephone conversation between Feng Dun and Wei Gaofan. "Only one of the original invoice manifests of the *Empress*'s true cargo still exists — in the hands of Yu Yongfu and Li Kuonyi."

Niu caught his breath and stubbed out his cigarette. "Yes. What else?"

"Ralph McDermid is going to pay two million

dollars to buy it from them." He described the arrangements at the Sleeping Buddha.

The Owl listened carefully, his mind accelerating as the fog that had obscured the situation evaporated: This was what the president wanted, and what he wanted . . . the objective proof. Wei Gaofan knew this and wanted the manifest destroyed. At the same time, the Shanghai couple — Yu and Li — were pawns, trying desperately to survive. Then there was the rich American businessman Ralph McDermid, who must also want a confrontation, although Niu was not sure yet exactly why or how far he would allow it to escalate. McDermid was willing to pay a small fortune to keep the manifest out of anyone else's hands. The rat who ran among all three was Feng Dun . . . pretending to work for McDermid and Yu Yongfu while his ultimate allegiance belonged to Wei Gaofan.

Feng was filth. Ralph McDermid and Wei Gaofan were worse. All must be stopped before they reignited the Cold War or started a hot one.

Thinking rapidly, he listened as Major Pan finished his report. Pan's willingness at last to hold nothing back told Niu that the spycatcher had finally committed his loyalty to Niu. In their culture, it was the ultimate compliment, and also the ultimate vulnerability.

Could he do less? "I understand, Major," Niu told him. "Perhaps more than you realize. Thank you for your fine efforts. You are on your way to Dazu?"

"My flight leaves in twenty minutes."

"Then understand this: Continue to observe

and do not interfere unless there's more trouble." He hesitated a fraction of a second, weighing the enormity of the step he was about to take. "If trouble erupts, I authorize you to help Li Kuonyi and Colonel Smith. Either you or Colonel Smith must retrieve the manifest safely. It's imperative."

The silence was like a held breath. "Is that an order, master?"

"Consider it so. If it becomes necessary, show my written instructions. You're working only for me, and you have my full protection."

There. It was done. Now there could be no turning back. It was he or Wei Gaofan — forward into the unknown future, or back to an unworkable past. And it rested in the hands of others. He fought off a shudder. But there it was. A wise man knew whom to trust.

Chapter
Thirty-Eight

Dazu

Jon awakened to a sense of claustrophobia, of bodies packed around like corn in a can. He grabbed his Beretta, sat bolt upright, and swept the big semiautomatic through the dim illumination. And remembered where he was. The Uighers' cellar. The air was pungent with body odors and warm exhalations, although only a half dozen fighters remained. All were sleeping. Everyone else had gone, including Asgar.

Heart still pounding, he lowered the weapon and checked his watch. The green glow of the dial showed 2:06 P.M. He had been asleep more than nine hours, which was astounding. He seldom slept more than seven.

He stood carefully and stretched. His muscles complained but not too loudly. His ribs ached. No sharp pains. His face felt fine. It would itch later, particularly when he sweated. Nothing fatal.

He padded to the steps. At the top, he raised the trap and climbed out into the satellite house. A new sentry stood guard at the window, while across the courtyard was movement in the main house's kitchen. Fighting off a sense of urgency, of a need to get on with it, he strolled outdoors. Strolling was something he did infrequently, too.

The sun was warm, the sky porcelain blue, and a gentle breeze stirred the willows and cottonwoods. The chilies that had been laid out to dry on mats around the dirt courtyard were an encircling carpet of scarlet. Their peppery scent filled the air, reminding him he was in Sichuan Province, famous for its spicy cuisine.

Asgar was in the kitchen, sipping a mug of hot tea with milk, English style. He looked up, surprised. "Are you mad? Why aren't you still asleep?"

"Nine hours is enough, for God's sakes," Jon told him.

"Not if nine hours is spread over five days."

"I've caught a few naps here and there."

"Yeah, you look really rested. Solid as a sand devil. Check yourself in the mirror. With that face, you can go to All Hallow's Eve without a mask."

Jon gave a thin smile. "Is there a phone I can use? I don't want to tempt fate in case someone around here is triangulating cell calls."

"Next room."

Jon found the telephone. Using the phone card Fred Klein had given him, he dialed Klein. It was yet another gamble. Public Security could be monitoring land lines, too.

"Klein."

Jon went into character: "Uncle Fred?" he said in halting English. "It's been so long, and you haven't called. Tell me about America. Does Aunt Lili like it?" Aunt Lili was code for possible monitoring.

"Everything's fine, nephew Mao. How's your assignment?"

"The first phase had to be postponed, but I can do it at the same time as the second phase."

There was hesitation and a note of disapproval: "I'm sorry to hear that. The second phase could be harmed." Concerned, Fred was reminding him that at the first sign of serious trouble at the prison farm, they would have to scrub the rescue. The meeting at the Sleeping Buddha remained their first priority.

"Well, that's worried me, too. I'll just have to see how it goes."

Another pause, this time as Klein shifted gears: "You must phone instantly when you have news. We can hardly wait. Did you find your cousin Xing Bao?"

"I'm in his house now."

"That's a relief. You must be enjoying each other, but this is costing you too much, Mao. I promise I'll write a very long letter first thing tomorrow."

"I look forward to it with pleasure, now that I've heard your honored voice again." Jon hung up.

Asgar called from the other room, "And?"

Jon rejoined him. "The priority remains the same. As soon as we have the manifest, I need to call Klein to let him know."

"Poor David Thayer."

"Not if we can help it. We'll do everything we can to get him out, too. Did you go to the Sleeping Buddha?"

"Yes, we did a thorough recon." He laid a deck of English playing cards on the table. "I left ten of

515

my best people behind to keep watch. They have walkie-talkies. Get some food, and I'll fill you in. Then we'll play some two-handed poker. If you don't know how, I'll teach you."

"Are you hustling me?"

Asgar smiled innocently. "I picked it up at school. Strictly amateur. Nice hobby, when one has time to kill." For a moment, anxiousness and nerves showed in his expression. And then they were gone.

"Okay," Jon said. There was no way he was going to sleep more now anyway. "Two-dollar limit, or whatever that is in your money. Straight poker. No wild cards. After I wash my face, I'm in."

Jon knew he was being hustled, but they had to do something to make the time pass. They had at least six hours to keep each other sane, before darkness arrived and they could begin their night's work.

Monday, September 18
Washington, D.C.

Fred Klein was puffing on his pipe angrily, and the special ventilation system was straining to clear the air, when President Castilla walked into his Covert-One office.

The president sat. His large body was rigid, his shoulders stiffly square. His jowls looked like concrete. "You have news?" No greeting, no preamble.

Klein was in the same bleak frame of mind. He put down the pipe, crossed his arms, and announced, "It took five of my best corporate and financial experts to ferret this out: The Altman Group owns an arms manufacturing firm called Consolidated Defense, Inc. As with many of Altman's holdings, this one's hidden behind a paper trail that boggles the mind — subsidiaries, associated companies, holding companies, satellite companies . . . you name it, the ownership winds through a quicksand intended to deceive. Still, the ultimate ownership is clear."

"What's the bottom line?"

"As I said, Altman and Ralph McDermid own the majority shares in Consolidated Defense and reap its rewards."

"This isn't particularly new. Altman's heavily invested in defense. Why do we care about Consolidated?"

"You're going to think this is a digression, but it's not: Let's discuss the Protector mobile artillery system. It was a millimeter from final approval. Then you decided that in our new world of terrorists and brushfire wars, heavy artillery systems like it were outdated. Often totally useless."

"The Protector crushes most bridges because it's too heavy. It can't be pulled out of the bog of a country road without major support. It certainly can't be easily airlifted. It's irrelevant or worse."

"It's still irrelevant," Klein assured him. "But that was an $11 billion contract that just evaporated. Consider this, the Altman Group at last count had some $12.5 billion in investments. That's serious money for a private equity firm. But Altman's accustomed to making big money — more than thirty-four percent returns annually over the past decade, particularly through timely defense and aerospace investments. On a single day last year, Altman earned $237 million. Impressive, right? Also dirty. Consolidated Defense is the army's fifth-largest contractor, but they took Consolidated public *only* after the September 11 attacks, when Congress skyrocketed its support for hefty defense spending, and *only* after a massive lobbying effort by that golden Rolodex of theirs paid off in Congress's initial approval of Consolidated's cornerstone weapon's program . . ."

The president stared, his expression grim. "Let me guess — the Protector."

"Bingo. The result was the $237 million bonanza."

"And —"

"And now Altman's assets will skyrocket billions and billions of dollars, if you and Congress approve the Protector and put it into production."

The president sat back, his mouth a thin line of disgust. "That bastard."

"Yes, sir. That's what Ralph McDermid's been up to. It's got nothing to do with the *Empress* directly. The whole thing was a setup to lead to nose-to-nose hostility between two continental giants with nuclear capabilities. If necessary, he'll wheel and deal us into war to prove the United States needs the Protector. Either way, once we board the *Empress* and all hell breaks out, he'll have proved his point. Congress will beg for the Protector, and he'll get his $11 billion."

The president swore loudly. "The only thing they didn't walk away with, because I clamped a lid on it, was publicity that would've scared the be-jesus out of the public and made it easier to win approval immediately."

"The way I look at it, it's damn immediate enough. All McDermid needs is for us to board the *Empress* because it's about to go into Iraqi waters."

"Oh, God." The president heaved a sigh. "Everything's on Smith's shoulders. What have you heard from him?"

"He called, but he had to use code." He paused. "I've got bad news, Sam. They weren't able to liberate your father last night. That's China time. Smith implied they'd try again tonight."

The president grimaced. He closed his eyes and opened them. "Tomorrow morning, our time — that's when they'll do it?"

"Yes, sir. They'll try."

"He didn't say anything more about breaking him out? Whether he has enough help? Whether he thinks he can do it?"

"I'm sorry, sir."

"Why couldn't he talk more?"

"I assume he was afraid to use his secure cell phone. Which meant he was on a public line that could've been monitored. It leads me to guess that the parachute sighting was hardly solid. The local authorities must not have located the parachute or any other evidence of insertion. With luck, they're skeptical."

"I hope you're right, Fred. Smith is going to need all the good luck he can get, and so are we." The president peered at the clock. "He's got four hours left, the way I count it, before dusk." He shook his head. "Four very long hours for all of us."

Monday, September 18
Hong Kong

Dolores Estevez hurried across the Altman Building lobby and out the glass entrance into the city's humid air and rushing people. Usually Hong Kong's carnival atmosphere energized her. Not now. She joined a queue of pedestrians frantically waving for taxis. But as soon as she raised her hand, one pulled up as if by magic. She decided God must have a soft spot for well-intentioned but late travelers.

She jumped in quickly. "The airport. Hurry."

The driver started his meter, and the taxi inched into traffic. They crawled for a few blocks, until the driver muttered in guttural Cantonese and swerved the vehicle into a narrow alley.

"Shortcut," he explained.

Before Dolores could protest, he accelerated, and they were halfway along it. She sat back nervously. Maybe he knew what he was doing. One way or another, she needed to reach the airport where the big boss was waiting, probably annoyed already. She was both terrified and excited by her new assignment — his official translator at someplace called Dazu in Sichuan. They wanted her because she could speak several dialects. She felt comfortable in Cantonese and Mandarin, although she had found the real thing in the field was not exactly the same as speaking in her graduate classes or in L.A.'s Chinese restaurants. She was also nervous about her English. No matter how hard she tried, she had not completely lost her barrio accent.

She was still worrying when the taxi screeched

to a halt near the end of the alley, the door opened, and strong hands pulled her out. Too frightened to struggle, she had a vague impression of seeing a fellow Latina who looked amazingly like her. She felt a sharp pain in her arm, and blackness enveloped her.

Ralph McDermid reclined in his seat aboard the opulent corporate jet reserved for his personal use, sipped his favorite single-malt Scots whiskey — over ice, no water — and glanced at his watch for the tenth time. Where was the damn translator? He fumed and was waving the steward for another single-malt when a breathless woman stumbled up into the cabin. McDermid eyed her with outrage that quickly became appreciation. She was clearly Latina, one of those with high cheekbones, long, lean faces, and a touch of fiery Aztec in her eyes. Exotic.

"Mr. McDermid," she said in English with more than a hint of L.A.'s South Central barrio. It was an accent he would have taken as a sign of lack of education and ambition in a man, but in a woman, it was charming. "I'm Dolores Estevez, your translator and interpreter. I apologize for being late, but they gave me terribly short notice. Of course, the traffic was *impossible*."

McDermid detected a slight lisp. Better and better. Her body was magnificent in any ethnic or national category. Her name was delightful. *Dolores.* He rolled it through his mind. When this was over, and they were back in Hong Kong, she would probably jump at the chance to please the *über* boss.

"Completely understandable, my dear. Please sit down. There would be fine." He nodded at the plush seat facing him. She smiled, all of a sudden shy. At first he smiled back, then he frowned. There was something . . . familiar. Yes, he had seen her before. Recently. "Have we met? In the office, perhaps."

She beamed while shrinking back in the seat. Her shyness was refreshing. "Yes, sir. A few times. Once yesterday." A slight boldness. "I thought you didn't notice."

"Of course, I did." Still, as he smiled, he felt an uncomfortable twinge. Was every woman beginning to look familiar?

At that moment, the pilot poked his head into the private compartment. "Is everyone aboard, sir?"

"Everyone, Carson. You've filed our papers and the flight plan?"

"Yes, sir. You'll have about two hours aloft, all in all. Customs will hold you up some when we land, but your papers should get you VIP treatment. Weather looks smooth all the way."

"Excellent. Take her up."

As the steward arrived with his next whiskey, he offered a drink to his new translator. She crossed her legs with a flash of thigh. At that point, he decided he could do worse for companionship, and the prospect of having the manifest by morning made him feel like his old genial self. He rested his head back and gazed out the window. As the big jet rolled down the runway, he tried not to worry about what would happen. Hell, he was willing to pay two million dollars for the manifest. Of course he would get it.

Chapter Thirty-Nine

Dazu

Jon and Asgar spent the daylight hours analyzing reports from the Uigher scouts and working through endless scenarios they might face tonight, interspersed with poker. Asgar ended up winning a few dollars, which Jon considered a donation to international goodwill. His thoughts never left the coming missions. He was determined to succeed at both, while Asgar, whose Uigher pride was involved, was equally eager to strike a blow for democracy and freedom in China.

Both worried about encountering what they had not envisioned. The thought of failure was impossible.

According to Asgar's people, the usual rafts of visitors had come and gone around the Sleeping Buddha, enjoying the beauty and spiritual quality of the centuries-old art, while local vendors aggressively hawked postcards and plastic statues. A normal day. Thus far, there had been no sign of McDermid's people, nor of Li Kuonyi and Yu Yongfu, but the hills and mesas around the

Buddha Grottos were largely open, so it was possible they could arrive unnoticed at any time, particularly after dark, hiking or riding in overland in vehicles or on horses, or disguised as tourists or vendors.

At the same time, the news from the prison was encouraging: The lockdown was over. No pallet check tonight, and tomorrow morning the prisoners would return to the fields. The harvest season had begun — cabbage, beets, bok choy, tomatoes, as well as the usual rice and chili peppers. Asgar figured that had played a large role in the decision.

Once darkness had cloaked Dazu's rolling hills and valleys, Jon, Asgar, and a dozen guerrillas drove to the prison and hid their vehicles as before. Now they and two of the Uigher fighters lay flat in cover across from the no-man's land and chain-link fence. The prison yard appeared quiet. The mess hall was shadowy and still. The double doors in the rear wall were closed, the rutted dirt drive deserted. From the barracks, an occasional voice rose in mournful song or macabre laughter, but the governor and the guards made no showing.

All of this information was vital, since the prison was still on medium alert. Jon and Asgar had decided they would improve the odds of a clean, quiet escape for Thayer and Chiavelli if they sneaked inside. They planned to take the same hidden route in which they hoped to bring them out.

Motionless, growing tense, at last they spotted movement. One of the double doors had opened and closed. Or had it? Jon stared, trying to pick out a shape, a form, anything. Then he saw it — a wraith low to the ground, a cross between a snake and a cat, scrambling through the ten-yard-wide blind spot to the fence. It was a small man in the usual drab prison uniform. He looked up at them once, spotted Asgar, and nodded.

Asgar nodded back and whispered to Jon, "It's Ibrahim. Let's cover him."

Noise was an enemy tonight. The last weapon they would use was their guns, even though they had screwed on noise suppressors. It was a myth that "silenced" gunfire was silent. Although it was quieter than regular fire, each bullet still gave off a loud *pop*, like a low-grade firecracker. With luck, their hands, feet, knives, and garottes would be enough. Still, they raised their pistols, sweeping over the grounds, in case of the worst. Beside them, the two Uigher fighters did the same. They must protect this man who was risking so much.

Jon's heart held a slow, steady beat, while tension fought to accelerate it. Ibrahim continued to scrape away the loamy soil until he had gone down what looked like a foot. Moments later, he raised a square of wood about three-by-three. He dove into the hole and vanished. Almost immediately, the dirt moved on the other side of the fence. It shifted, shook, and another wood panel arose. Ibrahim's head popped out, disappeared again, and re-appeared on the far side of the fence. The channel was clear.

Asgar whispered, "Our turn."

He rose to a crouch and scuttled to the fence, with Jon and the two Uigher guerrillas close behind. Jon peered down into the hole. It was a deep depression that had been scooped under the fence and covered with the two wood squares that met just beneath the chain links.

"Go," Asgar said in a low voice. "I've got your back."

Headfirst, Jon scrambled down, emerged on the prison side, and ran after Ibrahim to the mess hall, dirt flying from his clothes. He slid inside and turned to aim out his Beretta. The Uighers had replaced the wood on both sides of the fence and were pushing dirt back over. As Asgar ran to join Jon and Ibrahim, the remaining pair outside produced brushes and meticulously smoothed the dirt, making the night's disturbance unnoticeable.

When the last Uigher bolted into the mess hall, Ibrahim led them at a trot through the shadowy kitchen and deserted mess hall. They peered out the windows. Moonlight illuminated wood walkways that united three large barracks, joined them with the mess hall, and branched out to other buildings, guaranteeing dry feet for the governor during rainy seasons. All the buildings were raised on three-foot posts, indicating the seriousness of the seasonal storms. There were no trees and no grass, just soil that had been packed hard by many feet.

Two armed guards patrolled this area, rifles over their shoulders, yawning sleepily, perhaps because they'd had to patrol last night during the lockdown, too.

Ibrahim consulted in a low voice with Asgar, who nodded and told Jon, "Be ready. When I say go, we run out to the right and slide under the barrack there."

Ibrahim waited until the guards were at the ends of their routes and their backs were turned. He and Asgar clapped each other on both shoulders in farewell, and Ibrahim raced out of the mess hall, but to the left. He made no attempt to be silent. In fact, his footfalls were thumps on the hardpan. Both guards revived from their walking doze and spun, rifles aimed.

Each barked the same Chinese word, which Jon figured must mean "halt."

Ibrahim froze. His head dropped in fake guilt.

The men approached warily. They relaxed when they saw his face. Their lips curled as they spoke mockingly in Chinese.

Asgar translated everything in a whisper:

"You stealing food again, Ibrahim?"

"Don't you know you always get caught? What is it this time?"

The first guard searched the trembling Uigher and pulled a jar from inside his shirt. "Honey again. You know damn well that's not for prisoners. We would've discovered it was gone, and then we'd have tracked it to you. You're the dumbest inmate here. Now we've got to take you to lockup, and you'll be talking to the governor in the morning. You know what that means!"

His head hanging lower, Ibrahim was marched to a small building at the far edge of the yard.

"What *does* it mean?" Jon asked, concerned.

"Detention for a week. Ibrahim's an operator. It's his contribution to the cause." Asgar looked both ways. "Now!"

As Ibrahim disappeared inside, Jon and Asgar slipped out the front door, ran full speed to the right, and dove under the barrack. They clambered underneath to the other side, jumped out, ran again, and dove again, repeating until they were three barracks distant, in another part of the camp. They lay panting beneath the last one, peering out at another group of barracks. The most distant one from the fence where they entered was straight ahead.

Asgar breathed in deep gulps. Jon's heart pounded, and his face itched. But all he could think about was . . . in that barrack was David Thayer.

They studied the new area. Again, there were wood walkways uniting the buildings. Two more guards patrolled 180 degrees apart. As soon as the guards' backs were turned, Asgar nodded, and they ran once more, this time lightly.

The barrack door cracked open without a sound, and a figure motioned them into the dark interior. He was in his early thirties, with a scar down his right cheek that looked as if it had come from a blade. The man put a finger to his lips, closed the door, and padded quietly off between pallets of snoring male prisoners. Shafts of moonlight from high windows illuminated the bleak, regimented scene, which looked as if it had sprung from some monochromatic moment in a Solzhenitsyn novel.

Jon and Asgar followed the prisoner to a door at the rear. He pointed at it and returned to his pallet. Jon and Asgar exchanged a look in the gloom, and Asgar gestured as if to say, "Your turn, if you want it."

This was David Thayer's cell. This last door in

the last barrack in the compound. A man who had been declared officially dead for decades. Whose wife had remarried and died. Whose best friend had married her and died, too. Whose son had grown up without him. He had missed several lifetimes.

Jon opened the door eagerly. This man deserved more than pity. He deserved freedom and every happiness the world could offer.

Inside was a tiny room. Two men looked up from where they sat side by side on wood chairs. Each held a small, lighted flashlight, a hand cupping the beam. Jon could see little more. He and Asgar quickly closed the door behind them.

"Chiavelli?" Jon whispered into the dark.

"Smith?" asked a voice.

"Yes."

The hands released the beams. The cell erupted in shadows and light. Both men were fully dressed. The one who wore the usual prison shirt and trousers was younger — muscular, with a gray buzz cut and gray stubble on his chin. He immediately crossed the room and pushed aside the pallet in the corner.

The older one stood up, tall and rangy, with sunken cheeks and bony shoulders. He was dressed in a rumpled Mao jacket over loose peasant trousers, a Mao cap on his head. Under it was thick white hair and an aristocratic face that was riven with lines, not from the sun but from more than eighty years of life. Around his waist was a belt with a small pack. He was ready to travel. *David Thayer.*

Chiavelli said from the corner, "Asgar?" He was

on his knees, where the pallet had been. "I could use some help."

"Certainly, old man."

Asgar crouched beside Chiavelli, as Chiavelli explained what needed to be done. With their fingers, they worked loose and removed four-penny nails from the floor where Thayer's pallet had been.

Meanwhile, a warm smile wreathed David Thayer's wrinkled face. He extended his hand. "Colonel Smith, I've waited a long time for this. Wish I could think of something profound to say, but my heart and mind are too full."

"Actually, I was thinking the same thing, Dr. Thayer." He shook the hand. It was dry, warm, with only a slight tremble. "It's an honor to meet you, sir. I mean that. We're going to get you out of here. From this moment on, consider yourself a free man."

"If it's not too much trouble, I'd like to meet my son."

"Of course. The president sends his greetings. He wants very much to see you as soon as possible."

Thayer's smile widened, and his eyes shone. "I've hoped that for more than fifty years. Is he well?"

"From everything I know, he is. You have two grandchildren. Both in college. A boy and a girl. Patrick and Amy. You'll be going home to a beautiful family." Jon thought he heard a sob catch in Thayer's throat.

"Let's go!" Dennis Chiavelli called softly from the corner.

A panel of the wood floor was gone. It had been dropped down into the opening. David Thayer explained the Uighers had dug tunnels years ago, so they could move freely among the barracks.

Jon and Thayer hunched next to Asgar and Chiavelli, as Chiavelli explained urgently, "We go out as quickly and quietly as possible. Looks like the governor's laid down the law about the guards getting too lax, so we have to be damned careful. If a guard hasn't been bribed and tries to stop us, we jump him silently, without lethal force if we can, and we stash him, dead or alive, in the mess hall where he won't be found until after roll call tomorrow morning. If our luck holds, they won't figure out before then we're gone."

"We'd better be far the hell away by then anyway," Jon said. He looked at Asgar. "All of that sound right?"

"With an emphasis on nonlethal. My people have to stay behind."

Chiavelli frowned. "Why are they still here anyway?"

Impatience was written on Asgar's face. He dropped feet first into the hole and took out a small flashlight. "If we pulled off a mass escape, the Han would come down on us and all of Xinjiang like the Great Wall. It's better we remain a bloody nuisance, and *we* pick our times and places to strike. Besides, we slip people in and out of the prison when we need to. The network here is useful. Come on. We need to move as if the devil were nipping our heels."

Jon helped Thayer down into the opening. The moist, earthen hole had been scooped out into a tunnel about four feet high. They had to stoop, but it was a luxurious exit compared to Asgar's tunnel back in the Shanghai *longtangs*. Chiavelli, the last down, reached up and pulled the sleeping pallet across the hole. He angled the wood panel back up into place and tweaked it to the side so it would hold.

"One of our people will fix it so it's unnoticeable again," Asgar explained.

They headed off, almost doubled over, Asgar in the lead. Following were David Thayer, Jon, and Chiavelli. Jon watched Thayer for signs of pain or exhaustion from the strain of the bent-over position, but if he felt either, he gave no indication. The dirt walls closed in around Jon, and a sense of suffocation threatened to overtake him. He kept his gaze on Thayer's back. The tunnel writhed like a dragon's tail, interrupted by rough-hewn wood supports and occasional openings in the top where more wood panels indicated another entrance into another building. No one spoke, although Chiavelli sneezed twice, muffling the noise in his hand.

At last, there was a cool stream of fresh air.

Asgar breathed, "We're here." As they stopped, he continued, "We'll be coming up under the last barrack. After that is the mess." He looked at his watch face. "Right now, there should be no more than one guard patrolling between us and the final barrack. I'll handle him. If by any chance we're surprised by a second, which is possible tonight, Jon takes him."

"What do I do?" Chiavelli asked, frowning, eager to help.

Jon said, "Your job's to make sure Dr. Thayer stays safe."

Thayer protested, "Don't do anything special for me. I make it, or I don't. I'm too old for anyone to risk his life."

"You are old," Jon said bluntly. "But that means you'll make it harder on us if you try to do what you can't."

David Thayer said, amused, "So Captain Chiavelli becomes my bodyguard and my wet nurse. Poor Captain Chiavelli. It is a sad fate for such a brave man of action."

"No worries," Chiavelli assured him. "My pleasure."

"Here we go," Asgar whispered.

The panel above their heads had been unsealed and left ajar, the source of the fresh air. Asgar pushed it out of the way, and they climbed up, one after the other, into the crawl space beneath the barrack. Thayer was awkward but made it. Chiavelli replaced the panel and brushed dirt back over it.

Jon and Asgar took positions under the edge of the building, where the dimly lighted yard stretched between it and the mess hall. As Asgar had predicted, a single guard patrolled in a sloppy circle, his assault rifle slung over his shoulder and his head down as if half asleep.

They scuttled backward to where Thayer and Chiavelli lay. Thayer gave Jon a questioning look, but Jon shook his head, his fingers at his lips. They waited. The night air was chilly against their skin. The moon had retreated behind a gray cloud, and the shadowy prison took on an eerie, dangerous air. They waited tensely.

At last, the guard headed back in their direction. Again Jon and Asgar moved to the edge of the barrack. And waited. As the man's feet moved past, Asgar sprang out like a mountain cat and smashed the butt of his pistol down onto the guard's head. And it was over. Asgar started to drag the man under the barrack, where they would tie and gag him and smuggle him into the mess hall to hide.

Then it happened. A second guard marched out from around the next building. He saw Asgar bent over his collapsed comrade. For a long beat, the new guard stared, puzzled, his routine-dulled brain unable to comprehend and react. Abruptly, it penetrated. He grabbed his assault rifle, which was slung over his shoulder.

Just as he spun it over into his hands, Jon jumped out from under the barrack behind him and reached to clamp an arm around his throat. The man immediately slammed back the butt of the rifle. Jon saw it coming and dodged, but he lost his grip on the guard.

The man whirled around, aimed his rifle at Jon, and tightened his finger. At that moment, Dennis Chiavelli blasted out from under the barrack, racing shoulder down, like a battering ram. He crashed into the guard, pushing him a good six feet, while trying to yank the rifle from his hands. But the guard managed to pull the trigger.

The rifle fired. The noise was like a crack of thunder. It seemed to shake the buildings and explode up into the starry heavens.

Fear shot through Jon. "Hide him. Quick!" He kicked the guard in the chin, knocking him out.

At the same time, a voice shouted in Chinese, then another. There were questions in the voices. The old man straightened up onto his feet. He bellowed into the night, his voice strong. Jon had no idea what the words meant, but they were confident. The old man laughed, and there were responding chuckles in the distance.

"I told them I was an idiot," Thayer whispered as they quickly bound, gagged, and blindfolded the two guards. "I said I nearly shot myself in the foot by accident and begged them not to report me." He chuckled again.

"Nice save," Jon said in a low voice.

"Jolly right," Asgar agreed.

Chiavelli said nothing, merely smiled.

With the fear of being caught goading them, the four rushed the two unconscious guards toward the mess building. Two Uighers were waiting there, the door ajar. Inside, one of the Uighers asked Asgar a question.

Before Asgar could translate, David Thayer did: "They're saying they'll hide the guards, if we like. We should leave before the moon comes out again."

Jon nodded. "Tell them yes. Thanks, Dr. Thayer. Okay, let's get the hell out of here."

At a trot, they retraced the path Ibrahim had led them on, from the mess hall to the kitchen and finally to the rear double doors where another Uigher beckoned them to hurry even faster. The moon, approaching full tonight, was still low as they trotted out into the blind spot to the fence where the Uighers on both sides had already reopened the passage.

Asgar swiftly crawled under, but David Thayer suddenly stopped. He stared out through the chain links as if in a trance.

Jon looked all around. The hairs on the back of his neck were starting to rise. They'd had fairly good luck so far. Now was not the time to test it. "Dr. Thayer? Your turn. You go next."

"Yes," he murmured. "My turn. Astounding. Truly astounding. I used to be a big Dodgers fan. I understand they're no longer in Brooklyn." He looked at Jon.

"They're in Los Angeles now." Jon pulled him toward the passageway. "The Giants left New York, too. They're in San Francisco."

"The Giants in San Francisco?" Thayer shook his head. "I'm going to have a lot to get used to."

"Come on, sir," Jon said. "Down you go."

"It's odd, but I'm reluctant. Foolish, aren't I? My mind and heart are very full." He straightened his spine. Years seemed to fall from him, and he stepped to the fence, dropped stiffly to his knees, and crawled under. Jon immediately followed, and Chiavelli once more protected their rear, gazing carefully all around.

"Can you run, sir?" Jon asked urgently.

Behind them, the Uighers were already covering the wood squares with dirt again. Ahead, Asgar was dashing across the open space toward the trees. Jon and Chiavelli helped Thayer to his feet and finally got him to run. The stars seemed particularly bright. Too bright. At last, when they entered the safety of the forest, Jon felt as if he had just won the gold ring on the biggest carousel. They had gotten the old man out of prison. Now the trick would be to keep him out, keep him safe, and get him to America.

They stopped in a grove so Thayer could catch his breath. Sweat streamed down his face, but he was smiling broadly. He pressed a hand to his chest and inhaled raggedly. "I never managed an escape before. I tried."

They stood in a knot, sheltered all around by trees, waiting for him to recover, as they watched uneasily everywhere. An animal scurried away through the underbrush, heading north. Thayer never stopped smiling, even as he panted. His brown teeth were dark in his face. Some were chipped and broken. Two of his fingers were crooked, as if they had been broken but never splinted, so had healed wrong, perhaps after torture. The heaving in Thayer's chest slowed at last, and they ran on.

Chapter
Forty

Monday, September 18
Washington, D.C.

The mood in the tomblike situation room was tense. An electric tension that sapped at nerves already frayed. Throughout the morning, the assembled joint chiefs, service secretaries, National Security Adviser, secretaries of state and defense, the vice president, Charles Ouray, and the president himself had been discussing, sometimes heatedly, the rapidly approaching moment when a decision would have to be made whether to board the *Empress* and risk a military confrontation with China. After each had summarized his readiness, Secretary of Defense Stanton brought up the larger matter of long-range strategies and appropriations.

It was then that General Guerrero had reiterated what he called the army's obvious need to enlarge their quicker, lighter concept to include heavy weapons for sustained campaigns against strong forces over large areas. He cited several examples of weapons, including the Protector mobile artillery unit, as vital to be approved and put into production.

"You're alone on this today," the president told him. "At the moment we have a crisis to face that none of that can help us with."

The general nodded agreement. "Yessir, you're right."

The president turned to Admiral Brose. "What *can* you give us, Stevens, that'll make the Chinese and their submarine back off before all hell breaks loose?"

"Not very much, sir," the admiral admitted, his tone uncharacteristically gloomy.

Air Force General Kelly said, "For God's sake, Brose, you've got the whole damned Fifth Fleet out there. One carrier-based Viking, or even a Hornet, should scare the crap out of them."

Secretary Stanton chimed in, "Doesn't the *Crowe* have antisub choppers, Admiral?"

"Yes, to both comments," Brose said. "Or was it three? In any event, what you gentlemen seem to forget is that this isn't a military question, it's a political nightmare. We have far more weapons than we'd need if we could attack. Hell, barring advanced capabilities we're not aware of on that sub, the *Crowe* can juggle the situation on its own on at least an equal basis. But attacking first is precisely what we can't do. Isn't that so, Mr. President?"

"In a nutshell," the president agreed.

"So what I have to offer is a cruiser. I've got the *Shiloh* steaming full tilt. If it can get there in time, that might scare them off."

The president nodded calmly. This was to be expected and did not especially disturb him. His manner exuded quiet confidence, except for his right hand. The fingers drummed reflexively on

539

the table in front of him. "Thank you, Stevens. All right, where do we stand? Our attempt to secure proof of the *Empress*'s potentially lethal cargo by using the SEALs failed. We can't attack first, or we'll lose what credibility we have left that we're a nation that wants only peace and respects the rule of international law. I am, of course, still pursuing diplomatic avenues. But that pretty much exhausts our options, with one exception."

He paused to choose his words carefully, while his fingers continued their reflexive drumming. "Earlier, I mentioned an ongoing intelligence operation designed to secure proof of the cargo. I can report that I have high hopes of a successful conclusion to that effort, within hours."

The buzz in the room was excited. Emily Powell-Hill asked, "How many hours, sir?"

"Can't say for certain. You should know that the effort is inside China, and of course it's risky. Plus, there are enormous difficulties in running a mission on the other side of the world as well as having to contend with the vast distances of China."

"May I ask who's making this effort, Mr. President?" the vice president asked. "I'm sure all of us would like to pray for their safety and success."

"Sorry, Brandon, I'm not going to reveal that. I can tell you our man's close to success, but how close I can't be certain. Which leaves us faced with a simple, if potentially devastating decision. If I fail to hear from inside China in time, the *Crowe* will stop and board the *Empress* before it can reach Iraqi waters, which, in practicality, means before it enters the Persian Gulf. Exactly how many hours is that, Admiral Brose?"

The chairman of the joint chiefs glanced at his watch. "Seven, Mr. President. Give or take an hour."

Tuesday, September 19
Dazu

After a harrowing run through the forest, constantly looking over their shoulders, Jon, Asgar, the two Uigher fighters, and the two former prisoners reached the Uigher unit. A few minutes later, the entire group slipped out across the fields toward their hidden vehicles. They climbed aboard. With Asgar driving, Jon, Chiavelli, and Thayer took the limo, so Thayer would be more comfortable. Three other Uighers piled in back, their assault rifles bristling like porcupine quills. The rest of the Uighers divided themselves between the Humvee and Land Rover.

With the limo in the lead, the team drove off at a sedate rate in an effort to attract as little attention as possible. At the same time, they watched all around for pursuit, aware of every light, every boulder, every possible threat.

Jon studied the luminous green dial of his watch. "Where's Alani and her group? Aren't they still supposed to escort Chiavelli and Dr. Thayer to the border?"

"They're at the hideout," Asgar told him, his voice clipped, as if waiting for more trouble.

"Meaning, you want to give Chiavelli and Dr. Thayer a vehicle and some of your men to get them out of China?"

"That's the plan."

"No way. We don't know how many men Feng

or Li Kuonyi will bring. We need everyone. Besides, your people won't get back in time. We'll have to keep Chiavelli and Dr. Thayer with us until we actually walk into the mountains. Then we'll stash them somewhere safe and pick them up again when we leave."

Asgar thought a moment. "Okay, makes sense. Besides, we'll be able to use Chiavelli and perhaps Dr. Thayer. Can you shoot, sir?"

"A long time ago," Thayer admitted from the backseat. "Exactly what's this new mission?"

"We can't risk you, sir," Jon stated flatly.

"Absolutely not," Dennis Chiavelli agreed.

"All right." Thayer sighed. "But at least tell me what it is."

Jon related the highlights of the meeting at the Sleeping Buddha, the goal, the stakes, and the danger.

"This is for the human-rights agreement?" Thayer asked, his wrinkles rearranged in a frown. "Then it's vital. It's one of the most important pieces of legislation of my son's administration."

"Agreed," Jon said. "These are global stakes."

David Thayer took off his glasses and pinched the bridge of his nose in a gesture Jon had seen the president make. Then he slumped back as if exhausted. He stared out the window, a half smile on his old face.

Jon turned around in the front seat so that he was facing forward again. He glanced over at Asgar, and Asgar shot him a look of relief. Then both men resumed their careful watch for trouble. They drove past farmyards covered with rice grains spread out to be dried in tomorrow's sun, just as the red peppers had been. Unhulled rice was everywhere, even piled against walls and fences, like brown snowdrifts. Handmade wood tools leaned against the walls, too. There were penned chickens and pigs and vegetable gardens. Heavy wood vegetable buckets often sat neatly at the end of a row. And, of course, there were water buffalo, heads dangling, muzzles almost touching the ground as they drowsed.

Time ticked slowly. Too slowly, increasing the tension. They drove into a village, and Thayer roused himself. The houses were more prosperous looking, roofed with blue-black curved tiles and boasting two or more chimneys. At the same time, the road became a pavement of large stone slabs that appeared to be hundreds of years old. Thayer told them he had been brought occasionally out to do work around here, because of his clerking skills.

"See the chairs at the edge of the pavement? This road is like an extended living room," he said. "Villagers sit out here at tables to play cards, drink tea, and gossip. They lay their rice right on the pavement to dry, too, and bicyclists roll over it as if it's not there. No one cares. To the Chinese, rice is ancient. It's like the moon and stars. Nothing can destroy it."

Jon turned back to check on the president's father. His worn face still appeared tired, but even in the shadowy backseat, his expression clearly was happy. And he obviously felt like talking. A good sign.

"How are you feeling?" Jon asked.

"Odd. Strange. My emotions are jumpy. They're like gremlins, impossible to control. One moment,

543

I feel like laughing, the other like crying. I've reached the age where I cry rather easily, I'm afraid."

Jon nodded. "That's normal. How are you physically?"

"Oh, that. I was a little tired for a while, but now I feel fine."

"Were you ever tortured?"

Thayer frowned. He took off his glasses and pinched the bridge of his nose. Again, the same gesture Jon had seen the president make. But as Thayer did it, Jon again noted the two broken fingers. He suspected there were other broken bones, too, out of sight under the old prisoner's clothing. Ribs. An arm. Maybe a leg. No way to tell without a thorough workup. If they survived, the first order of business would be to make certain he had a physical.

Jon resumed his watch on the dark countryside.

Thayer gazed out the window, too. He was clearly enjoying himself, despite the danger and the stress inside the car. "The Chinese are a fascinating people. They're constantly repeating myths and creating new ones. Once, when one of the Communists' aqueducts was leaking badly in the mountains around here, they told the peasants living downhill that it was a new, scenic waterfall. That way they convinced them to keep working their farms, even when it wasn't safe."

"The Chinese culture entwines nature and myth," Asgar agreed. "Did they survive?"

"Yes. The aqueduct was fixed in time." Thayer continued, "Almost all of their natural phenomena have one or more legends. It's a perfect tool to keep

544

people ignorant. Science as we know it simply doesn't exist out here. But it's a beautiful way to live, too. They speak in a kind of poetry. A great tree is a transformed god. A rainbow is a cause for rejoicing. Heaven is alive on earth. But when that ignorance was transferred to Beijing, it caused a lot of problems."

"Wasn't Mao a peasant with barely an elementary school education?" Jon asked.

"Yes, and under him, other peasants ran the country. Some were actually illiterate. Couldn't read the reports they had to put their chops to. They knew little about mass production, factories, science, or even agriculture outside their own farming areas. Five years after Mao took over, the nation nearly starved to death because of ridiculous Politburo policies. In prison, we ate anything. Birds, insects, grass. After a while, there wasn't a weed left or bark on the trees. A lot of us died." Thayer shrugged. "But that's enough about that. Now that the impossible has become possible, I've got a reason to live long enough to meet what's left of my family. I suppose I'm growing greedy, but I don't care. Afterward, I can die in peace."

While they had been talking, Asgar had been on his walkie-talkie, checking with the drivers of the two other vehicles. None had seen any tails or surveillance. There was urgency in their voices over the crackling machines as they kept watch and stayed in touch.

"We've had word from inside the prison," Asgar reported over his shoulder. "They haven't missed those two guards yet, and they don't know you chaps are gone. Luck is with us so far." His gaze returned to the road. The caravan was climbing into the hills.

The tension in the limo relaxed a shade with the news. Thayer described the area of Baoding Shan, where they were headed, and the Sleeping Buddha, where the exchange was to take place for the *Empress*'s manifest. "Sometimes Baoding Shan is translated to mean Precious Summit Mountain, other times it's Treasure Peak Mountain. Near the foot of it is where the Sleeping Buddha and other figures are carved into the rock, like at Mt. Rushmore. They're painted, too."

"I heard they're a thousand years old," Chiavelli said.

"Nearly," Thayer informed them. "The ones around the Sleeping Buddha date back to the thirteenth century. Whoever planned the grotto had a real understanding of beauty. It follows the natural line of the cliffs. They're crescent shaped and solid rock, but around them is thick vegetation — trees, bushes, vines, flowers. Very green and lush. The cliff itself is part of a gorge."

"Tell me what you think of the Sleeping Buddha as a site for an exchange," Jon asked. Fred Klein had faxed him maps and descriptions. Still, there was nothing like hearing it from someone who had been there.

"For Li Kuonyi and Feng Dun, it will be full of possibilities. For you, probably the possibilities will make it difficult, since you want to take the manifest from whoever ends up with it. The Sleeping Buddha is massive, but it's in an overhang, and around it are a lot of different carvings, some of epic Buddhist stories. Many are at eye level, which means they're good places to duck inside and hide. There are other statues in dark caves and carved temples around there, too."

Asgar spun the wheel to miss a wild dog that had darted across the road. "You're absolutely right in every detail, Dr. Thayer. Couldn't have given a better report myself. But how do you know all this?" he asked suspiciously.

"Our prisoners are sent to clean and repair the Buddha art. I was interested, so sometimes I was allowed to go, too. In Chinese culture, the old are respected simply because they've managed to live a long time, even if they are prisoners."

At last, the trio of vehicles parked off in the trees. The Uighers jumped out and piled brush on the cars to camouflage them. Thayer walked around, stretching his legs, while Chiavelli accompanied him, keeping close watch.

"Time to go," Jon told the two at last. He gave Chiavelli the limo's keys. "Asgar's written out directions to the hideout. If we're not back by dawn, you'll have to take him there yourself."

"No problem. Then what?"

"Asgar's sister, Alani, will smuggle you both to the best border."

"Got it. Good luck." Chiavelli looked at him a moment, understanding passing between them, and he ushered Thayer toward the limo.

As they climbed into the front seat, Thayer's voice became shy. "Did you ever meet my son, Dennis? What can you tell me about him?" The captain's answer was lost with the closing of the doors.

The Uighers finished camouflaging the limo.

With weapons, flashlights, and maps, Asgar led them off onto a path filled with shadows and dark trees and plants that brushed against them. The fecund scent of growing things was all around them. One of the Uighers had been to the grotto, and he gave his opinions, which Asgar translated for Jon. Avoiding the usual routes, they climbed uphill single file, trying not to stumble on loose stones or fall against rocks into the brush.

As the trail flattened, Jon said, "Asgar, when we get near the Sleeping Buddha, we'll stop just above and to the side. We'll use the vegetation for cover."

"You give the orders this time, my friend."

"We'll take positions where we can see anyone who comes down from the entrance steps as well as whoever stops in front of the Buddha. My intelligence agrees with what Dr. Thayer said — there are a lot of places to hide among the statues and carvings. That's going to make our job even harder. Spread your men out so we can watch as much of the grotto as possible."

"Sounds like a bit of a challenge," Asgar said dryly. "How long do we have?"

"No way to know. The 'meet' may end up being at dawn after all."

"Daylight won't be kind to us. If you're planning to get the manifest out of China, we'd jolly well better be halfway to the border by sunrise."

"I expect everything to blow up long before then. Daylight won't be kind to them either."

They lapsed into silence. The group kept their voices low and their footsteps careful as their path headed downhill. As Thayer promised, a riot of vegetation surrounded them. Above, the moon illuminated the tops of trees and bushes and created black, impenetrable shadows beneath. Ahead waited the Sleeping Buddha, where Jon would face Feng Dun and Li Kuonyi once more, and where, one way or the other, the mission would end.

Chapter
Forty-One

The Arabian Sea

The communications technician turned from his radio controls. "It's the *Shiloh*, sir. They want our exact position now and our estimated position in ten hours."

Lt. Commander Frank Bienas leaned over the radioman. "Send our present fix. I'll work out the estimated. But tell them ten hours won't cut it."

Bienas sat down and went to work on the chart. The radioman sent the exec's message to the approaching cruiser and leaned back to wait for the response. He stretched in his seat, nearing the end of his watch and aching from the long hours they had been putting in. Bienas continued to plot the *Crowe*'s projected course and finally sat back, too, shaking his head.

The radioman was listening on his earphones. He called over his shoulder, "*Shiloh* says ten hours is the best they can do to get here. They're pouring on all they've got already."

"You tell 'em by then we'll be in the Gulf, and that's way too chancy. They need to be here in under six, or they might as well go home and bake cookies." Worried, he announced, "Anyone wants me, I'm on the bridge." He made his way up and out to the dark deck and on up to the bridge, where Commander Chervenko had taken charge an hour ago.

When Bienas entered, Chervenko's night binoculars were directed toward the distant running lights of *The Dowager Empress*. "She's picked up a knot in the last hour. Like a dog smelling home."

"The *Shiloh* says ten hours," Bienas reported.

Chervenko did not turn or lower his binoculars. "Brose did the best he could. Trouble was, the Fifth Fleet's too far south, and we're moving away from them. They'll never reach us in time."

"Not much they could do we can't anyway," Bienas decided, sounding tough and optimistic.

"Except be twice as formidable." The skipper was realistic. "What's the sub doing?"

"Holding steady. Hastings says he's picking up what sounds like prepping for attack. There's activity in the forward torpedo room."

"They know we're close to showdown time, Frank. We can't let the *Empress* get into the Persian Gulf. We'd be vulnerable to land-based air attack, torpedo boats, you name it, and no telling who'd get enthusiastic and want to join the act. Tehran might decide their interests were involved, too, and then we'd have one hell of a swell party."

Bienas nodded grimly. He stood shoulder-to-shoulder with the commander, staring out through the night at the running lights ahead as both ships sailed steadily closer to confrontation.

551

Dazu

"There it is." Asgar's voice was low but full of uncharacteristic awe.

He and Jon stopped among the thick canopy of trees and heavy underbrush. They had come to an opening slightly above and to the side, on the same flank of the mountainside as the carvings. Although they could not see the full scope of the thousands of pieces of rock art that extended hundreds of meters, the painted Sleeping Buddha itself and the statues around it spread before them in a breathtaking panorama, glowing in the candle-wax moonlight.

The other Uighers stopped to stare, too. The giant Sleeping Buddha reclined on his right side in the center of the horseshoe-shaped cliff. Its back sunk into the cliff, the Buddha was more than a hundred feet long and almost twenty feet high, a rendition of Prince Sakyamuni sleeping the sleep of the Enlightened as he entered Nirvana. Puny next to him, life-sized statues of Bodhisattvas and period officials wearing hats stood in a stone stream so close they could touch him. Protected from the weather only by the rock overhang that David Thayer had described, the timeless Sleeping Buddha was in full, spectral view.

Where they had stopped was a good place to set up watch. Jon and Asgar dispersed the Uighers into the undergrowth and found positions for themselves near each other, to make issuing orders easier. Under a tree, they began the wait, which could be long or short. In either case, Jon kept his excitement under control. He had been close to taking the manifest before, and each time he had

552

failed. He would get no other chance. He dismissed a shiver of anxiety and studied the display of carvings, memorizing it, so if either group arrived and hid, he would have the panorama firmly in mind. He could afford no more mistakes.

Other carved figures in various niches stretched around the stone crescent. Stone statues guarded the dark openings of caves. Low, painted steel fences separated most of the carvings from the public, which would arrive tomorrow morning. No one was around, not tourists, not vendors, not spiritual seekers, not police. The darkness stirred only with a light wind, small animals rustling away, and night birds flapping into hiding.

"When *do* you think someone's going to appear?" Asgar kept his voice hushed. "Morning's not so far away."

"No idea. As I said, the meeting was to happen by daylight, but my instincts tell me they'll show up long before then."

"Better be before the tourists."

"I hope so. But Li Kuonyi and Yu Yongfu might want the cover of crowds. Still, they must realize by now that Feng Dun will kill anyone in his way to get the manifest, so crowds won't be much help. No, they'll expect something underhanded from Feng, which tells me they'll arrive early. Early enough to be here before Feng, so they can set a countertrap."

But despite Jon's carefully thought-out assessment, he was wrong. Less than a half hour later, there was movement at the top of the stone stairs on the other side of the Sleeping Buddha. Jon focused his night-vision binoculars. There were five men, three of whom Jon recognized from Hong Kong and Shanghai — part of Feng Dun's gang. All were armed with what looked like British assault rifles. But Feng was not among them.

"Damn," Jon breathed.

"What is it? Trouble?" Asgar stared through the night to where Jon was watching the men make their way down the stairs into the valley and the crescent of carvings.

"Feng Dun's not with them," Jon said. He stopped and stared. He swore. "That's one hell of a surprise."

As the five men continued downward, another man had appeared in the moonlight and started down, too, carrying a medium-sized suitcase. Ralph McDermid himself.

"It's McDermid. The big honcho we think masterminded the whole deal."

"The muckity-muck himself? Isn't that odd?"

"Maybe not. Feng's gotten the manifest only once. He's botched it every other time. McDermid might've decided to take no chances. He's probably decided that Li Kuonyi and her husband would tend to trust him more. If the two million isn't legitimate, they know he can't stall and blame someone else to gain time. On the other hand, maybe he's here because he no longer trusts Feng."

"He might've bribed his people away from him," Asgar said.

"Right. Still, I don't like unexpected developments from the enemy. It usually means I've missed something."

The armed band continued to descend warily

and in open order, looking as if they were guarding against an ambush.

McDermid halted the group at least twenty feet above the grotto floor and motioned them to hide facing the Sleeping Buddha. The Altman CEO used a bush for cover.

Asgar said, "Looks as if McDermid expects Yu and Li to come down the stairs, too. He'd be able to confront them there."

If that was what McDermid had in mind, this time he was the one who was wrong. A burly man appeared first, walking alertly alongside the Sleeping Buddha in the moonlight. He came not down the stairs but emerged from somewhere to the Buddha's right, from among the statuary, just as David Thayer had suggested was possible. Through Jon's binoculars, he saw what appeared to be a 9mm Glock tucked inside the man's waistband in front.

Li Kuonyi followed onto the grotto walkway. She stopped beside the burly man and gazed all around. She wore a sleek, black pantsuit and a high-collared hooded jacket against the chill of the mountain mists and carried an attaché case, where the manifest likely was. Jon strained to see her face, but her high collar covered much of it, and her hair was hidden beneath the hood. Still, he had no doubt who she was. He would not soon forget the image of her drinking alone in the silent mansion in Shanghai.

The man who walked close behind as if afraid to be alone was somewhere in his early thirties, with a boyish face and a slim, wiry body. A man who watched his weight and took very good care of himself. But not now. Strain showed in his glazed eyes and furrowed brow. He looked dissipated and frightened. Days with little sleep had taken their toll on the man Jon suspected was Li Kuonyi's husband, Yu Yongfu. He wore a crumpled Italian suit that was probably custom made, a wilted regimental tie loose at the throat, scuffed dress boots, and a wrinkled white-and-blue-striped shirt. He stayed close behind his wife, his gaze darting nervously into every shadow.

A fourth person — another man — glided out of the dark to join them. Jon did not recognize him. Slimmer, his eyes had an unnatural gleam, like a bipolar patient in a manic state. Clearly another enforcer and far more dangerous.

With Li Kuonyi in the lead, the four walked past the Sleeping Buddha and peered up the stone steps.

She set the attaché case on the ground and called out in English, "Feng? I know you're there. We heard you. Do you have our money?"

Monday, September 18
Washington, D.C.

Admiral Stevens Brose announced, "Three hours, sir."

"Don't you think I can count, Admiral!" the president snapped. He blinked and took a long breath. "Sorry, Stevens. It's this waiting and not knowing what, if anything, is happening. We've been down to counting minutes before, but those were attacks initiated by an enemy, and all we could do was use everything we had to stop the attack. This is different. This is a confrontation we

556

initiated, where we can't use *anything* we have, and soon I'm going to have to give an order that could send us, China, and the rest of the world into a war none of us will be able to control. There's someone in China who wants that, and he'll be there to act — retaliate — as soon as we move on the *Empress*."

They were alone in the situation room. The admiral had requested the meeting, and the president had thought it best to talk where no one else could hear them. All the high-ranking military and civilian defense personnel were already walking on nails, and the talkative West Wing staff was oddly silent, as if holding their collective breath.

"I don't envy you, sir."

President Castilla gave a humorless laugh. "Everyone envies me, Stevens. Haven't you heard? I'm the most powerful person on earth, and everyone wants to be me."

"Yessir," the admiral said. "The *Shiloh* isn't going to get there in time."

"Then may God, and our man in China, help us."

Tuesday, September 17
Dazu

There was an electric pause as Li Kuonyi and her terrified husband waited for Feng Dun to appear.

Through his binoculars, Jon watched Ralph McDermid's emphatic but whispered orders to his men. From the distance and in the green glow of night vision, Jon thought the Altman CEO was telling them to stand by, on no account to do anything without his signal.

Then McDermid stood up from beneath his

bush and descended the stairs, smiling and carrying the suitcase.

He had nearly reached the bottom, when Li Kuonyi announced, "That's far enough."

"She's speaking English," Asgar noted.

"If her gunmen don't know English, then it's a good way to make certain they don't really understand what's going on," Jon said.

"Who are you?" she asked McDermid suspiciously. "Where's Feng Dun?"

"I'm Ralph McDermid, Mrs. Yu. I'm the one who's going to pay you two million dollars." He patted his suitcase.

Jon saw Yu Yongfu whisper in his wife's ear. Her eyes widened, as if Yu had confirmed McDermid's identity. "Is that the cash?"

"Indeed, it is," McDermid said. "Is the document in your attaché case?"

With the toe of her shoe, Li touched the case. "Yes. But before you have any ideas about taking it from us by force with the men you've hidden up there, you should know the case is booby-trapped. I'll trigger it the moment you make one wrong move. Is that clear?"

McDermid smiled at Li Kuonyi as if she were the most delectable woman he had ever seen. As if he enjoyed every moment of doing business with her, and Jon understood for the first time the false face McDermid showed the world was, to him, simply business. Even in pleasure, it was no doubt business. And, of course, all business was pleasure, a game to be won, the higher the stakes, the better. Life as transaction. It was an automatic reaction, like breathing.

"Perfectly," he told her in his genial voice. "You'll want to count the money, of course."

"Of course. Bring it down here and return to where you are now."

McDermid descended the final few feet, laid his suitcase flat on the ground, and climbed backward, never taking his gaze from Li and the three men, while above him his hidden gunmen waited with their assault weapons aimed.

A sense of excited expectancy radiated from the couple even from where Jon, Asgar, and the Uigher fighters watched from the hillside. The husband and wife glanced at each other, their eyes alight.

Li Kuonyi told Yu, "Examine it, my husband."

His face eager, Yu squatted and unhooked the clasps on the suitcase. For a moment, Li Kuonyi and the two bodyguards took their eyes off the hill to watch the suitcase's lid being raised. That was their mistake.

As if on signal, Feng Dun arose from the thick shrubs on the slope above where McDermid's five men lay, an assault rifle in his large hands. He fired, and the long bank facing the Sleeping Buddha erupted in a barrage of automatic fire. The noise was volcanic, shattering the stillness of the night, as the bullets whined and screamed, hailing down on Li Kuonyi, her husband, and their two body-guards. None had a chance.

Li Kuonyi's throat was nearly severed, blood spouting as she fell. As bullets riddled his chest, Yu Yongfu surged up then collapsed over the suitcase. The beefy bodyguard was still trying to under-stand what was happening when he was cut down.

Only the second gunman managed to get his pistol halfway out before he slammed back against the low steel fence in front of the Sleeping Buddha and catapulted over in slow motion, blood spraying out from bullet holes throughout his body.

On the hill between Feng's men and the floor of the valley, the five who had arrived with McDermid lay dead in the undergrowth, too.

As the valley turned sepulchral with shocked silence, McDermid froze where he stood, his mouth open in shock. Feng and a dozen men burst from the bushes and spilled down the steps.

Ralph McDermid screamed, his face a deep, choleric red: "I told you to stay away! I *told* you I would handle it! What have you done, *you idiot!*"

"What have I done, Taipan?" Feng said as he reached the corpses. "I've made certain the manifest will not fall into American or Chinese hands. I've earned two million dollars. Perhaps most personally important, I've eliminated an insolent, worthless, rich American."

As Feng fired a short burst from his assault rifle, McDermid's eyes opened wide, as if in understanding. The bullets riddled his heart and flung him backward, arms outstretched. He fell, sprawled, on the stone walkway. Feng laughed, kicked away Li Kuonyi's corpse, and grabbed the attaché case.

On the hill above and to the side, Jon and the Uighers had had no time to stop the bloodbath. Asgar swore and waved to his men, who were already aiming their AK-47s at Feng and his killers.

"No!" Jon said instantly. "Tell them to hold their fire. Tell them to stay hidden!"

"He'll get away with your manifest, Jon!"

"No!" Jon snapped. "Wait!"

The Arabian Sea

Commander James Chervenko lay on his bunk in his quarters, but he was wide awake. He had left the bridge to Frank Bienas two hours before, with what he knew was the unneeded order to call him the moment there was a new development. In any event, to check in no later than 0400 hours. He had gone below ostensibly to sleep, although he had known from experience that was hopeless. Still, the semblance of normalcy helped calm the crew, and the time alone gave him an opportunity to think carefully about how best to handle the Chinese submarine.

When a call from the *Shiloh* was put through, he took it instantly. The news was terrible: The *Shiloh* was definitely not going to reach them in time.

"How long do you have, Jim?" Captain Michael Scotto asked.

"Less than three hours."

"You at stations?"

"Not until I absolutely have to."

A brief silence. "You're cutting it fine."

"It's dark, and radar tells me they're running on the surface. They can pick up our activity. I won't be the one to pull the trigger until I'm ordered to."

"It's a risk. If they decide to start it . . ." Scotto on the *Shiloh* let the sentence trail off.

"I know, Mike. I'll take that risk, but I won't start it."

"Good luck."

"Thanks. Get here as fast as you can."

561

They broke the connection. Neither commander needed to say more. Each knew what was involved. In a naval engagement, anything could happen, and the *Shiloh* might still be able to help. If not, it could pick up survivors, if there were any survivors.

Chervenko had barely closed his eyes to try to catch at least an hour of sleep, when his intercom came alive: "Sir, the sub's diving. Sonar says they sound like they're running fish in."

Chervenko's lungs tightened, and his stomach knotted. "On my way."

He jumped up, splashed cold water on his face, combed his hair, straightened his clothes, put on his cap, and left the quarters. On deck, he stared aft but saw nothing.

On the bridge, Bienas nodded ahead toward the running lights of *The Dowager Empress*. "She's picked up more speed. Close to her top fifteen."

"The sub?"

"Sonar confirms she's arming."

"Moving in?"

"Not yet."

"She will. Let's go to stations, Frank."

Bienas nodded to the specialist on the ship's intercom.

He leaned to his microphone. His young voice quavered with nerves as he bellowed: "Battle stations! Battle stations!"

Chapter
Forty-Two

Dazu

Asgar waved his hand frantically to stop his Uighers from firing down the slope at Feng Dun and his men. Some wore Chinese army uniforms.

Jon stared, shocked, at the soldiers, while Asgar stared at him. "Are you mad, Jon? Feng's going to get the money *and* your manifest!"

But Jon had been watching the events carefully. He shook his head, disgusted he had not seen the truth earlier. But then, neither Ralph McDermid nor Feng Dun had either.

"Doubt it," Jon said. "It's a trick. Has to be."

Asgar was more confused. "A trick? *What* trick? Feng and his people murdered everyone, and now he's getting away with your bloody manifest and two million dollars!"

Jon shook his head stubbornly. "No. Keep your men alert. Watch."

Down in front of the great Buddha, Feng crouched before the attaché case while his men stood at equal paces around, guarding, nervous excitement on their faces. Gingerly, Feng picked up

563

the case. He weighed it in his hands. He tilted and rotated it carefully. Then he laughed and said something in Chinese. His people laughed, too.

Asgar explained, "He says there's no bomb in it. It's too light, and nothing heavy moves inside. He never believed there was a bomb. Li Kuonyi would never destroy her only real weapon."

"He's right about that."

As Feng prepared to open the lid, his men stepped back, not yet ready to trust. Feng lifted it and stared eagerly inside. Nothing happened. No bomb, no explosion. But Feng's face twisted in a scowl. He shouted an oath and hurled the case away. It landed quietly in the brush.

As Feng barked something in Chinese, Asgar looked at Jon, surprised. "It's empty!"

Jon nodded. "Had to be. As I said, Li Kuonyi produced another of her tricks."

There was no manifest at the Sleeping Buddha tonight. Down in the crescent, Feng jumped to his feet and strode to where Yu Yongfu still lay facedown over the suitcase of money. He kicked the corpse over onto its back and crouched. He licked his fingers and rubbed Yu's face. Grimacing, he stared at his fingers. He shouted another curse.

"What the devil is he doing *now?*" Asgar wondered.

Cold eyes glittering with fury, Feng hurried to where Li Kuonyi lay on her back, staring up at eternity. He bent over and repeated the same ritual. When he finished, he slumped on his heels, as if defeated. Then he sprang to his feet and spoke with disgust to his men.

"So that's it!" Asgar stared at Jon as if he were a magician. "It *was* a trick. Li and Yu's trick. It's *not* them. Those poor people are imposters. Perhaps some of her fellow actors, that she hired. They and the two guards were sacrifices, scene decoration to make the real Li Kuonyi and Yu Yongfu's ruse believable. But — ?"

"Yes," Jon said. *"But."*

As he spoke, down below Feng hunched again and searched the dead woman. When he stood once more, he held a small object.

"What the deuce did he find?"

"I'd guess a miniature microphone, receiver, and speaker. That's how Li put on the charade, and why she was the only one who spoke."

In the valley, Feng seemed to realize the same thing. He raised his head and scanned the mountainside above the Sleeping Buddha. When he saw nothing, he whirled and barked more orders in Chinese.

"He's telling them — "Asgar began.

Jon jumped up, shouting, "Now we fire! Fire! *Fire!*"

Asgar echoed the order in Uigher, and their part of the hillside erupted. All twenty-two assault rifles opened a blistering fire on Feng's trapped men and soldiers.

Monday, September 18
Washington, D.C.

The low sun of late afternoon probed through small gaps in the heavy drapes that shut off Fred Klein's office in Covert-One's new headquarters from the outside world. Still, the outside world loomed large in Klein's office. His face, haggard from lack of sleep and missed meals, bristled with a ragged six-day growth of gray beard too rapidly turning white. His heavy, red-streaked eyes appeared permanently fixed on the ship's clock on his wall. His head was cocked sideways in the direction of the blue telephone.

Had there been anyone to see, they would have thought him paralyzed, hypnotized, in a trance, unconscious, or dead, because he had not moved in so long. Only his chest rose and fell slightly as he breathed.

When the blue phone rang, he jerked alert and nearly fell from the chair as he grabbed the receiver. "Jon!"

"He's not called?" the president asked. Disappointment and tension radiated from his low voice.

"No, sir."

"We have two hours. Or less."

"Or more. Ships can be unpredictable."

"The weather in the Arabian Sea is calm and clear all the way to the Persian Gulf and on to Basra."

"Weather isn't the only variable, Mr. President."

"That's what scares me, Fred."

"It scares me, too, sir."

Klein could hear the president breathing. There was a slight echo from the other end of the connection. Wherever he was calling from, the president was alone.

"What do you think is happening? In . . . where is Colonel Smith?"

Klein reminded him, "Dazu, Sichuan. At the Sleeping Buddha."

The president fell silent. "They took me there once. The Chinese. To all those carvings."

"I've never seen them."

"They're remarkable. Some are nearly two thousand years old, carved by great artists. I wonder what we'll leave of use for those alive a thousand years from now?" The president was silent again. "What time is it there? At the Sleeping Buddha?"

"The same as it is in Beijing, Sam. China gerrymandered their time zones into a single one to make it convenient. It's about four A.M. there."

"Shouldn't it be over? Shouldn't we have heard? Not even a word about my father?"

"I don't know, Mr. President. Colonel Smith knows the time frame."

Klein could sense the president's nodding. "Yes, of course he does."

"He'll do his best. No one's best is better."

Again the affirmative nodding somewhere in the White House, as if the president were sure it would all work out, although a large part of him feared it would not. "I have to get the manifest, and then I have to get a copy to Niu Jianxing in Beijing. But now it's too late, isn't it? There's no time to get even a copy to China and hope that's enough to convince the hard-liners. They'd laugh at a fax, or at a copy sent over the Internet. They could be too easily counterfeited. Or at least, if we're right and there's someone inside Zhongnanhai who wants war, there's no way he'd have to believe anything short of the actual manifest."

"Jon will think of something," Klein said reassuringly. But he had no idea what that could be.

Neither did the president. "In an hour, maybe

less, I'll tell Brose to give the order. We're going to have to board the *Empress*. I don't see any way around it, dammit. You did your best. Everyone did their best. All we can do now is hope and pray the Chinese back off, but I don't see that happening."

"No, sir. Neither do I."

The silence was longer. The voice that finally came was sad, tragic: "It's the idiocies and tragedy of the Cold War all over again. Only this time, the weapons are more advanced, and we may be standing alone. In two hours, we'll know."

Tuesday, September 19
Dazu

At the base of the mountains, where the trail led up and over into the valley of the carvings, David Thayer slept, tired by the unaccustomed activity and tension of the night. Chiavelli watched the old man, the Chinese-made AK-47 given him by Asgar Mahmout resting across his lap in the dark interior of the battered limo. He had been greatly impressed with Thayer's ability to keep up and suspected that his exhaustion came less from activity than from tension.

The tension, especially here under the stifling branches and brush hiding them, of doing nothing but waiting was affecting even Chiavelli. He found himself dozing, only to jerk awake to the beating of his own heart. He took longer and longer to distinguish between dozing and being awake each time he opened his eyes. This time, as he awoke with a painful whip of his neck, it was only seconds before he knew he was actually awake, and that the sound in his ears was not the pounding of his heart.

It was many feet walking on the road. Heavy feet, booted, and moving in an all-too-familiar rhythm. Marching feet, coming toward them.

David Thayer had heard them, too. "Soldiers. I know the rhythm. Chinese soldiers, marching."

Chiavelli listened intently. "Ten? Twelve? A squad?"

"I'd say so." Thayer's voice was shaky.

"On the road, no more than five hundred yards away. A quarter of a mile."

"We . . . we're off the road," Thayer decided nervously. "The brush and branches should hide us."

"Maybe, but what are they doing here at this hour? It's oh four hundred. Four A.M. They couldn't have discovered you're missing, or there'd be an army out there. They wouldn't be walking. No, these guys are after someone or something else, and I've got a bad feeling."

That scared the old man, but he tried to hold up. "You think it's about Colonel Smith and the Uighers' mission. But how could anyone know? It's more probable they have no connection at all to what's happening at Baoding Shan."

"Can we take the chance? Do nothing?" Chiavelli answered his own question: "Absolutely not. If they're heading for the valley, they'll blindside Jon, Asgar, and the Uighers."

"We've got to help!"

"I'll try to hold them here. At least, to slow them down."

"What about me?"

"Stay here, keep quiet, and you should be safe. If I don't come back, you'll have to drive yourself to the Uigher hideout."

Thayer shook his head. "Unrealistic. I haven't driven anything in fifty years, Captain. And the last time I counted, two guns were always better than one. That hasn't changed. You're not protecting me by leaving me alone. Give me a gun. I haven't fired a weapon in fifty years, either, but one doesn't forget how to aim and pull the trigger."

Chiavelli stared at the white hair, the parchment skin, the determined look. "You're sure? The worst that'll happen if they discover you here in the limo is they'll send you back to the prison farm. Klein's extraction team should be ready by now. It's smart for you to stay here and keep your head down."

Thayer held out his hand. "I have a Ph.D., Dennis. I'm officially smart. Give me the gun."

Chiavelli stared. Thayer seemed completely calm. There was a stray moonbeam that glowed through the brush. In its light, he could see Thayer's eyes were smiling, as if mortality and death were longtime companions. Chiavelli nodded, understanding. Of course, the old man was right.

Chiavelli put Jon's 9mm Beretta in the gnarled hand. The hand was steady. Then he opened the car door on his side, which faced away from the road, and cautioned Thayer to be quiet. They slid out through the camouflage covering and hid behind it. The moon was directly overhead. They raised up enough to see the road was a luminous white ribbon and soon spotted Chinese soldiers approaching at a brisk march. There were ten soldiers of the People's Liberation Army, led by an infantry captain.

Chiavelli whispered, "How many men in a squad of PLA infantry?"

"I don't know."

They had no more time to think about that. Chiavelli took careful aim with the AK-47 and squeezed off a single shot.

The first of the marching soldiers cried out and dropped to the ground, holding his leg and writhing.

At the same time, Thayer held the Beretta in both hands and fired. The bullet struck the road twenty feet in front of the column, sending up a geyser of dirt. The nine soldiers jumped into the undergrowth, dragging their injured comrade with them. Seconds later, they returned a barrage of fire in the general direction of the limousine, but not directly at it.

Chiavelli whispered, "They don't know where we are yet. They're firing wild."

A voice barked in Chinese, and the gunshots ceased.

Chiavelli and David Thayer waited. Sooner or later the soldiers would have to advance, but the longer they remained hidden, the better. Thayer's face seemed flushed. Chiavelli had that heightened sense of reality combat always brought. A light sweat covered him.

Another bark, and Thayer shuddered. The nine rose in unison from the brush lining the road on both sides and charged, their moonlit white eyes searching for the enemy, and shooting as they came.

Thayer leaned around the rear of the limo and fired three quick shots. His aim was better this time, and a cry of pain from the brush rewarded him. "Maybe we *can* drive them off," he exulted, perhaps remembering all the pain of more than fifty years of captivity far from home.

The soldiers dove for cover in a panic, leaving the man Thayer had hit trying to crawl from the road on his own.

They were as poorly trained as everyone in the service had told Chiavelli to expect. Obviously, they had no combat experience. He doubted whoever was barking orders would get them to charge again in a hurry.

Chiavelli and Thayer stayed down, out of sight, counting the minutes and waiting. Time crawled. Twenty minutes, and still no attack. Good minutes, since they kept the squad away from the Sleeping Buddha. Then Chiavelli caught a silvery flash. Moonlight had reflected off something, perhaps the dial of a wristwatch. He had an uneasy feeling, then a sensation of sound and movement. Suddenly, the bushes seemed to be crawling toward them, not ten yards away.

"Fire!" he whispered wildly. "Open fire, Mr. Thayer! *Fire!*"

His AK-47 on top of the car, he ripped off a long string of bullets as the Beretta screamed with gunshots next to him. But the angle was bad, and they had to stay up on their toes in order to see well enough to aim.

Suddenly, two shots exploded into the limo. The hot smell of burned metal singed Chiavelli's nose. Shots sounded from behind. Voices shouted in Chinese.

Thayer's skin turned as ghostly white as the

moon. "They're telling us to freeze, drop our weapons and surrender, or they'll kill us. We can still —"

"Absolutely not. *Forget it.*" He had promised he would keep the president's father safe, and a return to prison was better than being dead. As long as they both remained alive, he still had a chance of being able to continue to protect him. "We've held them a half hour at least. Sometimes a half hour can make all the difference."

He gave the AK-47 a shove and let it fall on the far side of the limo. He raised his hands high over his head.

Trembling, David Thayer dropped the Beretta and put his hands on the top of his Mao cap. His few hours of freedom had ended. "Alas," he whispered.

The eight soldiers in front, supporting their two wounded, rose from the brush and advanced. They picked up the discarded weapons, grinning as two more soldiers appeared behind Thayer and Chiavelli. Apparently, there were twelve men in a PLA infantry squad.

The officer — a captain with his pistol out — stopped in front of them, speaking angrily. Thayer translated, "He's asking who we are. He's figured out we're Americans. He . . . oh, God." He glanced at Chiavelli. "He wants to know whether we're part of the spy team with Colonel Jon Smith."

In the valley of the Baoding Crescent, Feng Dun's surviving gunslingers and soldiers had taken cover and were beginning to return a weak, sporadic fire.

"Cease fire," Jon told Asgar.

"You're sure, my friend? Some are still alive and kicking. Shouldn't we go down and mop up? At least, make sure that monster Feng Dun is dead. I'm fairly certain I hit him."

"No! Fan out and search the slopes wherever Li Kuonyi could have hidden but seen what happened. The survivors will run away now."

"You think — ?"

"She and Yu are up there somewhere with the manifest. Let's *find* them."

Asgar gave the order, urging his men to sweep through the vegetation at a dog trot, circling around Feng's remaining men. "It's less than an hour until dawn, and that firefight will have been heard halfway to Chongqing."

"I know." Jon trotted ahead over the difficult terrain. He looked left and right at the long Uigher line as they searched. He knew their chances were slight, plus time was running out. They had little time to locate Li and Yu, get the manifest, and somehow send it to Washington.

Suddenly, gunfire echoed from less than a hundred yards ahead. Jon wrenched his head around, staring at a spot directly above and to the left of the Sleeping Buddha. Gunfire from an assault rifle — and response from a single pistol.

"Hold it," Jon called to Asgar. He crouched in the brush.

Asgar raised his hand to stop his fighters and lowered it palm down to tell them to go to ground and be quiet. He whispered, "What do you think, Jon?"

"Feng maybe?"

Asgar grimaced in regret. "We should've hied ourselves down to examine the bodies in the valley."

"There wasn't time. We had to try to get to Li Kuonyi first."

"If it's Feng, it seems we failed."

"Maybe. Maybe not."

Motioning his men to move quietly, Asgar joined Jon. Minutes later, the line of Uighers approached a clearing. Asgar signaled to stop at the edge where they could retain cover. Jon nodded to their left. The clearing ended at the cliff above the crescent of carvings, where someone looking down would have a direct view of the valley as well as the slope and walkway in front of the Sleeping Buddha.

"Li Kuonyi could've seen everything from there," Jon said.

Asgar sighed and nodded.

On their right, an assault rifle fired a short burst of three from a towering rock formation, where clusters of large boulders jutted above the trees and brush. It was some fifty yards from the edge of the cliff, overlooking the Buddha valley.

The gunfire was answered by a single pistol shot from a grove of trees closer to the edge, directly in front of where Jon, Asgar, and the Uighers hid. The bullet exploded sharp, deadly stone chips from the rock formation.

"Look," Asgar said.

Only ten yards from the cluster of rocks, closer to where Jon and the Uighers watched, was a smaller rock group. A large tree had fallen across the boulders, and Jon saw movement behind it. As he studied it, the assault rifle squeezed off another short burst from its higher vantage point, detonating wood splinters from the fallen tree.

A low, mesmerizing voice Jon had hoped never to hear again said in English, "A neat trap, Madame Li. As good as any I've seen. Your hired hands killed many of my men, but — unluckily for you — failed to kill me."

Li Kuonyi, her musical tones as calm as if she were greeting a visitor in her Shanghai living room, spoke from behind the fallen tree, protected from the rear by the rocks. "I also failed to get the money. I expect you have that, which makes me surprised that you returned."

Feng said, "I still need the invoice manifest, and I suspect, dear lady, you've run out of ammunition. You should be dead, and I'd have it, except for your friend over there in the trees. I wonder who he could be?"

Asgar whispered, "Why are they speaking English?"

"Damned if I know," Jon said. "Maybe Feng's got some men hidden somewhere that he doesn't want to know what they're saying."

Li Kuonyi was mocking: "There are many things you don't know, Feng."

A man's voice sounded nervously from next to her: "You should've kept the manifest when you had it, Feng. None of this would've happened. No one would've been hurt."

"Ah? A pleasure to hear you again, *boss*. Foolish of me to believe you'd kill yourself, even for the future of your family. But, then, your salvation was Madame Li's doing, wasn't it? My mistake. I knew who the man was in your house long ago."

Li Kuonyi said, "You always did talk too much, Feng. Since you say you want the manifest very much still, we might be interested in the money in your possession."

"All business as usual, Madame? The same arrangement as before, I trust. McDermid's two million in exchange for the manifest."

"Of course."

"Then we have a deal. Does the woman do all your talking now, *boss?* Ah, well, we can't all be men."

There was a scramble of movement in the smaller rock formation. Yu Yongfu stood up, red-faced, pushing away Li's restraining hands. "I am as much —"

The savage explosion of bullets ripped down from Yu's throat to his crotch. Blood sprayed black into the night. A furious return fusillade from the nearby grove nearly drowned out Li Kuonyi's agonized scream.

In the silence, came a single word: "So." Apparently untouched by the shooting from the grove, Feng paused, all banter gone from his voice as he continued, "Now you know *my* deal. Think hard, Li. Your friend's pistol will run out of ammunition long before I do. There's no two million dollars for you. I offer you your life. Throw out the case with the manifest, and you live."

Jon whispered fiercely, "Keep me covered. Don't open up until you hear my voice or hear me shooting, unless you absolutely must."

"What are you planning, Jon?" Asgar demanded.

"I'll circle behind those rocks, climb over, and take Feng from the rear."

"We could attack. There's nearly twenty of us left."

"It'd still be hard to dig a man with an assault rifle and plenty of ammo out of those rocks. We don't know what other weapons he might have there, too. Maybe he's got men as well. We could send Li into a panic if she thinks she's got even more enemies, and the manifest could be destroyed. It's too big a gamble."

Before Asgar could protest again, Jon had slung his MP5K over his shoulder and disappeared back through the trees. As he circled, he had more than one reason for making the attempt to stop Feng Dun. To fire the angry fusillade at Feng, the shooter in the grove had come out from behind a tree, and he had seen her face. *Randi Russell.*

He had no idea how she had gotten here, but Feng was right. She would run out of ammunition before he did. And if the Uighers attacked, she could be caught in the crossfire.

The Arabian Sea

Admiral Brose's voice was steady over the bridge loudspeaker: "Give me the *Empress*'s position as of this minute, Commander."

From where he stood on the dark bridge, Jim Chervenko could see the lighted bulk of the *Empress* sailing two miles off the *Crowe*'s port bow. Appearing to move at her full speed, she was continuing on her steady course across the moonlit sea for the Strait of Hormuz, the Persian Gulf beyond, and Basra, Iraq. He nodded to Frank Bienas, who took the fix from the navigator and relayed it to the admiral.

"By our calculation, you have less than ninety minutes before she enters the strait," the admiral said after a moment.

"That's how we calculate it, too, sir," Chervenko said.

"You've moved into position?"

"She's two miles off our port bow."

"The submarine?"

"Run her torpedoes in, and moved up with us. They have the *Empress* off their starboard, but they're submerged half a mile closer, cruising behind her where they have a clear fix on us, too."

"Your Seahawks are armed for antisubmarine and ready to launch?"

"Yessir."

The admiral maintained his calm voice, but the series of questions he would never have normally asked a raw lieutenant in his first command, much less a decorated commander with years at sea, betrayed his nerves.

Brose seemed to read his thoughts. "Forgive me, Commander, it's a nasty situation."

"None nastier, sir."

"The battle plan?"

"Move to stop the *Empress*. Send off the boarding detail. Keep the freighter between us and the sub, which will force her to come to our side where the choppers can get a clear shot. Otherwise, we play it as it lays."

"All right, Commander." A slight hesitation. "You'll have the order to board within the hour. The *Shiloh* should be there in three hours, give or take. I'll try to give you air cover at the last minute, but the timing is difficult. Hold out as long as you can." A hesitation again, as if reluctant to end the connection. Finally, a hearty, "Good luck." The admiral was gone.

Commander Chervenko looked once at the clock above his command post, then again focused his night glasses on *The Dowager Empress*, plowing ahead through the bright moonlight and across the calm sea. Inside his grim mind, he was counting down.

Chapter
Forty-Three

Dazu

The night felt heavy around Jon, oppressive. He crept among the shadowy boulders of the giant rock formation, inching higher and higher. His special canvas shoes gripped the stony surfaces, while his night-vision goggles enabled him to follow crevices, rain channels, and ledges. Sometimes he had no choice but to jump and scramble up the face of a boulder. Other times, a scrub tree allowed him to pull himself straight up.

"Time is wasting, Li," Feng Dun said, his cool voice so close Jon expected to see him any second. "Your husband's dead. Your bodyguards are dead. You've obviously run out of ammo. Your friend out there somewhere among the trees is alone and will run out of ammo soon, too, and then there'll be no one to stop me. This is your chance. Toss out the attaché case, and I'll walk away."

From her hiding spot, Li Kuonyi laughed bitterly. "And where would I go? Without a great deal of money, how would I get myself and my children out of China? I might as well burn the manifest myself. I *will,* if you don't leave."

581

As her bitter voice talked, drawing Feng's attention, Jon crawled faster up the rocks until he was sure he was higher than Feng.

Feng's laugh was nasty. "Sorry, Madame Li. Only the Americans want the manifest untouched. Please feel free to burn it. If you don't, I will. But that won't save you or help you escape China."

She suddenly understood. "*Wei Gaofan.* That's who's behind this! My father's benefactor. My *husband's* benefactor. *He's* the one who must have the document destroyed. He's the one you *really* work for!"

"Trusting us is your only chance. Otherwise, you know your fate."

Jon reached the highest rock. He unslung his MP5K, climbed silently over, and found a good position with his back against the top boulder. As a dark wind whistled around his ears, beneath him spread the mesa and Buddha gorge, a panoramic vista of shadows, vegetation, and monumental statues shining in the unearthly glow of moon and stars.

Feng Dun was kneeling behind a boulder not twenty feet below. His assault rifle rested on a lip of rock, aimed toward where Li Kuonyi hid. Jon took off his goggles and stared down at the top of Feng's head. His red-and-white hair seemed especially brilliant in the delicate light, the only spot of color in the black-and-gray rockscape.

At the same time, Feng's head was also a perfect target. With one satisfying bullet, Jon could shatter it like a melon. His trigger finger flexed. Simmering fury at the people Feng had killed himself or ordered killed knotted his chest. . . . Avery

Mondragon. Andy An. So many Uigher fighters. The pig Ralph McDermid. Even poor Yu Yongfu. Then there was the violent conflict that was waiting to erupt out on the Arabian Sea. Jon fought to control his rage.

He said loudly enough for all to hear, "You're not Madame Li's only chance, Feng. Give it up. Surrender now, and *you'll* live."

The advantage had flipped. For an endless second, Feng Dun did not turn. He did not move. Faster than the strike of a cobra, he whirled and dove to his right, heedless of sharp-edged rocks. His strange hair disappeared into shadow, while his face radiated outrage and disgust. At the same time, he fired his assault rifle, releasing a sweep of bullets that rushed toward Jon.

Jon grunted with satisfaction. He squeezed off a single burst from the MP5K. The bullets slammed into the mercenary's trunk, stopping his turn as if he had collided with a tank. The impact slammed Feng back against the boulders like a sack of rice. He recoiled forward, pitched over a smaller boulder, and rolled downward, starting a small avalanche.

There was a moment of shocked silence. Across the clearing, Asgar and his Uighers burst into the open and surrounded the fallen tree and rocks where Li Kuonyi had taken refuge. Their weapons were aimed, but Asgar stopped their advance.

Excitement surged through Jon. The manifest was in reach again. They would have the proof, and he could phone Fred. The *Empress* could be stopped, its deadly cargo offloaded, and the crisis ended . . . if there was time. He sprinted down among the rocks, dodging and leaping obstacles, until he reached the clearing. He dashed to the Uighers at the fallen tree.

Behind the log, Li Kuonyi sat with her back against a rock. She wore a sleek, black pantsuit and high-collared hooded jacket identical to that worn by her double, dead in the valley. Hers was torn, disheveled, and stained with blood, apparently from her husband's injuries. Her left hand gently cupped his dead face. Her right hand held a cigarette lighter, already in flame. She had no weapon, but the original invoice manifest lay open on top of her closed case, next to her right hand.

When she saw Jon, she smiled. "So? The American who wanted the manifest so many days ago. I should've realized."

"It's over, Madame Li," Jon told her. "Your husband's dead. You have no one left to deal with but me."

Her hand stroked Yu's immobile face. It was a mask of marble, of death. "He was a fool and a coward, but I loved him, and the deal remains the same. The two million American dollars and your Uigher friends to help me and my children leave China. In exchange, you get the undamaged manifest you have worked so hard for." She paused, her gaze stony. "Otherwise, I burn it."

Jon believed her. He glanced at his watch. One hour and ten minutes. By now, the *Crowe* would have cleared for action, waiting only for the final order to board the *Empress*. There was little hope he could get the manifest to the president in time to send to Beijing — unless something had changed or would change. A storm. Other navy ships arriving. Another nation interfering. Anything to slow the ship's arrival at the strait.

Too much had already been sacrificed for him to give up now, and too much was at risk not to make the final effort. "Did your men find the money?" he asked Asgar.

"They did. In a crevice near where Feng was shooting. Still in its suitcase. And it's all there. Real money."

"Give it to her."

Asgar's voice was suddenly tense, "I don't think so, old boy."

Jon glanced at the Uigher leader, and then turned again to see what Asgar's gaze was focused on at the far edge of the clearing. His throat tightened. They did not need this. A line of eight men in the uniform of the People's Liberation Army stood just inside the trees, their weapons aimed into the clearing. At them. The soldiers were too late to help Feng, but not too late to kill Asgar, Randi, and everyone else.

Monday, September 18
Washington, D.C.

Every eye in the White House's subterranean situation room was angled toward the head of the polished table, where President Castilla stared up at the wall clock.

"One hour, sir," Stevens Brose said.

"Less," corrected Secretary of Defense Stanton.

Vice President Brandon Erikson said, "We can't wait, Mr. President."

The president turned his gaze to Erikson. "They're ready? The *Crowe*?"

585

"They've been ready for a full half hour," Admiral Brose said.

The president nodded. Continued to nod. His gaze returned to the clock. His face hardened. "Give the order."

Instantly, the secure room galvanized into action. Brose snapped up the receiver of the telephone and issued orders.

Tuesday, September 19
Dazu

Asgar made a quick motion, and the twenty Uighers spread out to face the eight soldiers across the clearing. They stared at one another, hands on weapons, pointing.

"We outnumber them better than two to one," Asgar said in a rush, "but I don't dare take them on. We don't know how many more are nearby, and a firefight in which we kill a squad of PLA troops will guarantee Draconian reprisals against my guerrillas and all of Xinjiang. The payoff's not worth the sacrifice. Sorry, Jon."

Jon answered quickly if unhappily, "I understand."

"If there are no more than we're looking at, we can at least protect you as far as our hideout. My people there will help you get David Thayer out of the country."

"Appreciate it. Thanks. Why aren't they moving?" They were statues, armed and ready. An impenetrable line perhaps, but they could still be gotten around. They could still be shot. Why did they not fire first? Were they afraid, because they were outnumbered?

"They're not worried," Asgar decided. "As I said, they may have more troops coming up."

At that moment, Jon sensed motion on his other side. He spun on his heel. "Randi."

Randi Russell appeared, her face grim. "What can I do?" Her blond hair was dyed black, and she wore a crumpled business suit. She, too, stared across the clearing at the silent Chinese soldiers.

"Where the hell did you come from?" Jon asked, but his heart was not in their usual banter. The troops would not wait much longer.

"I flew in with the late Ralph McDermid, may the bastard rest in hell. He needed an interpreter."

"Lucky for us and Li Kuonyi he did. You've been with us from the start?"

She nodded. "Lurking up here. After the blood-bath below, I spotted Feng moving in on the other two. So I opened fire to drive him into the rocks."

"I owe you again."

"Don't mention it." Trying to be light, but not succeeding. "This cargo manifest the woman has . . . that's what you need?"

"Yes." Jon gave her the highlights, concluding with the standoff in the Arabian Sea. "McDermid set the whole thing up with Li Kuonyi's husband. Somehow, a Chinese politico got into the act, too. God knows what's going to happen, but it's not good. Not for peace . . . not for the future . . . not for the world. Sorry you got caught in this, Randi. Asgar's right. He can't risk the future of his people. There's no time left to change anything anyway." He turned to Asgar. "You and your fighters better get away while you can. If you can."

"You're not coming?"

"That'd only put you in greater danger. Uighers don't have the world's only superpower to protect them. We do." He clapped him on the shoulders as he had seen Uighers do. "Take the two million. You can make better use of it than Li Kuonyi, the Chinese government, or us."

"Sorry it worked out this way. Bad show all around, but perhaps we can do this again someday. Do it right." Asgar gave a signal, and before Jon and Randi could blink, he and his men had stepped into the trees and vanished.

Now there was no protection at all from the Chinese soldiers.

"Jon," Randi said quietly, nodding at them.

They did not pursue the Uighers. Instead, they parted, and an officer stepped through the line, walking across the clearing toward them.

"That's what they were waiting for," Jon said.

"A captain. Infantry, from the insignia," Randi agreed.

Jon, Randi, and Li Kuonyi stepped away from the fallen trunk. Kuonyi clutched the manifest in one hand, the cigarette lighter in the other. It was no longer alight.

The captain's expression was stern, his step authoritative. He glanced to the right, toward where the dead Feng Dun lay in his own blood. He slowed and stopped, his expression uncertain. A pudgy little man, also in the full uniform of the PLA, appeared from the rocks behind Feng.

As the new man walked steadily toward the infantry officer, Randi whispered, "He's wearing the insignia of the Public Security Bureau — internal security and counterintelligence."

"Swell. The Chinese KGB."

Major Pan Aitu had watched the first act of the drama at the Sleeping Buddha from behind the statue of a ferocious dragon that guarded the entrance to the Cave of Full Enlightenment. As the action had progressed, he had circled around, following it.

Night-vision binoculars had enabled him to study the band of Uighers who had attacked Feng Dun and his gangsters, including a few PLA soldiers, which had told him much. The clothes, faces, and weapons of the twenty-odd hillside guerrillas had made him smile his benign smile. Disciplined Uighers, with AK-47s. He had long since decided Colonel Smith had made his escape with the help of an unknown Shanghai cell of Uigher resistance fighters. Now they were here, too, where the elusive Feng Dun had murdered Yu Yongfu and the rich American, McDermid, to obtain the cargo manifest of *The Dowager Empress*. Could Colonel Smith be far away?

Pan's admiration for Li Kuonyi's cunning had increased ten-thousandfold. But if Wei Gaofan were to be defeated, Pan would still need to intervene. The appearance of the depleted squad of infantry only confirmed his decision.

Now as he stood before the captain, who was staring uncertainly at his PLA uniform, his rank, and his internal-security insignia, he said mildly, "I am Major Pan Aitu, Captain. Perhaps you know of me?" He looked the tall captain up and down.

The captain regained some of his martinet air. He held his ground. "Captain Chang Doh, and yes, I have heard of you, Major."

"Then we can dispense with the preliminaries. You are, I believe, under the personal orders of a commander who's a friend of Wei Gaofan. You've been unofficially detailed to aid Feng Dun, whom you can see is now quite dead. Under his completely illegal orders, you have lost PLA soldiers, both wounded and killed."

The captain's face went ashen. "I cannot speak of my orders, Major."

"Oh? There are many more soldiers hidden among the trees under *my* command. At the same time, I myself have written orders to investigate and, if needed, prevent the activities of the late Feng Dun. To assuage any doubt, here are my papers." He handed Niu Jianxing's authorization to the captain.

The captain read slowly, as if he hoped the documents would disappear from his fingers. Unfortunately for him, the orders confirmed that Major Pan was operating in his capacity as a counterintelligence and internal-security officer for the member of the Standing Committee who was in charge of such operations. The captain, on the other hand, was in the weak position of being merely an infantry officer working for a personal friend of a member of the Standing Committee, who was not in charge of the military.

As Jon, Randi, and Li Kuonyi watched, the infantry captain returned Major Pan's papers, took one step back, and saluted smartly.

"Looks as if the major's won the argument."

Li Kuonyi relit her lighter. "You can have the manifest before he gets here. I want passage to the

United States for myself and my children and asylum. Otherwise, I burn it now."

"No two million?"

She shrugged. "That was for my husband. I'm an actress, a good one. I'm already becoming known in America. I'll earn my own millions."

"Done." Jon grabbed the manifest and the lighter at the same time, before she changed her mind.

When the major reached them, he smiled at Jon and introduced himself in English. "I'm Major Pan Aitu, Colonel Smith. It's my pleasure to meet you at last. You've been most interesting to investigate. Unfortunately, there's no time left. Give me the cargo manifest."

"No!" Randi said instantly. She snatched the lighter and flicked it on. "I don't know why you want it, but —"

Jon stopped her. "Turn it off, for now. There's not enough time to get it to Washington anyway so the president can send it on to Zhongnanhai. Let's hear what our fellow agent has to say for himself."

The diminutive major's eyes flickered. He pointed to where the eight soldiers were disappearing into the trees. "They're now under my orders. Did you know that Captain Chang took two prisoners? One is an American captain, the other an old man. I can guarantee you, them, the two ladies here, and Madame Li's two children quick passage to the United States. We're on the same side in this, Colonel."

"Why help Li Kuonyi?" Randi asked.

"Let's just say I admire the lady's intelligence, resourcefulness, and artistry. I also admit that she's a complication we don't want. None of what's happened can or will become public. In your country or in mine. But success is slipping away, even for me."

Jon considered. The major did not want the manifest destroyed. There was nothing more China could gain unless they *did* want the *Dowager* boarded. A decision had to be made, and only he could make it. America had nothing more to lose and everything to gain.

He asked the critical question: "Do you have a way to stop the cargo ship before it's too late, Major Pan?"

"Yes."

He handed Pan the invoice manifest.

The major turned on his heel, motioned them to follow, and ran across the clearing and through the trees to another open space where a helicopter waited, its motors silent. Pan spoke into a walkie-talkie. As they closed in, the rotors roared to life.

The Arabian Sea

The moon was at its brightest as the *John Crowe* moved across the long, slow swells to close in on the *Empress*, still steaming ahead at full speed toward the Strait of Hormuz, which was faintly visible in the distance. The boarding party stood in the lee of the *Crowe*'s aft superstructure, armed, ready to lower the boats, ready to motor to the Chinese freighter.

In the communications-and-control center, Lt. Commander Frank Bienas paced, stopping every few minutes to lean over the shoulders of the radio, radar, and sonar specialists. He was peering at Operations Specialist Second-Class Baum's radar screen, when Hastings on sonar boomed, "Sub's moving!"

Bienas barked, "How fast?"

"Looks like full speed, sir."

"Heading toward the *Empress*?"

"Sort of, sir, yes."

"What the hell does 'sort of' mean, technician?"

"It means she's angling in toward the *Empress*, but her course'll take her around the stern."

"So they're heading for our side, armed and ready?"

"Maybe, sir. I guess so."

"Then say that, damn you!"

The shocked silence was broken by Hastings's stiff words, "I can't tell you where the sub's headed, Commander. Only her speed and course."

Bienas flushed. "Sorry, Hastings. I guess I'm kind of strung out."

"I guess we all are, sir," Hastings said.

The executive officer activated the intercom to the bridge. "Jim? Looks like she's coming to our side, full speed."

On the bridge, Jim Chervenko acknowledged the message, his gut tight: "Okay, Frank. The moment she comes 'round, let me know."

"Aye-aye, sir."

Chervenko switched off the intercom and stared astern. Then he bent to the intercom again. "Sparks? Open a channel. Hail the freighter." He straightened, watching the hard-driving freighter no more than a half mile away now.

The intercom squawked. "They're not responding, sir."

"Keep trying. Let me know when they do." He pressed another switch. "Ready, Canfield?"

"Yes, *sir*."

Chervenko nodded to himself, recognizing the young lieutenant's eagerness to go into battle. He remembered when he had been like that in what seemed now another world. "Put one across her bow. And Canfield?"

"Yessir?"

"Don't hit her."

A pause. "No, sir."

Chervenko raised his night binoculars to focus on the fast-moving bow of the *Empress*. He listened to the five-inch fire and watched the geyser erupt no more than a hundred yards ahead of the bow. A rewardingly large splash. That should shake their shorts.

He counted: One, two, three, four . . .

The intercom squawked again. "He's responding," the radioman said. "He's demanding to know the meaning of our aggression."

"Tell him to cut the crap, stop dead in the water, and prepare to receive a boarding party. Tell him I better not see even a tin can go overboard, or I'll put the next round from the five-inch down his gullet." Chervenko suddenly felt nervous. He studied the *Empress* again. When it slowed, he let out a breath. So far so good. He was about to give the order to lower the boats, when there was another signal.

Frank Bienas's agitated voice burst out: "The sub's come around, Jim! Submerged. Torpedoes in the tubes."

There it was. Sweat broke out on Chervenko's

594

forehead. He bellowed, "Prepare for evasive maneuvers. Send off the Seahawks!"

Out of the corner of his eyes, he noted that the *Empress* was hardly moving. She was almost dead in the water, barely gliding ahead as she rose and fell on the swell. But the main target of his gaze was astern, where the telltale trail of a torpedo could appear any second.

He saw no torpedo. What he did see was a giant shape rising ghostly in the moonlight, a monster emerging from the depths.

It was the Chinese submarine. As Chervenko watched, incredulous, it moved slowly toward the *Crowe* five hundred yards astern and a few hundred yards closer to the stationary *Dowager Empress*.

The intercom announced, "He's hailing us, sir!"

Chervenko's eyebrows shot up to his officer's cap. *Now what?* "Pipe him onto the bridge."

The stiff, vaguely angry voice said in stilted English, "Commander Chervenko, I believe. This is Captain Zhang Qian of the People's Liberation Army submarine *Zhou Enlai*. I have received orders from Beijing to join you in boarding the outlaw vessel *Dowager Empress* to search for and destroy any and all contraband cargo. I am further instructed to place a crew aboard the vessel to sail it and its personnel back to China."

Chervenko did not move. He stood there gazing out over the dark Arabian Sea, the intercom in his hand, and told his heart to stop thundering. It was over. Thank God, it was over. Someone had done their job. Someone . . . probably many . . . whose risks and sacrifices he could only imagine and whose names and faces he would probably never know.

"I'm at your service, Captain," Chervenko said politely. "And, of course, once the contraband is destroyed, we will be pleased to escort the ship back to Shanghai. Wouldn't want an outlaw vessel like this one to slip away or fall into someone else's hands, now would we?"

Epilogue

Beijing

The heads of the ten men seated around the ornate imperial table in the Zhongnanhai meeting room turned in unison to the door to the left of the general secretary. They watched as a slender man in the uniform of a lieutenant commander of the PLA navy entered. He whispered in the ear of the general secretary, and the secretary nodded.

When the young officer left, the secretary explained, "We have good news. It's over. The captain of the *Zhou Enlai* reports the boarding of the *Empress* by parties from the *Zhou Enlai* and the American frigate *John Crowe*. Many tons of contraband chemicals were found. The contraband is destroyed. The officers of the cargo vessel are in our custody, and the ship is returning to Shanghai, escorted by the American frigate."

A murmur of both approval and relief traveled around the table. Wei Gaofan said, "A close thing, but must we allow an American frigate to escort our ship?"

"I expect," the secretary said mildly, "the frigate captain insisted. Under the circumstances, we can

597

hardly protest." His eyes were tiny points of black stone behind his thick glasses as he fixed his gaze on General Chu Kuairong at the far end of the table. "How could this have happened, General Chu? An illegal enterprise of such unimaginable danger conducted by our citizens under our very noses?"

"I believe," Niu Jianxing said, "I must be the one to answer that, Secretary."

Wei Gaofan interrupted angrily, "None of us can be expected to answer for all the failures of those who conduct actual operations."

Niu did not look at Wei. He addressed the room in general. "Our colleague Wei appears to want to pass the culpability down to those least able to defend themselves."

"I resent — !" Wei snapped.

The secretary cut him off: "If there's an explanation, Jianxing, tell us."

"There is," Niu said quietly. "A simple explanation of various forces — a weak businessman, the greed inevitably fostered by free-market economics, the conspiracy of certain Western corporations, and the corrupt arrogance of a member of this very committee."

As the Owl enunciated the last words, there was a shocked pause. Then the room erupted in outrage, protest, and shouted questions directed back at Niu.

Wei Gaofan, his temple-dog face choleric with rage, shouted, "Such a statement is tantamount to treason, Niu! I call for a vote of censure!"

"Which one of us are you slandering, sir!" Shi Jingnu demanded.

"It's unconscionable!" called one of the youngest members.

598

"Unless," the secretary said quietly, "Niu can prove his accusation."

The room instantly was silent, questioning.

Someone muttered, "I can't believe it."

"Believe it," General Chu growled, his unlit cigar rolling around his thin-lipped mouth.

Niu pushed himself away from the table and walked to the door. He opened it and beckoned.

Still in his PLA uniform, Major Pan Aitu marched inside. Niu escorted the pudgy spy-catcher to the table and stood beside him. "Major, detail your investigation, if you please."

In his gentle, completely expressionless voice, Pan laid out the conspiracy from Donk & LaPierre's approach to Yu Yongfu with the contraband deal, to Li Aorong's and Wei Gaofan's involvement, until Jon Smith had at last handed the only existing manifest to Pan, who had faxed it from Dazu to the Standing Committee.

Wei Gaofan's hard face paled. Still, he grumbled, "It seems, with the tragic death of Li Aorong only an hour ago, all those named by Major Pan are dead. Except for me, of course. I categorically deny —"

Pan gazed steadily at Wei. "Not all of them are dead, sir. Li Kuonyi — without father or husband — is alive. Many of Feng Dun's men survived. The captain of infantry is, of course, alive, as is your friend, the general, who sent the captain to help Feng Dun retrieve the manifest. All have given me official statements."

For a moment, Wei Gaofan did not move. His features seemed to melt, but his jaw clamped tight. "Niu Jianxing has forced them to lie!"

"No," the secretary said thoughtfully, studying Wei as if seeing him for the first time. "There is only one liar here."

The color suddenly returned to Wei's face. "Niu Jianxing and the general secretary are destroying China," he announced to his colleagues. "What Yu Yongfu did is an example of the disease they'd bring home to the People's Republic. What I did was to awake you and the Party to what's happening to the great Revolution of our fathers. Of Mao Zedong, Zhou Enlai, Chu Teh, Deng Xiaoping. I will *not* resign. I will leave this room with all those who agree with me, and we shall see *who* the Party supports!"

He raised his massive body onto his spindly legs and stalked to the door. For a moment, he stood there, the door half open, his back to his colleagues, waiting. No one followed.

The secretary sighed. "Tomorrow I'll call for a vote of the Central Committee and the Politburo. You'll be stripped of all posts, all prerogatives, and all honors. You'll be expelled from the Party, Wei Gaofan."

"Unless," Niu Jianxing suggested, "you choose to do as Li Aorong told his son-in-law. But you must act quickly."

"You could think of your family," the secretary suggested, although his voice did not sound hopeful.

Wei continued to stand there silently. Finished, he nodded and walked out.

Monday, September 18
Washington, D.C.
Four hours after the cargo of banned chemicals

was discovered aboard the *Empress* and destroyed, Charlie Ouray invited Vice President Brandon Erikson over to meet with the president. Then he ordered Air Force One readied for a flight out to the West Coast, took a call from Ambassador Wu, who had just returned to the embassy on Connecticut Avenue, and headed downstairs to the situation room, where President Castilla was on the phone with his wife.

"It's a pretty darn good ending, Cassie," the president was saying. As soon as he saw Ouray poke his head into the room, he beckoned him inside. "You'll be able to make it, darling? I'm sorry about your having to cancel the dinner in Oaxaca, but . . . yes, I know you're as excited as I am. And the children? Wonderful! Wonderful! I'll see y'all then." He hung up, beaming.

Ouray waited for the president to look at him again. When he did, he reported, "The ambassador called, Mr. President. He wanted officially to thank you, and he gave me a message for you from Niu Jianxing — the Owl."

"That's nice. What's the message?"

"Niu sends his greetings and expresses hope that your health continues to be robust."

The president burst out laughing.

"What?" Ouray asked. Puzzled, he watched the president laugh harder. He began to smile, then to chuckle as he replayed the message in his mind. At last he held his sides, laughing, too. The merry sound filled the big, soundproof room, banishing the shadows of the last week.

"Oh, God." The president wiped his eyes.

"Priceless," Ouray agreed.

601

"We needed that. *Robust*. But from them, it's a vote of confidence."

"An expression of hope for the future."

"Hell, Charlie. He figures he's got me broke in, and he doesn't want to have to go through it again anytime soon with someone new!"

Chuckling, the two men leaned back in their chairs.

Ouray observed, "Well, sir, I guess we can say the same about him."

"True, true." At last, Sam Castilla's expression grew serious as his mind returned to the next task. "Just wanted you to know that Justice is getting ready to bring charges against Jasper Kott. It's going to be a mighty big scandal."

"Can't brush it under the rug."

"No, Charlie. Wouldn't be right." There was one more piece of business that had to be taken care of. He sighed, preparing himself. "Is the vice president on his way?"

"Better than that, he's here." Brandon Erikson entered the situation room with a broad smile on his handsome face. Behind him, the military aide closed the door. As always, his sable-black hair was brushed back impeccably, and his wiry body was encased in a tailored three-piece suit. He exuded his usual charm and energy. "My congratulations, Mr. President. A magnificent display of statesmanship."

"Thank you, Brandon. It was a close thing."

The vice president took his usual seat in the middle of the long table to the president's right, directly across from Ouray. He nodded pleasantly to Ouray and focused on the president. "I won't ask for the details of how you pulled it off, sir, but I suspect we have an unsung hero or two in our intelligence agencies."

"There's that," the president agreed. "We also had a lot of help from inside China, particularly from a high-level politician. Our work with him gives me a lot of hope for our relations with China."

Erikson grinned. "I suspect you're being modest, Mr. President."

Sam Castilla said nothing.

The vice president blinked and glanced around the silent room that was essentially sealed from the rest of the White House. Not only windowless and soundproof, it was constantly swept for bugs and illicit cameras. "Is everyone else late? I assumed we were having a post-crisis assessment session."

The president studied Erikson's face, looking for what he had missed. "There won't be anyone else, Brandon. Tell me, would your friend Ralph McDermid be as enthusiastic about our success as you are?"

Erikson looked from the president to the grim-faced Ouray and back again to the president. "I have no idea how Mr. McDermid would feel. I barely know the man."

"Really?" Charlie Ouray said.

Erikson did not miss the absence of his title or any of the other usual courteous forms of address for someone of his lofty position. His left eyebrow cocked. "Is something wrong, Mr. President?"

The president's hand slammed down on the table. Ouray jumped. Erikson looked startled and a little afraid.

Castilla growled, "You know damn well what

603

McDermid would've thought. You know *exactly* which intelligence agents are unsung heroes."

"That, sir, is preposterous!" Erikson retorted, as angry as the president. "I know —" He seemed to suddenly hear the president's exact words. "He . . . *would've* thought?"

The president said curtly, "Ralph McDermid's dead. Altman's board of directors is right now running around like vultures with their heads cut off to come up with a plausible story to explain it. And it won't help. McDermid's dirty deal is going to come out — I'll see to it. They'll be jumping ship faster than you can say Arthur Andersen."

"Dead?" Erikson repeated, his expression shocked. "It's going to . . . *come out?"*

"Your secret pal Ralph McDermid was shot to death in China," Charlie Ouray told him. "Murdered, I'm told, by one of his own hired thugs."

The vice president blinked, recovered, and said cagily, "Horrible. How tragic. What was he doing in China? Some business deal, I expect."

"Shit, Brandon," the president exploded. "It's *over.* You've been caught with your hands deep in other people's pockets. I expect your resignation on my desk by morning!" He nodded to Ouray, who pressed a button under the table.

Erikson sputtered, "My . . . my *resignation —"*

Two disembodied voices filled the room, one of them the vice president's:

"Don't get sarcastic. We need each other. You're a valuable member of the team."

"I'll stay that way only as long as I'm behind the scenes."

"It's not as bad as you think. In the end, neither

Smith nor the CIA woman damaged us or our project."

"That the CIA may have you under surveillance doesn't concern you? Even if it's not related to our deal, they've traced at least some of the White House leaks to you. That should bother you one hell of a lot."

"I think that's enough." Ouray stopped the tape. "I'm sure Mr. Erikson recalls the rest."

Erikson's hands were folded in his lap under the table. He blinked as if he did not know where he was. Then he drew a long breath. "I suppose I could claim that wasn't me . . ."

The president hooted. Ouray rolled his eyes.

Erikson nodded slowly. "All right, but doing favors for an important backer in a future presidential campaign, while possibly reprehensible, is hardly a crime, or all of us would be in prison. You may not like me now, Sam, and it's certain you can shut me out of everything until your term ends, but I doubt you can force me to resign."

"It's a lot more damning than that," the president said. "If you recall the entire tape — made by the CIA, incidentally — you'll realize you implicated yourself in an attempt to cause an armed conflict with China, in which American military personnel would no doubt have been killed. You also helped to ship illegal contraband. I believe some if not all of that skirts treason. It may be treason. Of course, Justice will have to make the ultimate decision about whether it's actionable. Preliminary reports tell me you're heading for criminal trial."

Ouray pursed his lips. "*I'd* say it's treason."

Erikson looked from one to the other. "What do you want, Sam?"

"Don't call me Sam. Not anymore. I told you what I wanted. You can claim ill health. Family responsibilities. You want to devote your time to exploring a campaign for president. That'd be partially true, anyway."

"Is that all, *Mr.* President?" Erikson asked bitterly.

"Not quite. You can make a good show of exploring the possibility, but in the end, you won't run for president, for senator, for dog catcher. No public office ever again. *Not ever,* even if you're not charged."

"And if I choose to run anyway?"

"I'll see to it you get no help from the party. Believe me, no one's going to want to be even seen in the same room with you."

Erikson's expression hardened into stone. He stood. "You'll have my resignation tomorrow." He turned to leave, then turned back. "You know, I'm not quite as bad as you think. I never really agreed with your policy of weakening the military. I did only what I thought best for the country."

"Bullshit," Ouray said. "You did what was best for Brandon Erikson."

The president nodded. "And along the way, you lost your benefactor, too. If the Altman Group survives, no one there will ever put you in their Rolodex again. You don't fit the profile. In your case, mixing business and politics almost caused a war. That can really hurt a bottom line."

Tuesday, September 19
Vandenberg Air Force Base, California

The morning was warm and hazy with sunshine

as the air force jet swept in over the Pacific. From a window, Jon studied the Channel Islands, ringed with tendrils of fog, and the rugged coast with its white sands and dramatic cliffs. The highly secure base extended over nearly one hundred thousand acres of manzanita and rocket launchpads, pampas grass and missile silos, on a wide shelf that jutted into the glistening ocean.

"We used to drive up here occasionally with Mom and Dad, to study the wildflowers," Randi told him.

She had a window seat, while he sat across from her, on the aisle, where he could rotate and see out several windows.

"Lovely, isn't it?" she continued. "There's something about the sun and the ocean that I find endlessly appealing. If . . . when . . . I ever settle down, I'll come back here. What will you do, Jon?"

About fifty miles southeast of Vandenberg was Santa Barbara, where Randi and her sister, Sophia Russell, had grown up. Santa Barbara was also where Jon had gone to lick his wounds and decide what to do with his life after the Hades virus had killed Sophia.

"Settle down?" he repeated. "You're making me shudder. Why would anyone want to settle down?"

"Why, indeed?" asked David Thayer. "Take it from me, people put too much stock in it. Footloose and fancy free, that's my idea of life now." He grinned, his crevices rearranging themselves in a face that shone with curiosity and eagerness. His thick white hair was combed neatly back, and he had new tortoiseshell frames for his glasses. "Goodness, I've been settled down more than fifty years. I've decided to spend the rest of my life on the go."

The three smiled at one another as the jet touched down and sped along the runway. They were dressed in casual trousers and shirts supplied by the U.S. embassy in Beijing. David Thayer had been surprised by plastic zippers, which he had never seen. Velcro fascinated him. He had ripped open and closed the Velcro straps that fastened his new athletic shoes several times. He had never ridden in a jet. The air force pilot gave him a thorough tour of the cockpit, trying to explain how much of the craft was computerized these days until he finally realized Thayer had no real understanding of computers. Thayer assured him he would buy a book and figure it out himself.

After Jon had reunited with Thayer at the embassy, Jon demanded he have a thorough physical exam. But Thayer did not want to take the time, explaining politely he would rather watch television, which was also new to him. Still, he was persuaded, and the doctor found healed bones indicating past traumas, what appeared to be an iron deficiency, an eye that should have cataract surgery soon, and obvious dental needs. Then Jon, Randi, and David Thayer had piled onto the jet, heading home to America.

The events of the past week remained very fresh — raw — in Jon's mind. That would not change for a long time. When he returned to Fort Detrick, he would write a full report for Fred. That often helped.

Jon had noticed that Randi had been studying the president's father from the time she first met him. At last, as the jet rolled to a stop, she asked, "Aren't you bitter, Dr. Thayer? They stole your life. Doesn't that make you even a little bitter?"

He gazed back from the window, where he was leaning forward so he could see Air Force One clearly. "Of course I'm bitter, but I've got other things on my mind, too. There he is!" He pressed his face against the glass. "I see him! My son. My *son*. There's my daughter-in-law! There are my grandchildren! I can't believe it. They all came. *They all came to see me!*" His body trembled with excitement.

The jet stopped, and David Thayer unsnapped his belt and headed for the door. Jon and Randi did not move. As he waited for the stairway to be rolled up and the copilot to unlock the door, he turned and came back. There were pink spots on his sunken cheeks. His eyes sparkled. He shook their hands, thanking them again.

"I hope you can understand, Ms. Russell." He patted the top of her hand as he continued to hold it. He glanced back occasionally, eager for the door to open. "I never would've survived if I'd allowed myself to be full of hate every second. There were a few good things among the bad. For instance, I learned the price for hubris was humility, and I learned I didn't have all the answers. Still, if I could go back and change what I did that got me into that mess, I would. But since I can't, I'm going to make the most of what time I've got left. The Chinese have a proverb that goes something like this: 'What a caterpillar calls the end of life, wise men call a butterfly.' "

"That's beautiful," Randi said.

He nodded. "I know." He squeezed her hand, punched Jon's shoulder, and hurried back to the door. He glared at the copilot. "Are you ever going to open this damn thing?"

"Right now, sir." He spun the lock, and the pneumatic door lifted and swung out.

The stairwell was there. The old man moved onto it without another look back. Jon and Randi watched him descend and brush away an aide who obviously had planned to escort him over to Air Force One. The president, his wife, son, and daughter were waiting in its shade. Thayer moved straight toward them about ten steps and suddenly stopped.

"Look at his face," Randi said.

"He's afraid," Jon agreed.

"It's hit him all at once. He doesn't know whether they'll like him."

"Or whether he'll like them. Whether he can live such a different life."

The president and his family gazed at one another, some sort of message passing among them. Without a word, they hurried across the tarmac to Thayer. He slowly opened his arms. The president reached him first, stepped into his embrace, and wrapped his own arms around him in return. They held each other a long time. The president kissed his father's cheek. Soon everyone was there, too, talking, laughing, introducing themselves, hugging.

As their jet backed up, Jon and Randi turned away from the windows.

"Back to Washington," she said with a sigh.

"Yes. It'll be good to go home for a while."

About the Authors

Robert Ludlum is the author of more than twenty internationally bestselling novels, including *The Bourne Identity* — the basis of the international hit movie — and *The Scarlatti Inheritance*. His books have been translated into thirty-two languages and, with over two million copies in print, are the standard by which all works of international suspense are judged.

Gayle Lynds is the coauthor of two previous Covert-One novels, *The Hades Factor* and *The Paris Option*, as well as several bestselling thrillers of her own: *Masquerade, Mosaic, Mesmerized*, and the forthcoming *The Coil*.